DATE		

CONCLAVE

By the same author

SON OF SAM

Lawrence D. Klausner

CONCLAVE

McGRAW-HILL BOOK COMPANY

New York   St. Louis   San Francisco
Toronto   Hamburg   Mexico

1 2 3 4 5 6 7 8 9 DO DO 8 7 6 5 4 3 2 1

LIBRARY OF CONGRESS CATALOGING IN PUBLICATION DATA

Klausner, Lawrence D.
Conclave.
I. Title.
PS3561.L332C6   813'.54   81-5960
ISBN 0-07-035028-0   AACR2

Book design by Roberta Rezk.

to my parents

Harold
(1911–1956
and
Esther
(1910–1980)

and to Mandi:
Your mother has never
stopped loving or
searching for you.

Author's Note

This is a work of fiction, whose characters and events emanated solely from the author's imagination. While the historical references to the innermost workings of the Holy See are factual, the events portrayed are not to be interpreted as bearing reference to reality. It is not the author's intention to impugn the selection of any Pope, past, present, or future.

I would like to take this opportunity to thank Nadine for giving of herself at a time when a lesser woman would have been consumed by a tragedy beyond comprehension. It is a debt I cannot ever adequately repay.

Sincere appreciation to Rosalee Simensky, and to Naomi Ribner.

And, finally, my utmost thanks to David Prager for his exhaustive effort in the construction of this book.

And behold another beast like a bear stood up on one side: and there were three rows in the mouth thereof, and in the teeth thereof, and thus they said to it: Arise, devour much flesh.

Daniel 7:5

Prologue

Knuckles white, the small man held the envelopes under his arm as a sinner grips a crucifix. His thick black shoes ground audibly against the pavement as he paced deliberately, watchfully down the deserted sidewalk. Dawn had not yet wrested possession of the earth from night.

A lonely breeze funneled through the empty corridors of downtown Prague, penetrating the lone figure's sweaty collar. As he approached the corner, casting a furtive glance behind, his fingers slid over the surfaces of the two large envelopes. He located the serrated edge of the postage stamp affixed to the one only and withdrew that one, pausing tensely before the dark red post box. He listened. Headlights heralded a gasping hiss of tires from the opposite corner. Urgently he grasped the cold metal handle and thrust the packet through. The dull thud of its drop echoed in his ears.

He stepped quickly away from the box and off the curb as the headlights turned toward him, revealing in their glare his leathery, careworn features. The vehicle rolled slowly up the street and pulled alongside him, the soft rumbling of its engine punctuated by a sharp click as the rear door swung open. From within, a voice spoke in precise Russian: "Comrade Inspector Motykia, we are instructed to convey you to headquarters immediately. Please step inside."

The Czechoslovakian inspector hesitated almost imperceptibly before entering the Russian automobile. The mail drop, he realized with relief, had gone unnoticed.

Motykia had been a Czech police inspector long enough to recognize the sensitivity of the documents he carried—and the danger in which they placed him. His thirty years' experience with the Czech Security Bureau told him this matter was being handled by the most select and covert elements of Soviet Intelligence. It followed that with the completion of his assignment he would become a liability to them. In the solitude of his windowless office he had made single photocopies of the documents with exactly this thought in mind.

"Your report, Comrade?" the Russian asked only after the car door had been secured.

"Completed." The Czech nodded, noticing he had been clutching the remaining envelope so tightly that it had begun to crease.

When the vehicle turned the corner, Motykia caught a glimpse of the post-box flap still gently waving from his deposit like the curtain of a confessional.

The next day the inspector's obituary would praise his long and dutiful service, abruptly ended by an unfortunate accident.

Dawn had already begun to dispel the darkness that shrouded the gray concrete suburbs of Moscow and rendered its buildings indistinguishable, braced row upon row like tombstones against the night sky.

The slow tolling of a bell initiated a trickle of Soviet citizens that soon became a torrent in the early morning streets. The first rumbling trains and buses began the reawakening of downtown Moscow's huge brick-and-steel office complexes, punctured at purely functional intervals by small expanses of glass.

Deep within one of these structures was a chamber in which the light and activity had continued unabated through the night. It was a room where powerful men wielded razor-sharp scalpels against the unsuspecting limbs of the world. Revolutions had been plotted around this polished table, assassinations had been formulated here, warfare had been planned and perpetrated from within these soundproof and totally secure walls.

At the head of the table, Soviet Chairman Maksim Shaposhnikov leaned thoughtfully to one side, one thick hand slowly stroking his jowl, piercing eyes scowling. Before him stood a slight, sunken-cheeked official, whose long fingers manipulated the controls of a recording device. Two somber men sat attentively at either side of the long dark-grained table, their reactions carefully attuned to the chairman's lead.

These men were Shaposhnikov's private team, a discreet quorum that commanded his personal force to strike at his bidding with lethal silence. They provided the extra aces with which to outmaneuver opponents and, if need be, dispose of them. There flickered before the chairman now the possibility of acquiring a hot political card to strengthen his hand. The magno-electricity of power crackled in his palm; its potency was matched only by the consequences of failure. Power, Chairman Shaposhnikov had learned through decades of gripping its pinnacle with an iron fist, was always filled with calculated risks.

He nodded for the standing agent to proceed.

"Gentlemen," the slight official began crisply, "our devices at Czechoslovak Security have provided us these recordings, their transfer executed without external knowledge." As he adjusted the correct button, a momentary hum preceded the recorded voice:

' . . . the last forty-eight hours, sir. I came directly upon completion of my research.'

'Good, Comrade Kakol. We are interested in what your investigation has revealed. Have you completely verified our manual suspicions?' It was the voice of Inspector Motykia.

'Yes, Comrade Inspector! It is exactly as we thought.' The second voice bristled with eagerness. 'All of the records were believed destroyed years ago by the retreating German armies, yet two documents have miraculously survived.'

The standing figure interrupted the tape recorder's progress momentarily to interject, "The second speaker is one Edouard Kakol, a police researcher assigned to the original case . . . an expendable." With an abrupt gesture, he switched the tape back on.

' . . . the partisan ledger shows that on that date in April 1943 twelve marriages were performed by the unit's Commanding Officer. It was difficult, but I was finally able to confirm the location of his unit on the exact date and time in question. They too match, beyond doubt. His unit was at Decin on the date referred to, and the marriage was recorded in both the official and the Commanding Officer's ledger.'

Kakol's eager voice raced on excitedly. 'And I might add, Comrade Inspector, that I have checked and double-checked every shred of evidence.'

'Then there can be no error?' Inspector Motykia's manner was much more grave.

'No possible error!' rejoined the other voice. 'Brandano Cardinal Michalovce was married!' There was a long pause. 'He spent at least two days leave—alone with her—before the incident that resulted in her death at the hands of the Nazis. His identity was conveniently changed after 1943, but the proven fact remains. You have the remaining pages of the lost ledger in the envelope, along with his change of name. I have taken the liberty to include the exact times and places for you.'

'I see. Excellent.'

'Oh, there's one more detail. Look here.' There was a shuffling of papers. Motykia spoke next; even his voice rose in excitement.

'A Jewess! A Jewess no less!'

His voice resumed its sober quality. 'Comrade Investigator Kakol,' he began, 'has anyone else been told of your findings? ... '

'No one, Comrade Inspector ... as you instructed ... '

The thin man abruptly stopped the tape and spoke to those seated. "This we can verify." He had the clipped tone of concealed self-congratulation. "Their movements were carefully monitored, as follows: 4:22—tape completed; 4:26—Motykia's call put through to us; 4:33—KGB vehicle connection at Czech Security Bureau. No persons entered; no other phone calls made. Complete documentation is before you."

The gray-haired Shaposhnikov nodded slowly as he spoke: "This Motykia will have to be eliminated."

"Already accomplished, Comrade Chairman," came the brisk reply.

"And this Kakol as well, I assume," one of the aides put in.

"His disposal will be performed presently. No need to arouse unnecessary suspicions by coincidental accidents; we had Kakol dispatched on official duty. His disappearance will remain unknown for some weeks."

"Excellent, excellent." The Chairman leaned forward and drew deeply on his cigarette. "Then it seems, with these documents, we have acquired for our own interests what we might term . . . an ally."

A smile flickered briefly across the features of the gaunt-faced agent. "The threat of exposure provides an iron lever with which to move this somewhat less-than-holy cardinal."

In the pause that followed, all eyes were on Shaposhnikov, whose palms came slowly to rest on the tabletop before he spoke. "This is perfect! It is what we have been waiting for; we can initiate 'Project Conclave.' "

At the Chairman's enthusiasm, the others seated at the table came suddenly alive. "Our Italian comrade must contract with a professional. When we have the full cooperation of the cardinal, the funds will be transferred," said one.

"But, Comrade," the other aide objected, "we can only initiate this project with the expiration of the new Pope."

"Excuse me, Comrade Torchnoi," interrupted the thin official with his terse, metallic speech. "Our sources indicate this process may be—shall we say, *can* be—hastened?"

1

The sticky warmth of the Italian summer night crept into the tight neckline of his dark clothing. He was lost in the shadows that clung like the moist air to the building's facade—a shroud of darkness that rendered him virtually invisible. Still as a panther on silent haunches, he monitored his surroundings.

The side street, chosen for its scant lighting and its possible escape routes, was completely deserted. The faintly luminous dial of his watch indicated that the prearranged hour had arrived. As if on cue, a Mercedes limousine turned the corner onto the rain-slicked roadway. It glided soundlessly to a halt beneath the lone lamppost down the street at precisely 3:00 A.M.

A cat slunk in his direction, hugging the safety of the wall. It paused, then continued onward, brushing his legs as it passed. He twitched his knee reflexively, his concentration unbroken.

The headlights died, leaving a momentary memory of amber on their filaments. From his baggy pants pocket, he removed a miniature penlight and pointed it at the limousine. He pressed the switch twice and a thin beam of diffused light reached out for the vehicle. A few seconds passed; the headlights blinked twice in response. He pressed the penlight once more, and replaced it in his pocket.

A loud click echoed in the silence. The passenger door opened. Hidden by the mass of the shiny black vehicle, a lone cloaked figure stepped out, looked about, then slowly paced down toward where he had seen the light, remaining in the very center of the roadway as he had been instructed to do. The hidden figure surveyed the entire scene; confident that all was proceeding as planned, he began to move forward.

Silent and invisible, he paralleled the other's movement. Peering out from the darkness, he studied the newcomer's features. The intermittent light revealed only a frail figure pacing nervously down the road. Identification had to be certain before he could proceed.

"*Stop where you are*, please," the voice commanded from the shadows in sibilant Italian. The cloaked man complied instantly, eyes riveted forward. "Now step this way."

The figure stepped gingerly over broken bricks and scattered debris. As he moved to within a few meters of the hidden voice, he stepped through a swath of dim light reflected from an alleyway. It revealed an elderly, darkly clothed man.

"Halt. Please remove your hat," came the final demand.

Silver hair gleamed in the pale light, in sharp contrast to the shadows that accentuated the long-boned jaw and nose. The crow-webbed eyes, tensed with fear, still shone with a certain defiance. A high, white collar showed conspicuously in the night. There was no doubt; it was he.

"Good evening, Comrade Cardinal. I am happy to see that you have followed my instructions."

A brief nod was the priest's only reply. His eyes strained in an attempt to identify the speaker, but he could discern only the vague shape of a burly man.

"Comrade Cardinal, the Church will soon go through a major change. The world's 700 million Roman Catholics will embark on a new path. . . ." He stopped.

"Yes?" the cardinal questioned in a tone that wavered with curiosity.

"That's not important now," came the dry reply. "What is important is that the Pope is old and tired. His reign is rushing to an end. Latest medical reports indicate that he will be meeting his creator in a matter of weeks, certainly no longer than three months. When this occurs, the Princes of the Church will be called to the Apostolic Palace to elect a new leader." The cardinal unconsciously rubbed his fingers together. "When a two-thirds majority plus one—or a total of seventy-five votes—is amassed for one man, a new Pope will be named." This was all common knowledge. But the whispered words that followed went to the very core of the cardinal's being: "Are you ready, Cardinal Michalovce, to assume the Papacy?"

The words that sprang from the darkness hit the cardinal like a sledgehammer. How could anyone predict the outcome of the conclave? "Impossible!" he muttered.

"No, my dear Cardinal. We are in a position to determine the papal successor. We are preparing. . . . All will be ready a month from now. When the white smoke curls from that small chimney atop the Sistine Chapel, it will announce to the world that Cardinal Michalovce has been proclaimed the Holy Father."

The cardinal's voice caught in his throat. "Me?" He began to move forward, then stopped. "Impossible! Are you a madman? You would violate our sacred conclave?"

From the shadows, the voice answered unhurriedly, "Believe as you will, my dear Cardinal, but be assured that I speak the truth. You, Bohuslav Tabor, will be named."

A slow chill went through the priest. The name Bohuslav Tabor had not been spoken since 1944. He had thought it had been forever lost in the ruins of the war. The shock of hearing it shot through him, opening old wounds. He trembled with the pain of it. "You cannot . . ." he fumbled angrily. "They mustn't. . . . "

"Have no fear, Cardinal, the name of Anya Anelovicz, or should I say Anya Tabor, will not return to haunt you after forty years of peaceful rest. On the contrary, our people will see to that zealously, with your help, Comrade Michalovce."

The cardinal's veined hands opened as if they were reaching out to touch something. For a fraction of a second he pictured her again, her soft madonna's features smiling tearfully at him before she melted into his memory. There was no one, nothing else in the world, that could have distracted him from his calling, his work, his life. It was a failing from which he had thought he could never rise. But rise he had. Now, he could not permit them to destroy the work he had done in the Church, and was yet to do.

Yet he could not permit the desecration of her memory. He felt as if they had ransacked his soul like thieves combing through a stolen purse. His hands dropped to his sides. "How?" He shook his head.

"That no longer matters. What is of importance here is that we can assure your future Papacy."

"That is impossible." He raised his prominent chin.

"Have faith, Father," came the cool reply.

Could the Russians perform such a miracle, he wondered? Could he, a Czech cardinal, really become the Pope? The horror of the thought made him shiver. The choices were narrow. Could he face expulsion from the Church? Could he dare to imagine himself the Holy Father? With only a few words, it seemed, the communists had both crucified and sanctified him. In the grim solitude of the abandoned side street, only one option remained. It beckoned like a beam of light.

"What do I have to do?"

The hidden figure answered as he had been instructed: "Do? Comrade Cardinal? You must simply follow your normal routine. . . . You are a Prince of the Church. You must act as such. When the conclave begins, things will progress in the normal fashion and in the end you will emerge as Pope.

"Your task will be simple. A short time before the cardinals go into seclusion, you will receive further instructions. Your position will not be endangered and there will be no detection."

"How? How can it be done?" the cardinal questioned again.

"My dear Bohuslav, this we cannot divulge."

The figure could not have answered—there was no reason for him to know, so he hadn't been told.

"All you need to do is perform a simple operation at the appropriate time." He paused. "All is agreed, then. Have you any further questions?"

No answer was necessary. A dropping of the priest's eyes was sufficient reply. But the cardinal did have a question . . . a question that had to be answered: "And assuming all goes as planned and I am elected Pope, what then will your masters ask of me?"

"Ask?" was the reply. "What will we ask? Nothing . . . nothing, really. Simply your understanding in dealing with us. We are not as terrible as the Church believes us to be. All we ask for is your indulgence, as the leader of the Church, in certain matters.

"And, Comrade, a visit by the new Pope to our country might go a long way in repairing the damage the Church has done. Is that too much to ask? We desire little; we offer you the throne of

Saint Peter." He had said all there was to say. He would answer no more questions.

"Comrade Michalovce." The unseen KGB agent resumed using the cardinal's proper name. "We are making preparations. We will move by the end of the month. Goodbye."

Tottering slightly, Cardinal Michalovce turned slowly and walked back to his waiting vehicle, his head pounding.

By the time he was seated in the luxury of the limousine, he was worried whether the plan, whatever it was, could be successful. He sat silently for several minutes. Finally he instructed the driver to return him to his apartment at the Vatican. Tomorrow he would be leaving for his homeland, as the state-arranged visit to the ailing Pope had drawn to an end.

The powerful vehicle backed down the street until it reached the main avenue, then swung east, picking up speed. It would be a half-hour's drive along the highway, through Rome, across the Tiber River to the Vatican. In the distance, flashing red lights atop a radio tower prompted him to switch on the passenger's radio. He turned the dial, finding soothing music to calm his nerves. This worked its magic for several minutes.

Suddenly the soft music stopped and was replaced by a series of high-pitched beeps. An announcer's voice crackled excitedly in Italian. "Pope John XXIV is dead! The Vatican has announced that at 12:52 this morning the Holy Father expired in his sleep. After a lengthy illness, Pope John has been taken by his Maker." In the background, the somber tones of organ music set the mood. Cardinal Michalovce crossed himself, reciting a silent prayer. The vehicle sped on into the night.

It came to him a few minutes later.... "He said they would be ready in a month. They won't have that time now!" He relaxed, believing he was safe. It was impossible for them to be ready in such a short time.

Someone else would be elected Pope. The thought struck him with a wave of relief, followed by a dull echo of sorrow, some of it for himself. At least, he thought, breathing deeply, the name Bohuslav Tabor would die and be buried forever, along with Pope John.

Josef Borzov, a member of the KGB since 1965, had completed his assignment. The meeting with Cardinal Michalovce had gone exactly as planned. The cardinal had agreed to cooperate—he really had no choice. Now Borzov had to inform Moscow that things would proceed as scheduled, and make final contact with the highly trained professional they had hired to carry out the project covertly and efficiently.

Borzov watched as the cardinal departed. Turning in the opposite direction, he left to return to his car by a predetermined route.

Unknown to both the cardinal and the Russian, they had been under close observation from the moment Josef had planted himself at the meeting place. Despite his thoroughness, the Russian had failed to detect the presence of the third party.

In ten minutes the KGB agent found his vehicle, a nondescript Fiat, not unlike others parked on the street. His watch indicated 3:45 A.M., fifteen minutes before he could call in his report. He spent the time thinking of the one question that had plagued him from the very beginning: How could they possibly alter the ballots? He knew that there existed a solution—but what was it?

At precisely 3:59 A.M., the agent opened the glove compartment of the vehicle. Behind the plastic door was a radio-telephone. As he lifted the receiver, the pretuned frequency was picked up automatically by a special aerial atop the Soviet Embassy in Rome. The designated KGB representative, flown in from Moscow, asked for his code name in Russian. When he responded, the transmission was relayed to KGB Headquarters in Moscow.

In another minute the Director of Operations was on the line. "Comrade Borzov, has everything proceeded as planned?" inquired the metallic Russian voice.

"Yes, Comrade. Everything went exactly as instructed. The cardinal will cooperate fully."

"Good." The satellite-relayed message sped into outer space and back. "And the hired professional has received all relevant instructions?"

"Affirmative, Comrade," was pronounced carefully into the micro-transmitter. "The Professional has been engaged pending our payment." There was a long pause in the dark auto before the next command crackled through from Russia.

"You will please take the next available flight back to Moscow to submit a detailed report."

"Yes, Comrade, the very next available flight."

"We shall be waiting for you, Comrade. Goodbye." The connection was broken. The Russian replaced the receiver, then closed the glove compartment.

With that phone call, the plan was locked into action. Payment to the Professional would now be released. The key to the entire operation had been the cooperation of the Czech cardinal. Now that it had been secured, the plan could proceed.

Josef Borzov was forty years old. Not past his peak of usefulness to the state, to the hired Professional, he had already outlived it.

He turned on the ignition, bringing the motor to life. As he switched on the headlights, their brightness was reflected by the vehicle parked directly in front of his. In the glow he glimpsed movement: a man walking slowly toward the front of his car. The figure halted at the edge of the shadows and stared directly through the windshield.

It was not until a hand adorned with a large, bulbous ring rose from the man's side, securely grasping an automatic weapon, that the Russian was able to identify him. Instantly, he threw his vehicle into reverse; the Fiat jumped backward, striking the auto parked directly behind. Sounds of breaking glass and bending steel reverberated as the vehicles locked together.

Reaching to shift the car into first gear, Josef's eyes caught his adversary one last time; the ring glinted under the barrel of a gun pointed directly at his face through the windshield. His hands came up in a vain attempt to stop the deadly projectile.

Josef never saw the spiderweb-like pattern that radiated across the windshield as the bullet pierced the glass, then passed through his palm and entered his face just below his right eye. His head was thrown back by the force of the bullet, hands covering his face. Another bullet instantly followed the first, striking the Russian squarely in the mouth and shattering the base of his skull as it exited. Bits of torn flesh and bone splashed against the rear seat. The bullet spent itself in the cushion, almost unmarked.

Walking on, the figure replaced the automatic in a shoulder holster, turned the corner, and was gone. It was over in a few seconds. Josef's body went completely limp as he bled freely onto the vinyl carpet.

The sound of shots being fired burst upon a sleeping man in his second-floor flat. He bolted upright, each report sounding like a hammer blow striking an iron spike.

Clearing his head, he waited for a second series of shots; there were none. He hastily pulled on his pants, partially stuffing his shirttails under his belt. He took no time to put on his socks, but slipped into his shoes, grabbed for his pistol and ran for the door.

In moments he was down the steps and out onto the street. He looked about. The street was deserted. Maybe it had been a dream, an all-too-vivid one. He considered returning to his apartment but decided to investigate further, around the block.

Moments later the first sounds of sirens invaded the neighborhood. He watched as two police cars raced by and turned the corner. As he followed them to Josef's car, he saw what had happened. The web-like pattern of broken glass indicated his initial presumption had been correct: There had been a rubout.

Another police car, this one unmarked, skidded to a halt at the edge of the growing crowd. Out jumped two sharp-suited detectives who waded into the milling mass of onlookers.

The crowd gave way less willingly to the unshaven man in shirttails and baggy trousers. At a hastily strung rope barrier, a policeman barred his way.

"Let me through. I'm a detective," the man demanded.

One of the on-duty detectives looked up, then walked to where the policeman and the intruder were standing nose to nose. "It's okay, officer. That guy is one of us."

"Need a hand?" the stubble-bearded officer asked after ducking under the barrier.

"Not really, Barzini," answered the working detective.

"I heard shots, so I figured . . . " he began, becoming aware suddenly of his appearance, pausing to tuck in his shirt.

"Thanks, Lorenzo, but we have everything under control here. Why don't you relax and get back to wherever you were?"

Detective Barzini poked around a few more minutes, and decided to head back to sleep. He thought he overheard one of his colleagues musing to another that "that guy couldn't figure out a parking ticket," and wondered indignantly if they were speaking about him. But such thoughts evaporated when he overheard the officer who was examining the victim's wallet gasp in astonishment. "This man's carrying Soviet diplomatic papers! Better call the chief."

It would take the Italian police some twenty-four hours—until they had recovered and examined all the physical evidence—to notify the Russian Embassy.

By the time Moscow was informed, the transfer of funds to the Professional's numbered Swiss account had already taken place. It was irreversible. Borzov's elimination, while unexpected, was not considered inappropriate; the project was far too important. The Professional was hired because of his reputation and unique skills. He needed to operate anonymously, and the elimination of Borzov, his only contact, fulfilled that need.

When the first light of dawn broke across the eastern sky, its color crowned St. Peter's just as it had centuries before. Cardinal Michalovce stood contemplating the majestic scene. The ritual for the deceased Pope had already begun; the faithful were streaming into the great square to pray.

The cardinal could not know that a complex series of events, intricate and precise, had already been set in motion with a momentum as relentless as the movements of the planets and stars across a darkened universe.

2

With her first reachings for him Eugenia awakened. Her mind groped through the thickened numbness of sleep, glancing off something raw; something hurting. She struggled to remain asleep, her mind recoiling into its own depths, wrapping itself in a protective cloak against the searing pain of consciousness. Her body, stretching for warmth to soothe her imaginary wounds, found only the coldness of an empty bed. She bolted upright with the shock.

A rush of pain, then a dizzying numbness, and consciousness flooded back. He was gone, dead; there was no return. She closed her eyes and fell in a heap toward the foot of the bed. At first her sobs were soundless; gradually she became conscious of her wretched cries as if they came from another. Hearing herself, she halted, stood suddenly, and dragged mechanically to the bathroom. Tears fell from her chin, splashing onto her hand clutching her robe closed at the throat.

Mrs. Motykia gazed at her disheveled image in the mirror. She did not remember herself as so disturbingly old; eyes red and sleepless, face furrowed with grooves deepened through the years of worry as the wife of a state security officer.

She had been rent with anguish for days. As if in a stupor she had been piloted through the funeral by the friends and relatives who surrounded her, holding her steady through a tear-drenched haze.

But the emptiness that followed had wrung her heart out. Now she stood before the mirror searching for a reason to exist.

Life reasserted itself slowly. She had been an inspector's wife for thirty years; had lived with the ever-present possibility of his death through most of those. Straightening, she began to gather strength. She would not be one of those wives who crumbled without her husband, who lived through him and was lost without him. Through years of late nights, decades of long and difficult assignments and risks, strength had become a necessity. "An inspector's wife," she repeated as if it were a litany; she would not fail him now.

Compulsively dressing, she wiped her tears away and smeared on a touch of makeup. She forced herself down the stairs and out into the cold open air.

These were perhaps her first moments of complete alertness since the news had come. She was awake.

Her face flushed in the early morning chill of suburban Prague. She walked with steps that appeared deliberate, but with no conscious direction. Every few moments a rush of remembrance would shiver through her. Wincing, she forced it away. "Go on, Eugenia," she insisted with stubborn determination; her dignity must set an example for the others.

She walked endlessly, alone with her thoughts, fighting the pain that rose like a deep chill. Eventually she found herself at Turgenev Park. Perhaps she had headed there unconsciously; it had been one of their favorite spots as lovers. Now at a slower pace, more gently, she turned to amble down the long slate square, gently touching the brittle hedges. With heightened awareness, she heard sounds of youngsters playing, a woman with a squeaky carriage, found the scent of roasting pretzels. In the empty fountain, only a film of rainwater covering its bottom, a leaf was embedded in the stiff mud. They had often come here in spring.

She watched an old man lying on a bench. For a moment it was he, unshaven, napping on the couch in front of the television, a Sunday afternoon. The old man groaned and pulled his coat tight, breaking her reverie. She sat on the fountain's edge and wept for hours.

Returning to her apartment, she found the door ajar. Inside, a middle-aged man wearing an overcoat stood with his hat in hand.

It took a moment to recognize him; he was one of her husband's colleagues.

"Sorry to startle you, Madame Motykia. I am here to pay a condolence call and to convey the respects of your husband's friends and comrades at headquarters. You had left the door open. I entered because I thought something might be amiss when no one answered."

"Oh, that's all right, Mr. Korchnoi," she said, regaining her composure. "I must have left hurriedly; I needed to get out for a while."

"I understand. It was a terrible tragedy. We shall all feel this loss. We wanted very much for you to have this." He handed her a bronze and wooden plaque dedicated to the long and diligent service of Zavar Motykia to his department and to the state.

Inspector Korchnoi left shortly, not wanting to burden the grieving woman with reminders. He'd already spoken overmuch of the senseless tragedy of the accident.

It was not long afterward that she sensed it, with the intuitive awareness that only a housewife can have. As she puttered aimlessly, dusting, straightening, trying to keep busy, she sensed that things in her home—drawers, letters, possessions—had been touched.

With this suspicion fermenting in her mind, a singular thought occurred, as if stirred from her innermost recesses. Zavar's death had been caused by an automobile accident—the car had struck an abutment. But he had been driving alone, she realized with a start, something he was never permitted to do.

Her confusion mounted. Coupled with grief, the fear she now experienced would paralyze her if she allowed it to. Pouring a cup of coffee, she struggled to resume her daily routine. She felt she had to get out.

The hollow sound of her leather shoes against the rough gray concrete treads leading from her third-floor, state-constructed flat, created the impression that more than one person was on the stairway. It was merely her imagination. Reaching the lobby, she turned to the row of steel post boxes that held the tenants' daily mail, key in hand.

There were two letters for her, the first from the State Security Police. The sight of the second struck a blow to her mind that left her reeling. Gasping, she stuffed it in her vinyl bag and darted back up the stairwell to the now-precarious asylum of her apartment. There could be no mistake: she knew his handwriting as she knew her own.

Back inside her apartment, she opened the official envelope first, its contents merely a set of forms to be filled out, entitling her to a widow's pension; the inspector had been killed while on duty. The second envelope lay alone in the center of the kitchen table awaiting her decision. Her eyes searched its surface. There was nothing save the postmark, dated the same day as his "accident."

For the distraught woman, it was an omen from the recent past to be treated with loving care. Finally, gingerly, but with determination, she grasped the plain envelope, slowly tearing it open.

An hour slipped by without her rising from the hard wooden seat. She was too stunned to act or even to move. Four photostatic sheets, their grayness dull against the white surface of the kitchen table, remained where they had fallen from her trembling fingers. The short attached note from her husband was brief but each word seared her with pain. Its hurried scrawl simply instructed her to keep the documents safe. Because he had said to, she would.

Where could the documents be hidden so that the expert prying eyes of the State Security Police might not search them out? The answer lay just outside the door of her apartment. She wrapped the envelope and its damning contents carefully in waxed paper, then used the heat of her iron to seal it into a weatherproof packet. Taking a roll of tape with her, she stepped across the hallway to the garbage disposal chute. Her husband had previously hidden documents there, so it was logical for her to do the same. He had broken a small hole in the uppermost tier of hollow concrete blocks that sat above the metal door jamb. Since the hole was above the level of the light fixture, it was virtually undetectable in the dimness of the anteroom.

Once she had wedged the envelope inside the hollow chamber and meticulously replaced the concrete, the block appeared merely cracked, not broken. Satisfied that the document was safe, she returned to her room to mull over the significance of her unexpected legacy. Hours later, the swelling anger she felt had found its focus. The link between these documents and her husband's sudden demise was unmistakable. She would devote all her remaining strength to making full use of the information provided by . . . a memory.

3

El Al flight 71, arriving from Tel Aviv at 1400, flashed on the Arrivals/Departures board. Interested travelers and relatives stopped, looked at the bright overhead display, and went on their way. No one took special notice of a priest amidst the crowded space before the giant board. Da Vinci Airport was bustling; the passing of the Pope had filled seats on each incoming flight, as people wanted desperately to be in Rome when the new Pope was consecrated.

In fifteen minutes the 747 would begin unloading at the International Arrivals area. It would take at least half an hour for the passengers to disembark and pass through the notoriously lax Italian customs. During that time, the priest would make his way to the single exit from the secure area in order to be there when the first of the tired passengers walked through.

By 1500 hours six priests that fit the description of Father Kottmeyer had been hailed without response; a seventh approached. "Father Kottmeyer?" the waiting priest shouted in German.

The father stopped and looked about. "Yes?" he questioned, as he looked for the source of the voice.

"Over here, Father! Over here!" Separated by a railing, the caller motioned for Kottmeyer to meet him at the end of the corridor. The German father acknowledged with a positive nod of his head. Bag in hand, he soon reached the end of the sectioned-off area and was greeted there by a smiling but unfamiliar priest, a large man, close to his own age of thirty-six.

"Good day, Father Kottmeyer. Welcome to Rome." The priest welcomed the newcomer with a businesslike handshake. "I'm Father Schmidt of the Vatican library staff. The bishop has sent me to ensure that you don't get lost in our city. I'll take you to the reception center." The priest scooped up Father Kottmeyer's single piece of worn luggage with one large hand and began to steer him from the terminal with the other.

"But, Father, I don't have to report for a few days. I thought I'd have time to do a bit of sightseeing before I begin work."

"Father Kottmeyer, since the Pope has been taken by the Lord, the Vatican is in turmoil. The bishop has asked for you immediately. Should I tell him that you have requested a few days for purposes of self-indulgence?"

Father Kottmeyer's eyes dropped, heavy with shame. He followed his guide out of the terminal without another word of protest.

The two clergymen walked along the pickup area of the sidewalk to a waiting lineup of taxis. The driver at the head of the queue popped out of his vehicle to assist them. Both priests slid inside while the driver deposited the suitcase into the taxi's cavernous trunk.

Father Kottmeyer's escort turned to him, smiling. "Father, I hope you don't mind, but I'd like to make a brief stop at my apartment. I neglected to bring a report that I will need this afternoon. I can instruct the driver to take us past the famous Spanish Steps. I'm certain that you'd like to see them before you get buried in your work."

Father Kottmeyer's eyes betrayed his interest. "Certainly," he replied, "if it is at all possible, I would love to see them!" His high-pitched voice revealed his avid desire to explore the city.

His escort turned to the elderly driver, and gave an address, along with directions that took them slightly out of their way. First they would pass the Trevi Fountain and then the Spanish Steps. The taxi, which seemed as decrepit as its aging driver, jumped into gear and jerked forward onto the complex of roadways that circled the airport. It took only a few seconds for the experienced hack to find the exit, spinning the wheel in what seemed a reckless way to the cautious German father.

Father Kottmeyer spotted a second taxi hurtling toward the

same exit. His right hand found the armrest molded into the door panel and he gripped it tightly with both hands, his knuckles turning white as the two vehicles almost collided.

At the last possible instant the second vehicle skidded, narrowly avoiding the taxi in which Father Kottmeyer was huddled. Their driver gave a brief exclamation of triumph, for he had just beaten another driver in a classic game of "catastroph." He looked into his rear-view mirror and grinned at the cursing, gesticulating hack.

Kottmeyer relaxed his grip on the armrest and sank back into the hard cushion that passed for a passenger seat. His escort chided him: "Take it easy, Father. . . . You'll just have to get used to that kind of performance. It's normal throughout Rome. These taxi drivers think they're American cowboys!" Father Schmidt seemed amused by the furrows of tension around his companion's lips and eyes.

It was Kottmeyer's first visit to Rome, and the ride through a bit of the countryside gradually relaxed him. The relentless midday sun shone fiercely on long rows of hand-tended vegetables. Men and women toiled together to harvest the produce from the rich soil. Here and there a farmhouse, its tiled roof glinting, stood at the center of a family's plot of land.

The scenery changed as the city itself drew near. Ancient Rome was built on seven hills, and Father Kottmeyer tried to pick them out as the taxi continued on its way. Traffic was sparse, for it was the time of day when all Romans disappear and shops and businesses throughout the city close, not to reopen until four. Not only tradition, it is necessity—for the heat of the day makes transacting business virtually impossible. Romans lose themselves in unknown places, relinquishing the city to the tourists. By one in the afternoon the city is asleep, save for the cafés that cater to both resting Romans and weary visitors. In the vehicle the two priests regarded the phenomenon differently: one with the wide eyes and reverence of a pilgrim; the other with the calculating perceptions of a shrewd planner.

The taxi approached Trevi slowly, as crowds of tourists hurried to their afternoon meeting places. At last a final corner was negotiated and the vehicle fell in line behind a horse-drawn carriage; to the right stood the famous fountain. Father Kottmeyer studied the giant statues darkened by pollution, and noted crevices worn by the falling water. Youngsters splashed in the fountain-pool as a lone policeman tried unsuccessfully to keep them out. The coolness of the water was too tempting; as soon as his back was turned, the children tumbled in once again. Another minute and the historic site was lost to view as the taxi made a quick turn. Only the memory of the stone gods, framed against the towering building's backdrop, remained.

Three streets later they came to another fountain, crowded with ever-present tourists. Beyond, stretching upward to a church on a street above, were the Spanish Steps. The time-honored steps were no longer like those seen on picture postcards. They had been invaded by an army of peddlers selling pictures and leather goods. There were no flowers, no brilliance; the site had become merely another tourist trap.

A busload of Japanese sightseers flowed out of a side street and hurried to the fountain. Around their necks hung the latest cameras and assortments of photographic gadgetry. Instantly they busied themselves snapping pictures of the scene and of each other. They were laden with bags of gifts, purchased in the most exclusive shops, for relatives and friends who would no doubt visit the same sights next year. The strength of the almighty yen had surely replaced that of the floundering dollar, Father Schmidt remarked. The Japanese obviously realized that nations no longer needed to conquer other nations; they simply bought them.

Schmidt tapped the driver's shoulder indicating that it was time to proceed to the address he had given. Once away from the Steps area, the streets were practically empty. Within five minutes the cab drew up in front of a typical Italian apartment house in the older section of the city. Once again the priest spoke in Italian to the driver, who turned the meter off.

"Come, Father Kottmeyer," he said in German. "We'll have some refreshments at my flat. There's a perfectly marvelous view of the Vatican from the sitting room." With that, Father Schmidt exited, removing the valise from the cab's trunk and paying the driver the indicated fare and appropriate gratuity; he doubted that the driver would note either priest. Lifting the suitcase in a fist that bore a large oval ring, he quickly entered the courtyard with Father Kottmeyer at his heels.

"What a lovely court," commented the father as he followed

behind. "Don't tell me the Vatican puts its clergymen up in quarters such as these?"

Schmidt stopped and turned to Kottmeyer, whose eyes had resumed their exploration of the ornate trappings of the small fountain and greenery. "Father, I hate to disappoint you, but, this isn't where I live. I just use the courtyard as a shortcut to the building at the rear. It saves time." Kottmeyer laughed out loud at the perpetual dilemma of a priest's minuscule salary. Schmidt returned a knowing smile.

They resumed walking through an archway and up a set of stone steps until a single, metal-faced door suddenly loomed before them. Even during the height of day, little light filtered through the small, sooty skylight two stories above. The priest found the keyhole, pressed the key through. The lock protested for an instant, then opened with a clunk.

He threw the door open, its unoiled hinges sending another eerie sound down the dingy hallway. "Welcome, Father," his tone rang hollow, "to a place of rest." He stepped aside, allowing Father Kottmeyer to enter. What lay inside was predictable—simple interior, a flat complete with modest furnishings.

The sitting area lay straight ahead. High windows at the far wall flooded the room with light, tightly drawn face-high curtains obstructing any view. Father Kottmeyer heard the door close and lock behind them as he walked forward. He reached the curtains and drew them aside. There in the distance, across the Tiber, was the Vatican, the dome of St. Peter's dominating the tiny religious state.

Father Kottmeyer felt lost in his gaze for a long moment, then turned slightly, suddenly aware of the other priest close behind him.

"That's odd," the father said, slightly disconcerted. There was something unfamiliar about his escort's expression. He looked at the other's hand: "Your jewelry—have the Italian clergy taken to wearing rings?"

"Why?" The other frowned. His fist bore a large, crested golden ring with a stone in its center. "I see you wear a jeweled cross on a chain, don't you?" He reached forward to examine the ornament.

Father Kottmeyer gasped as the priest's hand firmly grasped

the neckchain while at the same instant took a quick step behind and jerked it tightly about his throat, dragging him down backward. His breath left his lungs in a sudden rush.

Only a stifled scream escaped him before the ringed fist produced a thin needle and struck a single deadly blow at the flailing priest's neck. A sharp explosion against his skin brought excruciating pain, making it burn as if a blow-torch had been set against it. His struggle against the strangling chain abruptly ceased as his body stiffened with the first involuntary spasms of approaching death. His legs went out from under him and he fell heavily to the hard floor. He convulsed one last time—then it was over. His face was frozen in a contortion of anguish, jaw muscles locked tight, unseeing eyes bulging. The Professional stepped back, and, with his ringed hand, removed a small dart from Father Kottmeyer's swollen neck.

He looked back once, then left the room. In the dimness of the bedroom he quickly stripped off his priest's costume, a disguise that proved convenient not only in its anonymity, but also in concealing much that was unpriestly within its folds. He reached for a plastic apron and slipped it on. He then placed a plastic bag on each foot, securing them with tight elastic bands at the calf. Finally, he pulled on a pair of surgical gloves. Now ready, he returned to the dead man.

Kottmeyer hadn't moved . . . his expression remained unaltered. The poison dart had been dipped in nicotine—one of the swiftest and deadliest of poisons. Its effect upon the nervous system is instantaneous and irreversible. Within two or three seconds after simple contact with the skin, there is collapse; in an additional five . . . certain death.

The peculiarly clad man proceeded to undress the dead priest, neatly laying out each piece of clothing alongside the prone figure. When he had completely stripped the dead man, he carried the body to the bath, dumped it into an oversized tub, and turned on a trickle of warm water.

Using a surgeon's scalpel and saw, he expertly dismembered the body. Blood intermingled with the warm water, then flowed to the drain at the tub's lowest point, a darker river within a river. The Professional severed each hand from the arm at the wrist, and each fingertip from the finger. The fingertips were flushed down the toilet one by one; hungry sewer rats would eagerly devour them in the maze of lines running beneath the city's streets.

As he worked, he packaged the remaining pieces in plastic bags. He neatly severed the head from the trunk, then stripped the skin off. Next he cut the skull into four pieces, the jaw in two. Finally he packed and sealed the body's trunk in a dark plastic garbage bag, and placed it in a cardboard carton along with bits of refuse.

When this skilled surgery was completed, the remains of the former Father Kottmeyer lay neatly stacked next to the bloody tub. During the early morning, "Father Schmidt" would make a series of short trips outside his flat to deposit his carefully wrapped garbage deep within the cans that Romans placed alongside their curbs for the early morning pickup.

Even if the police found a package or two, without fingertips for fingerprints, or a skull, they would be at a loss to make any identification at all. They would be forced to write it off as the work of some terrorist faction or Mafia killing. The Professional felt perfectly safe in the identity he would now assume, that of the recently dismembered Father Kottmeyer.

The white tub sparkled after fifteen minutes of scrubbing. The surgeon's gloves and the plastic apron and bags were burned piece by piece in a wastebasket near an open window late that night, any traces of smoke lost in the darkness of a moonless sky. He scrubbed the two tools clean. Once he dropped them in the Tiber, there would be nothing to connect him with the crime. Hands disinfected thoroughly, he rinsed himself to the elbows in a basin of rosewater to dispel any remnant of odor. A paper towel wiped the moisture from his fingers and was disposed of.

The Professional leaned back in the room's only chair and gazed out the window at the steeple tops that pierced the sky over Vatican City, reaching upward like imploring fingers. In the distance the spires were indistinguishable from the clusters of television antennas that crowded the fashionable apartment rooftops outlying the city. Still further out, only the rough-hewn hills preserved a sense of Rome's venerable antiquity.

He poured himself a glass of red wine to dispel the tinge of bile at the back of his throat, and rose to reinspect the bath for any telltale bits of flesh or stray traces of blood. Finding none, he raised the glass and spoke aloud: "A toast to the late Father Kott-meyer—may God bless the old one in death, and the new one, in life." After taking a sip, he tilted the chalice and slowly poured its contents into the tub. The wine ran down the drain in dark rivulets like the blood that had preceded it.

Tomorrow he would begin the second phase of his plan, which was to become Father Kottmeyer in actuality. It was vital that he place himself in proximity to the Sistine Chapel. Anytime within the twenty-four hours directly preceding the cardinals' se-clusion in Conclave would do, as he needed no more than five or ten minutes alone there to accomplish the required task.

He had already completed a psychologically as well as physi-cally exhausting portion of the plan. What remained to be done, he hoped, was for the Vatican itself to carry the balance of the plot through for him.

A temporary "Official Identification Card" had been issued to Kottmeyer in Jerusalem. By stapling four color photographs to his folder, he would provide the Vatican with the only current pictures of Father Kottmeyer in existence. Prior church records of new personnel were carried by the individual priests to their new assignments. Tampering with sealed official Church documents by a member of the clergy was unthinkable—after all, who would want to impersonate a priest, and for what possible reason?

Across the Tiber River from the grandeur of the Vatican, a soli-tary priest walked deliberately down a broad avenue that led to one of the three ancient river bridges. Off in the distance, the dome of St. Peter's rose to command the morning sky and domi-nate the city's skyline.

As he walked, he joined others who were also making their way to the Vatican. In his pocket was an official pass made out in the name of one Father V. Kottmeyer, Assistant to the Curator of Relics. No one would notice a tiny slit at the base of the photo-graph that was sealed into the pass. It had taken nearly six hours to substitute his photograph for Father Kottmeyer's, yet it was time well spent. With this document, he had acquired free access to almost any section of the Vatican.

The time had come for the security officers and others in and about the Vatican to become acquainted with him. Father Kott-meyer's transfer from Cologne was to take effect in two days.

Now, with the death of the Pope, his services might be needed a bit earlier. He was unknown, this being his first assignment outside Germany. In the confusion caused by the ceremonies of the next week, the Professional could move about freely in his place. It was necessary for him to perform specific tasks; then he would simply fade away.

His steps carried him across the stone bridge. On his left, the Vatican beckoned a scant kilometer to the south. The sun broke across the dome of St. Peter's, creating a backdrop akin to the beginning of an opera—all that was missing was Verdi's hand in orchestrating the necessary score. The blueness of the sky was an endless eulogy of color. It was a fitting time for death. . . .

4

Surprisingly, the broad, gray stone steps that spread out before St. Peter's were almost devoid of people. Angular wooden barricades had been set in place by the Italian Security Forces minutes after they had been informed of the Pope's expiration. Their instructions were to permit only authorized and properly identified Vatican staff members to pass the police line; the general public would be denied access until nine that morning.

In front of the shallow steps lay the nearly circular plaza, enclosed by an ornate stone colonnade. These stones had seen centuries of the faithful gathered in mourning at the passing of their beloved Holy Fathers. The worn and ancient steps had borne rivers of their tears. Even at this early hour Romans were already a sea of black-clothed bodies, each one trying to push forward to gain a better vantage point. There was nothing yet to see, but being first, nearest to the cathedral's entrance, was the uppermost thought. The Pope's body would lie in state for another two days, but that fact did not deter them. To be even a microscopic portion of the impending drama was reason enough for each to be present.

The bogus Father Kottmeyer had managed to thread his way forward through the growing mass of humanity until he reached the central monument, the focal point of the historic plaza. Finding a coign on which to stand, he slowly surveyed the scene. To the west lay St. Peter's, rising in the morning sky to dominate the entire site; its awesome size diminished all else. On its left lay the Pope's apartment. News teams were already scurrying to set up their array of cameras atop a low roof that faced that corner apartment. From that location they would soon record this latest page in the ongoing chronicle of man's mad rush into history.

The day promised to be another scorcher, especially for those packed together here. Even at this early hour, the temperature added affliction to their grief and brought forth beads of salty perspiration on the foreheads of the mourners. Those of the throng who could reach the two grandiose fountains to Kottmeyer's right were moistening bits of cloth in it to cool themselves. These two fountains could not begin to accommodate the more than half-million souls that would be crowded into the plaza before the day ended. By nightfall the Red Cross would have carted away nearly three hundred of them, most suffering from heat prostration.

After a while, the Professional resumed his movement toward the steps. His priestly attire acted as a magic wedge, parting the packed crowd before him. A line of khaki-clad soldiers, mixed with a sprinkling of Rome's finest, stood on the far side of the wooden barricade in small clusters. A space in the temporary railing served as an entrance. A group of nuns was just being passed in; he waited behind the last member of the identically attired women.

A young sergeant allowed the last nun to pass, then turned to the waiting priest. "Sorry, Father. No one can come through without authorization," he said in Italian.

The priest replied hesitantly in the same language: "Please speak slowly; my Italian is poor. I am German."

The soldier began once again, this time more slowly. "Father . . . a pass, you must have a Vatican pass . . . a card to enter!" He gestured, forming a rectangular shape with his fingers.

This time the waiting priest seemed to understand and produced a temporary Vatican foreign identification card. The soldier compared the picture with the face of the clergyman before him who stood, poised, carefully studying the soldier's expression and movement, readying himself for any possible detection. The pass was handed back, the soldier saluting as the priest was ushered through. Father Kottmeyer's pass indicated that he was an important official.

The priest climbed the steps that led directly up to the great doors of the cathedral. The eternal fiery orange sun, and its accompanying oppressive heat, bore down on his bare head and covered shoulders, intensifying his tension. Reaching the entrance, he passed into dim, comforting marble coolness. He paused to let his eyes adjust—the darkness of the interior was in sharp contrast with the harsh early-morning brightness. A quick glance at his watch indicated it was 8:45 A.M., nearly time for the endless river of the faithful to begin pouring inside. For now, though, the silence was profound.

He walked on, approaching the statue of St. Peter. A lone, aged nun was praying silently, her wrinkled hand and bent fingers barely touching the statue's right foot at a place where untold millions had caressed it before. The saint's foot had been worn smooth, the toes seemingly melting together.

He continued toward the Tomb of St. Peter, standing majestically under the awesome, curved expanse of the basilica ceiling. Even in this semi-darkness, its sheer enormity dwarfed everything beneath it. Beyond was the altar, cutting completely across the nave. Above it was an architectural masterpiece, a golden circular stained glass window with a single snow-white dove at its center. The window was breathtaking in its brilliance, its brightness framed by the building's soft, dark interior. The stark light fell on the altar and on the small golden crucifix atop the simple white linen covering.

Far behind him, the resounding opening of the great doors signaled that the hour had arrived for the mass of faithful to enter. The movement of their thousands of pairs of feet ruptured the silence. Like an invading funereal army, they flowed in and dispersed throughout the vast cathedral. In moments, a dark line of humanity had formed to file, one by one, down a narrow stairway to the area where former Popes had been interred.

The priest turned right, paralleling the way he had entered, stopping briefly to view Michelangelo's *Pietà*, frozen in its yearning pose behind the thick sheets of bullet-proof glass that protect it from crazed humanity. Of course the protection had come, in a matter of speaking, after the fact, only installed after massive damage had already been done several years earlier. Since then it had languished in its case, a vision of consummate compassion shielded from the touch of the humans it was meant to inspire.

While the Professional seemed to dally in reflection upon the vanquished Jesus, his alert mind registered details, measured distances, calculated alternative routes. There could be no flaws, no unforeseen circumstances, no intricacies left unprepared for. The procedure must be as certain as his steps, which rang with striking regularity against the marble floor.

The time had come now to move on to the Vatican library to assume his role as part of the staff. As a German priest, a newcomer to the Holy City and not particularly fluent in Italian, he could expect his initial assignment to be relatively minor, while his position would grant him entry to most of the Vatican.

His cover was perfect. Father Kottmeyer was nearly the same age as his counterpart and was totally unknown at the Vatican. The father had studied in Europe, then at the Art Institute in Chicago, where he had spent four years learning about restorations. He had devoted another seven years to study at holy sites in Jerusalem.

The Vatican had published a series of short articles by Kottmeyer on fresco restorations from 1978 into the 1980s. They proved to be interesting, from a purely technical standpoint to a handful of Vatican experts. Thus, when the death of an assistant created an opening, he became the logical choice—almost by default. There simply wasn't anyone available to fill the position located anywhere outside the United States, and the possibility of placing an American in even this minor Vatican post was unthinkable. It would take perhaps another fifty years before an American would be considered for any responsible position within the Vatican Curia or library:

The choice of Father Kottmeyer, after much discussion, was finally approved and transmitted. He deemed it a great honor, and had accepted quickly with the proper degree of humility. He had been given a month to tend to the loose ends of his own affairs before reporting to his new position. In that time, the Vatican experienced the passing of an era.

When he reached the area of the Vatican that was restricted to authorized persons, a guard, not recognizing him, blocked his entrance. "Can I be of help, Father?" he quickly asked in Italian.

The Professional stopped and showed his pass. The guard examined it, then directed him to a reception center housed down the entrance corridor in room nine.

A single long table and a couple of chairs were the only furnishings in the high-ceilinged room. Seated behind the table was a priest who looked as old as St. Peter's itself. The living relic didn't look up from the ledger he was reading until Father Kottmeyer had stopped before him. Then he simply held out his wrinkled hand for the envelope the father was carrying. When Father Kottmeyer didn't respond immediately, a simple, "Envelope, please!" was barked in his direction in Italian.

Once it was in his possession he tore open the paste seal, without inspection, and removed the carefully prepared documents. He spread them out before him, making three piles as he examined each paper. When all were carefully read, he placed each pile in a separate envelope and used a paper clip to place a photograph on the face of each one. He handed the fourth photograph back to the waiting father and began to speak in German: "Father Kottmeyer, welcome! We've been expecting you. Our prayers have been with you for a safe and swift journey. However, we are saddened that you could not have had the opportunity to arrive here at a happier moment.

"Please go on to room number ten with this photograph and card." With that, he handed a typewritten pass to the waiting priest.

The bogus Father Kottmeyer began to turn, then stopped and spoke in German to the relic who was still riveted to his throne-like seat. "You speak German very well, Father. Perhaps you are a fellow countryman?"

A smile shone through the rows of wrinkles that partially hid his small mouth. He answered once again in German. "No, Father. I am an Italian! However, in a position such as this, I have come in contact with people who speak many different languages, so I have learned a number of them. Nevertheless, thank you for the most gracious compliment."

The standing priest had one more question. "How many languages do you speak, Father?"

"Sixteen!" was the reply, as he turned back to his day's tasks. He wished no further discussion on the matter, having gone through similar explanations in English, French, Spanish, Greek, and a dozen other tongues. After almost fifty years devoted to language-related assignments, he was weary of such conversations.

The Professional, sensing that the discussion had been terminated, pivoted and walked through the high doorway. These familiarities might prove helpful in acquiring freedom of movement in the Vatican. He turned right and saw room ten clearly marked several paces diagonally across the hall.

His knock echoed softly, but received no reply. The father opened the wooden door and walked inside. Again he was taken back by the sparseness of the furnishings. Two working priests were at their desks; one looked up, then asked: "Yes?"

"I've been told to report here with this card and photograph." He held them up.

This priest, too, appeared to have been born to his office, as he had to be well over sixty and walked with a pronounced limp. "Come here!" he commanded as he led Kottmeyer to a square machine located in one corner of the room. The elder priest held out his arthritic hand for the small color photograph and the typewritten card, then carefully placed them together in a stiff piece of folded plastic. He switched on the machine, inserted the plastic sandwich in the appropriate slot, and in a moment retrieved it from another slot at the bottom of the machine. It had been transformed into an official Vatican identification card, embossed with a golden Vatican seal.

The priest handed the card, which was still warm, to Father Kottmeyer and instructed him on its uses. Once again the speech had been given so many times that it had been memorized down to each word's proper inflection. It ended with a cold rote warning: "This is a most valuable document. If it is lost, or stolen, report it immediately to security! If you should require a Vatican passport in addition to your personal identification card while working in an official capacity here, Bishop Bartoleme, the chief librarian, will see to it that one is obtained for you. Now you may return to room nine." With his little speech completed, the bent priest returned to his desk, caring neither to hear nor to answer any questions. Father Kottmeyer was free to return to the reception area, room nine. His true identity now perfectly concealed behind a flawless plastic card, he had almost gained the unrestricted access and safety he would require to complete the project. Like dominoes, or like beads, one by one the pieces were falling into their places, preordained by the Professional's meticulous planning.

At the reception room he was greeted almost immediately by a breathless young priest who had apparently been sent to receive him. "Father Kottmeyer? I hope you're Father Kottmeyer! I'm sorry I'm late. I am Father Schumacher. I will take you to the bishop. He's been waiting for your arrival." He shook the father's hand firmly, hoping his German, although somewhat hesitant, would make the new arrival feel at home. "Please follow me. I'll try to familiarize you with our intricate system of hallways. Don't worry, though, it could take a lifetime to learn!" They closed the massive wooden doors behind them, then proceeded to the administrative wing of the complex. Beyond was the library, with its books and research center. The Vatican museum, archives and library were all interconnected. Bishop Bartoleme, chief administrator, ruled with an iron hand; and even a Pope dared not question his methods, nor his results.

The Professional followed Father Schumacher down an endless succession of corridors; he walked intently, studying details, always alert to any possible detection and to any detail that he could use to advantage. They finally reached the archives, that ancient bastion of Catholic history, and passed symbolically from the present to the past. Off to the side stood the chief administrator's office, and beyond it a solid cypress door. Father Schumacher approached, stopped, and then knocked softly. From within came a resounding voice—a voice as commanding as a thunderclap. So far all had progressed flawlessly. But now the Professional was about to encounter a living legend.

5

Elongated early-morning shadows sprawled across the narrow sidewalks of the ancient city. The stillness was disrupted by the grinding of the municipal garbage trucks as they attempted to consume the mountains of trash generated during the weekend. It was Monday, and eleven-year-old Maria Crisanti was on her way to school. She was already feeling the heat in her heavily starched uniform, but she quickly forgot any discomfort as she spied Rocco Marrero stepping into the street barely ten meters away. Her heartbeat took up the pace of her steps as she ran to his side. Even at eleven, she had a woman's instincts.

"Rocco," she began as she reached his side, "mind if I walk to school with you?" Her question had been the same each morning since he had moved into the working-class neighborhood the previous fall. Love bloomed at first sight for them both, the problem resting not with her, but with his inability to handle the still new, yet exciting, situation. He chose merely to pretend she didn't exist . . . even if his body knew she did.

"If you'd like, you're free to join me. The equality of the working class gives you that right." His father's political leanings often crept into his speech. The youngster's education and indoctrination had begun long before he had the opportunity to choose a path for himself. Rocco wasn't a man, yet he had to exist in a totally male-oriented society. His emotions, his actions, were all patterned after a rigid set of rules. To pass beyond those unwritten limits would attack his very manhood before he had even reached it.

They walked together along the street, carefully stepping around the still-uncollected trash. Each of them watched the sidewalk, being certain not to step into anything that might mar the mirror-like shine of their attire, painstakingly acquired the night before by their respective mothers. Rocco feigned indifference, but periodically snatched a glance at his companion. Their eyes met from time to time, quickly dropping back to the ground when caught.

The din cascading down the street from the approaching garbage truck soon made it impossible to speak, even if either had been inclined to conversation. Maria seemed oblivious to the noise, her thoughts concentrated on her companion. Suddenly catching her shoetip on a raised sidewalk square, she tripped and fell to the hard concrete surface, her books sprawled before her. She scrambled to right herself from an embarrassing position. Rocco looked down momentarily, his eyes catching a glimpse of the panties that covered her soft buttocks, just as she pulled her skirt to her knees.

Their eyes met once again. His face flushed and he quickly ran to retrieve her fallen texts. The situation was perplexing— what was he supposed to do about the sudden hardness that was pushing against the front of his pants?

Rocco quickly gathered together the strewn books and was about to return them when his eyes fell upon a small package lying atop a single cardboard box. Anything that might prolong returning to her side at this moment would be a godsend. He picked it up, examining its shape and the tight knot that held it together.

Maria was impatient for him to return and finally came to his side. "What have you found, Rocco?"

"Nothing," he answered, not wanting to look at her. The growing hardness had spent itself and, no longer needing the object to occupy his attention, he threw it back to its original place where it would be picked up in moments by the garbage collectors.

Maria reached down and retrieved it, tearing at its wrappings. In moments she had exposed what was beneath the brown paper exterior—a plastic bag with some sort of bone in it. Rocco held out her books, but her concentration was on the object. A feeling of revulsion swept her as she made out the row of teeth that ran along one surface of the bone. She threw it down with a barely suppressed scream.

Rocco reached for the object still encased within the small clear plastic bag. "What are you so afraid of?"

"It's someone's teeth!" she sobbed out to him. "It's someone's teeth!"

"So what?"

"Rocco, it's teeth from a mouth."

"Okay, so it's teeth, so what?" Rocco resumed walking, carrying both their books and the plastic bag in his hands. He hurried, not wanting to be late, and Maria quickly composed herself and caught up with him. They turned north on Via Contado. He was still examining the fragment as she took her books from him. With a degree of compulsion that she didn't quite comprehend, she brought herself to look again at the wrapped object. It was grotesque, yet fascinating.

"Let me see it again, please."

Rocco held out the object; her eyes examined it, but she didn't reach out to take it from him. She withstood it as long as she could, but finally turned away in disgust.

Rocco had proved his manliness by being able to cope with this bit of the macabre. "I'm going to bring it to school."

"Whatever for?" she questioned.

"To show Mr. Esposito in science. I bet he'll give me extra credit for bringing in these rotting teeth!" He placed the packet in his knapsack, then they quickened their pace. It would not do to be late, for any reason.

The first tones of the giant bell atop the church indicated that they scarcely had enough time. Their thoughts were on being prompt, not upon the jaw fragment that was resting in Rocco's sack. It would be almost 2:00 P.M. before Rocco's science class, where he would present Mr. Esposito with the intriguing item.

After an initial examination, Mr. Esposito tried not to convey his shock as he briefly questioned the boy. Leaving the class in the charge of a monitor, he then took the plastic bag to Father Cardichon, the Headmaster. The father quickly called both children to his office and repeated Mr. Esposito's inquiries. When the responses were the same, he acted.

A call was immediately placed to the bishop. He was apprised of the existing situation and his guidance asked. The revelation that the grisly find was not only human teeth but also a half segment of attached jaw left but one possible course of action.

Father Cardichon's next call was to the police department. By 3:30 P.M., two uniformed members of the department had arrived at the school. The officers examined the object, then questioned the two bewildered youngsters; after ten minutes, they knew the matter would be taken out of their hands. This dilemma was a problem for homicide.

The incessant double rings of the bedside telephone clamored in wanton disregard of his peace. He had fallen into the comfort of his undersized bed hours before, after an entire day of unproductive legwork. The case was going nowhere fast; the chief inspector would soon order it dropped. Other cases with greater chances of satisfactory conclusion were waiting. Results were all-important, and this one seemed unlikely to justify any further expenditure of either time or manpower.

His hand found the blaring instrument and lifted the receiver to stop the sound. He spoke slowly into the mouthpiece: "Hello?"

"Hello, Lorenzo. How's our newest star detective doing this fine morning?"

"Shit, Giorgio. Haven't you anything better to do than wake me up in the middle of the night? Have a heart! I just got off a little while ago," he pleaded as he allowed his head to sink back into the luxury of the feathery pillow.

"A little while ago? Are you kidding? Lorenzo, it's nearly eleven-thirty. Where the hell have you been all day?"

The detective's eyes shot to the alarm clock that sat next to the telephone. Its dial indicated the time was 6:45 A.M. but the rays of light that filtered through the window's blinds belied that. The familiar ticking of the clock was absent. He had neglected to wind it before he had fallen asleep!

"Holy Maria! What time did you say it was, Giorgio?"

"Eleven thirty-five to be exact, Lorenzo. You belonged back here half an hour ago. What happened . . . one of your girls too much for you?"

"Shut up, Giorgio." His friend was always teasing him for his chastely sequestered sex life. Giorgio was a real playboy, but Lorenzo was far too devout a Catholic to engage in such nightly transgressions. "I haven't gotten any sleep in a couple of nights. I've been working on that shooting in the pasta warehouse. If I don't come up with something fast, the chief is going to pull me off the case."

"Sorry to be the bearer of sad tidings, but he already did. I've covered for you so far today. Move your ass, lover, and get yourself down to St. Catherine's school. Seems some kids found some bones in a plastic bag in the garbage this morning."

"So?"

"So they brought the bag to school and it turns out the bones are human."

"Who the hell said they are?"

"The school's science teacher said they are."

"How the hell does he know? Is he an authority on the subject?"

"Lorenzo, don't argue with me. Just get yourself over to St. Catherine's as fast as you can. It's probably nothing, but at least you can say you were on the job. Move your ass, okay? I'll meet you there in half an hour with the car."

The detective was already in motion before the conversation ended. His feet hit the cool floor as he raced to the bathroom and turned on the shower, mumbling an incoherent invocation that sounded more like a string of profanities than a morning prayer. Then he hurriedly dressed, slinging on his shoulder holster and climbing into his rumpled jacket. There was no time to shave.

The bureaucrats at headquarters had not yet recognized his "unique qualities." Until now, they had not seen fit to place a really important assignment before him. There was little dialogue between him and the other men save for Giorgio, who had graduated the police academy with him nearly twenty years earlier, and for whom Lorenzo had written papers that barely salvaged his friend's grades.

The careers of both men were nearly mirror images, though their personalities were opposites. Giorgio, a playboy, laughed and lucked his way through the required three years on foot patrol, despite the exhortations of Lorenzo, a devout Catholic who took his job seriously. After Giorgio barely passed the competitive exams, thanks to Lorenzo's coaching, they were assigned together to a detail in plain clothes.

A year later, using Lorenzo's careful headwork and Giorgio's daring, they solved an important case by breaking a political terrorist ring. When the arrests withstood prolonged trial and public scrutiny, making the department look good, the chief inspector appointed them homicide detectives as a reward. But once higher in rank, they fell into a bureaucratic morass. The best cases were given as largesse to other detectives, and they were left with the mundane, mindless, or "impossible" ones.

By now they had put in more than their mandatory penance time, and their impatience grew with each passing day. Although the department hummed with the rumor that a major shakeup was imminent, it had proven to be nothing but speculation so far. Any changes were slow and at best inconsequential. They had no reason to believe that any sanctimonious new chief inspector would care to reform the system. But Lorenzo would be passed over because of his religious devotion, regarded widely as a personality quirk. And while Giorgio was well liked, his verve was equally threatening to his stodgy superiors, who considered him a flash-in-the-pan.

Musings on the injustices of the system were abandoned as Lorenzo slammed his apartment door behind him. Tugging his tie up around his unbuttoned collar, he ran down the flight of stone steps that led to the unkempt courtyard and rushed out to the street to hail a passing taxi. "Step on it!" he ordered. "I'm a police officer . . . and this is police business!" he shouted as an afterthought.

The driver urged the taxi on, not knowing that the urgency in the order was a result of the detective's simply having overslept. In ten minutes, the vehicle came to a screeching halt in the center of a flower-bordered cul-de-sac that lay before the middle-class school. Detective Lorenzo Barzini jumped out and threw a five thousand lire note at the driver, calling out for him to "Keep the change." He then ran around two unoccupied police vehicles and quickly disappeared into the school's interior, leaving the taxi driver cursing, for only the fare was covered by the single note.

The disheveled plainclothesman mistakenly entered the school through its chapel entrance. He lurched through its heavy door, footsteps clattering against the floor, before he became cognizant of his surroundings. He halted to pull off his hat and nod hastily toward the dais.

Realizing immediately that the chapel was empty, he began to dash off again, only to notice two small children kneeling in prayer, staring up at him. He fidgeted a moment, feeling some remnant of shame for his disrespectful conduct in this house of God—a lingering feeling from his childhood at a school not unlike this one. Only his had been considerably poorer, and stricter!

He gestured with a finger over his lips to the children, who returned to their earnest prayer; then he crossed himself, as he knelt in the pew nearest the hallway.

From down the passage a group of men emerged: two policemen, the senior priest, and the school's headmaster. The detective sprang to his feet as they approached.

"What's this?" growled the headmaster. Unshaven and hastily dressed, the kneeling detective resembled a derelict. "Listen my dear sir, the chapel is closed to the public at this hour: this is a private school. . . . "

"Er, excuse me, Father. I'm the detective, that is, I was told that there has been an unusual occurrence here." He held out his hand momentarily, and thinking better of it, fumbled for his identity card. The two uniformed officers glanced at each other, suppressing smiles.

"Oh, I see. I'm so sorry, Detective . . . "

"Detective Barzini, Father, at your service. Please excuse my appearance, Father, I was, uh, on decoy duty." He threw a scowl at the still snickering policemen. "Now, what seems to be the trouble here?"

"Yes, Detective Barzini, there seems to be a calamitous mistake. Two of our children have been hounded by these officers about something they had the misfortune to stumble upon on their way to school this morning."

The detective chose his words carefully. He had been raised in an environment that demanded complete reverence toward the clergy, and he still shuffled a bit in their presence. He assured the father that no charges had been made and that the officers were merely performing their duties under a unique set of circumstances. "I must beg your indulgence, Father, for a few moments. I'd like to speak to the officers in private. Then I'll be in a better position to answer any questions you might have."

Father Cardichon, the senior priest, nodded his approval and returned with the headmaster down the hall toward their study.

Lorenzo got right to the point. "All right, boys, what do you have?" The first officer presented the anxious detective with the plastic packet. The detective inspected its contents closely, then suddenly grimaced and pulled back.

"Ugh, where'd they dig this up?"

The first officer answered, "The kids claim they found it on a pile of garbage on the way to school."

"They probably did."

The officer seemed astonished at the detective's statement. "Aren't you going to question them? You just can't dismiss the possibility that . . . "

"That what? That they killed someone, then chopped off a piece of his jaw and happened to bring it to school for show and tell? You guys have to be kidding. How old are they?"

The second officer now joined in: "He's thirteen, she's eleven."

"So we have a pair of eleven- and thirteen-year-old axe murderers on our hands? Do you guys want to go to the chief inspector with an ingenious creation like that? Just type up your reports and put them on my desk after you end your shift. I'll take over from here." Without waiting for a reply, he headed down the hall toward the headmaster's study. The officers turned and left, happy to be rid of this pompous and disheveled older detective.

Detective Barzini strode directly to Father Cardichon. He was anxious to create a positive image, to dispel the impression of disarray and lateness.

"Let me assure you both that this won't take long. I just have a couple of questions for everyone. Rest easy, I don't believe for a moment that these children had any hand in any crime."

The father answered, "I'd be amazed if you did."

The young detective pulled a chair over to where the two children were seated. Rocco and Maria tried to sink into the leather couch and bury their fear as he sat and faced them. Lorenzo tried to reassure them, smiling his broadest and most theatrical grin. His inquest began with their discovery and ended with Mr. Esposito's realization that the teeth weren't animal, but human.

The detective retraced the sequence of events that had led to the finding of the jaw fragment. Their frightened expressions confirmed for him that these two children had no possible connection with the crime, if indeed there was a crime. When Lorenzo had gone as far as he could at the school, he asked that the children be allowed to show him the exact location at which their bizarre discovery was made, offering to take them home in his police car, just as soon as Giorgio arrived with it. He assured the father and Mr. Esposito that the matter wouldn't be a bother to them in the future, thanking them for their time, interest, and cooperation, and making a special point of asking Father Cardichon to relay his thanks to the bishop.

At that point a soft knock at the study door announced Detective Giorgio D'Annunzio, who strode in dressed in his habitual immaculate outfit, in marked contrast to the unkempt Barzini. His face was handsome and rugged, and he had painted on his usual half-smile, which had a certain deceiving charm to it. People tended to believe him on sight and he took full advantage of this to lull many a criminal into a false sense of security. The subterfuge enabled him to overcome countless barriers, particularly in his nightly trysts with the ladies.

"Sorry it took so long, Lorenzo. The inspector grabbed me about some case I had two or three weeks ago. I just couldn't get away from him. You know how he is when he gets started about man hours. You have anything here yet?"

"No, nothing, really. We're taking these kids back to the scene. If there was anything there this morning, it's probably gone by now. The garbage trucks have deposited it all wherever the hell they usually do." Aware after the fact of his mild profanity, he quickly glanced at the father, who made it a point to look away. Lorenzo then motioned to the waiting youngsters to get up and follow him. "Father, Mr. Esposito, thank you both again for your help." He gently shut the study door behind him, then led the other detective and the two children outside.

The heat of the late afternoon continued to be oppressive. Rome was returning to normal following the afternoon lull. Tourists invaded the streets in force. The noise of heavy traffic once again returned to the ancient causeways. Lorenzo loathed being forced to work the streets, but was certain that once he broke a really important case he would rapidly rise to a position of real authority within the department. Look at Chief Inspector Ugo Maggiore, a shining example of a buffoon who had made good. The inspector had literally bungled his way through a major narcotics case and had somehow come out smelling like a rose. There had followed a meteor-like rise within the department. Lorenzo had hoped that if an oaf like that could enjoy such a promotion, a person of his own intelligence had nothing but promise in his future career. But he had never anticipated that on his way he would become hopelessly mired in the self-serving bureaucracy that made up the higher echelons of the corrupt police force. The dead end had left him frustrated and self-righteous. His once-burning self-image as a white knight of the law glimmered less and less. He had been chided for his dedication, rebuked for his almost devout perseverence, thwarted, more often than not, by his own department. But Lorenzo Barzini was a stubborn man: the more he was thwarted, the more pertinacious he became.

Within five minutes the two detectives had driven the now excited youngsters to the exact spot where they had first found the wrapped package. The area, as expected, had been picked clean by Rome's sanitation force. A small crowd of curious neighbors drew in about Rocco and Maria, who were by now exhibiting a degree of bravado not apparent a short time ago in the headmaster's study.

"*Sure we found it!*" announced Rocco as he swaggered about. He had become the center of attention and was making the most of it while he could. "Maria was afraid, but you all know me! I just picked it up and took it with us! I knew the police would be interested in it!"

Maria stood off to the side answering questions that the detectives asked from time to time during their search. She was content to allow Rocco to have center stage, for she knew that from this point on, he would be forever in her debt. She'd always know the truth about how it happened and he'd never forget that fact.

Detectives Barzini and D'Annunzio searched the area thoroughly, covering a series of contingencies that might have preceded the children's discovery, but they found nothing. What lay ahead, on the one hand, was a great deal of basic detective investigation, and on the other a forensic workup to determine something about the person the jaw fragment had once been a part of. The latter would be handled by Giorgio, and the former by Lorenzo, who somehow consistently got stuck with the legwork. Even Giorgio's assistance could not be counted on until the inspector made the final personnel assignments. The bureau was backlogged with cases.

They both looked at Rocco, whose part—aside from bringing the object to school—was inconsequential, and watched him give a performance worthy of an Academy Award. The melodrama had reached its pinnacle when Detective Barzini called Rocco to him. Taking the youngster aside, he explained that it could be calamitous for him to further discuss the incident. After all, Rocco was a vital part of the investigation, and indiscriminant disclosures might hamper the detectives' job.

Rocco, proudly convinced that he was essential to the police investigation, agreed to remain silent to everyone except Maria. He shifted from proud relayer of information to trusted guardian of official secrets.

The detective and the youngster parted, Lorenzo making a prominent display of shaking Rocco's hand and loudly thanking him for his assistance. "Rocco, we couldn't have gotten this far without you!"

The boy's heart filled with pride. It was a day that would stay with him for a lifetime. By the time he and Maria were married, they would have built it into something far out of proportion; it would be something to tell their children . . . and their grandchildren. Yet they themselves would never know the real significance of their gruesome discovery that morning.

It took nearly a week for a forensic artist, working with the forensic pathologist, to come up with the first tentative sketch of the victim. The description they arrived at could fit countless people in Italy, and untold thousands anywhere in Europe, but it was a starting point. The inspector chose to disregard the importance of discovering the dead man's identity and simply assigned Detective Barzini to begin a superficial search through the current Missing Persons File. As with other seemingly unsolvable cases, the manpower problem dictated that only minimal effort be expended unless Barzini came up with something specific to go on.

That evening Lorenzo and Giorgio stopped at Salvatore's a popular bar and hangout for off-duty cops. While the more sophisticated Giorgio was a seasoned drinker, Lorenzo was not. It required only a couple of rounds before he began to speak loudly and with little inhibition.

Giorgio, carousing with the other officers in the bar, paused to offer a salute: "Here's a round for the Jawbone Man; a down-in-the-mouth case if I ever saw one!"

The seated officers responded with appreciative laughter, encouraging further commentary of this nature: "The guy really took it on the chin, eh?"

"Perhaps he flapped his jaw a bit too much," chided one of them, "so take a lesson, D'Annunzio."

Much raucous banter followed, but the capriciousness of the laughter began to annoy Lorenzo. To him, this was a matter of considerable gravity.

With exaggerated bravado, engendered perhaps by his third round of drinks, he stood dizzily to offer his dissenting viewpoint.

"This is no laughing matter, fellows. If we drink to anything, then we should drink to catching the murderer!"

"Lorenzo, you must be joking," shouted Giorgio. "There's not a shred of evidence!" Already Lorenzo had set himself up for a ribbing. The others would fuel the drunken debate.

"*Just* a shred!" joked one of them. "But not exactly a case to sink your teeth into, Barzini." The burst of laughter that followed was slightly delayed until all the tipsy policemen had caught the pun.

"Wait a minute, wait just a minute," Lorenzo gestured haphazardly. "As officers of the law, we should insist that to every crime there exists a solution. . . . " There was a pause.

"And to every argument there exists a dreamer!" Giorgio boisterously scoffed, to gales of laughter.

Lorenzo puffed out his chest and flattened his mustache with both hands before he spoke. "No sir!" he bellowed. "Each sinner shall be discovered, and brought to pay in full. It says so—right there in *Matthew*!" His speech elicited exaggerated oohs and ahs, between surreptitious laughter. The detective's religious predilection had long been a bureau joke.

The mocking spurred him to even more outrageous biblical

pronouncements. Although he had no religious training past parochial school, he often wished he had; the quotes he spouted were completely fictitious!

But the religious inventions did represent his inner feelings toward his job. Police work was a substitute for the priesthood—its uniform was to him the nearest frock of propriety. An officer of the law should be second only to an officer of the Lord.

In the drunken argument that followed, Lorenzo found himself vowing to bring the villain to justice, and nearly coming to blows with his hooting fellow policemen. He stumbled out, shouting from the door that Samson had raised a jawbone and slain four hundred Philistines. As he rallied groggily, he recalled, somewhat disconcertedly, that Samson had used the jawbone of an ass.

"The dismemberment was to hide the identity," he speculated, grabbing Georgio by the sleeve the next day at lunch while chewing on a sandwich. His partner checked for traces of tuna on his cashmere sweater. "It must have been an important personage, then, eh?" He'd badgered his partner all day with such theorizing. "A terrorist killing, hmmm? Like maybe that Coca-Cola executive they kidnapped in Bolivia—what's his name, the one they never found? Hmmm? Hey, that's why no one shows in missing persons, eh? What do you think?"

Finally Giorgio managed to quell his persistence with the advice that he relax and take a rest. Lorenzo was forced to agree; he had racked his brain and exhausted his imagination to no avail. It was time to get his mind off it. To this end, Giorgio had offered the number of one of his many more-than-interesting "acquaintances."

Hovering over the telephone on his paper-strewn desk, Lorenzo stopped abruptly, arms folded, and stared at it emphatically, like the adversary it turned out to be.

"No," he said finally, after some deliberation. "No, not this time. I won't step into that bucket again. If I want a woman, I'll pick one myself." With that decision he reached for his rumpled hat and slammed the door of his office booth as he left, the opaque pane of glass rattling in its wooden restraints.

Outside the sun had not yet faded behind the treetops. Steep shadows ranged across the Roman squares like legions still at

their ancient maneuvers. Lorenzo wandered with the late afternoon crowd, sauntering past barred shop windows, stopping to
buy a bag of peanuts from a street vendor. He had been working
entirely too hard, he decided; this jawbone case had become an
obsession. This evening he would seek some diversion.

Stopping at a crowded sidewalk café, he selected a table and
ordered a light wine. As he eyed the other customers in a somewhat professional manner, he noticed an attractive young woman
alone at a table at the café's rear. Lorenzo quickly straightened
his thinning hair and tucked in his shirt over a slight paunch,
then turned to glance in her direction. Although she looked up
occasionally, he was unable to catch her eye. Gazing at her
thoughtfully, he lost himself for a moment in her olive complexion and the movement of her thick, black hair. Finally her dark
eyes flashed in his direction; as she noticed him, her lips turned
slightly in a shy smile. Just then, his eye was distracted by a
movement behind her: an elderly man at the table past hers was
removing his false teeth and dipping them in a glass of water.
The sight of the flesh-colored dentures flooded his mind with images of the jaw fragment he was working so hard to forget. He
turned abruptly away and shook his head, scowling. A moment
later, when the waiter placed his veal and peppers before him, it
seemed to him to be cut in the same disturbing shape as the jaw-
piece. Having hardly pierced it with his fork, he realized he had
no appetite. As he rose to leave, he saw the woman greet an attractive trim-bearded gentleman approaching her table. Another
defeat without beginning the battle.

Oblivious to the fellow pedestrians he jostled while hurrying on
his way, he accepted that there was no avoiding this case. It was
mired permanently in his consciousness, jutting out into every
waking thought like the teetering mound of files of a hundred
other unsolved cases. Unconscious steps drew him down darkened
streets. Like his random thoughts, the streets gradually merged
until his steps found direction, drawing him to the site where the
fragment had been found.

It was almost evening now; deepened shadows clung to the
building sides and the sun barely hovered over the hilltops. In the
narrow street where the two children had made their grotesque
discovery, it was already dark.

Without a clear theory to follow, Lorenzo's only direction was to re-examine the entire area meticulously, hoping to discover some previously undetected clue. He surveyed the building line closely, checking basement doors and service entrances, peering into curtained cellar windows.

Regarding vantage points, he concluded that the winding street was well hidden—it was not overlooked by any window lining the cobbled lane. An ideal drop-point, in all probability it had been carefully selected for this purpose. Only the small rear window of a bake shop across the corner viewed much of the block's length.

Judging by the apparent cleverness of the perpetrator and his obvious skill in dismemberment and disposal, Barzini began to realize that his adversary possessed a criminal mind of extraordinary proportions. This was a devious murderer, a killing machine, cold and perhaps even more than that.

A shudder traveled up his spine at that thought. Perhaps this was more than he had bargained for? He continued his intense investigation of the now-darkened street. All packaged refuse along the street and in the alleyways was examined, boxes torn open, bags carefully rummaged through. There was little to be discovered in this manner, and the process was tedious and often unpleasant. But there was no other method for literally digging up a lead where none existed. After an hour of scavenging, he hit paydirt.

In the inner seam of a garbage can, off the far corner, Lorenzo's sharp eyes spotted a long dark stain. He lifted the heavy can, dumping the contents out as inconspicuously as possible, and dragged it under a streetlight to examine it more closely.

Unmistakably, encrusted in a groove of the can was a long rust-red drip, the distinctive color of dried blood. Lorenzo withdrew his pocket knife and scratched away a tiny portion of the stain, wrapping the knife in a handkerchief to preserve the dried droplet for lab examination.

"Hey there, what do you think you're doing?" The loud, gruff voice rumbled from a nearby cellar doorway, where an enormous, pot-bellied workman waved a beefy arm in Lorenzo's direction. "Put down that can or I'll break your ass."

Lorenzo, taken aback, dropped the garbage container on his

foot. He jumped back and it rolled clattering off the curb, drowning out his attempt to explain himself while he limped backward.

"I'm the janitor here," the big man barked, sauntering forward. "Look what you've done to my garbage." The incensed workman, bellowing self-righteously and aggressively wielding an ornate table lamp in Lorenzo's direction, left no time for explanations. Upper windows were being thrown open, and a shrill voice was railing at the disturbance. The detective beat a hasty retreat down the avenue. "Filthy derelict! Show your face here again and I'll call the cops on you...." was bellowed after him as he scurried away.

But at least he'd discovered something: If the blood spot checked out as he thought, he would have two points of some proximity to plot; perhaps then his superior would allow him to continue the investigation. He would make sure to return with a squad car and some uniformed officers in the morning and take another look around. There were more questions to ask—perhaps even the municipal garbage man had noticed something.

With such thoughts rattling constantly through his head, Detective Barzini caught a bus and headed back downtown. The night had taken hold, couples arm in arm were filling the streets. Lorenzo would not share in the evening . . . this was a time for thought.

A cacophony of angry sirens woke the sleeping detective. His back ached from having fallen asleep draped over his cluttered metal desk. Stretching would simply aggravate the stiffness in his spine; he didn't attempt it. The spill of harsh light on the report before him reflected into his puffy eyes. He switched off the fixture to avoid straining his sight. "Coffee," he mumbled aloud. He needed something to clear his head. He had scrutinized the report time and again in an attempt to extract that one hidden clue that might have gone unnoticed, but that elusive element had continued to evade his grasp.

The detective slowly stood and, wincing with pain, walked across his dark office to where a small coffee pot sat on a single hotplate. Lorenzo hoped that there would be at least one cup of bitter liquid remaining . . . there wasn't. He'd have to add water to the used grinds, and suffer the aftertaste. As he replaced the refilled pot on the heating element, he caught a glimpse of himself in the small mirror on the wall. He looked terrible! Though hardly impeccable at his best, he looked now as if he had slept in his clothes; as, in fact, he had.

He stared blankly and tapped his pencil absently on the peeling tabletop. His investigation had turned up nothing new save the specimen of blood taken from the garbage can. It was progressing with torturous slowness. His dossier on this John Doe contained but one simple report. He was no closer to knowing the identity of the man than when he had begun when he was given the pitifully small piece of bone with attached teeth on that first day. If only the blood specimen, now in the lab, could give him a new direction. But he was convinced that there had to be more; something had been passed over. Sooner or later it would come to him; he would prove to his cynical colleagues that with pious dedication the clue would emerge! Time was growing short. If he couldn't come up with something soon, the inspector would have to reassign him to a case with a greater possibility for success. The practical aspects of police work took precedence over interest; results were everything.

His telephone rang and his hand found it instantly. "Detective Barzini here." He listened as the voice at the other end identified himself as a lab technician. It seemed that the detective's blood sample was nothing more than the remains of some poor baby lamb that must have been someone's dinner some forty-eight hours earlier. Nothing seemed to go right for him.

A glance at the wall clock showed it was now nearly midnight. His worn body ached with the need for rest and he could deny it no longer. The detective signed out for the remainder of the night and proceeded to his parked Fiat. In his hand he carried the neatly typed pathologist's report. Maybe by taking that document with him he would be able to come up with that elusive clue.

The sticky warmth of the ocean breezes had invaded the inner city, causing its occupants to sweat as they lay in their beds, and Lorenzo tossed and turned in an unfulfilling sleep. Thoughts of his own malfeasance crept into his subconscious as he fought to stay asleep. There was no reason to blame himself, yet he did.

The inevitable decision to drop the case was coming, but he still fought on. He had something to prove.

Somewhere within the innermost quadrant of his mind, a realization began to form. First it was there, then lost, then there once again. He tried to hold onto it, to bring it to the surface. His mind circled about, not quite able to grasp it. It was something about the teeth . . . the fillings . . . the coldness of the report. Then it surfaced, the one minuscule, important fact he had overlooked.

The detective bolted up off the damp sheets, opening his eyes wide to the soft darkness of the room. He ran it through his mind once again so as not to lose it forever. The fillings were unusual. He just knew they didn't fit anything normally seen in Italy.

Quickly, he moved to his small desk and switched on the high intensity lamp suspended above it, causing a halo of light to encircle its top. Flinging the report open, he turned the pages frantically until he found the one he sought. Coal-black eyes flew down the page, skimming item after item. Then he stopped—it was there, had been there all along. The anguish of the past two days was over. Lorenzo finally had something to go on. The dossier was no longer a mortuary box slammed shut.

His fingernail underlined the crucial notation in the pathologist's report, referring to the dental work:

> . . . filling material, rear molar: amalgam.
> frontal pre-molar: stainless steel.

"Steel!" he shouted aloud. "The frontal filling was stainless steel!" He snatched at the phone, fumbling through his listings with his free hand, then dialing furiously.

A long succession of double rings kept him hopping agitatedly about the bedroom, until he stubbed his toe on an ill-placed stool and sat down to rub his foot. When he retrieved the receiver a groggy voice had answered at the other end.

"Hello? . . . Hello?"

"Dr. Grippe? Lorenzo Barzini here. Just one question to ask you: steel fillings. When and where are they used? . . . "

"Hello?"

"Steel fillings, Doctor. Highly unusual, don't you think? Where do they . . ."

"Who is this?"

"Detective Barzini. . . . "

"Barzini! Do you have any idea what time it is?"

"Dr. Grippe, please excuse the disturbance. This is important police business. Only one question."

"It's three forty-five in the morning! What could you possibly want at this ungodly hour?"

"Steel fillings; the jaw fragment had a steel filling in the frontal pre-molar."

"So?"

"So they don't make them here, do they?"

"No. It has to be an old filling. Before 1960, I'd guess. They abandoned them after that; too hard, not enough give. Never used them here, though."

"Where? Where were they used?"

"Eastern bloc nations," the groggy dentist answered. "Rumania, Czechoslovakia, Germany, and for less than a decade. Stopped using them in the late 1950s." He paused. "Now, if you ever wake me at an hour like this ag . . . " His words were drowned in a profusion of gratitude from Lorenzo.

Now he had something to go on. He lay back on his bed with his hands behind his head and began to speculate.

The man he was looking for most probably wasn't Italian, or at least not a natural-born Italian. The chances were, he was born in a Communist country and was either visiting Italy or had emigrated to some Western country after 1958. Rivulets of perspiration ran down Barzini's face and bare chest as he copied his thoughts on paper, beginning his profile of the unknown victim.

In a couple of days, an artist would be able to come up with the vital final physical description of the victim. It was already certain that the John Doe was a male. Weight, age, and bone structure would all follow in due time. A profile of where he might come from would add still another dimension to what had been, until now, a dead-end dossier.

Lorenzo finally had something concrete to present to the inspector. He had a reprieve, if only for the moment. There was something compelling about the case, something almost alive, gnawing at his pride and compassion. He knew he couldn't put it aside, not until he had identified the subject, and placed him and its murderer to rest.

With a piece here, a possibility there, Lorenzo could continue to believe that it would all eventually become clear. He saw no choice but to view it with that kind of dogged insistence. For him, the disconnected beads of existence could only be strung together on the thin strand called faith.

The moon had barely fallen from the gray morning sky, chased by a heated orb of light, as he stepped from his apartment on his way back to police headquarters. He would confront the inspector with this new and revealing piece of information in the next few hours. It was inconceivable that his superior would refuse to permit him to continue on the case, now that it was beginning to take shape.

Hours later he had won a partial victory. The young man was given free reign for a scant seventy-two additional hours, with the tacit understanding that the case would be reevaluated at that time, in light of the immense caseload facing the inspector.

Lorenzo left the office in a state of excitement. The inspector, and what he stood for, were anathema to a working detective. Yet this was the era of computers . . . of budgets . . . of accountability. There were undreamed-of pressures pitted against those at the very top echelons of the department. Lorenzo could just barely comprehend them, for he hadn't yet been placed in a position where he was responsible for anyone besides himself.

The young detective jumped fully into the case with a vehemence even he did not quite understand. Founded in uncertainty, lacking a focal point, and vulnerable to a multitude of changes, somehow the case had become an obsession for Lorenzo. He wanted this one—for his pride, for his career, for his sense of self and spirit.

6

There, seated behind an enormous wooden desk piled high with countless dusty volumes and manuscripts, was the legendary Bishop Bartoleme. His office had taken on the character of its present occupant, a preeminent biblical scholar. From a valley between mounds of antiquity, a bent and knotted hand beckoned like a Michelangelo fresco come to life. Father Kottmeyer, it appeared, had taken upon himself to report to his assignment earlier than anticipated. Such a rare quality would certainly give the bishop a good first impression of the foreigner.

A slight rustling of brittle pages indicated the bishop had closed the aged tome of his attentions. From somewhere behind the paper mountains, a voice called to the visitor. "Come to me, Father. Walk around my desk, I would like to see just to whom I am speaking." His voice was powerful, unlike the bent fingers that had snaked out from the rubble of time only seconds before.

The imposter wasn't quite prepared for what his eyes encountered. The seated bishop hadn't looked up; thus the Professional's first view of him was of a hairless, gaunt, bone-like head, knotted with purple bulging veins, and topped by the small skullcap that symbolized his holy office. The supposed Father Kottmeyer's presence next to him was his signal to turn his gaze upon his visitor. The bishop wore a visage from the Church's dark past: a face of melting wax, aged and sagging jowls matching the layered flesh overlapping the slits that housed his colorless eyes. The bishop was a pure albino; this darkened sanctuary had served for three-quarters of a century to protect his imperfect eyes from the harshness of the day's light. Despite—perhaps even because of—those physical deficiencies, he exuded a tangible aura of grandeur, a deep poignancy of pious dignity. The bishop was the acknowledged patriarch of the Vatican, owing to his seniority and vast knowledge—although, as a mere bishop, he sat far below the cardinals who directed the Church's affairs.

Bishop Bartoleme's eyes searched the father's face and body. The Professional could sense a quiet vitality deep within the frail, seated figure. Having scrutinized the new member of his staff to his total satisfaction, the bishop stood slowly and began to speak in flawless German, "My son, it is with great happiness that we welcome you into our fold. We hope your stay will be long and productive. I have read your papers on fresco restoration with great interest. In fact, the techniques you described are quite radical as compared to those employed by your predecessor, Father Policastro.

"You will find that, no matter what you might have heard, we are not averse to change—only to change that is devised for the sake of frivolity." Father Kottmeyer knew the limits in this Vatican arena; the game was played by the bishop's ancient rules.

Bishop Bartoleme began a slow measured walk, his subordinate following. A tinge of hostility had colored the bishop's voice; a measured quality intended to imply, perhaps, that he had not really wanted Kottmeyer to fill the position. The fact that the German had been by far the best qualified person available hadn't deterred the bishop from his vocal opposition. Still, in the final analysis, the bishop's opposition to a non-Italian was overcome by his integrity; he felt deeply the responsibility of filling the position with the best candidate. Personal prejudices must be set aside for the good of the Church.

For the next half hour, Bishop Bartoleme led the new arrival on a tour of his crowded, but immaculate, office and workroom. Finally, the initial orientation gave way to a discussion of Father Kottmeyer's new duties. "Father, we shall start you out slowly, building upon your expertise. We have countless treasures in dire need of your services. The longest journey will begin here with the proverbial single step, my son. Let me return to my workroom for a moment to retrieve your first assignment." The priest

watched the bishop walk slowly, but with an almost defiant erect-
ness, to his inner sanctum. In five minutes he returned carrying a
small package wrapped in fine gauze. It was obviously a miniature painting of some kind. He set the treasure on a tabletop
and tenderly removed its wrappings. The Professional's mind flew
ahead, thinking of possible uses of the situation, as the damaged
work came into view. Both the frame and accompanying picture
had been defaced with spray paint. The tiny canvas, no larger
than six-by-nine inches, was almost totally obscured. Only a
small area at the uppermost right corner attested to what might
lie underneath the white enamel. The fraudulent Father Kottmeyer endeavored to display the requisite repulsion at this desecration, but behind his horrified mask his thoughts were on whether
he could restore the work with sufficient expertise to retain his
cover.

"Please, my son! This was a favorite work of Pope John and
we would like it restored to its former place in the Vatican museum.

"Take care with our picture of the Blessed Virgin. Time is of
no real importance, for haste shall have no value if the painting is
permanently harmed. Care, as you know, is our uppermost concern. But if it were possible, its restoration would make a fine and
appropriate presentation to the new Holy Father on his installa-
tion." The bishop stepped away, lingering for a last pained look,
then returned to his valley amid the paper mountains.

The bogus Father Kottmeyer followed the frail man back to
his sanctuary, almost as one of Christ's disciples might have followed the Holy Son himself. Yet underneath the composed exterior lurked only a disciple of death. The bishop, resettled in his
upholstered seat, began once again. "Father Schumacher will see
to your needs. He will assign you an apartment here at the Vatican along with a laboratory to work in. If you should require special materials, books, or anything at all, please see him.

"And, by the way, how is your Italian?" The conversation had
been entirely in German.

The imposter smiled, composed what he intended to say, then
began in practiced, halting Italian. "Sire, your German is much
better than my poor Italian, I'm sorry to admit." He carefully
spoke as if his command of the language were minimal; it might

be to his advantage that those around him believe he had difficulty understanding them.

"Father, you will have ample opportunity to practice our tongue while you are working with us. I daresay that in a matter of months you will be speaking just as if you were born here in Rome."

"I look forward to that," he answered in German. "I always thought Italian to be a most beautiful language, but aside from what was absolutely necessary for understanding Church business, I haven't found time to study it adequately. I've had to master English for my stay at the Art Institute in America, and Hebrew for my work at the Israeli holy sites. Now, I'll finally learn Italian . . . the right way!"

The ruse had worked; the bishop's eyes showed him that the old gentleman understood. His attention strayed from Father Kottmeyer; gnarled fingers found the pages of an ancient manuscript with a movement that was almost a caress. The interview had obviously ended.

The Professional returned to the desecrated Renaissance miniature. The painting was merely a beginning; the first key in an intricate plan for the imposter to worm his way into the bishop's confidence. If he could complete restoration earlier than expected, greater responsibility would be thrown his way. In the final analysis, he had to become vital to the bishop, if only temporarily.

He again bound the soft wrapping around the wooden frame, secured it with the silken bit of rope, and carried it tenderly to the office's exit.

Outside the door, Father Schumacher was waiting patiently, engrossed in the text he had been carrying. Schumacher had already been instructed to escort the new technician first to his room at the Vatican, then to a small laboratory in which he would work. The restoration was expected to take nearly a month of exhaustive work, and the father was to be given any assistance he might require. Vatican Restoration Department Head was a unique position that required one to work in absolute solitude—which was precisely why the Professional had chosen the unfortunate Father Kottmeyer as an essential cog in his painstaking plan. There would be no one looking over his shoulder.

It was not until his third day at the Vatican that the Professional was able to tear himself from his work as Father Kottmeyer, to view the body of the Pope lying serenely in state. The catafalque was austere and humble, a fragile monument that was taken down and resurrected as the need arose. A torturously slow march of faithful passed the expired body as the Tiber might amble on a lazy summer's afternoon. The father was able to break into the silent line simply by producing his official Vatican pass. The guards held up the human procession momentarily, allowing the father to step in and pause longer than the usual allotted period of time, the flow resuming as he left. Clearly, this document would be his key.

The time had come to commence the restoration process. Luck had been with him, for the exquisite picture proved not to have suffered any damage at all! In his maniacal haste to destroy, the vandal had chosen the single method that inflicts the least damage to a work of this type.

The Professional had spent the better portion of the day in research, combing through the meticulous, extensive files his predecessor had kept during his long tenure at the Vatican. The documents detailed a step-by-step account of method and result for each of the restorations Father Policastro had performed.

Three instances paralleled the situation facing him; in each, spray paint had been used to deface an ancient canvas and frame. Apparently the canvas could be fully restored with little difficulty, but the wooden frame would require more extensive work. Unknown to the general public, works of this nature, especially those in oils, have invariably been covered with layers of clear shellac. The enamel spray had never penetrated this protective coating to the brilliant oil below. The white paint could be easily removed with the use of delicate paint solvents. Once eradicated, the shellac coating could easily be repaired, and the painting would be none the worse for its sad experience.

The frame, however, was entirely another story. No shellac protected the ornately carved wood and exquisite gold leaf. Minute applications of special solvents would have to be painstakingly applied to prevent damage to the dry and brittle wood, which was extensively inlaid and centuries old. After much deliberation, the Professional decided that despite the wealth of technical information presently at his disposal, he was not equipped to perform a restoration of this magnitude at the requisite speed. He would have to find someone else to perform it according to his carefully devised schedule. Picture and frame would have to be transported from the Vatican to an outside expert. The picture would be his pass into the Sistine Chapel, something absolutely necessary for the plan to succeed.

Dashes of fiery sunlight burst through the gray patches of clouds high overhead, alternating waves of heat and coolness upon the tired city below. Passersby paid little attention to a lone priest as he walked through the main entrance of the Excelsior Hotel. The dry, artificial coolness of the lobby struck his face and evaporated the beads of perspiration from his brow. The priest stopped, seeking the bank of public telephones that stood near the main desk, and chose a unit at random.

"May I help you?" was the question posed by the almost sensual operator's voice.

"Yes. I would like to place a call, please, to 87–42–21!"

In a moment the soft voice invaded the line once again. "Please deposit one hundred lire, sir."

The priest responded by placing five telephone tokens in the correct slot, then waited patiently for his call to be put through. Finally the familiar ringing pattern of Italian telephones came through the earpiece. On the third set of double rings, the call was answered. "Yes?"

"This is Mr. Evans . . . I have a problem."

"Mr. Evans, please call 87–42–22 immediately." The connection was broken; only the steady hum of a replaced receiver remained.

As before, he heard the telltale clicks of the long distance switching equipment search for the proper exchange, then lock on it. Just as the connection was made, the operator broke in once more. "Please deposit three additional tokens, sir."

Soon after the token deposit, the double rings of the distant receiver struck his ear. As before, on the third ring the call was answered, "Yes?" It was a distinctly different voice from that of only a minute ago; even though the numbers were only a single digit apart, the phones would be streets, if not kilometers from each other. The conversation was brief, the time far too short to allow for a trace to be made.

"I have a problem"

"Yes?"

"I need the telephone number of an expert who restores oil on canvas and gold leaf, preferably someone in Rome. He must be able to work quickly, expertly, and above all, with the utmost discretion." His eyes scanned the area around the booth, always searching for anything amiss. "How quickly can you come up with such a person?"

"Call this number back in exactly one hour." The line hummed with vehemence, almost as a protest to the broken connection. The Professional checked his watch; it was 12:37 P.M. At precisely 1:37 P.M. he would place the call, keeping it short and to the point.

The priest slowly passed storefront after reflective storefront, seeming to scan each, then reject it in favor of the next as he deliberately made his way up the sloping avenue. Summer tourists crowded the Via Veneto, weary sightseers searching the many colorful sidewalk cafés for choice seats. Whether seated or walking, each eyed the others with passing interest and hidden desires. A priest could move unseen in this city, having no place among the passionate sensations that flowed with the wine. The priest's somber robes were the perfect disguise in a city filled with armies of men in the uniform of the Church.

The hour crept by; it was almost time for his call. Checking his watch, he chose a nearby hotel and strode through its ornate entrance.

A chill overtook him in the air-conditioned lobby as the cool air filtered through the layers of his attire. The sweat absorbed by his undershirt began to evaporate, leaving his skin cold. Less than three minutes remained. The priest made his way to the line of enclosed telephone booths, just to the left of the hotel's desk.

He lifted the hard plastic receiver and an operator's voice came on almost immediately. "Can I be of assistance?"

"Yes, please. I'd like you to ring 87–42–22."

As the moments passed, his heartbeat quickened. A delay in making the connection—not uncommon with Italian telephones—

could cause trouble. He couldn't be certain just how long after the appointed hour a call would still be accepted. As the last token fell through, the familiar long distance switching pattern began.

Finally a voice came on the line. "Mr. Evans?"

"Yes."

"Mr. Evans, I believe I have a solution to your problem. If you'd care to call 45–46–90, someone there may be of service."

The Professional felt no need to place the mechanical voice, which was probably disguised anyway. "Thank you," he replied. "Your payment will be forwarded in the usual manner." He broke the connection.

Hours passed. The sun had fallen from its seat of majesty in the Mediterranean sky. Safe within his apartment facing the Vatican only two kilometers away, the Professional began to dress. The afternoon had been spent in a cautious calm resembling rest, although even in sleep each eventuality played and replayed through his mind.

It was 9:00 P.M.; strolling Romans and tourists flowed along the city's narrow streets. The father was quickly caught up in the movement, like a single raindrop joining a meandering brook. His course was certain—another public telephone, this time in a busy restaurant for anonymity, as its phones were in constant use.

Through a network of small windows, he observed patrons of the eatery enjoying the abundance provided by a staff of hectic, uniformed waiters. The aroma of sauces and pastas hung in the air, tantalizing his palate. It was a splendid temptation he had to overcome for the present; he suppressed his gnawing hunger as he entered.

The gaudy and cavernous interior of the restaurant was crammed, its atmosphere humming with a feverish cadence. The telephone booth's glass door muffled the merry din as he shut himself in.

Raising the red plastic receiver, he inserted a token. His finger found the dimly illuminated dial and spun it clockwise six times, as if he were counting rosaries. The familiar set of double rings began. On the eleventh set, the phone was answered. The voice, apparently muffled, spoke in Italian.

"Good evening," he responded clearly, in English.

"Can I help you?" The muffled voice switched to English.

"Perhaps. I've been given your number by a mutual friend. I have an item that is in need of repair. I was led to believe that you could be of assistance."

"That might be possible."

The Professional smiled. "Good. Might I suggest we get together to discuss the necessary work?"

After arranging the time, he offered the art expert various rendezvous sites, careful to allay this unseen person's fears of a possible trap. There was silence for several minutes; the bogus priest surmised that a hand had been placed over the receiver, possibly to prevent his hearing a conversation. Then the muffled voice returned. "Mister? . . . "

"Mr. Greene. Mr. Charles Greene."

"Well then, Mr. Greene. Just inside the entrance to the Roman Forum, there is a small reflecting pool. Stand on the right side of that pool at precisely noon tomorrow . . . and please be prompt. I so hate to be kept waiting."

"The Forum at noon. I'll be there."

The full Mediterranean moon penetrated the wispy passing clouds, its brightness casting a fairytale enchantment upon the city far below. Business completed, the Professional had succumbed to fragrant temptation and dined in the restaurant. The meal had fulfilled the promise his nose had made to his palate. During his repast he had concentrated on the food; now his thoughts came just as single-mindedly back to his mission. The interlude had broken the tension, giving him a brief but nesessary respite.

A leisurely walk back to his apartment served to renew his energies, details of the project turning over and over in the deepest recesses of his mind. Nothing could be left to chance, for he could count on no one but himself. His current employers would seek to destroy him once the new Pope had been chosen; his knowledge would represent an unnecessary danger. Thus the most important part of his plan would be a foolproof escape; Father Kottmeyer would vanish, just as the warmth of the summer's breeze passes into fall . . . except he would never return.

The plan was progressing; what remained before the act itself was merely mechanics. All possible problems had been thought of, then dealt with. Every conceivable problem. . . .

The solitary black-clothed figure turned into the entranceway of a back street Roman apartment house. The sinister frock lost itself in the shadow of the weathered stone archway. Leather-soled shoes flapped against stone, the reverberations lost to the silence of the night. The assassin had returned to his lair to rest; to rejuvenate; to play his deadly covenant with the devil.

It was 11:45 A.M. as he walked from the Coliseum; he had plenty of time to keep his vital appointment. The oppressive heat had returned and the Romans had begun their midday ritual of dispersal.

A break in traffic allowed him to cross the hot asphalt street to the Forum's side. Two attractive female tourists, American schoolteachers, stared at the exceedingly handsome, well-dressed gentleman as he passed. They bumped against each other as their eyes followed him, each dreaming of something that wouldn't be. Each had been hoping to meet a suave Italian such as he, but alas, once again, neither had succeeded. Comically, it was almost as if a conspiracy had been organized to thwart them from losing their virginity in the ancient capital. The moment might have posed a splendid temptation for Mr. Greene, had he been able to read their minds. But all his cerebral attentions were on the hour . . . the location . . . the rendezvous.

The Via Labicana Viale sloped gently down. To his right was the ancient Forum; to the left, the wide street itself. Colorful graffiti and slogans of communist inspiration covered the walls facing the street. Four maps in relief explaining the rise and fall of the Roman Empire were horribly defaced. They commanded no more than passing interest from the group of Japanese tourists, cameras in hand, on their way to the Coliseum.

At the entrance to the Forum he waited on the ticket queue, then passed through to the ruins beyond. The coolness of the shadows beckoned as he stood, as instructed, to the right of the small reflecting pool, not much larger than a bathtub. In front of the pool stood a small stone statue of a delicate woman. Her gentle features were timeless and he quickly became lost in her beauty.

He was momentarily oblivious to the presence of a second

person who had taken a position directly opposite him. His eyes had dropped to the placid pool at his feet when he saw her in the mirror-like reflection. It was as if the statue had taken flesh and bone! He felt compelled to turn. Her face was even more radiant in life than her image shimmering in the coolness of the water.

"Mr. Greene . . . " she began, the name flowing from crimson lips.

"Yes?" he answered, not believing she could be the one.

"Mr. Greene, I believe you have a proposition for us?" Not waiting for an answer, she began to walk toward the Forum itself as he followed barely a step behind.

To anyone who might care to notice, they were a handsome, continental couple. Perhaps they would be taken for two movie stars out for a midday stroll, possibly a wealthy couple anxious to lose themselves in the relics of antiquity. A wandering eye might have construed the pair as lovers with their thoughts entwined in each other as their steps took them down to the remnants of Rome's glorious past. As they moved about the great open-air space, they stopped to point and gesture at various ruins. But these brief pauses had nothing to do with the ongoing conversation.

"Now, Mr. Greene, what have you brought us?" Her eyes, like emerald gems, played over the Arch of Titus without really seeing.

Her companion, tall and obviously European, removed a single color photograph from his pocket and passed it to her. It was a picture of the damaged piece of art. Almost immediately she identified it: the *Madonna Lita* by the master Leonardo da Vinci. It had been at the Vatican little more than a year, a gift from the State Hermitage Museum in Leningrad. It was known widely that the priceless piece had recently been vandalized by a crazed artist for some obscure reason; this had been her clue, since so little of the painting was visible.

"The spray paint. What kind was it?"

"Enamel with a fluoride propellant."

"And the picture itself. Was there any other damage aside from the obvious?"

"None. The normal layered shellac coating was present. It most certainly protected the oils beneath."

"The attached frame—I'm sure it wasn't protected."

"No, I'm sorry to say, it wasn't."

"Then," she finally looked up from the photograph, "this is the real problem. What would you have us do for you?"

"Restore the frame and painting in the absolute shortest period of time possible . . . without any publicity, of course." The mention of publicity was unnecessary, merely interjected to add emphasis to the task's urgency.

"Am I allowed a question?" He nodded and they resumed their leisurely walk about the ruins. "The piece is owned by the Vatican. Why don't they simply restore it themselves? They are perfectly capable of doing that type of work."

He chose to stop and face her, so he could carefully weigh her reaction to his answer. "You'll be restoring it. That's all you have to know!"

"Of course," she responded. A trace of a smile crept its way into the corners of her mouth. Her eyes returned to the picture, probing. He waited for her to speak again.

"What time frame do we have?"

"A week, at the outside."

"Impossible!" she countered, handing back the photograph.

"I pay for the impossible. Handsomely."

The woman turned away from him, looking across the ancient center of Roman life. There was no sound except for the whine of a passenger jet high overhead. The heat blanketed the city, stifling all possible sound. . . . The minutes passed slowly.

Finally making up her mind, she spun on her heels toward him. "All right, seven days. The fee is twenty-five thousand American dollars or eleven thousand pounds sterling. Five thousand will be payable in advance along with the painting . . . the remainder upon delivery of the restored work.

"On the sixth day an advertisement will appear in the *International Tribune* with instructions for Mr. Greene. One must be added to each digit of the listed number before placing the call. We'll name the pickup point at that time . . . agreed?"

"Agreed."

"Then call tomorrow and we'll arrange for the pickup. . . . "

"No need for that," he interrupted. "It's near. You'll be able to take it with you now." His hand found an envelope tucked neatly inside the light summer-weight jacket. Looking down for a moment he removed 25,000 dollars, and handed her the remainder still in the envelope. He had been prepared to go as high as 30,000 dollars, if necessary.

Her fingers gently wrapped around the valuable manila packet. She placed it in her purse. "All right, where is the work?"

He reached deep into another pocket and profferred a single key. "You'll find it in a pay locker at the Coliseum station. I'll expect the painting to be completed in seven days."

Nothing remained to be said. She turned and walked up the hill toward the Coliseum exit. His eyes followed her but he didn't move from where he stood.

As she reached the top of the hill, she turned toward him one last time to make certain he wasn't following. He was standing beneath the ancient archway wiping his brow with a white handkerchief. Thinking she was safe, she turned and vanished onto the street.

But on the signal of the handkerchief, an Italian woman, who had unobtrusively followed the couple at a discreet distance since they met by the pool, set off behind her. Camera and guidebook in hand, this second woman seemed but one of the thousands of summer tourists. In fact she was a private detective, hired to report to her client, a certain Mr. Greene, just where the unknown person went. Earlier that day the Professional had retained the agency—for an exorbitantly large fee, paid in advance—to help in a "blackmail case." The report would be ready shortly after the "blackmailer" had reached her home. It would be hand delivered to an address just on the city side of the Tiber and then forgotten. . . .

The meeting had lasted only half an hour, yet the tension had drained him. At 12:35 P.M., the heat of the day was building to a crescendo. He began walking in the opposite direction, toward the entrance he had used earlier.

He reached the small reflecting pool, then the exit beyond, and walked through to the now quiet street. Immediately to his left was one of the ever-present street vendors hawking Coca-Cola and lemonade. Hot, his mouth dry from tension, he stopped for a cold drink.

Emblazoned on the side of the portable stand were signs in

many languages. Prominent among the tongues was Japanese. The vendor's efforts obviously paid off: as Japanese tourists spilled from the insides of a giant tourist bus pulled up at the Forum's entrance, they clustered around the cart, buying Cokes. The Professional had learned the essentials of Japanese as quickly as he had mastered English many years before, when the American dollar was strongest. He listened to the Japanese tourists for a few minutes, relishing his ability to eavesdrop. But their conversations bored him; he finished his drink and drifted away.

He returned to his apartment to await the report. By 9:00 P.M. he had the information he needed, neatly typed, with an appended note thanking the client for this trust and for any further assistance he might require.

The name: Sienta Alighieri
Address: 12 Via di Terni
                       Ostia di Lido

They had more than earned the exorbitant 5,000,000 lire fee. The precious painting would not leave his sight for more than twenty-four hours. He looked out the large window toward the Vatican, the dome of St. Peter's a gray silhouette against a darkened sky. His mind was engaged in a series of silent maneuvers, in which he pitted himself against the security forces of the Church and of the Vatican itself. He was certain who the victor would be.

The humidity finally coalesced into a light veil of drizzle. Somewhere within the confines of the holy walls, the political deals were beginning. Discussions that would ultimately result in the selection of a new Pope were being held behind closed doors. Men a thousand miles away behind similar doors at the Kremlin understood that any such selection could only be a temporary one. Immensely powerful forces had already decided on the new head for all Christianity, and the Professional stood poised to carry out their orders.

The sky darkened angrily and the drizzle became a torrent. A billowing wind rose suddenly, forcing him to draw the shutters. Gods long past seemed to object to his presence in their city, yet were powerless to intercede. The room was dark, but his eyes were still able to distinguish outlines and features. He undressed and slipped between the bed's cool sheets. Only a few short moments later, his mind drifted into the comfort of a deep protective sleep. He would not remember the hostility of the night, for now his body and soul sought rejuvenation in sleep's black depth.

7

From his obscure position in a distant corner of St. Peter's the Professional, once again in the guise of Father Kottmeyer, peered out through a haze pierced by filtered light. Far off in the interior of the great church, a simple wooden coffin lay beneath the majestic dome. A multitude of mourners and world dignitaries were paying homage to the once absolute spiritual authority of the world's 700 million Roman Catholics. All that remained was for the final mass to be recited.

A golden folio of three Gospels lay open atop the plain coffin as Carlo Cardinal Cristiani read a brief address in four languages, extolling the Pontiff's long and productive life. When he had finished, one hundred scarlet-robed Princes of the Church con-celebrated the High Mass. When the last mournful tones of "In Paradisium Conducant Te Angeli" had faded into the far reaches of the semi-dark basilica, the coffin was hoisted upon eight stout shoulders and gently carried to the prepared crypt beneath St. Peter's. There the Pope was entombed among his peers.

Before the long ceremony was over, the late summer's sky opened as if on command. A lace-like drizzle began to fall, almost as a parting tribute to the dead Pontiff. The fine moisture seemed to exemplify the spirituality, simplicity, and strength of the man who for more than two decades had led the Holy See. In his memory was the strength of his deeds; no grandiose ceremony need elaborate upon their meaning to the world.

As soon as he was interned in his final resting place, the task of electing a successor to the throne of St. Peter commenced. The following week, a total of 110 cardinals would enter the ancient Conclave, but not before much of the politicking had been settled. Speculation would mount, long before the "sealing" of the Conclave, regarding which prince would inherit Pope John's tiara. Already the list of leading contenders for the Papacy contained six notable *Papabili*, each independent of any major church faction, able to rule from the necessary middle ground.

Father Kottmeyer watched the procession of cardinals leave the great church, eyes playing over the faces of those who, at this moment, could be considered front runners. One by one they walked in silence, aged and dignified leaders of a tradition, a history, a faith. In the serenity of the procession, the solemnity of their postures, each appeared to be as resolute as he was devout. The arguments, maneuvering, and infighting in which many would indulge in the Conclave were not for public display. By the time the entire cast of cardinals had assembled inside the Apostolic Palace adjoining St. Peter's, the princes would have taken three elaborate oaths of secrecy. They would pledge, under pain of excommunication, to remain silent on all matters pertaining to the election of the Roman Pontiff.

Within the hour the workmen had once again taken over practical control of St. Peter's. Preparations for the Conclave began in earnest, so that all could be ready by Friday.

The refreshing coolness of the fine light rain fell on the Professional's bare head and shoulders, soaking through his garments. He raised his face to the opened heavens, welcoming the moisture as it fell. The vast area before St. Peter's held scant trace of the vast multitude that had crowded in only an hour before. Steam rose from the pavement in mute protest to the falling rain. The quiet was broken only by the occasional sound of running feet as the last of the faithful scurried for cover. The imposter walked slowly through the mist, away from the great basilica, with his hands clasped in an attitude of prayer. The rain fell harder, forming ringlets of the hair on his neck. In moments he disappeared from sight, stepping through the fading light and falling rain.

Dawn had exploded in brilliance an hour earlier over the Czar's Kremlin. Almost two thousand miles to the southwest, the Pope had been laid to his eternal rest. The three most powerful men in the Soviet Union had been deep in discussion throughout the short summer's night and finally had come to an agreement. The plan would proceed as conceived. The Pope's untimely expiration had caused some inconvenience, but the plan remained viable. Cardinal Michalovce would still assume the Papacy within the prescribed timetable; any other choice made in the interim would prove to be merely temporary.

Chairman Maksim Shaposhnikov stretched his strong arms, signaling the meeting's end. He felt too worn to rise after the arduous night-long session. As Chairman of the Council of Ministers and First Secretary of the Communist Party, he had made the final decision that had set the plan in motion some six months earlier. It was now his option whether or not to continue, in light of the Pope's premature death. However, he alone knew that the chances of contacting the hired Professional were slim, even if he chose to terminate the operation. No one knew who the Professional was, or how he intended to place the single piece of necessary equipment in the closely guarded Sistine Chapel. In short, he knew that this meeting was politically expedient, but his decision was foreordained.

Seated opposite him was Marshal A. A. Tukhachevski, the powerful Soviet Defense Minister. The younger Marshal Tukhachevski was the sole representative of the Soviet Armed Forces in the Politburo. He leaned slightly away from the table, an alert observer more often than a participant, constantly on guard against placing the military in perilous conflict with the Party. He had risen to his lofty post by carefully treading the middle line in Soviet politics and by capitalizing astutely on his status as the first cosmonaut to orbit the earth. At age fifty-eight he had reached the pinnacle of his profession. His historic picture still adorned millions of Soviet homes, depicting a sturdy, youthful Air Force major in full uniform, hero of the Soviet Union, standing before his scorched spacecraft, emblazoned *Soyuz Sovetshikh Sotsialisticheskikh Respublik.*

Nearly twenty-five years later, that picture was all that remained of the Soviet Union's mad dash into space. The Americans had taken the lead in the early seventies and by the eighties their dominance was undisputed. Marshal Tukhachevski was a throwback to the once-glorious, if short-lived, era before the Supreme Soviet had opted not to expend the country's resources on space. Secure now in his lofty position, Tukhachevski posed little threat to Chairman Shaposhnikov.

Seated to the chairman's left was the less-known, but equally powerful, Dmitri Gvozdetskii, Chief of the Secret Police and Director of Security of the Central Committee. In his dual role, he commanded respect, if not fear, from Chairman Shaposhnikov. It was impossible to ascertain Gvozdetskii's position on any issue. The chief of the secret police simply listened, took notes, asked for qualification. His poker-faced review of Soviet policy had kept Shaposhnikov conservative in both ideology and practice. The chairman was never certain whether Gvozdetskii acted merely as a watchdog or was planning an attempt to purge him at some opportune moment of weakness.

Shaposhnikov had been surprised when Gvozdetskii offered no resistance to the initial plan. Yet he understood that the success of the venture could not be made public, and failure would be known only to the three members present. Gvozdetskii might merely be biding his time until some fatal miscalculation could be charged against his superior. Then . . .

"Further debate would be fruitless, Comrades," insisted the chairman. "The essential conditions of the project remain substantially unaltered. We shall proceed with the venture as planned." He stood with some finality, his eyes bristling under their heavy brows with an implied threat, then turned slowly toward the large windows that were just to his rear. He pulled open the slatted wooden blinds, flooding the darkened room with a dull morning glow.

His contemplation of the rust-colored Kremlin wall and Spassakya Tower nearby was interrupted by the bespectacled Gvozdetskii.

"Comrade Chairman, might I remind you that this venture was of your choosing . . . and was carried out entirely under your auspices. Neither Marshal Tukhachevski nor I, as the representative of national security interests, has had any hand in its formulation or subsequent implementation." The chief looked toward the seated Tukhachevski. It was evident that the younger marshal also eschewed any responsibility for the project, concentrating his attention on his notes and leaning physically away from the growing tension hardening between the two elder statesmen.

The chairman felt the hairs of his neck prickle as he weighed the implications of the Secret Police chief's statement. He had been maneuvered into a position of great jeopardy. The stakes were high, the rewards possibly staggering . . . but the penalty for failure would be severe, if not fatal.

Shaposhnikov never turned his head as the sound of the closing double doors reached his ears. He had been left alone with his thoughts, wondering once again whether he should have exercised greater caution. He'd have his answer in less than two months. Though never a reckless leader, he would not shy from striking boldly at a calculated weak spot. But in such daring, he knew, he'd always be alone.

The usual flow of early Monday traffic sped along the cobblestoned street built centuries before. A tall priest in black garb exited from the concrete subway station to view the near-perfect pyramid and intersecting portion of Rome's ancient wall. The cool green interior of the municipal park across the broad avenue soothed eyes assaulted by the hot morning's sunshine. The park's trees reflected the sun's brilliance and spotted the pedestrian walkway with mottled light. Fast-paced throngs hurried through the patches of dark and light, heading for the station to catch the hourly train to Ostia di Lido, where they would spend the hot day at its black-sand beach. Whole families carrying packages stuffed with food and seaside paraphernalia streamed toward him, filling the station with a cacophony of sound and a medley of aroma.

The Professional's wristwatch indicated that almost ten minutes remained before the train was to leave for Ostia, time enough to purchase a gigantic Jaffa orange from a street vendor for the twenty-minute trip. It would have to serve as a belated breakfast this hot morning. He paid half the indicated price while the vendor accepted the small coins without a murmur. Re-entering the station, the priest smiled as the corner of his eye caught an angry gesture motioned in his direction by the young fruit peddler. "See," he thought, "nobody has any respect for the priesthood any longer."

The cool darkness of the station's interior was welcome as he took his place in a slowly moving line that snaked somewhere to the right. A single ticket agent methodically inspected, then re-

moved, the second half of his transit stub as he reached the turn-
stile. He passed through, holding a small, worn valise above the
rotating partition, and stepped into the vast open air area of the
depot where eight sets of silver tracks ended at a single concrete
platform. Rickety doors of a rapidly filling train were opening,
and he hurried along toward its front, pausing briefly to survey
the interior of each of the five cars. He entered the foremost car
and walked directly to a vacant seat. Almost at that instant, as if
it was waiting for him, the train's very soul came to life. From
somewhere beneath the compartment's floor, the train's braking
compressors hissed fiercely. In another minute the hinged doors
closed and the electric commuter train rattled slowly from the
station.

His eyes glanced about the car, scanning one face after another. It was a typical midweek Italian crowd that ranged from
vacationing youngsters and families to Italian soldiers reporting
for their daily duty assignments. His eyes rested on a young
couple who were thoroughly engrossed in each other.

The priest began peeling the orange, its distinct citrus aroma
floating up to his nostrils. The tender meat of the fruit was slowly
exposed as a neat pile of orange peels grew on a paper napkin
carefully arranged on his lap. The priest took great care to pull
off each section without breaking the thin membranes. He
watched the couple over the back of the seat he was facing as the
sweet juice trickled down his dry throat.

Ostia would be the end of the line, but now, with a series of
ear-splitting lurches, the train pulled into the first of the nine stations. The girl fell against her boyfriend, her ample breasts
pushed flat against his chest. Oblivious to watching eyes, they
laughed, kissed, and laughed again. He groped for her, eliciting
another round of laughter that didn't end until he caught sight of
the priest's staring eyes. The young man instantly stiffened. His
girlfriend kept giggling until he whispered that a priest was
watching them. She cast a quick glance at the seated figure, then
followed her boyfriend's lead. For the remainder of the trip they
sat quietly, their gaiety suppressed under the father's constantly
watching eyes.

The ruins of Ostia's ancient Roman heritage slid past the
train's dirty windows as a pathetic reminder of a glorious era.

Stout chain-link fences surrounded each of the stone remains and protected them to some minimal extent, at least, from the ever-present threat of vandalism. Finally the train made its wide turn to the left, indicating it was approaching the Ostia di Lido station. The engineer let go with a long blast from his train's whistle to signal his approach to the railroad tower. This time the train slowed down long before it reached the platform, negotiating a series of complicated maneuvers. When it finally ground to a lazy halt, nearly everyone in the car was already standing, pressing toward the exits.

The train came to a complete stop; the accordian doors rushed open, allowing passengers to spill out onto the platform. The Professional left only after the crush of sweating humanity had passed through. He followed the crowd to the steps that would carry him down and under the train's tracks, then back up to the street level beyond the station.

Outside the thirty-year-old terminal a plaza crowded with vehicles greeted the passengers. Directly in front of the concourse was a queue of buses filling with the train's disembarked passengers. These vehicles would disperse their fares to the city's suburbs, returning to the plaza within the hour to greet the next train arriving from downtown Rome. The father chose to walk to the beach area some seven streets distant. The route would take him past a maze of closed restaurants and through a major shopping area. His first priority was to find a room for the night.

He purchased a copy of the *International Tribune* at a newsstand, neatly tucking it into a pocket of the valise. He resumed his walk toward the ocean, the strong scent of sea air awakening his nostrils.

Walking down a small sidestreet he came across a series of businesses open for the tourist trade. Seated at one small circular table was the dark, round-faced proprietor of a café and ice cream shop, his heavy jowls full of cappucino and day-old pastry as he spied the approaching priest. Father Kottmeyer stopped directly before the shopkeeper and placed his bag on the pavement. He asked in Italian, "I wonder if you might be able to help me?"

"Surely, Father, if I can," was the jovial reply. Pastry oozed from the corners of his mouth and he ran the sleeve of his shirt over his lips to clean them. The proprietor was secretly hoping that the priest wasn't looking for a free lunch.

The tall priest handed a small slip of notepaper, damp with perspiration, to the still-seated proprietor:

12 Via di Terni

"I'm on my way to visit an old friend from the Seminary whom I haven't seen in many years. Can you please direct me to this address?"

The paunchy shopkeeper studied the slip of clammy paper, then stood up, beginning a complex and detailed explanation of how to proceed, ornamented with elaborate gestures. "Turn left toward the sound of the ocean," he concluded; "the street you are looking for will cross the avenue one block before the boardwalk." To make certain the priest had the directions correctly, the paunchy shopkeeper ran through them a second time.

Father Kottmeyer thanked the man, who slumped back into his too-small seat, then picked up his valise and began to walk to the corner. In the distance, the sounds of metal gratings being raised for the day greeted his trained ears. Shops seldom opened for business before ten or eleven, and by two they would close for the afternoon respite. Ostia was slowly rising for a new week of trade, just as it had since the time the Romans had made it their most important seaport. Today it served as a pool of cheap labor for the shops, factories, and service industries of modern Rome. In the evenings the work force returned from the city to their homes in the working quarter of Ostia di Lido.

He turned right at the corner, his deliberately paced steps carrying him alongside an Italian version of an American supermarket. Even at this early hour it was teeming with noisy housewives trying to complete their daily food shopping as quickly as possible. The windows of the market displayed a multitude of posters advertising various cheeses, soda, sausage meats and weekly specials. A mother with several shopping bags in hand emerged from the exit, closely followed by three children equally burdened; shopping was a family outing. She frequently stopped to urge and scold them in harsh Italian, but her hollow threats worked only momentarily.

The Professional marched on as he had been directed, a short trip into the not-so-distant past. It was the Italy of the fifties, lost to Rome, yet alive here in Ostia. By this hour, almost all the shops on the avenue were open for the day's trade. The smells and noises promised great adventure for anyone who might sample the products found in their dark interiors.

A motor scooter repair shop loomed ahead. Used and broken Vespas and Lambrettas were parked in a neat row on the curb of the broad sidewalk. Already a small knot of dirty youngsters had gathered for their daily ritual. The dream had at its core a single thought: possession of one of these miraculous two-wheeled vehicles to somehow vault them into Italian manhood. The priest, as he wove his way through the growing crowd, went unnoticed.

At the last intersection he turned toward the ocean, still blocks away. His measured steps were slow as he meticulously surveyed the layout of the passing streets, buildings, alleys and shops. He donned a pair of oversized sunglasses, their tinted lenses keeping his anonymity intact as he neared the address. Just ahead was a street sign: *Via di Terni*. The never-ending sound of the polluted Mediterranean lapping against its blackened sands now droned barely a block away, its monotonous murmur like a constant symbol of life: a heart that continued eternally, free from the preordained halt of mortality. The sea would beat against the sands of the beach long after man passed from existence on earth; it would beat on when the new rulers of the world took their place for their short burst of life, then sunk into their own oblivion. Creation, life, destruction . . . the struggle raged on into futility as it had since reported in the first book of *Genesis.*

The late morning sun was reaching its zenith, the heat from above reflected by the pavement beneath his feet as the bogus priest turned the corner onto Via di Terni. The first building he passed was numbered 219; the second 221. It was apparent that he had gone at least two streets too far; he began to retrace his steps. Coming to the corner once again and crossing the avenue, he continued on the strictly residential street, lined with three-story homes and small apartment houses.

The buildings' numbers reduced by two with each structure passed—20, 18, 16, 14, until Number 12 was reached. When his quick glance up and down the uncrowded street convinced him that nothing was amiss, he adroitly slipped inside the building's entrance. A set of brass post boxes with call bells on top was just to the right of the front door. Box number three indicated that the occupant of the apartment was the one he sought, Sienta Alighieri. There was no indication whether she was married, or shared the apartment, or if in fact she lived alone.

The snap lock offered little resistance to a thin plastic credit card. The interior of the hallway had a single apartment entrance at its rear. Along the peeling left wall, a worn carpeted stairway rose to the dingy second floor.

He climbed silently upward to the landing. Directly in front of him was apartment number two. The curved wooden railing twisted around toward the right, then continued upward, a single hanging bulb providing little light. At the top of the last flight of creaking stairs was apartment number three.

The Professional followed the walkway as far as it would go. His eyes traced a steel ladder that intersected a dim emergency exit; he climbed the cold rungs to check it out. Reaching the grimy underside of the skylight, he pushed it up with his free hand. It slipped aside, exposing a tarpaper roof that gently sloped from the front of the building toward its rear.

He scanned the series of attached tarred roofs and noted that each one had an identical skylight protruding from a parallel position. If necessary, an entire network of escape routes was at his disposal.

The Professional now replaced the heavy skylight, carefully wiping clean any trace of fingerprints from the handle and ladder rungs as he retraced his steps downward. Stopping at apartment number three, he placed his ear against the thin wooden door and listened intently. Only the faintest of unintelligible sounds could be heard. The one thing the wooden barrier couldn't hide was the smell of chemical solvents: this was undoubtedly the correct place.

Within moments he was back out on the hot street. His eyes searched for the ever-present FOR LET signs that usually dotted an Italian resort area of this type. There were two close by, one directly opposite number 12, and another only two buildings away. He crossed the narrow street to the nearer building. Walking up a couple of stone steps, he knocked on the entrance door and found an almost immediate response. An older woman, dressed in black, peered out from her apartment doorway; spotting his priestly garb, she quickly fixed her soiled apron and hurried to open the glass door, inquiring willingly as to what was amiss.

Father Kottmeyer assured her that nothing was wrong, but that he just might be interested in renting the apartment, if it would possibly be within his means. As it turned out, two flats were available, and she gladly offered to show them to him. One faced the sea, and the other fronted the street.

The priest followed the middle-aged woman up a staircase to the second floor. She had hurried before him and unlocked the door to the rear flat. She held the door open for him to enter the bright spacious room.

While she hastened to the windows at the south wall, he surveyed the interior. She pulled the frayed curtains open, brightly illuminating the entire room. The view of the sea some four hundred meters beyond was breathtaking. Off in the distance he could see a series of rusting gray freighters arriving and disembarking from the port. Now, at high tide, they left their foamy wakes in the blueness of the warm sea. But the expansive vista did not suit his needs; he required the much bleaker view of the street.

"Magnifico." He smiled, to the landlady's approval. "But how much is it for a week?" He hoped to decline it, using budgetary reasons as his cover.

The woman calculated quickly, knowing that the priest would want to pay as little as possible. "I usually get six thousand lire a day," she meekly answered.

The priest stood silent for a time, looking wistfully about, then asked, "Would the other flat be as costly?"

"On no! It faces the front of the building, as I said before. There isn't any view at all . . . and it's on the third floor. But, it's clean, and I could let you have it for less than half the price of this one—twenty-five hundred lire a day."

"Do you mind if I see it?"

"Not at all, Father. It would give me no greater pleasure than to have you stay with us during your holiday. Please follow me." She closed the door, locked it, and led him to the next floor.

The flat was as she had described. Sunlight reflected through its windows from the southern row of buildings across the street. A quick glance told him he could almost peer directly into the apartment across the way. It was faultless for his purpose. "How much did you say?"

Once again she hesitated, then lowered her price. "Would two thousand lire be too much, Father?"

He tried to feign a look of embarrassment, answering, "Not at all. Thank you for being so reasonable. I'll take it for a week."

"I'm so glad, Father." She forced an uncomfortable smile. "I hope you are comfortable." But she remained, hands folded, with an expectant air.

"You'll want the 14,000 lire in advance." The priest nodded, removing his wallet and extracting the correct amount in worn bills for the waiting proprietress. Not until she had counted the money did she stop feeling a guilty lack of trust.

"Have a good vacation, Father," she exclaimed while handing him a key, then turned and scurried to the door.

"Thank you, Madam," he called as he lifted his valise to the bed.

"You may call me Madam Franchesco, Father. If there's anything you need, I'll be downstairs."

The Professional waited for the door to close, then discreetly approached it and placed his ear next to the cracked and painted wood. He could hear the receding sound of the matron's footsteps on the stairs. Once assured that he was alone, he placed the long key in the lock and turned it until the bolt caught tight.

Quickly removing his jacket, he returned to the valise, opened it and withdrew its contents. Fastidiously placing the items in order on the bedspread next to him, he focused his attention on a white towel that concealed a heavy object. Lovingly, he picked it up and unwrapped it to expose a 9mm automatic pistol. The succeeding hour was spent disassembling and meticulously cleaning the weapon. Each piece was carefully inspected before being reassembled, then dry-fired to assure flawless operation. A short perforated pipe-like device was tightly screwed onto the barrel. Finally, the lone ammunition clip was loaded with eleven hollow-pointed lead shells, rolled like beads between his fingers, and firmly snapped into the weapon's handle. He pulled the register back sharply, then released. It smacked forward, forcing the first shell into the firing chamber. Switching the weapon's safety on, he rested the pistol in the palm of his hand, sensually weighing it.

Next the priest went into the bathroom. Just to the right of a small frosted window was the watercloset. With a roll of adhesive tape and the cleaned pistol in hand, he stood atop the toilet and placed a series of white strips across the 9mm automatic. Then he carefully attached the weapon to the back side of the overhead water reservoir. He pressed the tape firmly in place and stepped off the bowl's edge. It was now safe from the prying eyes of his temporary landlady and available for use when the time should arise.

The Professional's caution meant that he must eliminate anyone who could possibly identify him. His need to control every detail made the fact that the priceless work of art had left his hands—and that at least one person could conceivably trace him—loathsome to him. This next step, then, was of absolute necessity.

Opening the *International Tribune* to the classified advertisements, he carefully inspected them; the one arranged for was not yet present. Still, it was only the fifth day. It was unlikely that the restoration had been completed, but his instinct and training always compelled him to cover even remote contingencies. Such fastidious planning had often borne reward. Once he had arrived at a rendezvous a day earlier than his prey anticipated. It resulted in his opponent's demise twenty-four hours before the reverse would have taken place. His techniques might have been considered unorthodox, but there was no question as to their efficacy.

The Professional fought the tedium of the long, hot afternoon as he watched the apartment building across the street. It wasn't until almost five that Ms. Alighieri exited from the front of the building. She returned within a half hour, burdened with a large shopping bag and an Italian bread tucked under her free arm. Dinnertime was approaching; evidently she had bought enough for more than one person. He had surmised that someone else had to be involved in the restoration process. The initial difficulty in establishing the necessary contacts indicated this; her large purchase had served to confirm it.

Daylight was gradually slipping away, although there would be another hour of subdued light before darkness enveloped Ostia. The visitor dressed once more, then left his room, securing the flimsy door behind him. In a moment he was on the street; quickly turning away from the apartment building, he began walking toward the sea.

The rhythm of the surf echoed faintly as he pursued its beckoning sound. Dark-sand beach, enclosed by a pitted concrete and chain-link fence, ran as far as the eye could see. Further to the west was the intersection of Via di Mar and the vast eternal sea itself. A great traffic circle and pedestrian walk made this spot the natural focal point of Ostia.

On the land side of the great circle quaint restaurants overflowed with tables onto the sidewalk, rapidly filling with their daily supply of endless tourists. Families were out for their pre-dinner strolls, which led, ultimately, to this intersection.

On the ocean side of the circle lay a great spherical terrazzo plaza and rotting steel pier that extended into the living sea. The pier should have been torn down years ago, yet it persisted as the city itself had: stubborn, frail with dilapidation, but sturdy with history.

Here was an entrance to the beach, if one really cared to make use of it at this late hour. At any other time of the day, a charge of 50 lire was imposed by the municipality.

The plaza also offered another enticement. Along the waist-high concrete wall, enterprising workers displayed and sold a variety of tourist goods, local handicrafts and assorted small precision industrial tools. Parked along the curb were a number of motorized vehicles whose backs were laden with conglomerations of roasted nuts, dried fruits, and hard candies. Vendors noisily hawked their wares to the flowing mass of people, creating a carnival atmosphere.

Now and then, individuals would stop to look, then haggle until a price was set. The father took his time walking along the periphery of the plaza as he moved from display to display. Small clusters of potential customers crowded about an arrangement of scales, drill bits, watches, and sundry items proffered on an array of towels and colorful handkerchiefs spread atop the coarse concrete parapet.

Threading his way quietly through the milling crowd, he finally found what he had been looking for. There, an interested patron was inspecting a pair of used binoculars. As was the custom, and also to show a passing interest, Father Kottmeyer approached the display—but stopped two to three meters away from it. A dark middle-aged and unshaven gentleman immediately noticed the priest's interest, his knowing face breaking into a broad, false smile.

The game commenced. In minutes, the young father and middle-aged vendor were engaged in a typical transaction, the unkempt salesman trying desperately to convince the priest that a second pair he had would be a much better buy. The father carefully inspected all three pairs offered, alternately holding each up to his eye and looking through the objective. He cast the third, cracked pair aside. Of the two remaining, neither was of exceptional quality, but either would suffice for its intended purpose.

Choosing one, he returned the other to the bit of cloth that served as a display case. Now began the time-honored ritual of Italian bargaining.

"Father, please be fair. You have chosen the best of the lot. l paid almost 50,000 lire for them and they're worth a great deal more!" The Professional picked them up again, inspecting them closely. Satisfied, he returned them to the cloth for what seemed to be the last time, and began to walk away.

"Father, please . . . " implored the vendor while taking a few quick steps after the departing customer. He stopped the potential buyer before the sale slipped from his grasp. "Please come back, maybe I can do a bit better for you."

The priest retraced his steps and returned to the haggling. Bargaining was to be expected; buyer and seller both knew that the final price would be about half the initial asking price.

It took a full ten minutes to come to terms. The Professional finally clinched the transaction with a "take it or leave it" offer, made by placing three bills totaling 25,000 lire on the cloth, and keeping his hand over them. The hand lingered over the bills for a minute, indicating the priest had gone as far as he would go. The seller's eyes were momentarily caught by the ornate gold ring on the priest's hand, but his interest fled as the hand withdrew. Looking up at the disguised Professional, then at the crisp bills, the vendor ultimately nodded his begrudging approval, and smiled even more broadly than before. He had garnered only a slight profit, but had managed to conceal that one of the lenses had a cracked retaining ring. The priest picked up his prize, turned and walked off to blend into the crowd.

He had structured the event in that precise manner. The priest would not be remembered other than as a tall, sturdy man of God. The item was purchased without undue debate over the price, and—just as importantly—without too little! Orchestrated in typical Italian custom, the tall priest with the large gold ring would surely be forgotten in a day or two.

Anticipating a long night, he stopped on his way back to his rented room to purchase a small repast to be consumed in his lair. By the time he was secure in the third-floor flat, night had conquered the day. Illumination from the apartments across the way provided sufficient brightness to permit free but unseen movement about his small, unlit room. He positioned the single armchair so that it faced the open window, yet was well enough back to remain hidden from view. Seated, he trained the binoculars on the apartment directly opposite.

Viewing almost all the interior with a sweep of his newly acquired glasses, the Professional found that it was not unlike the building he was in. The room itself had been set up as an artist's studio; with the glasses he could distinguish the tubes of oil paints, brushes, and easel on a table that stood against the east wall. Evidently the equipment had been recently utilized.

The woman rose from her bed with a rolled object in her hand and walked to the low gas stove at the far wall. He had to stand to change his viewing point so as not to lose sight of her as she moved about. She passed through a blind spot between the two large open windows of her apartment, reappearing on the other side. Her back was now to the windows; her body blocked his sight of her movement. In a moment she had finished. She stood to adjust a knob atop the porcelain stove, the loosely rolled object no longer in her hand.

What was missing from the scene was the accomplice he'd anticipated. Apparently whoever was in the venture with her was at some other location. Having seen enough to know exactly what had transpired, he began planning his next course of actions.

Hours later, lying awake in the sagging softness of the cheap rooming-house mattress, he turned over in his mind what he had visualized. His features reflected his exhaustion. It was well past

2:00 A.M. before his mind slid into the small serenity of an uneasy sleep. Even in slumber his brain never completely rested. It was alive, deviously running through plan after plan; its frenzied activity only subsided with the coming of the dawn.

A mind is a peculiar, magnificent mass of gray tissue that controls our lives through electrical impulses, transmitted at the speed of light. The mass may extract information from its innermost recesses, or may bury any of those chemical particles we call memories that it finds too painful to reconstruct. Then only in dreams can the buried live again.

And so the self-imposed discipline that allowed him to function even while asleep had been breached. Random thoughts seeped through the crevice, unconscious thoughts laced with bitter remembrance. His body tossed in the soft bed. The white pillowcase became stained with sweat, its pattern spreading as his face turned from side to side. His mind had drifted back to the time years ago when his whole world had seemed to cave in about him.

The grass was dark green that morning, the field long and lush and soaked with the night's moisture, the long panorama of Belgian hillside awakening from darkness with the red sunlight. He walked across the field behind the polished wooden coffin that bore his father to his final resting place. He was alone save for the six paid pallbearers and the single priest, who had chanted continously from the steps of St. Martin's church. The temple's Gothic design and sculpted figurines wove their long-forgotten images through his dream.

With a clang the lead pallbearer swung open the wrought-iron gate surrounding the tiny hillside cemetery. The cortege passed through. A neat rectangular scar had been cut deep into the hillside, a mound of fresh soil piled just to its right. The graveside service was brief; all proper phrases mouthed, the handful of moist earth was cast into the hole to strike the coffin's lid with a soft, heavy, empty thud like a final heartbeat.

With his father gone now, he was the last of his line. A dynasty had ended, for there would be none after him. Only a youth, he was sorry his father hadn't given him more time, but thus it was to be. Still, he had been schooled well, by a true Professional. What lessons were missing would have to be self-taught. But he had been an excellent student, and held no fear. He would carry on alone.

The boy slowly turned from the grave to the headstones that stood upright against the morning sky. All of his family had been buried here; he would be as well. The engraved names rumbled with memories of faces in the past. He stopped, looked down at his only inheritance: a golden ring with the family crest emblazoned on its face. Engraved deeply in the gold orb was the image of a striking panther, leaping at a one-carat diamond embedded in the ring's center. The ring and its bearer were all that remained of the family Van der Meersch-Maes.

His mind could never go on past that point. It would climb away from that juncture in time and space, reaching for some other vision. Some mechanism deep within the mass of gray tissue stemmed the trickle of memories.

Daybreak had given way to the heat of the morning before he finally stirred from his mental cocoon. That day, it was not a mortal priest who rose from bed, but a modern Beelzebub in mortal disguise. He was a macabre human machine intent upon one objective . . . absolute destruction.

His bare feet swung away from the comfort of the too-warm bed and struck the floor, the cool smooth boards sending a shiver through his body. Immediately his mind snapped into readiness. He had trained himself to be alert at an instant's notice, no cold showers necessary.

He completed his daily routine, dressed himself in his priestly vestments and emerged almost ready to go on stage for his daily performance. But on this day the role required an Angel of Death. He examined himself in the mirror, and put on a tinted pair of thick-lensed glasses. They were deceptive; optically perfect, their thickness and color merely served to disguise his features. If his steps were ever traced, a description of the priest would surely include his poor eyesight. At the Vatican, of course, the glasses were never used.

Now for the final prop—though this one was real. Standing on the dull white china commode, he reached up to remove his automatic. A slight tug and it fell free into his hand, striking the massive golden ornament that adorned his ring finger.

He removed the tape and rolled it into a ball, then slipped it into his trouser pocket, to be discarded later with care; his fingerprints were embedded in its sticky surface . . . and fingerprints would not be left behind. He used the small hand towel to wipe the bathroom clean of any unconceivable finger or palm traces, methodically moving about the single room and rubbing clean every telltale surface even knowing he'd do it again later that night. That finished, he removed any debris he might have brought with him. When he departed there would be no trail left behind.

He closed the door and locked it behind him, then quietly slipped down the rickety stairs.

The street was nearly deserted; only the earliest-rising workers were out. Languidly they made their collective ways to vehicles, or walked to the rail center for the 8:05 A.M. to Rome. Standing on the stone lintel of the rooming house, he squinted against the harshness of the light.

Emilio Pertini had been sitting in his small café since eight in the morning, awaiting a reply to the advertisement in the day's *Tribune*. It was always a nerveracking experience, living with the uncertainty of clandestine meetings, secret phone calls, illegal art. But it was lucrative beyond belief, much more than he could have hoped for as an aspiring young commercial artist.

He had worked for a Milan advertising agency, finding that being a junior artist meant little excitement and even less pay. Any chance at real money was tied to a slow progression of raises and advancement, years in the future. The hope for rapid recognition died slowly. As each year dragged into the next, the lack of prospects almost strangled the will. Emilio was a more-than-competent artist, but that mattered little in the world of advertising. A single quality eluded him; its absence had hampered him since childhood. He lacked aggressiveness. He was always overlooked, forever being unnoticed. He grew to believe that things would never change.

Then one afternoon, while he was eating lunch in a Milan park, his life had taken a new course. It had been an exquisite day, late in spring. The trees had shed their winter's drab coverings and were bursting forth in a shower of crisp color. Before him stood a fountain blowing translucent bubbles onto the pond's surface. But Emilio's mind cried with sorrow, for at thirty-five he felt his life passing quickly, unfulfilled. He had tried to pull his thoughts from an endless fantasy about what could have been, and had almost accepted a lackluster future of mundane work and loneliness. In his most despairing moments he would sometimes think that in dying he would finally have the freedom he so desperately sought, the release he had not attained in life from numbing mediocrity.

He stared out across the pool to the gently sloping knoll beyond it, a carpet of velvet dotted with lounging office secretaries taking full advantage of the spring's bounty. Here too, he was a total failure. Women never were attracted to him, even though he was pleasant, built well enough, and dressed nicely. His few and feeble attempts at intimacy with the opposite sex had ended in disaster. That day he was waiting in the park solely to watch a young secretary who had joined the agency almost two months earlier.

Miss Alighieri was an exceptional beauty, and though it seemed unlikely that she would have anything to do with him, that mattered little to a man who felt such a yearning in his loins. He had made it a point to walk by her desk a number of times. With each progressing week the daily frequency of his sorties had increased, until he was certain she couldn't have overlooked him. Still, a month later there had been no response on her part. She had looked up a number of times, then returned to her job. His level of frustration had grown, then gradually subsided as he realized that nothing in his life had altered. It remained meaningless.

Halfway through the two-hour midday break, he spotted her on the blacktop path that wound through the park. His heart rate increased as her steps brought her closer. In a few minutes she stood directly before him, having recognized him from afar. She smiled as she approached, and took the spot directly next to his on the wooden bench. He caught her movement through the corner of his eye, afraid to face her or even speak, fearing that her proximity would prove illusory.

It wasn't. In a moment she took the initiative and engaged him in conversation. By the end of the hour she had cleverly maneuvered him into asking her to dinner that very night. He spent the remainder of the workday in a state of euphoria, and literally floated about the office, barely able to survive until closing. Emilio then hurried home, dressed and arrived at her flat a full half hour before he should have.

His sweaty hand found her bell, and she invited him upstairs via the intercom amidst a flood of apologies for her tardiness and the paltry condition of her flat. It never occurred to him to wonder that a working receptionist would be able to afford an apartment in the most prestigious complex in Milan.

Her door was slightly ajar, the soft light from the interior beckoning him from the hallway. He timidly pushed it open to reveal the interior of the expensive flat. A familiar honeyed voice invited him to enter. From behind the bedroom door, she instructed him to fix drinks for both of them—a rolling cart filled with an ample liquor stock, glasses, and ice stood before the sliding doors that led to the terrace. The kind of drinks didn't matter . . . not for what she had in mind.

Then she appeared. Sienta was everything Emilio could have possibly desired, and more. She had dressed in a flowing black gown made of layers of silken material. It was revealing, yet not totally. Her high-pointed breasts swelled above the rim of the barely confining fabric, their crimson nipples fetching toward him. As she walked forward, the triangular patch of darkness nestled between her thighs was there, then gone. It was something he had never experienced, a primitive urge groaning from his depths.

When he handed her the measured drink, their fingers met for a delightfully lingering moment. That instant was a rebirth of his very life, a microsecond that electrically filled the void of his manhood.

They sat and chatted for a while, and dined at home rather than going out. The simple meal was ordinary, but for him it had been a dream come true . . . the consummation of a lifetime. After, on the terrace overlooking the city's lights, they'd kissed, tenderly at first and then with a zealous fervor.

When the morning's light fell softly across the sleeping lovers' faces, he awakened and turned toward her, half afraid that everything had been a dream. Seeing her there beside him, her sleeping features framed by a jet-black border of fine, luminous hair, he'd known that what he felt would never leave him. She had expertly led him through a night of pleasure, and in the end, she had made him feel like a king. He had not then realized that he was little more than a pawn.

In the succeeding weeks she would become everything to him. Little by little she gained control of his emotions, his thoughts, and finally, his every action. Her tastes were expensive, far in excess of their combined incomes at the advertising agency. Her "necessities" included the fabulous apartment, an expensive sports car, and all the other pursuits of stylishness. It mattered little, for he moved in with her almost immediately, soon becoming exposed to a lifestyle he had never imagined. He asked no questions as to the source of her wealth. The topic simply never arose, and he would never dream of prying, or doing anything that might upset her—in the least.

At the end of the second month, she announced suddenly that she would be leaving Milan for Rome early the next month; her funds were exhausted. Emilio was devastated, not knowing what to say or where to turn. He would follow her of course, go with her anywhere. In the end he did, but only under her conditions: She would use his artistic talents to make them a great deal of money.

She explained that her contacts in the art world were numerous, and from time to time she was asked to provide "display" pieces for various private art shows. Also, she said, she was commissioned to copy works so that the originals could be kept safe from vandals. Emilio had accepted her explanations, not really caring, for it seemed to be the only way he could remain with her.

Then, with equal abruptness, the pattern altered. She capriciously moved her studio from fashionable Rome to seaside Ostia. While he spent long hours working at their third-floor studio, she had remained in Rome for long periods of time "on business." When he finally approached her on that subject, she flew into a rage and threatened to have him arrested as an art forger.

Learning that his worshipped Sienta was merely using him was devastating; his anguish was excruciating, and he hoped it would kill him. But she had chosen well; they both knew he'd never have the strength either to leave or to turn to the police. He was hopelessly bound to her—torn between hate and that other illogical emotion.

Then, only last week, the most spectacular painting of all had been thrown into her lap. She was to restore a Vatican masterpiece for a fabulous fee. And she had a plan; the work would also be copied. Then, after it was both chemically and thermally aged, the duplicated copy would be substituted for the original. She could sell the original for a king's ransom, then vanish. The prize seemed worth the risk. Now here he was, waiting for the call that would set up the delivery. It could be dangerous business, but at this point he no longer cared. His life had ended the moment he understood the reason she had wanted him. He was merely going through the motions, waiting for whatever sexual favors she might bestow on him from time to time.

A young woman walking by caught his eye. Her body reminded him of Sienta's. Once again his mind searched the past. In the moment that followed he recalled a recent morning when he had gazed upon Sienta's sleeping body beside him. He could almost feel his hand reaching tentatively for her breasts, her rose-colored nipples. A single finger traced a circular pattern on the swelling, causing it to grow hard. Sienta stirred; his hand fell away. Her eyes opened, not with passion but with a look of disappointment. She spoke, but he could not hear her. Words filled his ears, but they were not hers.

"Do you like what you see?" questioned the young woman who had passed moments before.

He was caught unaware. "Yes . . . I mean . . . "

"May I join you?" she inquired.

His eyes lifted to her face. She was smiling.

"Please," he replied, barely leaving his seat.

The young woman quickly sat down, moving her chair beside him.

"Can I interest you in something other than your paper?" she inquired as her hand reached for his thigh under the small table.

Her touch was cold even through the fabric of his pants. He moved his leg away, uncertain of what she meant.

"I said, can I interest you in a warm afternoon? A lady needs something to fill her time. . . . And for you, a bargain price."

Emilio got up, his hands searching his pockets for an instant. He extracted a few bills and threw them on the table without counting them."No . . . no," he stammered. "Maybe some other time." He picked up the newspaper and hurried off. The girl shrugged her shoulders, then looked about. In the far corner of the shop was an elderly gentleman. She got up and slowly walked in his direction.

The Professional, in his priestly guise, had escaped the morning's heat by breakfasting in the Airport Hotel in downtown Ostia. The dining room was comfortably air conditioned, and it was a pleasant way to begin the day. An efficient waiter took his order, then hurried on to a group of tourists just down from their rooms. He expected better tips from the American tourist group than from an underpaid priest.

Opening his newspaper to the classified section, the Professional scanned the listings until he found the advertisement he sought. He folded the paper back and memorized the number given, mentally adding one to each digit.

He would not place the call until much later in the day. By then he would have retrieved the original piece of work, and would be ready to execute the maneuvers needed in acquiring the copy. Once again, he would leave no vestige of a trail—that was how he worked. It was a science, calculated to the most minute detail, the risks determined—and disposed of—with precision accuracy.

As the waiter approached, the father lifted his head from the *Tribune*. His appetite was back. As always, he would eat like a lion . . . but conversely, *before* the kill.

8

The Professional, clothed in his priest's disguise, sat in the safe darkness of the movie house. He had chosen to spend the hours until night could disguise his task in the air-conditioned comfort of a theater. It was nearly 9:00 P.M., time for him to place the call that would set in motion his plan for regaining the Vatican treasure. Rising, he carefully sidestepped into the aisle and walked up the incline to the theater's rear.

Exiting through the double doors past couples already queuing up for the ten o'clock performance, the priest made his way across the avenue to a sidewalk café, where he would purchase a sandwich and place the all-important telephone call.

The proprietor came up to him and smiled. Since the café was not busy at this hour, it mattered little if the priest occupied a table normally used for three or four persons.

The priest looked up and said, "I think I'll have a cheese sandwich and an espresso."

The proprietor began to leave but was called back. "And may I please use your telephone . . . for a local call, of course?"

The heavy-set Italian gestured to the far corner of the interior of the café as he walked inside.

The Professional followed the proprietor. At the far wall he found the telephone. At the fifth set of double rings, the familiar voice of the woman he had encountered at the Forum came onto the line.

"Yes, who is it?"

"I'm answering your advertisement in today's *Tribune*. From its content I assume that my merchandise is ready. What are your plans for its delivery?" The question was irrelevant; he had no doubt that they intended to collect their fee and then present him with a copy of the priceless Da Vinci painting. He played along, knowing that the scenario's finale would be quite different from the one they envisioned.

The woman answered, "Tomorrow afternoon we shall meet as before, under the Arch of Titus. You will have the balance of our agreed payment. I will present you with a key and instructions as to where your merchandise can be retrieved. Your painting has been brought back to its former condition; I'm certain you'll be satisfied with the results. Tomorrow afternoon at . . . three. Please be alone. You'll be observed the entire time. Understood?"

"Yes, I understand. The money is ready. I'll be there. . . . " He allowed his words to hang for a moment, then broke the connection. It was an appointment that none of them would keep.

It was still hot; the night air felt sticky. As he emerged from the café's interior, a hint of sea breeze swept across the city from the warm waters that bordered it. He took a seat facing the sidewalk. The city was first coming alive as the torpor of the day wore off; a trickle of people walking to their favorite restaurants by the shoreline would soon become a steady stream, and finally a torrent. Only then would he vanish in the flowing current of humanity.

The young priest ate slowly, watching the few tables fill up until his was the only one occupied by a single person. The owner finally approached. "Excuse me, Father. Will there be anything else?" The owner obviously wanted him to vacate the table; filled tables were much better for business. He paid the already waiting check and added a modest gratuity, then stepped out onto the sidewalk.

Immediately he dissolved into an anonymous member of the crowd, just one of many men of the cloth on yearly holiday. He headed in the direction of the ocean, four or five streets distant.

His steps were slow, yet purposeful. There was no need to make haste; the woman, along with any companion she might have, had no idea he had uncovered her whereabouts. She would

be feeling perfectly safe in her top-floor flat, possibly even cele-
brating tomorrow's impending coup.

As he approached the last street before the broad seaside
boulevard, his nostrils rejoiced in the sea's timeless scent. The salt
air brought a briskness to his seemingly tired gait as he turned
onto the Via di Terni, to the apartment house that had been his
haven for the past day and a half. Before he entered the building,
he paused to gaze upward at the open windows of the flat at
number 12. He watched the light from its interior dancing
against the limp curtains. Dark shadows moved, indicating life
within.

Quietly he slipped back into his building, not wanting the
landlady to know he had returned. As a rat might avoid the light,
he kept to the hallway's shadows, passing her open door without
being discovered. He deftly negotiated the stairs, then cautiously
entered his flat. Practiced eyes surveyed the room and saw that
everything was as he had left it. In the near corner of the room
his single suitcase still sat precisely aligned with the floorboards,
indicating the landlady had not moved it.

He moved about the flat, taking care not to touch anything
but what was absolutely necessary. His fingerprints were not on
file with any police agency, and he took great pains to retain that
advantage. In his business, that one spot or partial print could
end in his unmasking and capture.

On the only scatter rug in the flat, he laid the suitcase flat on
its side. He sprung the cheap locks and opened it. Inside he had
placed all the refuse he had created during his brief stay. He
would dispose of the suitcase and its contents before his final act
later that evening. And with its disposal, any trace of his identity
would be gone. He used the small towel to wipe all the surfaces
clean yet again, along with the room's doorknob both on the inside and outside of the small cubicle.

From one of the apartments just below his, a radio filled both
his room and the street with loud music, covering the sound of
his movements in the small flat.

He had one final change of garments in the case, clean and
free of the perspiration that had soaked through the shirt and
dark jacket of his priestly garb. Walking back to the center of the
darkened flat, he changed quickly. His weapon was checked, then

slipped into its holster under his left armpit. To hide it he donned a black cotton windbreaker and zipped it closed.

He was almost ready. He checked the flat directly opposite his one final time before putting his plan into motion. He took the binoculars to the window, stopping just short of the sill. From this vantage point he could observe the interior of the other flat without being observed from either the street or his own apartment.

For almost half an hour he kept vigil, making mental notes of the locations of all large objects within his view. The various paints, solvents, and artist's brushes were no longer on the small kitchen table. Apparently, their task had been completed. Now the table was covered with soiled dishes set for two persons. This fact, along with two wine glasses, confirmed his feeling that only two persons were involved. His disposal of them and immediate recovery of the Vatican's precious painting now seemed assured; he was dealing with professional art forgers, not killers.

When he had seen all he needed to, he returned to the center of the room, placed the binocular's lens down against the side of the suitcase, and gave the room one last, careful look. Mentally he went about the four walls, making certain that he hadn't missed any corner. He stuffed the last of his discarded clothing inside the suitcase, then reached for the binoculars. As he lifted them, the left lens retaining ring fell free and struck the rug, which muffled the sound as it hit. It rolled to rest against the suitcase's side, hidden from his view.

He wiped the binoculars clean of fingerprints and placed them in the center of the valise. With finality he closed the suitcase; the priest who was vacationing in Ostia ceased to exist.

A strange grayness hovered over Prague. Summer's warmth had fled—replaced, if only for today, by bleakness. The skyline of the city stood out against the monochrome of the heavens as the day began.

A cold sweat filming her heavy brow, Eugenia Motykia sat back from the window, protected from view. She had not left the seat for the past hour. Four stories below, a now-familiar figure passed through the courtyard, glancing up at the unlit windows of her flat. He had followed this pattern precisely, every fifteen minutes for as long as she'd been watching. His dress—which was not unlike that of her deceased husband's—and the manner in which he walked had given him away. But perhaps that was his intention all along: for her to notice, to fear. If so, he had succeeded.

She had first spotted him standing just outside the state food store, three days ago. His staring eyes had followed her as she moved out the glass doors and down the street. She could feel their glare burning into her back as she fought terror. Had he come to get her? Did they know? She couldn't be certain. But he had been there, more faithful than a shadow, ever since. Not caring much for anonymity, he had taken up residence outside her apartment. In response to the unseasonal chill, he was now wearing a dark trench coat, amplifying his conspicuousness.

The widow knew this routine well. Her husband had spoken of the psychology often used to make suspects so full of fear that they would give themselves away. Now as the object of that same tactic she swore not to break under the strain. In the semi-darkness of her small flat she had mentally examined the possible reasons for the secret police's interest in her. Her answers weren't too frightening at first. They probably believed that if she had something to be fearful of, she would run; maybe someone suspected that her husband had divulged information on one of his cases to her. In either event, if she did nothing and went about her normal routine as before, she was hopeful that after a few days they would leave her alone. Yet her mind turned over the possibility that somehow they knew about those mysterious papers her husband had sent her. It had not been until last night that she had begun to understand their fatal importance.

The televisioned Czechoslovakian news program, with its brief, flat statement that the cardinals of the Roman Catholic Church were about to enter Conclave in order to choose a new Pontiff, had meant little to her. She had watched as they filed into the centuries-old splendor of the Sistine Chapel. Then her heart skipped a beat as the camera fell upon the representative from her country, Cardinal Michalovce. His name on the documents, his prominence just at this time, her silent watcher . . . it couldn't be coincidence. That had to be why they were watching!

Long minutes passed; then, like a clockwork figure marking the quarter hour, her persecutor trod stolidly across her line of vision. Fear invaded her soul once more. She knew he was toying with her but was powerless to prevent her rising panic. A cold bead of sweat ran down her forehead and she sank back from the window as his face turned upward. He must have seen her, known she was watching; he slowed his pace to an agonizing crawl.

From the darkness of the unlit room her eyes searched for his, peering just over the line of sight that was necessary to keep him in view. It took all her strength to break free of his gaze; she could feel her will bowing to his. Panic slowly overtook rationality. Her thoughts reached out to her husband in a futile cry for help.

Eugenia's mind was speeding uncontrollably . . . anticipating the inevitable conclusion of this frightening scenario. It would all have been rehearsed to the minutest detail. At the chosen moment, there would be footsteps just outside her door, then a knock. She would take a few frightened steps to the door, unlock it, and let them in. They would "escort" her to the waiting car and drive her to the formidable building on the square—ironically, the same building where her beloved husband had served these many years. Then, somewhere in the bowels of that fearsome structure, she would be broken. It might take days, weeks, or even months. But time mattered little; in the end, they would have what they were searching for.

The figure was lost beyond the corner of the next building, but his disappearance afforded her little solace. She knew too well that he would be back on schedule. As the minutes passed she took hold of herself. Her eyes strayed to the door to the hall, across which was the room where the documents had remained hidden these past weeks. No doubt remained; there was nothing else they could be seeking.

Being careful to remain out of view from the courtyard, she rose from her chair and walked to the door. Her determined steps reflected her new, if fragile, resolve. Opening the door a crack, she carefully peered in both directions to be sure no one was watching. The corridor was free. Stepping out quickly, she closed the door behind her. In an instant she was across the open space and into the room that housed the garbage disposal chute. Here she would be safe, for the moment, from prying eyes.

Her hands reached up above the metal door jamb and tore at the fragmented concrete block until the hole materialized once again. Desperate fingers reached inside and found the waxed paper envelope she had made. Quickly she withdrew the package and hid it inside her blouse. In a moment the broken concrete had been replaced, the hole again rendered undetectable in the dimness of the room.

Checking the hallway once again, the middle-aged woman stepped out into the passageway. At that precise moment her neighbor's door opened. She froze. Terror gripped her mind and body. From her right a voice reached out to her.

"Eugenia, Eugenia, how are you?"

The voice was familiar, yet she didn't budge. Her eyes were on her own doorway and her mind on the illusory safety of her apartment. All she could think of was that somehow she must get back into her flat. The voice called to her once again; then a figure was standing in front of her, blocking her way. She clutched her bosom, trying to hide it, the envelope, terror creeping into her face.

"Eugenia, what's wrong?" Her neighbor's eyes searched her own. "Eugenia, what is the matter? Are you feeling well? You're sweating. Come." The woman put down her package and placed her stout arm around the widow's waist. "I'll take you inside."

Mrs. Motykia kept her arms tight across her chest as she allowed herself to be led the few steps to her doorway. She opened the door and spun to face her longtime friend.

"Magda, thank you. I'll be all right. It is nothing. I'm just tired. I've not slept well since Zavar's death." One hand left her breast and found the edge of the door. She closed it in her friend's face, then sank against its cool metal backing. Had she seen it? Once more the fear had returned.

Magda Steffin was taken aback by her neighbor's actions. "Poor woman," she thought. "What a lot she has gone through in the past few weeks! What with her husband being a secret police official, who would go to the funeral? Only his co-workers. No children, no friends, yes, it is sad." The woman turned, picked up her burden and cast a sorrowful look at the apartment's door, then walked down the hall to the stairway.

It took the widow a full minute to regain the strength needed to stand without the door's support. Finally she eased herself free and found her way back to her seat before the window. Only seconds passed before the secret policeman once again came into view around the corner of the building three stories below. The terror she felt now turned to rage as her eyes followed him across the compound. Her hands brought the precious envelope out of her blouse and placed it in her lap, but her eyes did not leave him until he again disappeared. Only then did she allow herself to look down at the documents encased in their waxed-paper protection.

A few tentative rays from the morning sun braved the somber overtones of the day. She was glad that she wouldn't have to turn on the single overhead fluorescent light. For the past three days she'd felt as visible and vulnerable as a player on the stage when the light was on. The darkness gave her the courage to tear at the tight wrapping of the package in her lap until the four pages of documents fell free. She threw down the waxed paper and reached for them, afraid of what she would find.

Her eyes carefully studied the photostats, this time more intensely than she had weeks before when the shock of their arrival had blunted her comprehension. Now, after the TV announcement about the Vatican Conclave, she knew she must decipher the message for which her husband had given his life.

On the first page, a copy of a ledger of some kind revealed that twelve marriages had taken place on a single day in March of 1943, among them one between Bohuslav Tabor and Anya Anelovicz, a Jewish woman. The two names had been circled in red. The site was a partisan camp in the Nazi-occupied area around Decin, adjacent to the German border.

On the same sheet was photocopied another page from the same ledger listing the partisans' casualties from a German air-raid attack. Included in the death list, again circled in red, was the same name, Anya Anelovicz; she had died only two days after the marriage.

The second sheet documented an official change of name made in 1946. Red circles drew her eyes to the name B. Tabor, and then to its counterpart for his new identity: Brandano Michalovce.

Following the name changes was a note from the partisan commander to his troops at Decin. It was dated 1943. The note was countersigned by B. Tabor, Lieutenant. The last page, a photostat of a hand-lettered parchment, was the most innocuous of the four. It was a simple certificate of ordination, again to the same Bohuslav Tabor, dated some years before the others, immediately preceding the outbreak of hostilities.

The photostat rustled in her hand. This man, this priest whose marriage was recorded in these ledgers, had violated his sacred oath. Now the web had been spun. Her life with her inspector husband hadn't gone for naught; she could put these simple facts together. It was apparent that at the war's end, B. Tabor had become Michalovce during the chaotic months following the German surrender. All Czechoslovakia knew of the cardinal's rise to power, and now he was in Rome helping to choose a new Pope. With the rules against a priest's marrying, how had this man risen to be a cardinal? Was it possible that not only should he not be a cardinal, but perhaps not even a priest?

Her fingers began to tremble and the papers fell back into her lap. It had become clear that her husband's involvement in this matter was the reason for the sudden interest in her shown by the secret police. But did they know of the existence of these documents? Surely not, for if they did, they would have taken her into custody and ransacked the entire apartment to find them. No, she understood that simple fact of logic. Well, if they hadn't taken her, then what did they have up their sleeves?

In the following hour the widow tumbled the pieces in her mind and finally arrived at a determination. They didn't know that her husband had made copies of the documents; they were merely playing with her as a cat plays with a mouse before the kill. Their open surveillance of her was calculated to make her panic, to make her break if the inspector *had* confided in her. Thus, if she did nothing to arouse their suspicions, it stood to reason that they would eventually tire of their game and go away.

But now an even greater problem had reared its ugly head. Her husband had died because of these scraps of paper. What then should she do with them? If she did nothing, then he had died in vain. Unless perhaps he had died to keep them secret? That didn't seem possible. They had apparently lain dormant since World War II. So there must be some reason for their current resurrection. . . . If she was taken and if she died, then the truth in the documents would die with her.

A glance out the window confirmed that the figure that had

hounded her for the past few days was back on schedule. This time her eyes followed him completely across the courtyard . . . followed him without fear.

Chairman Shaposhnikov's limousine pulled up in front of the administration building, which was set back from the venerable walls of the Kremlin. He abhorred these late-night meetings for, at seventy years of age, he knew that it was but a matter of time until someone younger pushed him off his lofty perch atop the Communist Party's hierarchy. It was nearly time for this to happen; a matter of practicality: Victory in the war against the capitalists could only be achieved by young, vigorous leadership. Almost six months earlier, a plan had been proposed that was bold and would strike deeply against the West. At first he resisted it. But as time went on, the implications of what success might bring won him over. He embraced it as a method of clinging to, of strengthening his hold on the chairmanship. But there had been complications, with first the death of his agent, and then the untimely death of the Pope. As he emerged from the vehicle, he understood the reason for the meeting. The plan would have to be revised; the question was, how? The Professional had not contacted anyone they knew of. In fact, while the chairman believed that the plan was still in motion, he really had no way of confirming it. The funds had been transferred and their loss meant little to the Soviets. Still, if at some later date they were found to have been wasted, it would not sit well.

The guards came to attention as he swept past them. Identification was not necessary; the chairman was a Russian institution. He walked directly to the waiting elevator, already almost half an hour late, a habit he had picked up from Marshal Stalin, who was always last to important meetings because it gave his opponents time to think and time to fear. Whether necessary or not, it was effective. The later leaders of the Soviet nation had never had the power to instill fear in their rivals. Molotov, Vishinsky, Malenkov, Bulganin, and Khrushchev had all tumbled from power, one stepping upon the fallen body of the other. None of them was feared the way Stalin had been. Gradually, Maksim Shaposhnikov had risen to the top, not only through political stealth, but through fear. Those who could not be won over could be broken.

Three floors below street level the elevator came to a stop. Its doors opened onto a large reception desk where two armed Soviet marines were on duty. Catching a glimpse of the elderly chairman, they immediately snapped to attention. The chairman never acknowledged their existence, merely swept past them and down the hallway. One of the marines reached down for a button on the panel before him to unlock the automatic gates blocking the chairman's path, opening them moments before he reached them.

Without breaking stride, the seventy-year-old leader walked down the very center of the hallway. In fifty meters the guarded doors of the conference room presented his next obstacle. He continued onward as a bull charges the matador's cape, his eyes fixed at the very center of the two doors, the marine guards in charge leapt at the door's handles, once again just beating him to the seemingly inevitable collision. He swept into the room, then stopped so that all could catch his entrance. He had been unannounced and the other two men were momentarily startled.

Marshal Tukhachevski jumped to his feet, a purely Pavlovian reaction reinforced over thirty-some-odd years of strict military training. The chief of the secret police, Dmitri Gvozdetskii, who had initially requested the meeting, also began to rise, then caught himself and merely looked up.

Before the chairman's entrance began to lose its effect he began. "Gentlemen, I'm so sorry I was detained. I know you will both understand, but affairs of state do have a degree of precedence over meetings called for some reason unknown to me."

Gvozdetskii wasn't intimidated by the chairman's display of bravado. He had requested the meeting because of the turn of events in Rome. He was about to seize the opportunity the nefarious situation presented, always keeping one eye on the chairmanship.

Tukhachevski, however, was more apologetic, hoping to retain the favor of both men. He valued his position and understood that a storm was brewing. As an opportunist, he knew that neither man had reason to fear him. He was the rival of neither, nor would he come to the aid of the vanquished. Rather, if it became apparent that either would emerge the victor, he would be ready to throw his support, and that of the armed forces, to the winner.

This was the middle ground, the safe terrain, and his philosophy had served him well; his lofty position bore testimony to its effectiveness. He would not risk what he had earned these past thirty years for any grand or devious scheme that promised less-than-certain results.

The chairman took his seat at the head of the conference table. Gvozdetskii, never moving, was on his left, and Tukhachevski on his right. The elder statesman chose not to speak for a full minute, until the silence had firmly riveted the attentions of the two other men on him. He cleared his throat, then began.

"Now, then, may I ask the reason for this conference, Dmitri?" the chairman addressed his secret police adversary.

It was now up to him, and he began the short speech he had rehearsed, knowing that the chairman had to be put on the spot, and Tukhachevski duly impressed. "Maksim"—Gvozdetskii had chosen to use the chairman's first name, something rarely done by anyone outside his immediate family—"I think we . . . you have a problem with your Professional. I've been waiting for some sign from our people in Rome that the endeavor is still in progress. But alas, there has been none.

"The funds have been transferred, and removed, with no sign that this person has decided to continue with anything. Our agent in Rome has been disposed of, which is understandable under the circumstances, and that seems to be the last we shall hear of this 'Professional.' He has not made contact with our people to acquire the electronics he needs to complete his end of the bargain. I am most rueful to inform you, Maksim, that all evidence indicates that he never had any intention of completing the mission." Gvozdetskii now placed his palms down on the long table, using them to propel himself into a standing position. He pushed the chair aside and began to walk away from the still-seated pair, staging his performance with much the same flamboyance as the chairman's forceful entrance. Dmitri launched his attack, realizing that if he failed, or showed any sign of faltering, the chairman would ensure his collapse into the bottomless pit already teeming with the broken bodies of others who had attempted unsuccessfully to unseat him.

"Comrade Chairman. I regret to point out the possibility that you have committed a serious blunder. At this moment you have no notion of the project's progress. You have authorized payment to a phantom and have placed the very security of the Motherland in serious jeopardy." He spun about as he reached the end of the table, at the furthest point in the conference room. His eyes found those of the chairman; the void between them instantly dissolved. Marshal Tukhachevski had been relegated to the position of observer, a position he prayed would not change in the near future. The longer he remained neutral, the better he liked it. He would have time enough to take sides.

"Once again, Comrade Chairman. Are you aware of the juxtaposition of the elements as they now exist?" The answer had been presupposed by the policeman.

But Chairman Shaposhnikov revealed no hint of fear. He had no answer to the question posed by his adversary, for he had no additional information other than what he'd already received from Rome. And he knew for certain that Gvozdetskii had at least that same knowledge at his disposal. Additionally, in the absence of any additional communiqués, it was perfectly reasonable to assume the worst. The secret police chief needed little with which to build an insurrection. In the inner circle of communist leadership it was no secret that Gvozdetskii had his sights on the chairman's seat. He had emerged from the pack as a feared adversary, not unlike the man he now set out to destroy.

Heart pounding, palms damp, the chairman nevertheless remained outwardly composed. He knew he must not falter. It was still possible that the carefully conceived scheme was at this very moment churning forward. True, no word had been received after the killing of the Soviet agent, but that proved nothing. Perhaps this blanket of silence should be interpreted as a shield rather than as an indication that the project had been abandoned, or, worse yet, exposed.

The chairman, had he been an American, could have competed in any poker game in the land. A master of the bluff, he used that skill to play out his hand to the end. There was little chance but to play Gvozdetskii's game and to beat him at it. He began walking directly at his adversary, something Gvozdetskii hadn't expected. Shaposhnikov was far from beaten; he was now on the attack. He continued until he had reached the far end of the table and there he stopped, staring deeply into the eyes of the secret police chief. "My dear Gvozdetskii, you are a capable man, yet not so capable as to see to your own health! Your network of intelligence has provided you with incomplete dossier, it would appear." He paused, giving his startled opponent a moment to ponder his words. To accent his complete mastery of the moment, the chairman withdrew a pack of his favorite English cigarettes from his jacket pocket and lit one. His doctors had cautioned about his continued smoking; it didn't help his heart condition. But it served in this instance for a calculatedly dramatic effect.

"It seems, my dear Dmitri, I have sources at my disposal that are unavailable to you." He was lying, but convincingly.

Gvozdetskii was stunned. How was it possible? His agents had assured him that nothing had happened to change the situation. He thought he knew everything. The chairman could be bluffing, but there was no way to be certain. Did the older man know something that had eluded the chief's men? Had he played his hand too soon? "Comrade Chairman," he began. The tone of his voice was now much more conciliatory, softer. The chairman picked up the change immediately, and Marshal Tukhachevski noticed it a moment later. As Gvozdetskii's attack faltered, Shaposhnikov exploited the opening, not giving the secret police chief an opportunity to continue.

"No, Comrade Gvozdetskii, it is now my turn to speak. It seems you have been ill-informed. Perhaps our illustrious KGB are not so efficient as they would like to have us believe?" A smile crept into the corner of his mouth. His eyes fell upon Marshal Tukhachevski, who was watching the proceedings with interest. The marshal was weighing the adversaries well and the chairman knew it. "The plan is proceeding as originally conceived. However, with the death of the Pope at such an inopportune moment, alterations in procedure have been inevitable. Your accusations, Dmitri, are groundless, and dangerously divisive to the party, I might add. We will have our Czech Pope, you may rest assured. Our Cardinal Michalovce will wear the ring of St. Peter; only the schedule has been adjusted, nothing more." He paused but met only a satisfying silence. Using his dramatics to the utmost, he spun suddenly and left as he had entered, striding directly to the conference room exit, throwing the doors open and walking through without looking back. As he walked on he glanced down at his watch. The entire episode had taken less than five minutes.

But the counterattack had worked: Tukhachevski had been won over temporarily; and Shaposhnikov had stifled Gvozdetskii's accusation. Understanding that he'd merely created a smokescreen, he knew something would have to develop in the near future. Otherwise, Gvozdetskii would again be ready to pounce. This tactic would only win him a delay, and not forever. He had staked his future in the party on this project now and would either ride its crest to victory or sink to defeat in its hollow trough.

He emerged on the steps of the administrative building and sucked in the cool night air. He was still in danger, and his position was even more tenuous than before. Standing and gazing at the inside of the Kremlin wall, a view afforded few in Russia, he could only hope that the Professional had not given up, that he would continue onward successfully. "In a way," he thought, "it is ironic. If he does complete his assignment, it will keep me in power, yet will cost him his life."

The limousine door opened as he approached and he slid into the rear seat. The driver didn't look back; the limo's engine sprung to life and the car sped off toward the gate that pierced the wall. There was no need to stop. By now the guards stationed at the exit knew the vehicle well.

The chairman spent a restless night knowing his destiny lay in the hands of someone he could only hope was at work 1,500 miles to the southwest in a small state called the Vatican. And the chairman dared not make any inquiry into the whereabouts of this hired Professional; doing so would tip his hand. Maksim had striven to appear confidently and fully abreast of the situation; now he had to live as if it were so. At times like these, he questioned whether it was all worth the many years of political intrigue. The dice had been tossed and their roll was still in spin. But what their spots would read was as yet unknown.

Night had begun to give way to a faint glow in the eastern sky. The restaurants, cafés, and tourist traps of downtown Ostia had been closed for more than two hours; their former occupants had already straggled back to their hotels. In the dimness of the still-early day, a solitary priest, suitcase in hand, walked between the city and the ocean. Ever cautious, he took care to keep in the building's shadows, even though there was little chance of encountering anyone at this ungodly hour.

Crossing the final street, he approached a wall, then stopped and looked about. There was no one in sight. The wall was merely waist-level, facing the sidewalk. He dropped his suitcase over it and watched it fall to the black sand of the narrow beach less than two meters below. Again checking the street in both directions and finding it absent of life, he followed the suitcase to the sand.

The powdery sand sifted into his shoes; he sank into its surface. Suitcase in hand, he walked to the water's edge, opening the valise as he moved parallel to the lapping, warm water. The margin of the beach sloped steeply to the sea, water caressing the sand with delicate strokes. As he walked along this edge of sea and land, he took what were once articles of clothing, now torn into unrecognizable shreds, out of the container and threw them into the waves. The sea swallowed up the bits and pieces.

In the time it took him to walk 100 meters down the beach, he had disposed of everything that had been packed into the valise. Heavy objects had been thrown far out beyond the small breakers. At last he came to a halt. All that remained was the case itself. It too was torn apart, the chunks dropped into the waiting waves. He looked back to the city as a hint of light was making its appearance from the east. It was now time to act.

He retraced his steps to 12 Via di Terni. Quickly, he climbed the stone steps that led to the front door and slipped inside, his shoes making the slightest trace of sound against the hard surface. The interior was lit by a single bare bulb that hung suspended from the high, peeling ceiling. He negotiated the wooden stairs that rose in the unlit interior's stairwell, making his way silently to the third-floor landing.

Careful not to allow any floorboards to creak under the weight of his body, he approached the door of apartment number three and placed his ear to its cold surface. He listened for any sign of movement from the flat beyond the door. There was none. He decided to wait a little longer, for there was no need to hurry.

In ten minutes his patience was rewarded. His sensitive ears began to pick up the first sounds of life from within. Words drifted toward him, words of passion, and the creaking of a mattress. The words began to flow more freely, more urgently. His opportunity had come.

He removed a small leather case from his back pocket and unzipped it. When opened, it revealed a set of sharp picks, the tools of an expert locksmith. In the dim light he examined the door's single keyhole, fitted into the doorknob. Selecting a single pick, he inserted it into the opening. Any sound the process might make would go undetected by the flat's occupants, evidently preoccupied with each other. In a few seconds the lock turned freely. He replaced the pick in its proper place and returned the case to his rear pocket.

His hand found the doorknob and slowly turned it. Allowing the door to open a crack, he examined its inner edge, making sure there was no chain to bar his entrance. Finding none, he was free to go inside, but instead he drew the door closed and stepped away from it.

He now began a practiced routine, drawing the 9mm automatic from its place beneath his jacket, the short, perforated, pipe-like device that would muffle the escaping explosion from the weapon's discharge protruding from its barrel. He switched off the safety. Resuming his position at the door, the automatic in his left hand, his right on the doorknob, he again turned the metal knob, freeing the door to move inward. It swung open with agonizing slowness until there was enough room for him to enter.

With the instinctive movements of a cat, in one smooth step, he stepped inside—reflexes alert, ready to move. But his years of training and expertise had taught him one perfect skill: restraint. An untrained killer might have burst in with his gun blazing, perhaps missing a crucial detail, or panicking. The Professional entered slowly, with quiet stealth; alert, calm, with the peacefulness of death itself. First he peered around, making certain he hadn't been discovered. In the darkness, his eyes probed the placement of the furniture, making mental note of the position of each piece. At the far side of the room, between the flat's windows, was the bed. It had been invisible from his apartment across the street. The sounds of lovemaking reached his ears once again and he watched the movement of two forms beneath the sheet.

Now the intruder raised the long barrel of the automatic as he moved inside. He closed the door behind him and turned the handle to the locked position. There was no sound save the heavy breathing of the couple some five meters from his stance. He noticed a chair against the wall behind him, and he grasped its back, lifting it up off the floor to move it forward. He set it down and eased himself onto its seat, never taking his eyes off the unsuspecting couple. He leaned back and relaxed, training the gun unerringly on the amorphous, moving form under the sheet.

In the darkness of the room his eyes sought out each object until he saw a package of butcher paper bound by string: the picture. Of course, he knew better. This was the forgery they would have presented to him, had he allowed it. A strange anger, cold and malignant, rose quietly within him, tightening his muscular frame as he remained motionless, watching their movements.

Faint glimmers of muted light drifted through the framework of the windows, revealing another canvas standing on an easel. Even in the dimness of the room, its beauty was unmistakable. *This* was the treasure, the *Madonna Lita*, the serene mother and the suckling infant whose aura almost penetrated the darkness. The disfiguring smears had been removed and the marked frame restored. No doubt remained that the forgery was in the package next to it.

Only seconds passed before his calm and resolute attention returned to the prone couple. This time his eyes would not leave them. With a slow, deep, silent breath, he rose. The floor protested gently. His fingers tightened on the weapon about to do his bidding as its gunsight rose. From somewhere in the street below a truck started up, motor racing. The time had come.

Days had slipped by; Barzini's case was mired in stagnation. The detective had avoided a purely routine interoffice request, sent down by Chief Inspector Maggiore, to appear before him. He knew what the Old Man, the chief, was about to do—pull him off the case—and Lorenzo hoped that by somehow avoiding his chief, the inevitable and frustrating conclusion might be forestalled long enough to make a convincing breakthrough. Lorenzo had gone through the motions of normal bureaucratic routine, signing in each morning and dropping off a perfunctory and loosely worded report regarding his progress with the case as he exited unobtrusively each evening. But he had fooled no one with this tactic. Each evening Barzini's immediate superior, a younger, aggressive little Sicilian named Paluzzo Antionelli, saw to it that his staff collected the reports and entered each on the division's new efficiency charts.

In the course of the week following the discovery of the jaw fragment, Barzini's record on that chart had fallen. The supervisory officer had brought the matter to the attention of Deputy Chief Antionelli, who had no love for Barzini—or any of the handful of older investigators under him. Barzini, a loner who had an unbending predilection for pursuing even the most dead-ended cases, often seemed most troublesome, as one of the least productive of the lot. Antionelli was determined to advance his administrative career by clearing the department of all those whose efficiency records were below average. By indulging in another stubborn vendetta, Barzini had made himself a prime target. Feeling he now had enough ammunition, Antionelli requested a meeting with his superior, Chief Inspector Ugo Maggiore, whom the division referred to disdainfully, and only occasionally fondly, as "The Old Man."

The police receptionist who sat outside the chief inspector's polished cypress door raised her head from her typing as Paluzzo Antionelli briskly approached. She swiveled her stool to greet him, the chair's rollers squeaking against the acrylic sheet protecting the tight-knit nylon carpeting that had recently replaced a worn woolen relic of World War II. The receptionist was careful to appear efficient whenever Paluzzo made one of his infrequent visits to the chief's den. It was common knowledge at headquarters that the Old Man was soon to retire, and it appeared likely that the ambitious young deputy chief would replace him.

The attractive receptionist would like nothing better than to remain in her well-paid position. The responsibilities were minimal when compared with the very real prospect of being reassigned to street duty after the departure of her current boss. As talk of the chief's imminent departure increased, his receptionist took every opportunity available to appear of value to Antionelli. Accordingly, she'd rearranged the chief's busy schedule to insert the meeting that Paluzzo had requested, knowing full well that the Old Man tried to avoid his deputy whenever he could. Of course, she tactfully let Paluzzo know of the difficulty his request had given her—just one in a series of carefully orchestrated ploys to make her appear indispensable to him.

The young woman swung her bronzed legs from beneath the typing stand, her navy wraparound skirt parting just enough to expose a delicious flash of thigh above her stockings. A smile crept onto her moist lips as his eyes dropped to the expanse of bare flesh. Another point in her little game: Paluzzo would remember this instant long after he'd forgotten any scheduling favors. "Deputy Antionelli." She stood to greet him. "You're a bit early for your appointment. The chief is still in conference with officials of the Motion Picture Development Board." Then softening her voice to a more confidential tone, she added, "I think they'd like his permission to use some of our men in an upcoming spy movie. They'll be at least another fifteen minutes. Might I get you an espresso while you wait?"

Antionelli took a seat at the oversized sofa and placed the manila folder he was carrying on the low table before him. "Yes, officer . . . "

"Just Angela to you, sir," she smiled and felt his eyes running along her body, following her movements as she turned to leave the room. Angela Cardone was twenty-eight years old, educated, slim and extremely attractive. She had been a graduate of some demand when she completed Rome's Police Academy some seven years before. Her sharp mind earned her placement in the chief inspector's office within that first year. Since then, she'd risen in rank, although always remaining the chief's personal secretary. She was now a lieutenant, a position of responsibility, with the chance to rise even higher within the department.

Returning with a metal tray carrying two small china cups, a plate of lemon peels, and a cup of sugar cubes, she leaned over to place them on the table, her loose white blouse falling away at the neck. His eyes immediately explored beneath the fabric and caught sight of her small breasts pushing against the barest hint of a lace undergarment. She did not have to look at his eyes to know where his attention was. As for her presumptuousness in bringing two cups of espresso, he hadn't noticed.

By the time the chief inspector's door opened moments later and Ugo Maggiore stood framed in the doorway shaking hands with the film delegation, Angela Cardone's image was firmly entrenched in the mind of the deputy chief inspector.

"Ah there, my dear Antionelli." The chief had said his official goodbyes to the delegation and promptly ushered his deputy into the inner office. "Sit down, sit down. No need for formalities in here." A broad smile dominated his fleshy, heavily lined face, below the shock of fine, white hair. Antionelli had the lingering impression that his chief's smile was, perhaps, too broad. Although Maggiore was a blunt man by nature and origin, deviousness was not unknown to him. Already a subtle tone of condescension had crept into the chief's voice as he spoke. "After all, it's no secret to me that you would not be among those to grieve for very long if I were to hang it up, shall we say, and relax on my pension." He raised his palms immediately to quell any protest to the offhanded remark. "No need to object, my dear Antionelli, I mean only to imply that within a few months, your placard may well be hanging on the door to this very office."

Antionelli straightened up . . . there was a thinly veiled sarcasm in the chief's inflection. "Chief Inspector Paluzzo Antionelli . . . ah. This is what you've always aimed for, isn't it? And very likely what you deserve, don't you agree, this title?" He paused in mid-gesture, indicating the boldly lettered name and title block resting on his desk, until he caught Antionelli's eyes. " . . . and all the crap that goes with it!" The chief emphasized the word *crap*, and Antionelli felt the hairs at the back of his neck prickle. "Like these lousy big-money filmmakers who act as if they own the department . . . " He stared directly at his subordinate as he completed his thought: " . . . and all the other idiots who come in here."

The chief looked away and swiveled his chair to a more relaxed position. He had made his point, retained his patriarchal relationship to his deputy. There was no need to push further and become adversaries. Leaning forward, he selected two ornate glass goblets from a tray perched atop a hand-rubbed serving cart that stood in front of the office windows. "This is one piece of furniture that upstart won't inherit when he moves in," thought the elder policeman. He filled the glasses to within a centimeter of their rims from a decanter of local red wine. The chief handed a goblet to the clearly uncomfortable Antionelli, then straightened

himself behind his massive eighteenth-century desk, another arti-
fact that would not be passed on when the changing of the guard
took place.

The chief's tone suddenly changed, "Now, then, what's so
damn important that you have to ask my secretary to change my
luncheon schedule just to fit you in?" The chief held up the iri-
descent goblet so that only his eyes peered over the circular rim.

The younger man took a deep draught of the sweet, sticky
wine, its alcohol content barely warming his throat on its way to
his stomach. He placed the glass masterpiece carefully on the
desk before him, making certain that its base rested upon a pad
of notepaper rather than on the highly polished surface, then produced the manila folder he had brought, placing it in his lap and
running his manicured fingernails along its sharp edge. "Chief,"
he began, his fingers stopping, then beginning anew the precise
pattern of movement. Having come this far, he determined, he
might just as well state his case bluntly. "As you know, sir, I've
been doing a study on the efficiency of our men. For the most
part the division has been performing pretty well, considering the
budgetary and manpower cutbacks."

"Yes, yes. I'm quite aware of those unfortunate cuts. However,
it's something you just have to learn to put up with these days.
The goddamn lira is getting it from all sides, what with the drop
in American tourism, the energy problem, and now those Arabs
buying up all the gold they can get their hands on. In a pinch,
our illustrious mayor would rather have another five hundred
cops walking their beats than a hundred good detectives nobody
can see on the streets. But, remember there'll always be a need
for guys like us."

"Yes, Chief. It's all very understandable. However, there are
many young officers in uniform who deserve to move up to our
division . . . and some detectives who should either retire, or be
placed back in uniform where they might exhibit some much-
needed productivity. Such transfers would surely increase our efficiency." Gathering resolve, the swarthy deputy chief opened his
folder to display its carefully prepared contents. "I have here a
list of five detectives who, without doubt, should be among the
first to go." The deputy held up a typed list, then placed it on
the desk facing the older man. When the chief made no effort to
grasp it, Antionelli used his finger to edge it a bit closer to him.

The chief's eyes finally fell to the sheet before him. He read down the list, reflecting on the men in question, then placed his goblet down atop the names. "I see that all these 'inefficient' detectives seem to be our oldest men . . . and I might add, our most experienced." The effort of his deputy to eliminate detectives who were among those the chief had known the longest, some of whom were aging, had struck a soft spot in the older man. He viewed it as an attack on himself. The veins in his neck began to bulge and his hands tensed, though he remained silent for the moment. He understood Antionelli coveted the chief's job and that the younger man made no bones about replacing all the so-called dead wood in the division once he assumed command. Yet to attempt to clean house before he was in that position was a bit too much for the chief. As an officer of the old school he understood the meaning of the word loyalty. He knew that he himself had never been the best of detectives and that he was in this lofty position merely because he had stumbled across a spectacular arrest. Yet the men on this list never grumbled or aired their wash in public. Loyalty such as theirs would not go overlooked. "Damn!" he burst, his right palm coming down full force on the desktop, his left hand following to steady the falling goblet. A few drops of crimson liquid splattered against the papers. This list would not be used as long as he was in command of this division. He would make certain that his deputy didn't misunderstand that point. "Antionelli, you can forget it!"

"But, Chief . . . "

"But Chief nothing! I'll have no argument on this matter. These men stay." He stood up in place, looking down at the seated man. "What the hell do you know about being a detective? You've never had your ass out on the streets. You've never had to crawl through a garbage dump after a clue, or had to shoot it out with some hardened criminal, or had someone hold a razor to your throat while you're trying to talk him out of slitting it. You're a—a college boy with a hot-shot background, a desk-type administrator. Let's not forget that the only reason you're here is because your family can pull strings, eh, Antionelli?

"Well, the men you've seen fit to place on this rotten piece of neatly typed paper came up the hard way. They were on the force while you were still in grade school. They're the best damn detectives we've got. They work with their hands, their minds, and their guts. Surely you know what guts are?" He now brought himself to a position where his both hands were on the desk's lip and his shoulders faced the younger man squarely. "They get the very pulse of a crime and dig. Five men, 120 years of experience and you want to put them out to pasture. Don't make me laugh."

"But Chief. . . . Just take a look at them. . . . Tucci, Palmero, Barzini; they've got the lowest arrest records in the division. Time has just passed them by."

The chief took a few steps to the window and looked across to the city below. "Yeah, take a look at them. They get the worst cases on your orders. You have them out there trying to solve the unsolvable. Maybe they do have the lowest arrest records, but sometimes it amazes me that they are able to solve even one of them." The Old Man spun around, hands on hips, and walked back to his subordinate. "And Barzini. What about him?"

Antionelli quickly slipped out the sheet that dealt with that officer. Holding it out before him, he pointed to one paragraph as if Maggiore could read it from where he was standing. "His daily reports are falsified. He's been doing nothing. He's on this case, the homicide and dismemberment with the jaw fragment, and he's pursued it to the exclusion of everything else. He should be putting time in on some of the backlog he's already built up. But this detective is a stubborn mule. Even though he's clearly reached a roadblock he continues beating his head against it. He refuses to follow the orders I sent to drop it, and he continues to fudge his paperwork." Feeling he had made his point, Antionelli paused and sat back, running his hand through his thick black hair.

Ugo Maggiore took a last step, then leaned over and grasped the top of the chair Antionelli was seated on. The strength of his upper arms and body was transmitted through his oversized hands and the chair creaked under the strain. "Barzini . . . I'll tell you about Barzini. He's been given a murder that ten of your new detectives wouldn't even know where to start on. So he'll stick to it because he's one of the old breed. And one thing a homicide detective will not do—a *good* homicide detective—is ever give up on a murder!"

The deputy inspector was shocked by his chief's sudden attack. Maggiore wasn't noted for making waves. Among the younger men, rumors circulated from time to time about their boss's lack of investigative skills. There seemed to be some lingering question about just how the chief had gotten where he now was. But such questions, when directed to any of the older detectives in the division, were never fully answered. The "Old Guard" in the department simply watched out for one another. Those few surviving detectives whose seniority extended back to the chief's original enstatement were unknowingly blessed with support behind closed doors.

Chief Maggiore turned his back on the younger man as a sign that he felt the matter was closed. Antionelli hesitated, uncertain if he should continue pressing the attack. His sunken black eyes peeked out of a blanched face. Wisps of long straight dark hair had begun to cascade onto his forehead, clinging to the first faint traces of perspiration that had appeared along his almost nonexistent brow. He folded his thin lower lip under his perfect front teeth, bit down, then spoke. "Chief, what then would you have me do with Barzini, as an example?"

Chief Maggiore took his seat once again. He needed time to think. Antionelli had thrown the ball into his court and he had to come up with something. There was that unwritten debt, and another thing, ego. He wouldn't admit defeat. Faced with Antionelli's chipping away at his authority, he struck out angrily. "Paluzzo, you still haven't allowed the essence of what I've said to sink in. Barzini is far from being let out to pasture. He's an example of the kind of man that I depend on. He's the very backbone of our division. This case he's on, he's to stay on! As long as he doesn't give up on it, we'll not give up on him."

"But, Chief. That is the very point I've tried to bring home to you. Barzini has gotten nowhere with it. He has no leads and yet he continues."

"And have you taken the time to speak to him about it? I don't mean reports from your 'efficiency experts.' I mean have you spoken to him personally? Haven't you learned that it's better for a supervisor to get involved man to man with his subordinates than to relay solely upon lifeless reports?"

"Sir, it wouldn't matter. Personal contact would achieve nothing. The facts wouldn't change. He has come up blank and that's all there is to it."

The chief stood up and walked to the door slowly. He didn't speak. His hand engulfed the doorknob as he turned back to Antionelli. "And so, my friend, you believe he's come up with nothing? You see what losing touch with your men has accomplished. Had you taken the time to question him about his investigation, you would have learned that his orders to continue on the case come directly from this office. He and I have been in continuous contact. In fact, he is presently on to an aspect of that 'unsolvable' case that may well prove to be the key to a major breakthrough." He paused for the desired degree of emphasis. "Now, I believe we've said enough on this particular matter, don't you agree?"

Antionelli's brow was now completely wet. He grasped the manila folder and gathered his papers, stuffing them inside the envelope. He thought better of bringing up any of the remaining four detectives at this time. Things hadn't proceeded as planned. He stood up wondering to himself—Barzini? A major breakthrough . . . impossible. That oaf couldn't break through a paper bag. The chief just might be—he was caught in mid-thought by the sound of the door being opened by the Old Man.

Slightly flustered, Antionelli walked into the outer office. The chief followed, placing his massive hand on the thin shoulders of his deputy. "Perhaps it would be best if you kept in more personal touch with our men, Paluzzo. If you find yourself tied up in an office such as this one, you'll be unable to reach out to them. Gain their respect now, before it's too late."

Antionelli shook hands with the chief, his somewhat limp fingers releasing their grasp almost instantly, then walked on through the office, letting himself out. The thin man paid scant mind to the chief's secretary, who had composed her best smile for the occasion. As the door slammed shut in front of her, the smile she had painted on her lips disappeared.

The chief turned to Lieutenant Cardone and said, "Angela, type up a memo requesting Detectives Bordoni, Scarpa, Tucci and Palermo to make appointments to confer with me in the next week. Also, get Detective Barzini on the phone and make sure he gets in here no later than five this afternoon. Make it clear that I want to see him in my office *today*. And, Angela, keep it discreet, please. We wouldn't want Antionelli to get wind of this, would we?"

Lieutenant Cardone responded to the Old Man's words with a lowering of her eyes, a slightly flush, and businesslike, "Yes, Sir. I'll get in touch with Barzini immediately," and reached for the interoffice phone.

9

The soft sound of the sea floated gently over the row of buildings across the street, then filtered into the apartment where the drama was about to reach its climax. The weapon's gunsight came to a stop parallel to the bare floor. The Professional's trained eye peered directly down the dull barrel to the short-haired figure on the bed. He fixed the sight on the back of the man's head. Scant light from outside the flat fell on the full breasts and thighs of the bed's second occupant. She moved slowly, expertly over the man, her hands playing across his heaving chest as she straddled his thighs. The soft creaking noises that came from the springs beneath them were lost as the truck that had warmed up in the street below now began to pull away. The Professional remained undetected, poised carefully in the deep shadows.

Her hands left Emilio's shoulders, chest, and nipples to play lightly across his stomach and onto his growing hardness. He responded, his fingers running alongside the whiteness of her thighs, careful to be gentle, as if Sienta were some fragile piece of ancient porcelain. Only his hands conveyed urgency; the remainder of his body had not yet begun to respond. She leaned over him, her heavy breasts hanging tantalizingly in front of his face. The Professional watched the scene, basking in his private irony. Their lust failed to excite him.

The man looked at the luscious flesh before him, the smoothness of the perfect mounds capped by a ring of darkness at the center of each breast. She leaned further forward, now almost touching his lips with her nipples. His hands left her thighs and ran up her sides, his fingers coming to rest on the classic ridge of her shoulders. Fingers tightened; the muscles of his forearms began to pull her toward him; his mouth finally tasted what had eluded him moments before. His tongue ran in circles around the darkened tip. Her body came alive, moving against him.

Her mouth was moist. Her wetness flashed a touch of reflected light toward the seated figure. He felt a stirring in his loins but paid little heed to its calling. His body remained rigid, poised, ready. He had caught his prey enveloped in their mating dance. His nerves tingled with a private ecstasy of power. His pulse burned toward only one purpose; his eyes glowed with a hunter's fire and his nostrils flared, not with the growing smell of sex, but rather with the heady scent of death.

Her mouth ran across her companion's lips, down his face and neck, playing briefly on his heaving chest. She paused a moment, toying with his mounting desire. She would give him that magnificent moment only when she thought he could withstand it no longer. Her thighs moved lower along his lean legs, her buttocks coming to rest against the insteps of his feet, now pinned to the crumpled sheets. Soft breasts pressed his thighs, and her warm mouth found his semi-erectness. His hands sought her head, fingers entwining themselves in thick, dark hair. As the urgency of the moment grew, his fingers gripped and relaxed in unison with the mechanical movement of her tongue and mouth. She reached up and pulled his hands away forcefully, pushing them firmly to his sides, retaining control.

"Please," he pleaded in a throaty, almost frightened whisper.

Her mouth came off him with a tantalizing slowness. "Soon, my love."

"Please."

"Wait."

"I can't. You know I can't. Please hurry."

A smile crept across her lips, then fled. Her body moved up slowly. She showed herself to him. His eyes followed first her face, then her breasts. Experienced hands found his full hardness; rhythmic fingers played along its length, running from base to fiery tip. Her commanding fingertips traced a raised blue vein, sending a sensual shudder through his prone form. He was smaller than other men she'd had and, what was worse, virtually impotent. It sometimes took her hours to bring him to a climax, a task she disdained. She understood what stimulation was required to give him pleasure and used that knowledge on those now infrequent occasions when she granted him the exultation her body could supply.

Her fingers continued to play along him. It will all be over in less than three weeks, she thought as she watched his expression change in the hint of light. By then I'll have received the final payment and will have sold the real treasure to that anxious Arab businessman. No questions asked. The two hundred fifty thousand in American bills! But still a bargain, one he couldn't turn down. On the open market it could bring over two million so he's paying barely ten cents on the dollar.

"Please," he begged. "Please. In another moment it will be lost."

"Yes, my love," she whispered back. The words flowed from her mouth, yet meant nothing. She moved slowly back along his legs until her thighs straddled his. Then she stopped. . . .

"Please," his voice pleaded, achingly.

She stood on her knees over him, his face just inches from her wetness. The power of her commanding image above him stirred his senses. Slowly, she tantalized his eyes with her liquid passion, then wriggled down to meet his straining member. Her hand guided him into her and she came to rest once again against his legs.

An anguished expression, mixed relief and urgency, danced across his features as he relinquished himself completely to her control. The warmth of her sex engulfed him, the refuge he so desperately sought. He belonged to her again, ready to serve whatever purpose she might desire, forever. He began to strain upward, trying to thrust himself further in. The walls of her body gripped him, caressed him. He writhed in an ecstasy that would be his last.

Sienta played the game, cooing convincingly at the appropriate moments, groaning and coaxing him on with fiery eyes and words. Within the month he would have fulfilled all her purposes. Then he could be discarded, if she so chose.

The dark-enshrouded form seated at the edge of the room's shadows aimed the perfectly balanced weapon unfalteringly, even as he reveled in the erotic drama, almost complete, before him. He had watched her toy with her mate insensitively, without emotion, like some long-legged spider ensnaring her insect prey. He recognized that she was like himself, using what skills she possessed to achieve the required result.

The thought weighed testily in his mind as he aimed at the skull of the thrusting, writhing male. Slowly, the Professional's arms locked. His reach extended, extending the perforated metal into the dimness. For a second the light glinted off its ugly muzzle. His finger began to tighten on the trigger.

Her breasts were gently bouncing to the rhythm of her movements. She was looking away from her partner's face, perhaps concentrating on the pattern of shadows on the wall that faced her. She wanted to avoid his eyes, fearful she might laugh at his pathetic efforts.

There was a tiny, almost imperceptible pop as the projectile exploded from the muzzle. It sped across the void, shattering the brain of the prone male, a stifled cry in his throat strangled. The head jerked against the pillow; the body jumped rigid, then collapsed. There would be little blood. In the mixed sounds of love and death, the spent cartridge fell to the floor.

Sienta Alighieri had played her part well. Below her, the figure had finally come to rest. She had completed a task she would never need to perform again, a thought that offered her some measure of satisfaction. Relieved, she could now shower any trace of him from her, then sleep. She whispered words spilling from her mouth: "My love, you were perfect." There was no response. She wondered if he had fallen asleep from exertion. Her fingers began to play with his moist hair, knowing this would soothe him into a deep sleep and leave her unbothered for the night's remainder. Her hand moved first along his sweat-dampened forehead, then reached lightly toward his temples . . . and found a sticky warmth oozing from the left side of his head, just in front of his ear. She explored further, probing the unfamiliar wetness. She felt the small entry wound, uncertain at first as to its origin. One hand cupped the back of his head and drew it off the damp pillow. Her eyes strained against the dimness of the room's light. Beneath the now heavy burden lay a pool of crimson darkness.

She uttered no scream. Rather, her eyes fell full on his face once more. There was something terrifyingly unnatural about everything; he had been moving only a moment before. Confused, she shook him vigorously by the shoulders. His head fell limply to one side, mouth slack, the slimy wound glistening clearly in the darkness. She stopped, wide-eyed, and drew away from him in hesitant fear. Suddenly she leaped off the bed, spun and gazed with naked terror in the direction the bullet must have come from.

In the corner near the door a dark form stood. He watched as her ears caught the sound of his movement and her eyes sought its source. Taking a few silent steps to his right, he emerged from the darkness between her and the apartment's exit.

Her eyes opened wide as she came to a stop in the semi-darkness. The shadows no longer shielded his identity. Terror gripped her. It was him; he knew everything. With desperation her mind raced ahead. Her searching eyes were riveted on the glinting weapon.

Why hadn't he killed her, she asked herself. He must have found out about the forgery, so it would serve no purpose to protest her innocence.

Did he want something else? Yes, something more. It was her. The thought rang through her with a jolt. Her survival dangled on that hope. She reacted: her one most powerful skill might be enough to save her. Sienta drew herself up, threw back her head, and with her hands grasped her firm breasts, pressing them toward him. Her nipples stood out with fear, erect as bullets. Trembling, she raised her chin haughtily and opened her lips as she edged forward. He didn't move. His eyes never left hers. Her vision slowly followed the line of his trousers to his crotch. There was the unmistakable bulge beneath the fabric that she had prayed would be there. One last time, perhaps, she could barter with her body, this time for her life. She was the personification of the Roman goddess-whore, begging for defilement. The Professional, hard-jawed, expression unchanging in the darkness, now began to let his gun barrel drop.

Her tongue caressed her ample lips, covering them with moisture. Soft hands slithered slowly along the length of her side. It was an invitation to pleasure.

"Do you like what you see?" she said, the lulling silken smoothness of her voice snagging on the crags of her fear. Quavering: "I'm yours, if you'd like." Another step was taken, the distance closed.

"I'm yours . . . the painting is yours. You have everything." Her tones reached forward. The space between them was now no more than two meters. "Come," she continued, her arms slithered up from her sides and reached out for him imploringly. "Come and take me," she whispered throatily.

Their eyes were locked together. She stepped close. "I'll make you feel as you've never felt before." The words dropped off her tongue and hung in the air for an instant before vanishing. His body, poised, his expression unchanging, spoke for him. Even as she stepped forward to reach for him she found a cold gunpoint pressed between her breasts.

A smile crept onto a corner of his closed mouth as she began to lurch away. The gun jumped in his grip. It hissed as it sent the deadly missile on its mission. The bullet entered the center of her chest. It shattered the small golden crucifix, suspended from a thin chain, that hung in the valley between her breasts as if to protect its bearer from harm. The bullet met the soft metal, tearing skin and cross at the same instant. It pierced her body, passed through her rib cage, and punctured her heart. She was lifted up by the force of the impact and thrown back onto the bed atop her accomplice's limp form, dead before she came to rest. The second spent shell hit the floor, the small sound loud in the silence.

The Professional paused over the broken bodies for a moment, then replaced the weapon under his jacket. The room was morbidly peaceful. It was as if the violence had been swallowed up in the soft blanket of night. Looking down, he searched for the two brass shell casings his gun had ejected. Finding them, he placed them in his pocket, then turned his attention to the paintings.

The butcher-wrapped paper package was the object of his interest. His fingers traced what lay beneath the wrapping. He carefully tore open a corner to investigate. Undoubtedly, this was the forgery. Next he walked to the canvas standing adjacent to the far window. Here was the true *Madonna Lita*. Up close its beauty was unmistakable. Its brilliance seemed to light up the room. He took a moment to study the composition. The compassion and serenity of the Madonna's face and soft searching eyes could almost subdue the bloody violence of the rent and naked bodies splayed across the bed only a few meters away.

He found the heavy wrapping paper and concealed the painting's delicate beauty with a thick, double layer. Next he quickly scavenged the room, covering himself with whatever clothing and plastic he could find, finally donning an artist's smock, and turned his attention back to the slain figures. He withdrew his keen surgeon's saw and scalpel from their pocketed leather case, and began quickly and skillfully to sever the bodies' fingertips from the fingers. Next, he cut through each prone figure's neck, severing heads from torsos. Blood oozed from the gaping wounds, quickly spotting the mattress. As he had done with the remains of the priest weeks before, he expertly cut through their jaws, removing both lower jaws and upper teeth.

Fingertips were methodically flushed down the lavatory, the bloody jaw and tooth fragments carefully packaged to be disposed of later. Identification was now rendered impossible.

But there were clues still remaining in the flat that couldn't be disposed of. The artist's materials, paints, canvas, solvents and stains all pointed to an operation any trained detective would surely note. And so, one last preparation remained. He removed the borrowed clothing and plastic bags, tossing them on the bed, then assessed what other materials were available for his use. He began.

Taking one of the dinner plates, he placed it on the floor in the midst of the artist's materials. Next, sheets of the local daily newspaper were arranged so that a layer of the rough paper covered the area, making a trail leading to the blood-soaked bed. He removed the dinner candle from its holder and lighted a match, melted the base, then placed the taper in an upright position in the center of the plate. It would serve as the fuse.

Several cans of shellac and solvent were splashed along the trail of newspapers leading to the bed. He poured the remainder over the mutilated bodies and mattress, and saved a considerable quantity for the dinner plate arrangement at the junction of the newsprint trails. The liquid overflowed onto the papers, an expanding pool of flammable material. Fumes wafted off the floor and reached his sensitive nostrils. The smell increased the intensity when he knelt unseen near the windows, shutting them tight.

Lastly, he took a plastic container of household ammonia and some detergent powder. Walking back to the bed, he placed the open container of liquid just under the mattress, then poured out the detergent, forming a mound of the snow-like material about the plastic container. He used his hands to pack the detergent about the base of the container, then stood up. The preparations were complete.

He lit the candle. Moving quickly but carefully, he collected the six grisly packages of chunks of his victims in a single parcel, then made a larger package containing both the genuine and the counterfeit paintings. Placing his ear to the door jamb, he listened for any telltale sign of movement on the landing outside the room. There was none.

His eyes had begun to tear from the combination of volatile vapors. It was time to leave. He opened the door and silently made his exit, closing the door tightly behind him. Worn wooden steps creaked under the strain of his weight. He had reached the landing of the floor below when he heard the sound of the apartment house front door. He stopped and listened. The clanking together of bottles indicated that the milkman was about to make his early morning deliveries. As the sound got closer it became apparent that he would be seen if he remained where he was.

The Professional retreated up the stairway, which afforded him a few seconds more before discovery. He looked up; the alternate escape route had to be used.

Quickly he climbed the ladder to the top, pushing off the hatch that blocked entry to the roof. He hastened up the last few rungs, pulling through his burdens, then replaced the hatch behind him. Below, the milkman had reached the landing.

Quickly the Professional dashed across the attached roofs, stopping at the last one. He pulled open the corresponding hatch and, after listening for sounds of life below, he negotiated the stairway to the street.

The coolness of the dark, early morning was welcome. Close to exhaustion, his lungs burning from exertion and the fumes he'd left behind, he stopped for a moment to draw a series of deep breaths, clearing both his body and his still somewhat foggy mind. In a minute he began to walk away. Sufficiently removed from 12 Via di Terni, he paused at varying intervals to deposit his tiny burdens in trash cans. He had completed placing the last packet when he decided to look back. It had not taken long to begin.

The candle had burned to its base, igniting the solvent that filled the plate. Adjacent shredded newspaper caught fire immediately. A trail of flame danced its way to the bed and leaped quickly onto the mattress, engulfing the bodies in orange and red heat. Fire dripped off the mattress onto the mound of detergent. A few seconds later the container of ammonia burst, followed by an explosion that tore open the windows of the top floor flat, showering the street below with deadly splinters of broken glass, burning wood and bits of floating fabric. Moments later the entire top floor of the eighty-year-old building was in flames. Even at two blocks away his face was lit by his handiwork. As he turned calmly, his ears were greeted by the first sounds of bells and sirens as police and fire vehicles raced to the scene.

Neighborhood people began running in the direction of the flickering light. By now the flats on either side of the stricken house were also engulfed. There would be little left of the flat's occupants, or their effects, when the fire brigade brought the inferno under control in an hour. The fire would be deemed arson from the outset, but its origin would remain unknown.

Dawn had already broken when he reached the plaza before the metro station. Noting the time in a nearby watchmaker's window, he knew he'd have ten minutes before the early train left for downtown Rome. He took a seat on a wooden park bench and turned to the sun. Its warm rays comforted him, giving him much-needed strength. He had to exert a great deal of willpower to pull himself up from the bench when the train's whistle signaled its approach.

He melted into the growing crowd of commuters that used the public transit facility, all intent upon reaching the train first in order to find a seat for the 40-minute trip to Rome's center. Finding one in a corner of the first car he fought to remain awake as the sound of the steel wheels on the track created a soothing concert of rhythmic sound. In minutes he lost the battle and his mind slipped off into a restless sleep.

Detective Barzini was aware of the trace of his own nervous perspiration. His squad commander had instructed him, in a tone that left no room for anything but compliance, to report to the chief's office before he went off duty. Normally he'd have gone back to his flat, showered, and shaved in order to present an appropriate image to his superior. But this time his sergeant escorted him directly to the chief's waiting room and did not leave until Barzini had knocked and entered.

Now, ten minutes later, Barzini was still waiting, unconsciously wringing his hands, acutely aware of the sweat-limp, somewhat unkempt figure he presented. His eyes hadn't strayed beyond the floor in front of his feet since he'd been told to be seated and wait. The chief's secretary hadn't spoken further, busying herself collating papers into neatly arranged piles.

He sat in silence, scratching the stubble on his chin thoughtfully, listening to the rustle of the police reports being sorted on her desk. Distracted thoughts skittered through his mind. Had his preoccupation with his jawbone case done him in? Perhaps they would only pull him off the case. But wasn't it irksome—shouldn't there be some reason for the gruesome deed? Why was the identity eradicated so meticulously if the victim was no one who would be missed?

Murder cannot be ignored, he insisted silently, grinding his fist into his sweating palm. It cannot be filed away in a drawer, another name without substance, dead and buried in some folder, stripped of all meaning. Lorenzo's thoughts grew insistent; his pulse raced angrily.

Man's actions must have consequences. Each life and every deed must possess some intrinsic meaning. They have to fit together, somewhere. It followed then, to him, that the fragment's discovery revealed some higher purpose. A clue, after all, does not jump out of nowhere. If it reaches my hands there is a reason for it. It can only be tossed to me by the finger of providence, he reasoned, while tugging forcefully at his tie. Otherwise there is no justice, no reason for justice, for law, for any of my efforts. His thoughts were interrupted by the slam of fist striking stapler.

As she finished fastening the reports, Angela Cardone's eyes fell upon the sorry individual seated two meters in front of her. She had heard fleeting portions of the argument that had occurred earlier in the day and now felt a nudge of pity for the man, understanding that his career could be on the line. Seated nervously by the doorway, he looked to her like a piece of machinery that had outlived its usefulness, soon to be cast aside. She remained silent, however, because she felt she had no control over the situation. And if by some chance she had, it occurred to her, she would have probably done the same thing. It would be better for the department, she supposed, if he would submit his retirement papers before being subjected to the indignity of a forced resignation.

The intercom broke the cloud of silence with a brusque command ordering Barzini into the chief's office, where the Old Man greeted him with his false smile and forceful handshake. "Officer Cardone," the chief called out, "You can go home now. Barzini and I have things to discuss. I don't think I'll be needing you again today."

"Yes, Chief," she answered, as she stood up straightening her skirt. The chief waited until the sound of the outer door closing reached his ears. He then returned his attention to the nervous detective.

"Take a seat, Lorenzo," requested the chief, his broad smile fading from his lips. Barzini waited for Chief Maggiore to get back behind the ornate desk and take his seat before slipping into the same chair that Deputy Chief Antionelli had occupied earlier that day. "You can smoke if you wish, Lorenzo. There's no formality behind these doors, for us."

"Thank you, Sir. I'd appreciate a glass of water if you . . . "

"Water?" the chief interrupted. "I think I can arrange something more palatable . . . for us both."

As Maggiore stood up, Barzini jumped to his feet by reflex action. "No, no, Lorenzo. Please, no formality here, and I meant it." Barzini allowed himself to fall back apprehensively onto the cushions of the armchair. Despite the river of cold air being forced into the room by the window air conditioner, Barzini could feel twin rivers of sweat trace their way down his sides.

In a few moments a smiling Maggiore walked from the bar to the seated detective. He handed Barzini a goblet of wine. "Eh, Lorenzo, like in the old days, right, when we were just a couple of new detectives against the criminals, and the bosses."

"The old days, yes. . . ." He reached out, grasped the glass firmly and brought it immediately to his lips, almost draining the glass in a gulp.

The chief, comfortably sipping his wine, had resumed his posture behind the desk. "I'm sure you want to know why I've called you here after a long workday, so I'll get directly to the point. Certain younger members of my staff have begun to question just what you're up to in that case of the, shall we say, the 'Jawbone of the Ass Case.' I've indicated that you're on to something and that seems to have quieted them for the moment. But. . . " He paused to sip from the goblet.

Barzini looked down at the glass in his hand, then raised it, quickly finishing the remainder. The Old Man's eyes followed him intently as he returned the goblet to the desk top. Realizing, in the heavy, uncomfortable silence that followed, that it was his turn to speak, Lorenzo said, "Chief, I've been giving this one all my time. It's become part of me. It's more than the time I spend at it during my tour. It's my spare time also." His voice was barely louder than a whisper, almost as if he were embarrassed at what he was saying. He was uncertain, yet continued: "I've come up with a couple of hunches . . . nothing concrete as of now, just some damn good hunches. Like when we were just starting out and that sergeant told us to go with what our bellies told us." His eyes came up for an instant, then fell away from his chief's. "I've already had a break in the identification of the tooth fillings. I know our victim was from an Eastern bloc country."

He was interrupted by the chief. "Yes, yes, Lorenzo. But you made that discovery days ago. What have you now? You had better come up with something stronger than the fillings. Are there any witnesses? How about Missing Persons; maybe they have something on file?"

Barzini tried to find his chief's eyes over the rim of the wine glass, but as their eyes met, he nervously glanced away. He continued, squirming slightly, unable to judge his boss's reaction. "Boss, there's nothing . . . nothing current enough to fit the age, sex, or time sequence of our man. Whoever he was, he wasn't coming home to anyone. Apparently, he just hasn't been missed. There hasn't even been an inquiry by an employer about a missing worker. I've even contacted some of our most reliable Mafia links." Lorenzo shook his head with futility.

"But we can assume one fact. Whoever the poor devil was, he must have been important enough to someone to warrant the dismemberment and disposal. So I'm figuring he's either a guy on holiday . . . or someone who wanted to get lost here in Rome. The city's big enough for a man to lose himself for a long time without being noticed." The chief inspector placed his glass on the desk blotter and sat back, his eyes scanning Lorenzo's lips. The words tumbled out of the detective's mouth. "And if that's the case, it will prove even more difficult for me to trace him."

"Well, then, Barzini. If you admit it's going to be impossible to trace him, why waste your time? God, man, there's plenty to do in our files without devoting your time to a dead-end case." The chief folded his hands in front of him and he brought them to his lips, resting his massive head on the clenched fingers.

"Sir, it's not a dead-end case . . . it's not impossible. And, above all, it's a murder. Ugo"—Barzini's tongue slipped—"it's a very special murder. You can count on that." Lorenzo's deep-set eyes gleamed with urgency above dark pouches caused by lack of sleep. "Someone's gone through a lot of trouble to make certain his victim remains unidentifiable. I've never run across anything like it before. Have you? Consider: It's not a Mafioso hit, because everyone would know who it was in a matter of hours; like the Tutino murders when they sawed off the heads, remember? It was designed as a scare tactic." The chief, his interest piqued, nodded in recognition as Barzini continued with intensity, "or, you remember the Barbato case—the body we discovered in the lime pit near the subway station—at least it was traceable, something turned up within hours. But this? There's something different about it; you can tell. After all these years on shit like this I've come to be able to smell it. It's something a good detective has. Chief, you understand. You have that same sense, don't you?

"Sure, it'd be easier to pack it all in. But you know about following through on the tough one, Chief. That's what good detective work is all about. Sometimes you have to go to sleep with it, putting in your hours until something gives." Barzini caught himself as he began to gesture emphatically with both hands. It was a plaintive gesture, as if to ask for a second chance, a gesture that might be made to a priest being asked to offer absolution. The chief looked away and shook his head for an instant.

"I must be crazy," thought Maggiore, "but I'm not going to pull him off it just because a little twerp like Antionelli wants it. No, a few more days, then . . . "

The chief stood up and walked to where Barzini was seated. Looking down, he placed a gentle hand on the detective's shoulder. "Okay, Lorenzo. You've convinced me. I'll give you the time you want . . . within reason. I won't pull you off it, yet. But, for Christ's sake, cover yourself better! Don't forget these college kids of mine are damn sharp. I don't want to hear any more stories about falsified reports. I'm officially overlooking it for the time being. Now get in step with the times. These efficiency experts are the wave of the future." His eyes turned away. "And we're close to being put out to pasture. Our days are numbered, in more ways than one."

"Yes, Sir," Barzini answered. The detective stood, shaking the chief's hand with both of his.

As they left the office together, the Old Man found himself experiencing a certain curious relief at having made the decision. Too many actions were being taken out of his hands by ambitious underlings. By sticking up for Barzini he felt as if he were strengthening his own authority. Carried by that same spur-of-the-moment feeling, he found himself softening his stern facade. He turned toward Barzini and asked lightheartedly, "Well, my friend, how about a couple of drinks at Gimberto's? We'll knock around the old days." The door slammed shut behind the two men and they walked down the now-deserted hallway, this wing of the building already closed for the day. Being an administrator had certain distinct advantages, but there was still something enticing about being a detective out on the streets. Once you left there, the chief was certain, you began to die. Barzini and he were a breed of discards and they both knew it.

It was long after midnight before Lorenzo found his way back to his flat. He collapsed on the soft, unmade mattress. He didn't even bother to remove his clothing. In the morning he'd be sorry for the evening's indiscretion; he never did react well to alcohol. But, he had his reprieve for the moment. Now he would have to take advantage of it.

Night had swooped in suddenly over Moscow. Its dark wings concealed the spires of the all-but-abandoned great cathedral that alone evoked a flickering remembrance of a dwindling magnificence. The day's passing went unmarked within the private communications room, dug deep in the bedrock of the Kremlin's foundation. There Chairman Shaposhnikov had spent the past ten hours, deep in troubled thought. The time spent wrestling with his dilemma went unrequited, for his diverse deliberations continued to be drawn ineluctably to the same conclusion: His position, his authority, even his personal safety hung by a delicate thread totally dependent on an unknown figure—an unknown somewhere beyond the pale of his control. It was a position that the Russian strongman had little taste for, yet one he remained powerless to alter.

The windowless room had suddenly grown stuffy. He held his breath and listened. The sound of the mechanical ventilating system reassured him. Sitting back in the leather-upholstered armchair, he allowed himself the luxury of a moment of physical and emotional relief. His breathing slowly returned to normal, his rapid pulse rate leveled. He sank into a trance-like state of meditation. It was a technique he'd learned fifty years earlier as a young Army lieutenant stationed on Russia's easternmost border with China. He'd taken time to master certain aspects of the culture of the barren highland's inhabitants. During the long winter, the monks dressed in such sparse clothing the fierce cold should have left them frozen. But instead, they worked long hours with barely a sign of distress. From these Oriental *bhikku* he had learned some of the mysterious arts of physical endurance through mental assiduity and discipline, qualities he had invoked often throughout his patient, steady, inexorable rise to power. Intense mental concentration became a facet of his prowess that left his opponents awestruck.

Russia was just emerging from civil war when his tour of duty ended, the communists solidifying their newly won position of complete power. In the background was the specter of a coming worldwide depression, and the base of all power was the Red Army. Shaposhnikov's rise within the Army was constant if not spectacular. Yet this slow upward movement served to protect him from the ravages of the numerous purges that quickly eliminated the ambitious.

By late 1937 his career within the civilian-political sector had begun. He resigned from the Army a major, and was appointed a deputy commissar for the Ukraine, responsible for utility vehicle repair. He held that position for two years, until the outbreak of

World War II. With the inception of hostilities in Europe, Shaposhnikov was recalled to active service, with the rank of colonel. Considered too old for a combat position, he was assigned to command a training division. The division was based in Stalingrad.

Fate would have it that the Second Ukraine would be encircled by the advancing Nazis. Surviving the bitter battle against all odds, Shaposhnikov was promoted again and awarded the Soviet's highest military honors. Thus, he was permanently assured a rung on the ladder that climbed into the very heart of the Communist Party. By 1947 he was once again a civilian, this time given an important post in the Ministry of Transportation. Along with the job came a seat in the Supreme Soviet. From that vantage point he would bide his time, allowing purges and natural attrition to take their toll of those above him.

Laboring behind the scenes he soon became one of the trusted members of Stalin's inner circle. Shaposhnikov posed no visible threat to the Premier's position, electing to remain unseen in the background for ten years before illness forced the aging Premier to entrust greater power to his subordinates than he wished. All the while, Maksim Shaposhnikov had maintained a low profile, hardly noticed by Western observers. When he was appointed Special Secretary to the Chairman in the late 1970s, surprised newsmen misinterpreted his selection as a tactical maneuver wrought by the feuding Soviet overlords. But Shaposhnikov's own steady hand would soon be clearly revealed at the throttle of his success. Until that point he had yet to acquire a serious enemy. Through the single year that followed, that condition would change drastically. In a manner reminiscent of Stalin decades before him, Maksim instituted a thoroughly systematic purge of any and all opposition. Within that year he became the most feared man in the Soviet Union.

In the mid-1980s, when the Western press buzzed with rumors as to Chairman Brezhnev's successor, the victor was already known within the highest echelons of the party. Shaposhnikov would close his hands methodically about the reins of power in the end. On January 1, 1986, Maksim Shaposhnikov was hailed as the new Chairman of the Communist Party and Premier of the Soviet Union.

But now he was beginning to feel the razor-sharp teeth of his single most powerful adversary, Dmitri Gvozdetskii. This young upstart refused to wait his turn in the wings as Maksim had. Any slip by the now seventy-year-old chairman would bring the jackals in for the kill.

Shaposhnikov slowly roused himself from his meditation, his faculties coming sharply into focus. It was clear that he would have to rely on the Professional to complete his mission, because contacting any of the Russian agents in Italy would surely alert the chief of the KGB. Unquestionably, he finally determined, I will have to play out my hand as if I were certain the mission is progressing as scheduled. So long as Gvozdetskii remains uncertain as to the true state of affairs, I am at an advantage. He is not yet ready to call my bluff. He took a shot of vodka from the bottle on the desk before him, allowing the clear fiery liquid to drain from the glass into his mouth, the solution warming, then burning his throat as he swallowed. His mind soon relaxed, passing from the moment into the dark eternal void that exists between the present and what is merely memory. Time seemed to slow, then to be suspended. He was once again kneeling before an altar in far-off 1924 China. His heartbeat slackened, and his breathing regularized. A cloud of serenity slowly engulfed his mind. Chairman Shaposhnikov never noticed a secretary slip out of the adjoining office. Outside, the near silent clicks of a telephone being dialed went unheeded.

Into the nearby phone receiver the low whispered voice of a bespectacled scribe conversed anxiously. "Comrade Gvozdetskii ... Yes, apparently sleeping at the moment. ... No, he hasn't placed a call, nothing at all. Nothing to our people in Italy or anywhere in the vicinity. ... No, Comrade. There were no calls received from them either. ... Yes, Comrade, of course. I shall continue my surveillance."

Outside, some three stories above, the black fist of a summer's storm gripped the sky, angry clouds born of icy winds in the Arctic Circle. Soon the storm would capture the countryside, beating Mother Russia into her classic posture, bent and aged under its heavy blanket of eternal snow.

Reclining in his chair, head thrown back, the chairman's thoughts wandered over brittle winter images. The bottle of vodka dangling from his hand slid slowly from his lax grip and clattered empty on the waxed floor. The future, its triumphs or consequences, would come inexorably as the winter, he had come to realize. It was beyond his power to control the forces of nature, if not of men.

10

The first rays of sunlight dispelled the night's heavy haze, creating a brilliant halo behind the drab skyline of Prague. The harsh light soon bathed the small suburban apartment where Eugenia Motykia reclined on the bedspread, her eyes semiclosed with the exhaustion that had finally caused sleep to overtake her. When the dawn's glare stretched its tendrils to her eyelids, they fluttered open, her body flinching with a restrained start. Unmoving, she lay squinting at the window, raising herself ever so slowly to peer over the sill and into the courtyard below. She knew only too well that the solitary figure was there, unmoving, barely concealed in the shortening shadows. She was surprised to discover that the sinking feeling, experienced each time she reencountered his presence, did not diminish with familiarity. To the contrary; along with her fear, it grew.

A week had dragged by since the surveillance team had taken up position outside her state-run apartment complex. At first she had hovered on the edge of panic. Then, as she had uncovered the reason for the state police's presence, her terror had slowly been transmuted into a mordant sense of determination. It was as if, in the ravages of despair, she'd seized on a mission to perform, an almost holy destiny she was now driven to fulfill by the aching emptiness of her shattered life. The task that remained was to somehow give meaning to her husband's death. There was only one way.

All through the bleak procession of days and nights that followed, her mind searched for a method of passing the documents out of Czechoslovakia, then to find the proper authorities. But to whom could she entrust them? Somewhere in the midst of her uneasy slumber the solution came to her. Today, Sunday, she would seek out those who would be in a position to transform the slips of paper her husband had died for into an avenging sword, to stab at the heart of the death-dealing secret police.

Hours slipped by and still she lay there, as if her soul were trying to soak up energy for the trying task ahead. Off in the distance a lone church bell rang: the solitary tone prodded her into movement. Within the hour she had bathed and changed clothes. Soon she would seek sanctuary in a time-honored refuge that the depths of her heart believed she could trust.

Standing before the bedroom mirror as she prepared to leave, her eyes fell upon the wedding photograph that stood framed on the dresser, and a wave of sadness overswept her. She picked up the photo and seated herself heavily on the bed's edge, lost in the melancholy weave of memory. Her image of thirty years past stood beaming at her in the photo, arm in arm with the proud and straight young police recruit in his finest. She searched his youthful features but found barely a trace of her Zavar as she remembered him in his last years; careworn and haggard after long hours, his face leathery and hair a thinning gray, his body slumping under the slow wear of tension wrought by his job and by the state. She clenched the frame tightly in her hands and bent over it, eyes moistening. Then, decisively, she forced back the tears and pulled her head erect. With a sudden motion she hurled the framed photograph into the far corner of the room, its glass shattering on the floor.

She had gathered all her resoluteness. There was nothing left for her, she realized, but to seize the moment and act. Determinedly, almost frenetically her steps carried her through the apartment. She wrapped a black woolen shawl about her head and shoulders as she had more than thirty years before. Her hands found the tightly wrapped envelope where she had placed it the night before, in a Bible that rested on the telephone stand. She tucked it into the bodice of her dress. It was a last reminder of her husband, something to be kept close to her heart for as long as possible. Buoyed by its presence next to her skin, she walked firmly out of the building.

The sky above her bore no trace of clouds when she emerged into the courtyard. Except for some young children kicking a soccer ball in a nearby doorway, the yard was virtually deserted. She allowed her eyes to dart about as she walked. When she reached the end of the paved court, she saw two of them. She walked straight toward them, heart pounding, hoping this show of bravado would fool them.

At twenty meters one officer recognized her and alerted the other. Instantly they split up and busied themselves walking as if to appear unaware of her presence. She continued onward with measured steps, unfalteringly. As she passed them, one took up position behind her while the second hurried to their vehicle, which was parked around the corner.

The officer jumped inside and grabbed for the communicator as first the suspect, then his partner, came into view. "Car 6 to Control, he hissed impatiently. When contact was finally established, he hurriedly relayed news of the widow Motykia's determined flight. It took several moments for supervisory personnel to assess the situation. Finally he was instructed to follow the pair by vehicle, reporting at designated intervals.

As soon as the radio fell silent, he pulled his portable communicator from his jacket pocket and called his partner. "Nandor, where the hell are you?"

"I'm right behind her headed for the church."

"Church?"

"Yes! Looks like the old lady is going to morning mass."

"Nandor, stay with her. I'll be there in two minutes."

The engine started at once and he sped off down the wide avenue, arriving a moment before she was swallowed up into the deep shadows of the gothic structure's interior. His partner immediately came to the car, a puzzled look on his face. "Well, you're the senior man. Do we go in there after her?"

"How the hell do I know?" he answered. "I'll call in and ask. In the meantime, you move it around back, just in case she's heading for a rear exit. She's on to us for sure."

He got on the car's radio once again and relayed the strange turn of events to his superior, Lieutenant Masaryk, back at police headquarters.

Eduard Masaryk was the day's duty officer at Prague's main police facility. Usually he enjoyed Sundays, a largely inactive shift.

The events of the next hour would dispel that image from his mind forever.

After the Czech field officer got off the radio line, Eduard called a Soviet KGB senior officer as he had been carefully instructed for this peculiar case. He was quickly put through to the chief of the local KGB unit, Yury Kulikovo, who appeared most interested in Mrs. Motykia's movements. Kulikovo instructed Lieutenant Masaryk to make sure the two men on the scene took no injurious actions unless absolutely warranted. Masaryk assured him that he had already left those same instructions with his men. Kulikovo, nevertheless, insisted that the orders be transmitted once again in his precise words. Lieutenant Masaryk shrugged and obeyed. He saw no sense in aggravating the KGB on this quiet Sunday.

Fifteen minutes passed with no change in the situation. Every five minutes the officer in the car radioed into headquarters, with the message relayed to the chief of the KGB. Unknown to the Czech lieutenant, the Russian was likewise relaying all reports back to Moscow as soon as they were received. In Moscow's Central KGB building, Dmitri Gvozdetskii, Chief of the Central KGB, waited in silence. His eyes nervously attacked the wall clock that hung just above the transmitting unit. At precisely 9:47 A.M., he acted.

"Instruct those foolish Czech amateurs to stand by. Then, Kulikovo, you personally select your best men and accompany them to that . . . " he paused, pronouncing the final word with distinctly disdainful resonance, "church. I have to know what she's up to. Understand?"

"Yes, Comrade Gvozdetskii," an apprehensive Kulikovo responded.

"You are to take charge. Do not allow those Czech incompetents to interfere; I don't trust any of them. Do everything yourself; I'll hold you personally responsible if there are any mistakes. Let her run if she will, but follow. Try not to stick out like a sore thumb. We will acquire the information we seek if, and only if, this pressure is asserted correctly, without abatement. Her breaking point is near. I'll get it one way or the other." He ended his string of admonitions with a precisely enunciated, "*Do I make myself clear, Comrade?*"

"Yes . . . Comrade Gvozdetskii. I understand fully," was the instantaneous rejoinder.

There remained nothing more than for the play to run until its final scene a thousand miles from Moscow. The slight, bespectacled chief of the all-powerful Soviet KGB was at this very moment devoid of any real power to alter the situation. Decisions would have to be left to the local KGB. He abhorred the helpless waiting. Thin, almost pure-white hands removed his glasses and wiped them on his tie. The cleaning was repeated time and again with precise movements while the men mechanically paced the tiny communications center. From the furthest point in the room, he glanced up at the wall clock, its second hand seeming to slow to a snail's pace. This little Czech goose chase, he was certain, could provide the substance for a potent move in Gvozdetskii's game of power.

Eugenia Motykia stopped at the top step, half turned to spot the officer tailing her down the block, then, clutching the envelope tightly to her bosom, hurried into the safety of the cathedral. Inside, the stone walls had retained the night's coolness; she drew her shawl close. Making her way through the smattering of faithful, she located a seat adjacent to the confessional booths. Ahead was the altar, adorned with a massive golden crucifix thrust forward defiantly from its silken white background. Services had already begun, the long rolling chants reverberating through the chapel in timid waves never quite rising to what they should be. She knelt, crossed herself, then slid into the wooden pew. She shivered once from the chill, but she paid no heed, her thoughts engrossed only in the task at hand. The service was familiar, yet shorter than she remembered it. Times had changed since her youth, yet the state had not been able to force the church from the hearts and minds of the people entirely. She found a measure of calm solemnity in the prayers and chants. They engulfed her in deep medieval tones, able to dispel much of the presence of danger that waited just beyond the cathedral's steps, cresting in the cavernous interior, a true sanctuary from her worldly fears. She sat unmoving and let the ancient ritual help strengthen her resolve.

By 11:00 A.M. the service was over. As the small flock got to their feet and began to file out she remained seated. Some individuals strayed to the confessionals, darting inside, emerging. Many kept their eyes to themselves, and moved skittishly away. Eugenia wondered how many of the nervous faces feared first the consequences of violating the state's desires, and their own consciences' only second. Eventually, it was her turn. She didn't hesitate; this was why she had come.

Inside the booth the darkness seemed to grab for the packet. She felt suddenly entombed in the quiet realm of conscience and truth. She placed her cheek against the wood of the cubicle's common wall with the identical booth on the other side. She could hear its occupant breathing, waiting for her to tap on the small hatchway that connected the two. Her fingers found the wall and she lightly struck the paneling. The priest on the other side responded by sliding open the wooden panel. The opening revealed a latticework of finely worked wood covered with a black lace overlay. It served to allow voices to pass through, but to keep the identity of the occupant secret.

"Father?" her voice questioned.

From the other side of the opening a young male voice invaded the privacy of the cubicle. "Yes, my daughter?"

"Father...I haven't attended a church in almost thirty years."

"But in the hour of your need you have returned to us."

His words seemed to calm her.

"Yes, Father. But only because I seek...help." She pressed her cheek into the wood.

"But, my daughter, you did come here. This is, after all, a place for confession, for spiritual comfort. You can speak to our Lord, through me." His voice understood her need to be heard.

"Father, I..." her voice wavered.

"Yes, my child."

"I am not here to confess my sins," she stammered, tears beginning to stream down her face. She started to remove the envelope from its hiding place, then stopped. For a moment there was indecision in her mind, as she watched her hands tremble in the dimness. "Father," she blurted out suddenly, "my husband has been killed by the state's butchers."

From behind the wall she could hear the occupant shift his weight. She understood what must have been flashing through the young priest's mind—the danger, the persistent religious harassment by the communists. And the special exuberance the authorities indulged in when making an example of disloyal clergymen. The priest must not only fear for his life if he agreed to help her, she realized, but in these times he must constantly be on the lookout for a police trap.

The clergyman's voice, barely audible, breathed through the opening. "Speak, my daughter. In this booth, before God, there is no fear."

Good, she thought, he is a man of principle. The realization helped her to risk more. In carefully rehearsed words, she continued, "He has been murdered by the police, I know it. There can be no doubt. But he has left a message, an envelope."

"Yes?"

"In it is the information that caused his death."

Again the priest moved in his seat on the other side of the wall.

"He has sent a message for the Church, a crucial one. Documents that must somehow find their way to Rome."

The father felt his heart plummet within him. He drew away from the opening, his body tensed. This is deadly, he thought, I mustn't allow myself to be drawn into it. He was afraid to give the wrong reply—who knew who might be listening, or to whom this woman reported? He heard his own voice whisper hoarsely, "My daughter. Here in this confessional we speak only of those things that affect . . . our mortal souls. What has happened is past. It is finished. Only God's love, and perhaps God's wrath, will see justice done. We concern ourselves with . . . "

"Father, this *does* concern us," she insisted passionately. "It concerns all of us as Czechs, as Christians, as people. I don't know if I'll ever have the opportunity to come here again. They've been following me." She knew he'd understand who the "they" were. "It is something that must reach the eyes of the Holy Father."

"The Pope?" Is this woman sane? he wondered. "Perhaps what you believe you possess is in fact nothing?"

"Father, my husband was an officer of the secret police. They killed him because he knew about . . . these—only for the knowing. Young man, I haven't been a religious woman for thirty years, yet I am asking you, in this moment, to use your faith. He died for this." Her hand withdrew the small package and forced it through the tiny opening. She felt resistance—perhaps his hand, not wanting to accept the burden it represented, blocked its passage. If it was a trap, then possession of whatever it was would be enough to cause his arrest. She pushed harder and the packet fell into the priest's cubicle. It lay on the floor, untouched. "Father, please believe me. Pass these to your most trusted leaders. They will understand. They must, there is no other way." Her trembling voice disappeared abruptly as she threw open the door and darted from the dark box into the church's brighter interior. Her steps clattered against the stone floor as she hurried toward the exit. When she reached the cathedral doors she heard the priest's door being opened. Its sound merged with the sound of her footsteps.

"Wait," he called to her in a stifled voice that died before it left his throat. The clergyman returned to the booth and slumped on the stool. On the floor before him was the packet, untouched, unopened. He nudged it with his foot to the booth's corner and then carefully placed his Bible over it. After staring down at it, motionless for a long moment, he withdrew from the booth, his eyes squinting out at the sunlight pouring through the open doorway.

Eugenia's determined steps carried her out into the brilliance of the morning's sun, where she paused, taking a moment for her eyes to adjust to the sudden light. She drew a deep breath, in it she could almost taste freedom. Then she saw them off to a side: these men who had killed her husband, who were determined to destory her as well. Drawing herself erect, she dispelled all doubts about what must now be done.

She pivoted and began to run down the broad steps away from her pursuers. As she dashed down the weathered stone steps, a flock of gray and white pigeons feeding there leapt into the air in a frenzy of beating angels' wings. Her shawl fell from her shoulders, but she refused to stop to retrieve it. This time she ran for freedom, eternal freedom.

Only an hour earlier that morning, local KGB Chief Kulikovo had had some difficulty rounding up his men. On Sunday, the

KGB, like other governmental agencies, gave its members a day of rest. Sunday could be considered a dead day. Thus, when Kulikovo asked for specific agents, he was informed that it would take half an hour before cars could be dispatched to retrieve them from the diverse locations indicated on their sign-out sheets. The chief instructed that all haste be made to locate and transport the men directly to the church, where he would meet them. They were to call him for exact instructions from their vehicles.

Before he left for the stake-out, he'd relayed a final call to Moscow. At KGB headquarters, in the underground Moscow communications center, Secret Police Chief Dmitri Gvozdetskii was waiting for his message. Quickly Kulikovo ran down the sequence of events for his superior, who seemed pleased with the preparations. But Kulikovo knew only too well that if anything went amiss, his head would be on the block. By 10:50 A.M. he was running to the familiar black KGB sedan, always waiting in a reserved space at the private rear entrance of the infamous structure.

Instructions were shouted at the driver as the car roared off. Immediately Kulikovo checked the vehicle's radio. It was working properly. He was patched through to an open channel, one assigned to him and the car that had been sent to collect his agents. He gave his instructions for the second vehicle to its driver, to be relayed to the agents after they were picked up and taken to the church. One man was to stay with the car and its radio, the second man to go off and find the agents. There would be no break in communication.

Ten long minutes later, the first of two KGB undercover agents, panting from his hurried preparations, tumbled into the car and immediately called in. The car careened around the narrow winding streets of the Old City, rushing to retrieve the second agent. It paused for barely a moment to admit him before screeching off toward the church. Above the whining tires and blowing horn, the agents listened to Chief Kulikovo's instructions. Although a sense of urgency was audible in his anxious voice, the chief informed them only that they were personally responsible for keeping the subject under tight surveillance. Any further specifics, they were succinctly instructed, would follow later.

At 11:21 A.M., Chief Yury Kulikovo's KGB sedan came to a halt behind the waiting Czech police vehicle. The two parked cars—the police vehicle a dark institutional blue, the larger KGB auto in shiny black—protruded prominently from the residential street. Kulikovo leaned out of the rear window and motioned the Czech officer over. The plainclothesman, seated in his police car, got out and ran to the KGB chief's window. "Has she left the building?" Kulikovo inquired of him.

"No, sir."

"Where is your partner?"

"I'm in contact with him, sir. He's stationed at the rear of the building in case she was attempting to lose us."

"Good. In a few minutes my men will be here. You'll stand by to assist us *only* if necessary."

"Yes, Comrade," answered the policeman, quite relieved that he would no longer be responsible for overseeing an operation that was clearly bigger than it seemed.

"Go, join your partner. Continue surveillance and keep updating. That's all. Give me your communicator. One should do for both of you. Now go!"

The communicator was relinquished through the open window by the Czech officer, who snapped to attention, sharply turned, and ran off. Kulikovo wanted this operation to remain in KGB hands and had sent the ordinary Czech officers out of the way to ensure that nothing would be bungled.

The officers and agency vehicles had attracted enough attention by now to inhibit general movement on the main street, Sunday strollers growing cautious with the awareness of a police presence. When the third car containing Kulikovo's two agents came streaking down the avenue, lurching to a halt at the far corner, any remaining onlookers melted into doorways or found alternate routes to scurry away on.

The two agents instantly jumped from the car. They had barely slammed their doors shut when the plainclothesman nearest them pointed up toward the church entranceway and shouted out, *"There!"*

Atop the stone steps stood a small but resolute figure, a frightened woman. But beneath her shawl the middle-aged face was etched not only with anxiety, but with a building determination. Eugenia Motykia was a woman with a vengeance, and now, with a mission.

Kulikovo had already stepped out of his car on the side street when the subject appeared. He had no time to bark a command to his agents before she began to run. She struck off boldly, away from the agents and police who immediately gave chase. Kulikovo scrambled off after them, realizing in a wrenching flash that his men were overreacting—their guns coming out of their pockets as they ran. He could hear them command to her to stop, yet she continued.

Without clear instructions regarding the purpose of this police effort, the agents were responding as they had been trained to; do not think, act!

"*Halt!*" they shouted, two voices as one. Behind them, Kulikovo's "Wait!" went unheard.

Without slowing her gait, she bolted into the roadway, two KGB men in hot pursuit. Kulikovo ran after them, trying to prevent the oncoming disaster. One of the men looked back for the moment and spied their master after them. His chase caused them to run even faster, shouting, "*Halt or we'll shoot.*" As before, the command went unheeded.

From around the far corner of the square a large flatbed truck, heavily laden with vegetable crates, veered into the roadway. The woman burst directly into his path.

The elderly driver's first reaction was to veer sharply away from the onrushing woman; then he caught sight of the pursuing officers and froze, staring for a couple of seconds at the unfolding drama he'd blundered into. One agent fired two shots in the air while running; the other stopped, both hands firmly on his outthrust pistol, striking the deadly pose to take aim. The driver spun his wheel and ducked with the shot.

Somewhere, someone screamed.

Eugenia, running full-tilt with her head down, did not see the vegetable truck until it was almost upon her. She stumbled, trying to avoid its path as it finally obeyed its driver's command to turn, swerving from her. The bullet that exploded from the agent's gun sizzled past her left ear as she fell. It struck the front tire of the swerving truck, sending it careening forward, uncontrolled. In desperation, the driver slammed his foot on the brake. The huge lorry screeched, then stopped in a deadening silence. In quivering protest it began to topple. The weight from the mass of high-loaded vegetable crates caused the vehicle to tip, then slowly roll onto its side with an enormous crash. Heavy cargo was thrown over, burying the woman under tons of shattered wooden crates and smashed vegetables.

There were more screams as people ran into the littered street. The two KGB men were first to reach the vehicle. The lorry's tires were still spinning as the vehicle lay groaning on its side. The driver's door tilted skyward as the dazed driver attempted to climb out of his cell. In an instant the Russian officers began tearing at the mass of debris that covered their suspect. They were still throwing aside the garbage when Yury Kulikovo climbed into the mess. He pushed them aside and grabbed at the soft mass of broken melons which oozed sweet liquid onto his hands and suit. In a minute he had succeeded in uncovering her face. The barest trace of serenity was on her lips, but a thin river of blood crept out of a corner of her mouth. She coughed only once.

The police chief placed his lips to her ear and spoke to her. "Mrs. Motykia, can you hear me?"

One eye half opened and she focused on him.

"Mrs. Motykia, whom have you spoken to?"

The lid closed.

"Who . . . ?"

The word died on his lips as he felt her body go limp. He looked up at his men, then barked, "Idiots, call an ambulance!" It was futile, he admitted to himself; she had already expired.

He stood and murmured under his breath, "No matter. Whatever she knew is now dead and gone."

A crowd gathered around the lorry. Some men had helped the vehicle's driver down and were attending to him. From somewhere in the distance the alternating wailing of sirens began, and drew near. Yury Kulikovo was helped off the rubble by the remaining KGB man, and he walked away, brushing the grime from his sleeves. The crowd parted for him, then closed about the wreckage when he passed through. He never saw a second figure emerge from the cathedral doorway, squinting from his position on the stone steps in the brightness of the noontime sun.

Father Hacha, drawn to the cathedral's doors by the sound of the shot, had observed everything. When the crowd parted, allowing the Russian to pass through, he realized what she had done. Whatever was in the envelope, still on the floor of the confessional, must have had great enough importance for this woman to give up her life for it. He ran back into the church, rushing to get his vestments, then returned to the street to administer the last rites to her.

He forced his way through the throng of onlookers and reached the body, still only partially uncovered. His eyes shut and his breath exhaled softly upon the realization that she was gone. Still, he knelt, grasped her hand, and recited the necessary prayer in a soft, hoarse whisper. He finished her last rites with the wail of the arriving ambulance as her only mourner.

Father Hacha did not remain standing in contemplation for long. Rather he returned directly to the small dark confessional cubicle and timidly peered inside. The envelope was still there waiting for him; he bent over and retrieved it. A moment's judicial consideration discouraged him from surrendering to his curiosity and opening the seal. Instead, he decided finally, he'd give it to Bishop Galen, who was visiting Prague from West Germany at this very moment. Whatever they were, whatever was meant by this, he would allow the bishop to decide the appropriate action to be taken. It would be dangerous enough to transport the envelope without knowing what its contents were, but to be so foolish as to involve himself further might prove fatal. But nothing would prevent him from transmitting this envelope now, despite the apparent danger. Had he trusted her, he realized, he might have been able to prevent her death. It was a responsibility that lay heavily on his conscience; his atonement would take a lifetime.

Envelope in hand, Father Hacha retired to his small room to the right of the sanctuary. He changed out of his priestly garb and went directly to where Bishop Galen was staying during his twice-yearly visit. Once he had passed the envelope on, he could wash himself clean of the entire affair.

By 1:30 P.M., a disguised Father Hacha slipped out of the side entrance of the cathedral. He walked along the crowded streets directly toward the cardinal's residence. He would have to get the bishop off to one side, alone for a few minutes. He would be careful not to involve the cardinal, for it was rumored that he had close ties to the state due to his brother's position as Minister of Education of the puppet communist regime. And besides, Bishop Galen would be leaving for Berlin within the week. He could safely take any packet out of the country without arousing suspicion.

His steps carried him into the midday crowd, where he went unnoticed. It was good he already knew the bishop, so he'd need no introduction. Father Hacha didn't understand exactly what compelled him to become part of this affair; he knew only that his conscience required it, and for him, such a calling was sufficient.

The sun bore down on his shoulders, causing him to sweat. In half an hour, he hoped, he'd be through with everything. The packet seemed to burn a hole in his skin where he'd taped it to his chest. His breast heaved as if some Roman soldier were prodding him with a pike. Cold sweat ran down his skin, the feeling akin to a river of blood being drained from some invisible wound. He turned the last corner to the cardinal's residence, set behind a formidable cut-stone wall.

Entering quietly through the servants' entrance, he prayed silently that his strange pilgrimage would soon be over. A single dark cloud invaded the summer's sky, momentarily blocking the warmth of the sun. The sweat on his body seemed to freeze, sending a shiver up his spine. He paused to outline the sign of the cross over himself in the belief that this ancient ritual would somehow protect him from the unknown.

11

The exhausted detective pulled unconsciously at the single graying sheet that had served to ward off the night's chill. Now discomfort from the growing heat made Lorenzo's still-sleeping figure stir.

Barzini's mind jerked haphazardly across the case's disparate details. His body twitched in a troubled sleep. As the heat rose, the dream-images that flashed through his mind grew more grisly. Foggy images of dismembered corpses and snapping disembodied teeth flickered through his restless unconscious, until a deeper dream enveloped him.

In his dream he is running, panting. His steps clatter down a narrow, cobbled alleyway lined with high walls, indented only with tiny distant windows. Lorenzo winds his way down the darkening alley frenetically—he is searching, frantically, rummaging through trash cans and peering into basement crevices. The garbage cans are waiting at every turn; each battered receptacle reveals, hidden in its slimy contents, a bloodied human limb. Feeling driven, he ransacks every container, the contents of each more gruesome than the last. Coarse laughter rings out from the tiny windows above: fingers point accusingly. Lorenzo stumbles forward. The alley is now vacant and the crevices blank. The trash cans disappear before he reaches them, or roll empty, lying on their sides. Running on with the growing weight of exhaustion, he sees nothing more ahead but the endless echoing cobblestone alley and its ever-narrowing walls. Lorenzo's despairing scream echoes in his own ear.

Off his bed with a jolt, the detective awoke to a scream that he finally realized came from his telephone. Disoriented for a moment, he finally traced the source of the double rings to beneath his bed. He pulled on the instrument's umbilical cord until he produced the black plastic irritant from its hiding place, and then snatched the receiver to his ear. "Hello?" he mumbled into the mouthpiece.

"Lorenzo . . . hey, Lorenzo, that you? Are you still asleep?"

The detective sat on the edge of the bed, the soft mattress folding against him. "Yeah, it's me. Who in Christ's name do you think it'd be, in this apartment?" he said, casting a furtive glance at the flat's disarray. "If anyone broke in here, I'd make him clean up before he'd be allowed to cart anything off." His annual spring cleaning resolution had now gone unfulfilled for its third year.

"You know what time it is?" questioned the voice at the other end of the line. "Don't bother to look, but it's nine-thirty. I've had to cover your ass again. What's your excuse this time?"

"Nine-thirty?" he barked as he stood up. "*Ave Maria*! Anyone notice, Giorgio?" Barzini carried the phone as he dropped his underwear and hurried toward the bathroom. "Be a good guy and give me half an hour. Tell them I'm onto something in the . . . Carbionalli case. Okay?"

"Carbionalli case? What the fuck is the . . . Oh, yeah, the boy-friend who got his balls shot off when the husband showed up unexpected. What the hell could you have come up with there? The missing husband? . . . Don't tell me you've found him after? . . . "

"No, Giorgio. I haven't come up with anything, but it's a great excuse if you can get them to buy it." Lorenzo tugged the phone wire to its limits so that he could just reach the rusty shower faucets. "Just half an hour, Giorgio."

"Yeah, yeah. I've already covered for you, Romeo. But sooner or later they'll catch on and transfer me, and you'll end up in the frying pan. Who the hell is going to take the heat then, Lorenzo?" The phone went dead in his hand.

By 9:49, an awake Barzini hurried from his flat, tugging on his tie and fumbling with his door keys. As he rushed to the archway leading toward the street, he heard a door shut overhead. In a moment the rhythmic patting of a woman's heels striking the tile floor on the second-floor breezeway reached him. It was the new tenant who had taken the flat directly over his. He had only seen her once, on the day she'd moved in. But that single glance had been enough. He was quite taken with her long, slender figure and smooth olive complexion.

The sharp clack of her footsteps moved down the stairway toward the courtyard where he had paused. Should he run . . . or wait? He'd linger.

She came around the corner of the stairwell and walked toward him, an inviting smile touching her soft lips as she saw him. "Hello." She cocked her head to one side. "Do you live here too?"

"Yes, yes . . . in flat 1-F." His eyes caught hers. They were magnificent, dark pools of magic glowing forth from the soft face of an angel. "I believe you are right above me."

"Oh, I see. Then you must be the detective that the landlord spoke of. I hope you don't mind the noise of my television?"

"Television . . . I hadn't noticed." He was searching for something engaging to say, but found himself stammering like some schoolboy struck by spring fever.

"I'm Theresa Manzillo," she said, holding out her right hand.

"Detective Barzini . . . Lorenzo Barzini," he responded, face reddening with his perception of his own clumsiness.

"So nice to meet you." She smiled as she started toward the courtyard's brick archway exit. "I always like to get to know my neighbors, especially a policeman; it's comforting to know that in case I ever need an officer I won't have far to look. Goodbye now, Detective Barzini, I'm sure we'll meet again." She spun on long slender legs and stepped out onto the sidewalk.

A warm breeze swept suddenly down the narrow street, catching the hem of her linen skirt and billowing it up over her knees. Tantalizingly dark, suntanned thighs were exposed to Lorenzo's view for an instant, sending a shiver of electricity down his spine. Her back to him, she bounced up on her toes and waved toward the corner, calling, "Iori . . . Iori . . . " then ran toward a silver Fiat that screeched to a halt in the bus stop across the street. Her long steps, as graceful and sprightly as a deer's, carried her to the sports car; she climbed in beside a well-groomed gentlemen who spun the wheel and spirited her off. Lorenzo wasn't sure if it was his imagination, but he thought he saw her turn and wink.

At the other end of the street was his car, one of the few Fiats left in the department's motor pool, a disreputable wreck. The deputy chief had assigned this derelict to him as a gesture of contempt, but Barzini relished the acquisition. Each scratch and rust mark was a battle scar to him, every ding or dent a medal of courage. He reveled in the old Fiat's dilapidation. After all, it had taken him years to get it. In his more flamboyant moods he'd don sunglasses, or sometimes pull a rumpled hat down over his forehead, and then drive it like a demon possessed. To Lorenzo it was his own vehicle; in it, he was an independent investigator *exemplare*.

He walked to the vehicle, sitting in all its dilapidated splendor in a no-parking zone. A small indulgence . . . using a forbidden zone for parking, knowing the official license plates would protect him. He climbed in, revved up the engine, and careened out of the space with the motor buzzing like a power saw on a tree trunk. A small child walking with his mother covered his ears as the car roared past, a cloud of black smoke billowing in its wake. Even as the little car pulled out, another immediately wiggled into the vacated space; parking was at a premium in Rome, and a space was always a space, legal or otherwise.

It took five minutes for Lorenzo to bob and weave through the city traffic, jerking forward past larger cars, swinging into oncoming traffic just long enough to scoot around vehicles or dart through a changing light. The car was so bedecked with Christian medallions and ornaments dangling from the sunshades and mirror that it rattled as he negotiated the narrow and congested downtown streets at ridiculous speeds.

Arriving at the Central Police Station, he swung into the lot and practically skidded down to the furthermost assigned stall, number 787. Someone had taken his spot. Damn, he thought, already they're trying to squeeze me out. He parked in the next available stall and placed his identity card on the windshield to keep it from being towed away.

Checking out the vehicle in his stall, he spotted an identity card with a golden shield emblazoned on its surface, signifying a chief inspector's car or a local detective unit. He was clearly outranked. Sighing, he walked through the lot to the main entrance of police headquarters, stopping at the newsstand on the way. He purchased the morning daily as a matter of routine, folded it under his arm and hurried into the building, running up the flight of stairs to Detective's Office Eight, Homicide.

The detective walked directly through the reception area to

his shared office. He didn't care to notice the lieutenant who was making note of Lorenzo's arrival time. It was his second late entrance this week.

His partner, the younger and more sharply outfitted Giorgio D'Annunzio, was waiting for him, pretending not to notice Lorenzo's late arrival. Finally he looked up from his paperwork, a sly smile on his boyish face, and kidded, "Okay, Lorenzo. Who was she this time?"

"How did you know?" Barzini gasped.

Giorgio looked up, startled at first, then laughing. "Don't tell me that our most famous detective has found a perfect woman?"

Lorenzo dropped his eyes, not knowing whether or not to answer. He'd taken quite a bit of ribbing from his peers in the department over the years. Because he was a bachelor, or his religious pretensions, or his general disheveled appearance. Not to mention his haphazard method and zealous persistence on the job. He could tell he was in for another round of roasting, but by now he had learned that if he played it close to the vest, he could keep everybody guessing.

"Well?"

"Well, what?" He played dumb to Giorgio's questioning.

"You know what! Who the hell is the broad?"

"What do you mean . . . broad?"

"Broad, you know, dame, chick—female, Lorenzo. Who is it? Come on, one of those tall skinny ones from downstairs in transport?"

"Now Giorgio, stop. Some things are best kept private."

"So there is someone, you old fox." D'Annunzio was agape. "Christ, they give him a car and suddenly he's a rolling Casanova."

Barzini'd already implied far more than was necessary to ignite a scorcher on the office rumor hotline. Hoping to change the subject now, he leaned forward confidentially and whispered, "Look, Giorgio, we'll talk later." He winked conspiratorially. "Meanwhile, I need to know how everything went here. Did the lieutenant say anything about my absence from roll call?"

"No, no sweat—never even asked. If he had, I'd have just told him that Detective Barzini's woman was keeping him in bed a little longer than usual this morning, sir." He continued smiling, testing to see if the verbal poke would strike home. "And he'd understand. After all, the lieutenant was young once too."

Barzini scowled and sat down, throwing the newspaper on the desk. "Enough, Giorgio." The paper opened revealing the morning headline, SUSPECTED ARSON. "I've had to put up with your women, haven't I? Now, I guess, you'll just have to get used to putting up with mine." It was his turn to smile. Even if she was merely a figment of his imagination, Lorenzo was sure that the entire division would know about his mystery woman by lunchtime, if he knew D'Annunzio.

The next hour was devoted to paperwork, routine, but required. But he knew how to convert the mundane to his advantage: If he complied enough studiously documented reports, it kept the bosses off his back.

D'Annunzio and Barzini exchanged forms, countersigning each in its proper place. Police regulations maintained that partners were to check one another's work sheets for accuracy: in practice they merely saved time and signed anything placed in front of them.

It was nearly noon when Barzini completed his work. His partner had finished minutes earlier and gone to the cafeteria for an early lunch. There he'd undoubtedly pass on the story of Barzini's girlfriend, adding spicy tidbits wherever necessary. Before 2:00 P.M. D'Annunzio would have him sounding like an insatiable Roman lover, the story blown out of proportion with each repetition. Barzini, of course, secretly relished his little ruse.

He straightened up in his chair, hands on his lower back, chest thrust forward to stretch the muscles that ached slightly from deskwork. Closing his eyes, he rotated his head slowly from side to side to relax his stiffened neck. When he opened them, his eyes froze on the newspaper that had lain to his right unseen for the past two hours. The headline leapt off the page at him. He read further: HEADLESS BODIES RECOVERED IN OSTIA ARSON.

The slow tide of realization washed slowly across his countenance; at first only his eyes responded, widening incredulously, eyebrows rising ever so slightly. In a sudden motion he swooped down on the paper with both hands and sprang to his feet. "Giorgio . . . " he choked out without realizing that his partner wasn't there. His mouth went agape. "Dismemberment!" he muttered aloud as his eyes raced down the article. The similarity to the jawbone case was inescapable. "Fingertips also removed, preventing identification," he read aloud with some conviction. "Ostia!" One hand snatched for the phone receiver, the other stabbed impatiently at the operator's button. "Ostia police department," he barked at the police switchboard operator, "detective division."

Moments later Barzini was dashing through the corridor, down the broad steps and out into the hot afternoon sun, running toward his vehicle at the far end of the lot. When he finally reached the car he jumped in, puffing and panting, and revved the engine. With one hand he spun the wheel to pull out and with the other, threw a kiss to the plastic Virgin Mary mounted on the dashboard—a gesture of thanks for this lucky break.

On the phone he had been told that Detective Alessandrini, in Ostia, was out to lunch and would return in half an hour to submit his report before resuming fieldwork. Barzini saw no point in waiting to call back—he didn't want to miss seeing him in person.

From downtown Rome it should take forty-five minutes to get to the Ostia Police Building. The route veers around the outskirts of Rome, zipping by pathways once trod by the ancient Roman legions en route to the sea. Twenty-five minutes after his departure, Barzini was speeding past the ruins of Ostia Antica, horn ablare as he howled down the highway. In another five minutes he had arrived at the crumbling police building.

He parked with a jolt and tumbled out of the driver's door in haste, forgetting to place his parking permit in the windshield. Running up the steps, without stopping for the officer attempting to point out that he had parked illegally, he rushed past the reception guard with a flourish of his identity card.

"I'd like to see Detective Emilio Alessandrini. I'm Detective Lorenzo Barzini, from Rome," he announced to the sergeant at the front desk.

"Alessandrini . . . I'll see if he's in. Please have a seat, sir."

Barzini had no time for formalities. He pushed open the gate that separated the reception area from a maze of offices. "You can't go in there without . . . " The sergeant's words were lost as the detective rushed inside, looking at the nameplate of each office as he strode down the corridor. An officer started after him, but Barzini paid no heed, stopping only when he reached the door marked "DETECTIVE E. ALESSANDRINI." Without knocking, he entered. Seated at the standard Formica desk was a square-jawed young man, working on an endless array of paper forms that were so familiar to the older detective. Barzini held up his identity card to the seated figure.

"I'm Barzini. Are you Alessandrini?"

At that moment two officers burst into the small cubicle. "Who the hell do you think you are?" one of them questioned as they grabbed Lorenzo.

The seated man jumped up. "Hey, what's going on here?"

"Emilio, this nut just ran through the gate," shouted the officer as he grabbed Barzini from behind. The detective's identity card slipped from his hand.

"Hey, he's a policeman, a detective from Rome."

"A cop?" they answered in unison. "Are you sure?"

Barzini shrugged off their grasp and bent over to pick up his card, holding it over his shoulder for the officers to see.

"Oh!" one of them said, "he *is* a cop." Barzini ignored them as they began to back out of the room. Seating himself, he faced the stunned detective and began. "I'm here about the headless bodies you guys pulled from that fire last night. I want to know everything about them you can tell me."

The young detective studied the concerned face of the Roman cop for a minute, as Barzini did the same to him, like two prize fighters feeling each other out before combat begins. "The fire. You came from Rome about the fire? Say, have you had anything like this that could maybe help me?"

"Maybe," answered the seasoned detective. "Maybe."

The hairs on Alessandrini's neck stood on end. Identification of the twin corpses had seemed impossible. The case had been dumped on him only because the senior detectives avoided ball-busters like this assignment. But here, seated in front of him in the crumpled garb of a weather-beaten, highly experienced detective was what appeared to be a godsend.

Alessandrini had become a detective only ten months earlier, after five years on regular patrol duty; he knew his superiors felt that finding either the victims' identities or the arsonist was only a step away from impossible. With this in mind, he had already begun filling out papers necessary to shelve the case, having gone through the routine motions called for: missing persons reports, fire records, modus operandi—all legwork and lengthy paperwork. A description of the headless torsos was already on the teletype to all Italian police units, and if nothing came back within a week, he would be able to move on to something else.

But suddenly, with Barzini's arrival, there rose new possibilities. "What do you have?" he inquired.

Lorenzo knew the routine well. Alessandrini would try to milk him for information without giving anything in return. But this case was his, and he intended to keep it that way. "Emilio," he began in a quiet voice with a confidential tone, "maybe we can help each other."

"Sure . . . what do you have?"

Barzini smiled as he leaned forward conspiratorially, "Right now I'm not certain I have anything that can help. But look, do you think I would have rushed here from Rome if I didn't think I had a possibility . . . "

"What kind of possibility?" Alessandrini had been hooked.

"Look, I'd like to get out of here and over to where you guys found the bodies. I'll know more when I see what's really happened. Then maybe I'll have something for you. Fair enough?"

Alessandrini, stroking his prominent chin, didn't have to mull it over for long. This case was clearly beyond his power to solve. If he even got part credit for its solution, he would earn a feather in his cap. This older detective with the flamboyant entrance must be on to something big, he figured. "Okay, a deal. I'll help you if you'll help me."

The two detectives stood, shook hands, and walked out of Emilio's small office back down the corridor past the waiting sergeant.

"Hey, Mr. Rome detective. Don't come busting in here again like you're any . . . " Barzini paid him no heed, passing him without faltering.

Lorenzo stopped at his car for a moment to take the summons off his windshield and hand it to Alessandrini. "Don't your men know better than to give a police car a ticket? Here, that sergeant can stuff it up his ass. Now, let's get going."

It was only half a mile to the site of the fire. All the way, Barzini remained quiet, allowing the young detective to bring him up to date. There was very little to go on. The flat had been rented to a single woman a month earlier, and a boyfriend had been seen living with her. "From their neighbors I've gathered they were painters. Lab reports verify this—paint and artist's materials on the site. They kept to themselves almost completely, and that's creating a problem in getting a sketch of him, although the landlady remembers her. The trouble is the landlady was burned in the fire and has bandages all over her face. It's going to be a couple of weeks before she'll be able to see well enough to help a police artist work on a composite, and you know what a couple of weeks can do to a memory. And, besides, composites are usually worth nothing."

Barzini nodded.

The stench of smoke lingered in the air as the automobile turned onto Via di Terni. A single fire truck remained in the middle of the street, hoses stretching up the blackened stone stairway into the ruined apartment building. Most of the facade of the three-story structure was gone, ripped away by the force of the explosion. Faces of the adjoining buildings were stained and watersoaked. Barzini stopped the car at the police barrier; the assigned officer recognized Alessandrini and indicated his permission to park there.

The two detectives got out of the car. The charred smell of smoke and ruin was even stronger now. Cautiously, they stepped over blackened bricks and rubble scattered in the street. A dank and pungent odor hung heavily in the air as the Roman sun bore down on the drenched debris.

They were greeted by the Ostia fire marshal, a large round man with a few strands of dark hair slicked back across his bulbous pate. "*Ciao*, Emilio," he began. "Back again?"

The two men shook hands. "Captain Chiabrera, this is Detective Barzini from the Rome police department. It seems that he might have something for us."

The captain held out his hand, "So, Barzini . . . could you be, perhaps, Lorenzo Barzini?" He was smiling. "I worked with you some . . . fifteen years ago when I was first starting out on the police force. I'm Chiabrera . . . Vincente Chiabrera."

"Ah, yes, Chiabrera." Lorenzo's face lit up. "I remember you. You were the one who made that big numbers bust, a rough one, am I right?"

The heavy-set man nodded with a nostalgic smile. "It still

hurts up there where I was hit, sometimes." He patted the fleshy area of his upper left shoulder.

Lorenzo nodded his recognition. "Oh, yeah, I recall now, a thirty-eight."

"Only a twenty-two." Chiabrera frowned with a minimizing gesture. "But I'd had enough of being a cop, so I took the test for the fire department. And now, as fate would have it, I'm back in the detective division, this time mostly rummaging through the crap people make of good buildings, usually for the insurance."

The men began walking toward the front steps of Number 12. "So, Barzini, I see you're a senior detective now, eh? What brings you out this way with my young friend Emilio here?"

"Well, Vinny, if I'm lucky, I'm chasing a hot lead. Can you tell me about the fire?"

'Sure, it's interesting. You see, at first we thought it was just a routine chemical explosion. You know, an artist stores solvents and paints in a closet, maybe something spills or leaks, the temperature goes up and"—he raised his bushy eyebrows—"boom, an explosion. But once we found these bodies, I began to dig a little further.

"In fact,"—he turned to Alessandrini—"I was going to call you, Emilio. I think we've got some piecing together to do here." The fire marshal chuckled cynically as he pointed toward the building shell with a hefty arm. "And I don't mean the bodies. You see, I was kicking around up there,"—their eyes raised to the blown-out section of roof and wall three stories above—"and came up with something very interesting. Sometimes you get bodies without pieces of hand or face, with fingers missing—occasionally even without heads. But two exactly the same, with fingers missing—too much.

"Now, we found the bodies pinned against the wall by the mattress. Mattresses contain flame retardants, by law, which helped preserve the remains. We figure the blast, which also blew away most of the fronting, must have been close enough to the bed to throw it against the far wall. That would put the source of the explosion around there." He pointed up to the visible edge of what was left of the third floor. "But the interesting thing is that the point of origin of the fire has to be further back, inside, where it spreads out and down." Chiabrera gestured toward the upper staircase landing with both hands.

"The condition of the bodies indicates foul play; this confirms it. Lab reports show it was a foamite explosion, gas released by a volatile chemical mix—point of origin, here. Fire, also chemically aided—point of origin, back there."

"A fuse," surmised Barzini.

"Exactly," the burly Chiabrera continued. "Somebody was pretty damn clever here. I found a pattern on the floor that could indicate a trail of flame like a fuse, that led to the bed. Whoever he was, looks like he killed the couple, then threw them on the bed, expecting the fire to cover up everything. And he'd have been right except for the explosion. If he'd just set a fire, everything would have burned up. But he set a time bomb in there and it blew the whole fucking building apart. The blast pinned the bodies against the wall behind the mattress, where we recovered them before they'd been completely consumed by flame. Conclusion: The decapitations were in no way a result of the explosion."

"Clear enough." Barzini was becoming agitated now; the connection was getting firmer by the minute. He thought out loud: "The decapitations were to obscure the identities, the fire and explosion were to mask the killings: I'm up against someone who really knows how to operate." The detective returned his attention to the two other men. "No explosives, right? He must have used anything available, straight out of their closet. Without a lucky break, it would have been indistinguishable from a natural fire."

"No doubt about it," said Chiabrera, "the perpetrator was a real pro. Probably used ammonia, solvent, detergent, paint— made himself a great little bomb. Too great. That's his only mistake. . . . Sometimes you're too good." They paused and gazed up together at the charred remains of the skeletal structure.

"We got here pretty fast because the station crew was just returning from another call when the blast occurred. They heard it and were on the scene in less than five minutes. The fire just didn't have time to eat everything up. A couple of hours after it was all over, one of our guys found the bodies. That's when they called me in on it . . . and the police."

"How can I get up there?" Barzini wondered aloud.

"What for?" questioned Chiabrera.

"To see for myself," he responded, beginning to pick his way around the snake-like pattern of canvas hoses that stretched up into the darkened interior of the building.

"Hey, Lorenzo. You don't have to. I've got pictures of everything. Every angle, and besides, my boys have torn what's left of the place apart. You understand; once we found two bodies, we couldn't be certain there weren't more. We really gave it a good going over. The pictures will tell you the story without getting yourself filthy or breaking your neck."

Alessandrini spoke up, feeling like the odd man out between the two old acquaintances. "Hey, make sure to send me copies. I'll need them for my investigation. It's an Ostia homicide . . . isn't it?"

"Yeah, you're probably right," agreed Barzini, his eyes already scanning the surrounding buildings and the faces of the curious. "Looks like you've both got your work cut out for you. Emilio, I'd suggest we get started asking questions of all the neighbors about anything they could tell us about the occupants, or about any local who might be capable of arson. You might just luck out on a reason for all this."

Alessandrini was anxious to allow the Roman detective to lead the way. He had suddenly been cast into a complicated investigation, one he didn't have the experience to handle. It wasn't simply a mopping-up operation any more. And besides, even if Barzini did come up with something, he'd get enough credit because this was Ostia, his precinct and his assigned case. "Good idea. We'll have a better idea of what we're looking for. Look, Barzini, how about you coming along. Then if anything sounds familiar to you . . . "

"Sure. So far it doesn't look like there's anything to do with my case, but, why not?" He winked at Chiabrera, guessing that the fire marshal already understood the manuever. "It was good seeing you, Vincente. Thanks for your help. Take care of yourself. Maybe we'll have a drink together, later?"

"Sure," answered Chiabrera. A smile lifted the corner of his mouth.

By 4:00 P.M. the detectives had made their way across the street, Alessandrini having already questioned many of the mustached old men, gangling children, and matronly housewives who had gathered at the police barricade to view and gossip about the spectacle. After canvassing the first house on the corner, Number 1, they began working their way back down the street.

By now the occupants of the block were expecting them, having learned of the investigation through the back-window grapevine. Often they were already waiting by their doors in their aprons, anxious to ask their nosy questions and offer fanciful theories. No one knew the couple, few even knew of them, and none had seen any unusual occurrences. But already most of the inhabitants of Via di Terni were convinced that this was vengeance wreaked by the dreaded Cosa Nostra. One group of teenagers was willing to swear that they'd seen a black sedan with a half dozen hit men pull up in front of 12 Via di Terni the previous night. Alessandrini scribbled down each version, trying to collect every conceivable lead. Barzini knew better.

When the pair reached Number 13, directly across from the burned out shell, they were greeted by the building's landlady; she had eagerly anticipated their arrival and was waiting with fresh coffee and rolls.

Mrs. DiGrigorio was ready to ask the same questions each of the previous landladies had. Between her pronouncements of what a tragedy it was and her sighs about how awful for the neighborhood, she poured coffee and offered homemade pastry. She wanted to know who the couple was and whether or not they were married, and why the police are never around until after a crime occurs.

Detective Barzini sipped the coffee she offered and played on her natural desire to talk, merely inserting a few key questions. "Can you tell me if you ever saw the couple across the street?"

The woman quickly crossed herself. "Hardly at all!"

"Can you possibly tell me anything about them . . . anything at all?"

"Well," as she looked about, "it's not that I'm nosy or anything, but I didn't think they were married. I'll bet it was the lady's husband who finally found about them having an affair . . . "

"Why do you say that?" Barzini pressed.

"Nothing, it's just that they kept to themselves all the time. Like they had something to hide."

This was something the detective had of course considered. In adultery cases, the husband often shot the wife as well as the boy-friend. However, he would usually await the arrival of the police. If this was truly a husband-killing-wife affair, the murderer had gone through a great deal of trouble for nothing. He could of course prevent an immediate identification of his wife, but how could he possibly explain her disappearance to children, relatives, and the like? No, there simply was too much expertise here for a crime of passion. "How about your tenants? Maybe one of them might have seen something? Are any of them home?"

"Tenants? No, I keep a strict house. I'm sure no one here would be involved in such goings-on. But, if you must?" She shrugged her shoulders and turned. "Some of them should be home by now." She went out to the entryway of the building and rang the bells of her boarders; as they responded, she called up the stairway for them to come down to speak to the waiting de-tectives. Five minutes later, they had all been interviewed, except for the occupant of the upper front-facing apartment. It seemed that Mrs. DiGrigorio hadn't seen the priest since she had rented the flat to him. Oh, he had slept in his bed, for she made it each noontime; but she hadn't heard him leave or enter.

"Are you certain he's all right?" questioned the detective.

"I certainly hope so. If he wasn't, how could he leave each morning?"

"I think I'd like to see his apartment," said Barzini.

"For what reason?" questioned Alessandrini.

"Because from his windows we can look into the mess across the street . . . without getting our shoes dirty."

The detectives were led upstairs. Mrs. DiGrigorio, using her passkey, let them in. The room was immaculate, orderly, and spotless, the open closet empty; there was not even so much as a smudge on the windowsill or a wrinkled towel. "Are you certain he was here last night?" questioned Barzini.

"No," answered the startled woman, looking about. "I thought that he was. But with the terrible fire and all, I haven't had time to come upstairs and clean up. I didn't see him when all the commotion started—but it was so noisy, that big boom and the fire engines and everything."

As she prattled on about the fire and the neighborhood's property values, Lorenzo began to feel the strain of the long hot afternoon. Alessandrini stood at the window, gazing into the wreckage from this improved vantage point, as Barzini sat and rubbed the back of his neck. The leads, and his patience, were thinning.

He was up against a pro, he realized, remembering Chiabrera's words, whose only mistake to date was that he was too good. The fire marshal's phrase lingered in Lorenzo's mind, full and heavy as grapes ripe for the plucking, hanging tantalizingly just out of reach. Then it hit him.

Too good; too careful . . . there was something wrong with this room . . . it was too clean! The perception hit him like a bolt from the heavens. He jumped to his feet, his eyes darting all around the interior space; then he stopped and stared across the way. This room had all the innocuous simplicity of a masterfully camouflaged lair!

Alessandrini spoke, interrupting Barzini's reverie. "Hey, Lorenzo, let's get moving. It's getting way past quitting time, eh?"

"Sure." Lorenzo grimaced, allowing Alessandrini to lead the way out the door. He had but a gut feeling to go on. But gut feelings separated good detectives from the street cops. Barzini gritted his teeth angrily as he began to close the door behind him.

And then something caught his eye. The one thing that was out of place, a small ring on the floor near the chair leg. He retraced his steps to the scatter rug in the room's center. As the landlady and young detective walked into the hallway, Barzini bent over and picked up the plastic ring with his handkerchief, and quickly stuffed it into his pocket. He cast one final glance out the window at the skeleton of 12 Via di Terni, whose burned timbers reached for the sky like the spires of ancient church steeples.

Lorenzo had come into possession of a piece of black plastic of unknown origin from an apartment that had been painstakingly gone over by its occupant to ensure that any such remnant would not exist. The puzzle, whose solution still eluded him, was now slowly coming into focus. This single clue might prove to be the piece that would unlock the mystery. As Lorenzo left the room, an alert observer might have noticed a renewed spring in his step.

12

Thirty-six days had passed since Cardinal Giuseppe Casaroli had emerged from the sealed Sistine Chapel as the cardinals' choice for Pope. The prelate had quickly taken the name of his predecessor, John XXIV, in a gesture intended to ensure continued solidarity among the conservative members of the Church. Sixty-seven years of age, a burly, robust man of seemingly tireless enthusiasm and compassionate manner, coupled with strident traditional religious ideology, Casaroli was the logical choice to succeed Pope John XXIV.

It had been widely reported in the world's press that the cardinals had chosen Casaroli after only four ballots. There was little opposition to the man. He represented stability, orthodoxy, scholarly acclaim and, above all, a quiet strength. Casaroli had studied beside Pope John for nearly twenty years and had been appointed to head numerous sensitive committees dealing with such controversial issues as divorce, abortion, contraception, and woman's place within the clergy. In each case he had guided the Church through to a position that moderated only slightly, but sufficiently, its firm traditional stance. In those twenty years the Church had flourished. Now the momentum that had been sought and gained by Pope John XXIV would be continued by John XXV. The Church anticipated another generation of growth and prosperity.

The vigor with which Pope John pursued his daily routine fit neatly into the machinations of the Professional, who took careful note of every move, every nuance, patiently awaiting a flaw to exploit. He would soon discover what he sought. Always studious and energetic, John quickly plunged into the daily Vatican routine, which was not unfamiliar to him. He had worked many years within the ancient walls of the city-state, and the respect widely accorded him helped the transition to proceed smoothly. Within the first few weeks, the Vatican had already resumed much of its normal schedule. The constant, watchful eye of the Professional carefully noted the new Papal routine. Pope John rose precisely at 5:00 A.M. underwent painstaking ministrations to his cleanliness and appearance, then immediately proceeded to his private chapel for the morning's prayers.

After half an hour he would partake of a simple breakfast in his study. This time allowed him to peruse the day's agenda and perform those adjustments deemed necessary. His secretary, Agostino Cardinal Guerri, would be at his side, advising him of state and clerical affairs of highest priority. Guerri and Casaroli, lifelong friends, had gone to school and seminary together. Now, as one began his new role of leadership, the other served as his advisor, companion, confidant. The Professional quickly observed that no one had audience with the Pope without first passing the close scrutiny of his ever-constant associate.

By 8:00 A.M. the daily routine of conferences, audiences, and public appearances had already begun. The Pope worked through to 11:45 A.M., when Cardinal Guerri would preempt any and all activities, not to be resumed until the afternoon. Pope John, accompanied by Guerri and assorted secretaries and policemen, would retire to his apartment for lunch and a brief rest.

The Pope's afternoon resumed at 2:30 P.M., continuing until the evening, when he always returned once again to his apartments to refresh himself and dress for evening mass. At 8:00 he retired for the evening, excluding those occasions when state functions required his attendance. Barring such, the Pope would eat a late dinner and then study privately until midnight. All through his rigid routine, Agostino would remain at his side.

The Professional studied his prey intently. Gaining proximity to Pope John would require a precision maneuver. Although Father Kottmeyer, as a member of the Vatican restoration staff, had access to almost every nook and corner of the complex, the Pope's apartments were an exception, a restricted area.

After studying the routine, the Professional began to shape his plan. On his daily return for his luncheon, the new Pope John followed a route that took him through a series of lower corridors leading back to his apartments. The final two passages were narrow, and if Father Kottmeyer was at work in one of these areas, the Holy Father would have to pass him at no more than arm's length. The place to strike had thus been determined. What remained was method.

A master in the use of chemical toxins, he had used various poisons effectively in the past. The one that acted almost instantaneously, undetectably, was concentrated nicotine. Its victims, like those of curare, appeared to have suffered heart seizures. To any observer, the Pope would have died naturally. Administration of a lethal dose is even simpler. Nicotine requires no syringe, no glass of liquid. It penetrates directly through the skin itself, in seconds. Any contact with the substance ensures immediate death.

In the guise of Father Kottmeyer, the Professional planned to position himself in the corridor, feigning work at a fresco. When the Pope left his office at 11:45 and proceeded into the passageway, the priest-workman would be waiting. When the Holy Father drew near, the priest would kneel. The Pope would surely offer the ring of St. Peter to a kneeling priest, and the Professional would lower his head to kiss the holy object. But the Professional's lips, carefully coated beforehand with liquid plastic, would be daubed with a tiny droplet of liquid death. Instead of kissing the ring, the bogus priest would plant his lips on the Pope's fingers. As he proceeded unknowingly down the corridor, the Pope would be doomed. Within heartbeats he would grasp his chest and collapse. Paralysis would follow in five seconds, death unerringly within ten. During the hysteria of the mortal spectacle, Father Kottmeyer would appear to be but another horrified onlooker. The frantic movement of security and medical personnel would provide ample opportunity to slip away unnoticed.

With the death of John XXV, the final stage of the program could be set into motion. It would take barely twenty-four hours to prepare. The opportune moment was selected: Friday at noon, less than three days hence. By then, Pope John XXV would have been the Holy Father for thirty-nine days. His reign would be mercilessly short.

The pressure was consuming all his faculties. The combination of sleepless nights and tense, wakeful hours had left the Professional so drained that his only refuge was sleep. Devoid of consciousness, his body remained motionless.

In his slumber the tension found release. It seeped through hairline fissures from the present into visions of the past. A young boy walking with his father, a fleeting remembrance; something for his mind to grasp, hold on to. Trees and lawns became real, bygone places and objects became suddenly familiar. A dog, silver-black, ran at their heels. There was a sense of joy, a long past euphoria not to be encountered again. From a bluff overlooking the emerald sea, the tall man spoke to him.

Still in sleep, his lips pleaded for the person he had loved above all others. In the small room a single ray of light stole through the drawn blinds and fell across his dry lips. "Father . . . Papa," he gasped.

Suddenly he tossed; the light burned across his forehead like a mark of black flame. He trembled; the dream faded. "Come back," he mouthed soundlessly. Raising his body, the light now behind him, his eyes opened, but as yet remained unseeing. Was he blind? The moment passed; the bare room came sharply into focus. He was back in his cell within the walls of the Vatican. It was a simple refuge, a base from which he could implement his plan.

His feet swung off the bed, all traces of sleep vanishing before they touched the coolness of the floor. His consciouness would turn fully to his committed course. His next few hours would alter irreparably the future of this spiritual nerve center of the world.

The stage had been set by careful preparation; now he would act this scene. But the script would not be wholly his—another hand would direct its final outcome. He washed and dressed.

The black fabric of his habit had grown all too familiar. His fingers found the string of glass beads and he allowed them to tighten about his fingers. A delicate golden cross weighted the rosary at its center. He held it before him; the shaft of light falling on its reflective surface caught and held his eyes. He placed the amulet about his neck.

He picked up his workman's case from the concrete floor,

glancing before he departed at the small painting of the face of Christ, grimacing in its unfathomed agony. The Professional wiped his forehead with the back of his wrist, squinting at the harsh rays being reflected through the windows. The Fates, like so many other Roman gods, seemed to hover with watchful eyes.

Tall and sturdy, the bogus Father Kottmeyer strode through the corridor housing the Department of Public Information offices. He pretended to be examining the ceilings, jotting a series of notes as a ploy to prevent any unlikely questioning of his movements.

The man in priestly guise peered inside the open portal to ascertain that the office was vacant, as planned. A quick glance down the corridor confirmed that it too was empty. Slipping inside the office, he closed the heavy, polished door behind him and quickly moved to the nearest desk. He set his wooden toolbox on the floor, and snatched up the telephone, speedily dialing a number that could be utilized but once. It was the key to his entire mission.

The signal raced through the maze of switches that connected this phone to another receiver somewhere in Rome . . . or elsewhere. The familiar double ring began. Once . . . twice . . . thrice. Then, before the fourth set of rings, the line was answered. "Yes?" The voice rang like cold steel. "Recognition signal, please." In a voice that darted like a dagger thrust, the Professional spoke the signal word: "Conclave."

Only a fractional pause preceded the rejoinder, "Where shall the delivery be made?" The taut answer was, as always, precision planned to shield his identity even (and especially) from those by whom he was employed. "Vatican Bookstore, under the philatelic exhibit; today, precisely at 17:25." The time selected immediately preceded closing. It would fit neatly into his careful contrivance to eliminate detection from both his intended victims and his co-conspirators.

"Acknowledged," the voice enunciated. "It will be there. Do you require any further assistance?"

"None." His hand hit the button as soon as the command escaped his lips; there was no need for further discussion. There would also be no time to trace the origin of the call.

He quickly replaced the receiver in its cradle and returned the instrument to its original position on the desk, ensuring that everything was as it had been before he entered. Somewhere down the hallway the sound of footsteps echoed. The rhythmic patter of leather soles striking the stone floor drew near. He lifted his workman's case and strode rapidly toward the doorway, reaching it almost at the same instant that an elderly monsignor turned the corner. The pair met face to face.

"Oh, my . . . Father, can I help you?" The startled Church official groped for words.

Father Kottmeyer stepped calmly aside. "No, no. Just checking for possible repair work. I'm from the restoration staff." He held up the sheet of paper with the indistinguishable markings. "I've only been here for a couple of weeks. I must be on the wrong floor. Sorry." Not allowing the monsignor opportunity to answer, he quickly took a step outside, turned left, and walked away.

The elderly churchman looked after him for a moment, then turned inside, the incident soon forgotten.

The Professional took the first stairway he came to, hurrying down to the first level. He smiled to himself. His Italian had been impeccable. Years spent with private tutors had served him well. He glanced at his watch—it was already 9:15 A.M.—then at the small containers arranged on the open wooden case he carried, holding brushes, artist's knives, tubes of colored oils and soft rags. He was about to complete his masterpiece.

The corridor was cool. Frescos adorning its walls had been laid there by the master Michelangelo centuries before. Every few years they were systematically cleaned and thereby given new life. Today's cleaning might be a few seasons premature, but its timing possessed a scalpel-edged accuracy. The location was ideal for his purpose. The Holy Father passed through this passage twice each day. In an hour the leader of the world's half-billion faithful would face a devil dressed in black.

The tools of his trade were laid out before him; not tools of destruction, but those used to restore life and luster to art inspiration. No one could know that these benign brushes, cloths, and swabs shielded deadly intent with their simple guise. Other members of the Vatican staff passed by. None paid him any heed. Clergy garbed in ill-fitting workmen's clothing were constantly at their jobs. Identification cards needn't be displayed within the Vatican's interior. Even if they had been, Father Kottmeyer was merely doing what he had been summoned to do. There was nothing amiss.

Two hours passed. A glance at his watch showed the time to be 11:56 A.M.; in less than fifteen minutes the Pope would pass along the corridor, returning from the morning's hectic duties. This morning's rigorous schedule would be his last.

The workman-priest bent over and laid his brush alongside the neat row of its fellow camel's-hair instruments. His eyes darted about, checking always for onlookers. Spying none, his steady fingers sought a bottle of clear liquid hidden among a score of other similar containers. He unscrewed its top, carefully placing it on the temporary wooden platform he had erected hours before. The Professional's hand groped for a cotton swab, then dipped the absorbent end into the liquid. He waited a moment, then brought the swab to his lips, carefully running the liquid over their surface. He waited for thirty seconds and ran the still-wet bit of cotton over his lips a second time. He took care not to allow his lips to touch for another minute, allowing the liquid coating to dry thoroughly. As he waited he closed the small bottle and disposed of the swab.

A member of the Swiss Guard walked down the hallway. The Pope would follow soon after. The priest cleaned his hands, awaiting the Holy Father's arrival. The innocent bit of cleaning material he held between his fingers hid a tiny vial of $C_5H_4NC_4H_7NCH_3$—nicotine.

There was no more waiting: His eyes caught sight of the Pope as he turned the corner some forty meters distant. The elderly Holy Father walked briskly toward him. He was speaking animatedly with members of his retinue.

Quickly the priest's hands brought the cloth to his mouth as if to wipe it clean. The unseen vial was pressed onto his plastic-coated lips. An infinitesimal drop of poison remained there. Safety was assured as long as his skin remained shielded from contact with the tiny fleck, glistening like a jewel.

The Pope drew near. His mellifluous voice could be heard above the hushed, deferring tones of the others. A few yards away, under the pretense of working, the Professional observed surreptitiously, eyes like those of a snake coiled to strike. Suddenly the Pope halted, his hand reaching for the wall. He leaned dizzily, head bowed, then coughed and cleared his throat loudly.

He took a deep breath and exhaled, a flush returning to his countenance, which had paled momentarily. Finally, to the sudden buzz of hushed voices, he began to walk forward once more.

The priest in workman's clothing stepped out into the Holy Father's path and knelt. He lifted his hand as if to ask for the Pope's ring, to kiss it. A minute droplet of death danced on his lip.

The Pope was no more than a step from him. He stopped, smiling as the color returned to his face, pale from his coughing spasm of just a minute before. Pope John held his hand out toward the young priest before him. The Professional began to bend toward the Holy Father's ring. Then it happened. The Pope's eyes widened; he stepped back. He drew stiffly erect, tense, and parted his lips as if to speak. In that fleeting second a strange look passed the Pope's countenance. The Professional knelt, heart pounding, tense with fear, the tiny glistening droplet still waiting to find its murderous mark. His eyes stared into the Holy Father's; in them the kneeling agent saw a flickering light of—was it—comprehension?

The light in Pope John's eyes faded to question, to confusion. His mouth widened as if to cry out. Only a strangled sound escaped his lips as his hands leaped up to clutch at his chest in obvious pain. He staggered to one side. Everyone was frozen in place. The Pope's fingers tore at his high white collar; the religious beads that surrounded his neck broke and fell clattering to the floor.

The Pope slowly spun about, his back pressed against the wall. Horrified aides rushed forward to catch him as he slumped, gasping for breath.

"Your Holiness. . . . " they shouted. "Quick, get a doctor," one called out. "He's having a heart attack!"

They laid him on the floor. His eyes rolled upward. His breathing became rapid, intermittent. A Vatican police officer dashed forward and fell to his knees. He closed the Pope's nostrils with one hand, then began rhythmically blowing air into the stricken leader's mouth.

For several moments, agape with amazement, the bogus Father Kottmeyer did not rise. His face tightened with creases of strain. Finally, as other officers began racing down the corridor from both directions, he slowly stood and stepped back. Unnoticed, he withdrew a chemically prepared cloth from his pocket and wiped his lips clean of the nicotine. He turned away from the crowd, bowed in a posture of grief, and using this subterfuge, took the opportunity to reach discreetly up to his lips. His fingernail caught an edge of the plastic and he pulled off the coating. It fell free and with it any possible remains of the poison. In another moment he was being pushed away by a member of the security force. A medical team ran toward the crowd.

"Let them through!" shouted someone in authority. "Everyone back. Let them do their work. Give the Holy Father some air." The medical aides worked frantically, administering injections of adrenaline, pounding vigorously on his chest, keeping up the artificial respiration. Only minutes later a doctor arrived and went immediately to work. The veins on his neck protruded in dark purple as he labored over the body. Finally he rose, slowly, and with a demeanor of intense seriousness pronounced the Pope dead in a voice that trailed off. The crowd stood back; everyone was silent. Prayers began as everyone present crossed himself.

Father Kottmeyer quickly gathered his tools and materials. It was time for him to leave. He began to walk away when a voice called to him, "Father . . . Father . . . you, in the workman's clothes."

He turned. A policeman was standing behind him. His hands tensed. "Yes?" the priest questioned.

The policeman's hand reached out. In it was a small cloth. "Father, you forgot this."

Father Kottmeyer took the bit of cloth. "Sorry, I . . . please . . ."

"I understand. It must have been a terrible shock."

"Yes . . . it all happened so quickly." This time the priest made the sign of the cross. The policeman followed suit. In another moment the priest disappeared down the hallway. He walked slowly, carefully dodging the increasing flow of panic-stricken officials summoned to administer to the deceased. "Is this God's will?" one cried allowed as he passed, searching the heavens for solace.

"Maybe, yes," the Professional muttered quietly.

It was 4:00 P.M. when Nadine Romanoff's telephone rang. It was the private intra-European line. "Hello?" she said coldly. "This is Chairman Shaposhnikov's secretary speaking."

"Nadine, this is Sergei Vlostoff. I'd like to be put through to the chairman. It's a matter of the utmost urgency."

"Hold on, Captain. I'll ring through to him." She put the call on hold and turned to the intercom. "Chairman Shaposhnikov, Captain Vlostoff is on the secure line. He requests to speak to you. Should I put him through?"

Maksim Shaposhnikov's last few days had not gone well. Pressure from Dmitri Gvozdetskii increased as each day passed without contact from the hired Professional. Everything in Rome had slipped into limbo. Until this moment there had been nothing but waiting, and ever-increasing tension as time crept forward. They did not yet know how far the Professional had progressed. Subtle questions were suddenly being asked; questions without apparent answers. Next week the Central Committee would be in session, ostensibly for discussion of the next Five-Year Plan. However, if no word was forthcoming from Rome, Shaposhnikov understood that quite possibly the conversation would turn to the plan. His career and quite possibly his life were in jeopardy. His hand slowly pressed the intercom lever.

"Nadine, put the captain through." He now reached for the desk phone and brought it to his ear. There were clicks as the electronic hold was released, then as his secretary replaced the receiver in its cradle in the outer office. The signal light on the dial blinked off, ensuring that no one was listening in. He spoke slowly. "Sergei, is it you?"

"Yes, Chairman. It is I. I have called to be the first to offer my congratulations to you."

"Congratulations? For what?"

"Comrade Chairman. Haven't you heard? The Pope . . . he's dead. You said I should inform you of that fact if indeed it should occur."

The Chairman bolted upright almost carrying the receiver off the desk. "Dead? How . . . dead? When did it happen . . . who was present?" A barrage of questions followed without pause as the captain at the other end struggled to respond. Finally the chairman halted sufficiently for the captain to catch his breath.

"Comrade Chairman. The Pope had a heart attack at noon, Rome time, as he was returning to his apartment for lunch."

"Heart attack? Are you certain of this, Vlostoff?"

"Unquestionably, Comrade Chairman. It is now coming over

Vatican radio. Our people within the Vatican confirm it."

"Thank you, Vlostoff." The chairman sat down and began scribbling some notes. "Please, if any other news breaks in this area that warrants reporting, call immediately." He hung up the receiver. The chairman's hands came up to his lips. He was thinking. In five minutes he called for his secretary.

Nadine Romanoff was thirty years old, blonde and strong. She had been assigned to the chairman directly after putting in three years in the Soviet Army, where she had been a language specialist. Nadine worked first as a translator of both English and French. After four years in that assignment, she was promoted to assistant appointment secretary to Shaposhnikov. The young woman quickly advanced to chief appointment secretary and in another year was made personal secretary to the chairman. Unknown to Shaposhnikov, Nadine Romanoff was in fact an internal agent of the KGB, and reported directly to director of security of the Central Committee and chief of secret police, Dmitri Gvozdetskii. At the very moment that the chairman had buzzed for her, she had been speaking to Gvozdetskii.

"Yes, Chief. Captain Vlostoff just got off the line to him. I'm not certain where he was calling from but the conversation lasted for nearly fifteen minutes. I will keep you informed of anything of value . . . as always." A second ring on the intercom brought a quick end to her conversation.

Nadine quickly pushed her chair aside and walked into the chairman's office. The heavy-set Shaposhnikov met her at the door, handing her a slip of paper. "Miss Romanoff, deliver this message in person to Marshal Tukhachevski. There will be no reply. Please return at once. If the Marshal is not available, I wish you to return the message to me only. Is that clear?"

"Of course, Comrade Chairman," came the reply in her businesslike manner. The secretary took the slip of folded paper and hurried off through the heavy office doors. Maksim Shaposhnikov smiled. This was just the item to spring on the Central Committee. This will take the wind out of my opponent's burgeoning sails he thought to himself.

The chairman's secretary walked briskly down the narrow corridor that connected the executive offices with those of the armed forces. In the opposite direction the same lane would have taken her to the offices of the dreaded Secret Police. As she walked on, her fingers opened the slip of paper. She glanced down at its message only once, fleetingly, in the portion of the hallway least visible from both cameras at opposite ends. This time, the glimpse was sufficient. It read, simply: "Tukhachevski, our Professional has struck. All proceeds as planned. Maksim."

To her it meant virtually nothing; nothing she could comprehend. But as a private communication between the defense minister and chairman, she would report it to Gvozdetskii with all due haste. The meaning would doubtless be clear to him.

She walked directly to the military officer who stood guard outside the electronic doors of the office of the defense ministry. Comrade Romanoff was immediately recognized.

"I have a message for Marshal Tukhachevski," she said, drawing to a halt.

"For personal delivery?" he asked.

"Of course. Is the marshal in?"

"Yes, Comrade."

"Then please let me through!"

The guard withdrew his electronic entrance card from his breast pocket and inserted it in the computer terminal beside the door. A few seconds later the heavy metal door swung open; Nadine stepped through. Ten feet from the doorway was another guard sitting beside an illuminated box. The woman walked directly to the station, familiar with the routine.

"Comrade Romanoff, do you wish to gain entrance, or to deposit something?"

"I wish to hand deliver a message to Marshal Tukhachevski." Once acknowledged she placed her right hand, palm down, on the face of the box. A bank of light ran under the glass and electronically read her palm- and fingerprints. In seconds the configuration was cross-referenced, the identification was completed, and the doorway behind the seated policeman opened automatically. Without another word she walked through.

A frequent messenger to the inner sanctum of the military's Kremlin Headquarters, she was always annoyed by the constant monitoring, cross-referencing, and rechecking. Perhaps it was necessary, but who could possibly break in? Security was just too strict on the many levels above.

Ahead was the office of defense minister. Outside his offices an equally comprehensive set of security checks were performed before she was permitted to gain entrance. She stood at attention outside the marshal's private office for five minutes before being admitted.

Marshal Tukhachevski looked up and smiled. Even though he was approaching the age of sixty, his face had lost none of its handsome character. He was little less attractive than he had been thirty years ago, the popular space pioneer that every Soviet citizen remembered from the glory days before America regained the lead in space exploration. He quickly rose. Dressed in a short-sleeved shirt, his powerful arm muscles strained against the blue fabric. He sported a powerful chest and a youthful waist. His hair had turned silver and was still full and flowing. The Marshal was the kind of hearty, dashing officer that women fell in love with on first sight.

Nadine Romanoff, however, was not among them. She had her job to do, and that transcended anything else.

"Comrade Romanoff. What a pleasant surprise." He always began their meetings with that ploy. Nadine, as usual, kept a discreet social distance.

"Marshal Tukhachevski, good day. I have a message from Chairman Shaposhnikov. He has instructed me to deliver it to you in person." She handed him the folded piece of paper. The marshal clasped it and left it unread.

"My dear Nadine. Why so formal? Have I not expressed ample interest . . . "

"The chairman wishes me to return promptly. He said there would be no reply."

"In a moment, please." The marshal turned away from her and opened the message. The light in his eyes remained hidden from hers. With composure, he faced her again. "You may leave, Comrade," he pronounced. Apparently the message had had a positive impact on him. "The chairman was correct. There is no need for a reply."

"Good day, Comrade," she said as she let herself out. Returning to the outer office of Chairman Shaposhnikov, she spoke into the intercom. "Comrade Chairman, the message has been delivered as you instructed. There was no reply. Will you be needing me now?"

"No, thank you, Nadine," he said in a distracted tone. "Please see to tomorrow's appointments."

"Yes, sir," she replied as the connection was broken. The chairman had other things on his mind.

Marshal Tukhachevski sat down as soon as he heard the door close behind the chairman's secretary. He reread the message before spinning on his seat and despositing it in the electric shredder at the side of his desk. A soft whirling sound came from the mouth of the instrument as it ground the small piece of paper into pulp. "So the plan is working," he thought, congratulating himself. "I was wise not to take sides. The old fox has seemingly conquered the young wolf once again."

The marshal had played his hand correctly. He had left his options open until it was time to align the military with the winning side. Having no love for the chief of the Secret Police, and privately frightened of his ever-increasing power within the Central Committee, he was quietly pleased with the outcome. If Gvozdetskii ever gained power, even the sole representative of the Armed Forces could be vulnerable. Anything was possible when dealing with that jackal. No, he would be much happier to have the elderly Shaposhnikov triumph; after all, Maksim was a known entity. Only the unknown was feared.

His hand reached for the intercom. "Captain Korbet," he began, "please call a meeting of the division leaders for tomorrow at . . . 10:00 A.M. in my office. Instruct them to be prompt.

"Yes, Comrade Marshal." Korbet was a young and efficient aide. At 10:00 every key member of the defense ministry would be in the marshal's office. The captain would see to it. Then Tukhachevski would inform them of the plan for the first time. He would skillfully lead them as a shepherd would lead his flock through a narrow mountain pathway. By the conclusion of the meeting, the marshal would be able to offer the support of the Soviet Armed Forces to the chairman. It would create an unbreakable bond between the two men, a bond with which even Gvozdetskii would not tamper.

The Armed Forces would always align itself with the most powerful faction. It was, therefore, never in a position to set policy openly, but always in a position to influence it. Now the chairman would owe the marshal a favor, a boon. By such favors, empires were built, or tumbled.

Nadine Romanoff looked about the small office. The clock on the far wall ticked off the moments: 4:50 P.M. In the past quarter hour, the chairman had been in conference with an administrative aide. The second secretary had been called inside the inner office to take notes, leaving the security guard standing stone-faced at the doorway. Reaching to her right, she turned on a small desk radio. The music was brash but discordant and sorrowful, the product of a new breed of Russian composers who, buffeted by the tide of socialist realism, surreptitiously smuggled influences of newer waves from the West into their compositions.

The psychodynamics of the music were of little import. All that concerned Miss Romanoff was that the sound would serve as a shield for the phone call she was placing on a special line hooked directly into her receiver. The line was activated by pressing a hidden switch and dialing the appropriate code.

"Hello, please put me through to the supply central," (code name for Gvozdetskii, should she be overheard). She continued with the voice of authority, "Tell him the office manager is calling." The code enabled the call to go through to the chief of the Secret Police without delay.

The unmistakable file-edged voice of Dmitri Gvozdetskii broke the silence. "Comrade N?"

"Yes, Comrade." She turned down the harsh music and whispered, "I have just delivered a message to Marshal Tukhachevski."

"And?"

"The marshal made no comment but did not appear troubled. It was important: He didn't continue to make a pass at me after reading it."

"Mmmm." He paused. "And?" She so hated his "And?"

"It read, 'Tukhachevski, Our Professional has struck. All proceeds as planned. Maksim.' There was no reply."

There was a silence for a few seconds. Then, "Very good, Comrade. Please keep in touch with us." He broke the connection without awaiting an acknowledgment from her.

She replaced the receiver and turned the radio off. The guard never moved. He was merely a fixture, not a spy. By now he was used to the fact that whenever a secretary wanted to place a sensitive telephone call, she would switch on the ever-present radio on her desk. When the call was over, the radio was switched off. He saw nothing unusual in the arrangement. It was not his job to think, just to guard.

Nadine Romanoff returned to her end-of-day routine. In another half hour she would be relieved of duty. Until then, she would confirm the next day's appointments, as requested.

Dmitri Gvozdetskii replaced the telephone receiver. The message had been clear. The chairman had been informed of the death of the Pope; so had he. But perhaps the Professional had had no part in this. It was entirely possible that the Pope had died from a heart attack, as reported. If that was true, then the chairman had placed his neck in a hangman's noose, having made his play for the support of the Armed Forces. Gvozdetskii, understanding full well the strategy of Tukhachevski, knew the marshal would play along with the apparent winner. Now he too was vulnerable.

For now Gvozdetskii could only wait. Even if the Professional didn't act, and succeed, Dmitri would have lost his momentum, and permitted a relationship to solidify between the chairman and the Armed Forces. If the Professional did succeed, the pair of them could become practically invincible. To prevent this he would have to find a way to turn the latter possibility into a personal victory. Perhaps by claiming credit for it. This could be accomplished by sabotaging the mission, and then rescuing it from the brink of failure, with his own resources. He smiled. Those about him feared this thin-lipped half smile, half sneer. The edges of his narrow lips merely edged upward at the extreme ends. No, he would not relinquish the driver's seat, not yet. His whip would remain poised to strike the pair plunging ahead before him. If they won, he would make sure that they won nothing. Then he would merely replace his whip in the coach's boot to await the next opportunity to tear at their skin. And he knew there would be a next time.

Turning to a communications officer he commanded, icily, "Get me our top man in Rome, and keep me informed on the latest news regarding the real cause of the Pope's demise. And contact Colonel Torchnoi, who is to report to me immediately . . . for special assignment."

But the chief of the Secret Police had other things on his mind at the moment. The documents the Czech inspector must surely have copied were still missing. They had to be found.

The problem had plagued him for the past week. Gvozdetskii was after all a policeman; so was the Czech. Thinking alike, Gvozdetskii would have made copies of everything critical to serve as a kind of insurance policy. Now those documents were of utmost importance. If they fell into the wrong hands it might mean that the Soviet Union would have lost an opportunity to control the keeper of the ring of St. Peter.

As he paced, Gvozdetskii ran his wrinkled handkerchief over the surface of his already polished glasses. It was an obsessively nervous habit, one of few that marred his otherwise undaunted facade. From time to time he would stop, eyes quickly darting about as if to catch anyone who might be watching. No one ever dared. He'd then return to the circular movements with his thin fingers. Time was moving painfully slowly, too slowly to suit him.

The events of the previous month in Prague had slipped out of his control. His agents had not only failed to find the telling documents, but had also allowed their victim to kill herself. That was the trouble with trusting anyone other than oneself, he reflected sourly.

The problem had been turning over again and again in his mind since Mrs. Motykia had died. Now he placed a call to Chief Kulikovo.

"Kulikovo, this is Dmitri. What have you come up with?"

"Nothing new yet, Comrade Director." The voice at the other end of the line seemed apprehensive, its volume wavering with uncertainty. Gvozdetskii was known to be brutal, sometimes even savage in his treatment of failure.

"Kulikovo, there must be something." He paused and stared at the second hand of the clock that hung on the room's sterile beige wall. It seemed to move with agonizing sluggishness. A tiredness in his knees made him slump down into the seat behind him. "You are a fool. There has to be something. She ran, didn't she?"

"Yes, Comrade Director. She ran."

"Why? There is a reason. And since there was nothing on her when you searched, it then stands to reason that the documents were either at her flat . . . " He stood up and shouted into the phone, " . . . or she had already passed them on. There can be no other explanation. That was why she went to the church with these documents, where she would feel they would be safe."

"Yes, of course, Comrade, we have investigated this thoroughly. We have questioned everyone. We cannot apply any physical pressure to the clergy."

"Hear me out! This information was of vital import. The facts have international implications, and the inspector knew it. He was a policeman, just as you are supposed to be. He understood that his mere knowledge of the matter made him a target for elimination.

"Thus, with that knowledge and clear understanding of procedure, would you expect that, judging by her reactions, he had said nothing to his wife? If he had made a copy of the papers, to whom else would he entrust such material?"

"Yes, Comrade Director. Of course you are correct."

Govzdetskii became furious. "Don't you dare patronize me, Kulikovo. You're not some KGB fool. Think!"

"We are trying, Comrade," stumbled Kulikovo. "We know that the only people she would have felt safe in giving those documents to would be members of the Church."

Gvozdetskii broke in. "No, not just a priest. She knew their importance. If it was given to anyone, it would be an important member of the Church."

Suddenly Yury Kulikovo interrupted his boss, "And I can tell you who that was."

"You know?"

"Of course—it must be," answered the KGB chief in Prague. "It had to be Bishop Galen. He was on his monthly visit from West Germany."

"Where is he now? shouted Dmitri, his face visibly spotted with beads of sweat.

"He's long gone."

"Then the documents are out of our control." Gvozdetskii felt his shallow chest tighten. "I'll speak to you later, Yury. Everything we've spoken about will of course remain with you and you only."

"Of course, Comrade Director."

With a slam of the receiver, the conversation was ended. Gvozdetskii made a mental note that Yury would have to meet with an unfortunate accident in the next week. He, too, had become a liability, and thus expendable.

His eyes riveted themselves once again on the hands of the wall clock, but soon lost their focus as he drifted into his thoughts. If he had recovered the documents he would have scored a coup. Now they had passed from his control to that of the Church, a matter of no small consequence. Of course if the plot was exposed, the government would deny everything, labeling the information a capitalistic deceit. Yet the inference could be enough to shake things at the top. He would have to be sure his position was sturdy when it shook.

He stood and walked to the doorway, his face showing a trace of a smile. The doors parted and he walked swiftly down the corridor to the elevator. The cubicles lining the corridor remained silent until the open doors closed behind him. As they clicked shut, the clerical and police workers along the corridor could feel the tension lift. For a short while, until the director returned, they would be able to converse.

A tired Lorenzo Barzini was midway through his drive back to Rome when he heard the report of the Pope's death. Now he sat sullenly in the jam-up, contemplating. The Holy Father was dead, after such a short reign. Why? It was an unanswerable question that rattled about his head along with his more recent queries concerning the brutal murders he was tracing. Quickly his mind returned to what had ensued this day. The Ostia bodies were obviously connected to the jaw fragment case. Clearly, whoever had engineered the double killing was no amateur.

News of Pope John's death had flashed over the airwaves of Europe within minutes of the Vatican's announcement. Almost immediately Bishop Galen was informed. He froze in his chair, his hand instinctively reaching for the cross hanging about his neck. It was as if God had chosen him to be an actor in some sinister movie.

"Are you all right, Carl?" questioned the monsignor who acted as his full-time aide. "Can I get you anything?"

Bishop Galen looked up. His eyes were blank. "No . . . no. Please, just leave me alone. Please."

"Surely. I understand." The monsignor backed away silently.

The hours passed. Night slowly crept upon Berlin, finding Bishop Galen still seated in his office. His mind turned over the information contained in the shocking series of documents that had been given him in Prague.

He had understood at the time that he might have to inform the Vatican authorities of their existence. But now the day had exploded upon him so quickly. It wasn't up to him to question why. He was in a quandary, a paradox. Attempting to bring the comfort of God's word into a nation controlled by beasts, and now he would be asked to jeopardize the Church's work by denouncing its leader in another communist country.

He would journey to Rome for the interment of Pope John. Once there it would be a matter for Vatican security or the College of Cardinals. Whatever the method, Cardinal Michalovce's future would be out of his hands. The sooner it was over, the better he would feel.

Bishop Galen rose, his legs nearly locked from minimal circulation over the past five hours of contemplation. He walked slowly to the open windows and took a deep breath. The air was cool and dry—he imagined from the new vigor it gave him that it must be the air of freedom.

The bishop's palms felt clammy. He had spent his life in open devotion to his Maker, and never engaged in any clandestine practice. His new espionage-like role fit him as poorly as a nun's habit. In another few days it would all be over, he hoped. When he felt his hunger returning to him, instead of this gnawing in his gut, it would be a good feeling.

The official announcement of the Pope's death hadn't yet been made, but already it was buzzing everywhere. The Vatican bookstore had remained open as the multitude flocked to purchase mementoes of John's too-brief reign. By 5:15 the store had nearly been bought out.

A tall handsome priest watched the busy entrance from the courtyard. As far as anyone was concerned he was reading a small Bible. As he fanned through the pages his eyes glanced over the faces of those waiting in line to gain entrance before closing. The courier could be anyone among them. The package needn't be big, he thought. Just large enough to house the necessary papers, ink, and electronics. In all the entire burden would weigh no more than two or three kilos; it might be as large as two loaves of bread.

The priest looked at the watch on his wrist. It was 5:17. Time was running out. If the material was to be delivered on time, it would have to reach the appointed spot eight minutes from now. It was time for him to become an unobtrusive fixture within the bookstore. He wanted to observe the person who made the drop.

The priest tucked his Bible under his arm, picked up a handled wooden box, lowered his head, and began to walk toward the entrance. Halfway down the line was a man in a loose-fitting blue suit. From its cut, the priest surmised it to be foreign. The man stared straight ahead at the neck of the person directly in front of him. He carried a briefcase of slightly wider girth than normal, his fist clenching it tightly. The small pulsing muscles on his hand revealed his identity to the sharp-eyed Professional. Clearly this man, with carefully restrained agitation, carried something important.

The priest mounted the two steps that led to the shop's illuminated interior, without protest from anyone in line. The faithful were accustomed to priests' walking to the heads of lines, particularly within the Vatican.

The inside of the shop was bathed in artificial light, incandescent bulbs highlighting a series of framed photographs of the last six prelates, on sale for the princely sum of 1,000,000 lire. Outside the city-state, at any street merchant's stand, copies of these same "official portraits" were available for half the price. But for those who had come to Rome, to St. Peter's, only something purchased in the Vatican could be considered truly blessed.

The priest began to browse through the shop, always taking a position from which he could simultaneously observe both the philatelic exhibit and the entrance. Once again he checked his watch. It was 5:24—still no package under the case.

His eyes left the watch's face. The foreign-looking man he had spied waiting outside had now finally entered. Only his stiffness revealed his carefully restrained nervousness. He slowly looked about, first at the pictures on the wall, then at a series of statues that lined the high row of shelves behind the glass counter. The Professional turned to examine an engraved chalice, but his attention was focused in the mirrored plating of the exhibit. He watched as the man pressed calmly to the center of the group of customers who were pushing to pay for whatever they could lay their hands on. Shielded by the crowd, the courier stepped toward the exhibit of Vatican City stamps. He placed his bulky attaché case before him and withdrew his wallet from his pocket. As he withdrew his money for the sales clerk, only the Professional noticed the man's knee bend slightly forward, depressing a panel on the case.

The time was now 5:25. At that moment an announcement came over the loudspeaker. "The shop will close in five minutes." It was repeated in French, Spanish, and English. The press of the crowd increased. Already the outer doors were being swung shut by two burly guards.

Father Kottmeyer moved toward the glass case. His eyes played over the remaining customers' faces. None of them seemed interested in the movements of the priest. The tall churchman stopped at a display of books and began leafing through one.

He was now directly over the package. As he fanned through the books, the shop was being cleared of much of its throng. From across the room a voice called out, "Father, Father, we're about to close."

He looked in the direction of the voice. A pretty young Italian clerk smiled. "Father . . . "

He appeared startled, letting the wooden box he carried drop directly over the package. A faint click was lost in the vastness of the room as the box settled to the floor. In a moment he gathered up the wooden container, heavier than before, and walked toward the smiling clerk.

"Father, you'll have to leave," she said. "I'm sorry, but we're closed."

Reaching inside his breast pocket, he removed his Vatican identification card. "Just another minute," he said.

She immediately recognized the official seal. "Oh, I'm sorry. Of course." She waved away one of the guards who was walking toward the pair. "It's all right, Victor. He's an official of the Library." The guard came to attention and saluted. The priest acknowledged the salute with a nod of his head. He was playing for time. If he could wait inside the shop for another five minutes, the guards outside would have emptied everyone from the courtyard. No one would be able to identify the person who had retrieved the precious package.

A uniformed officer saluted as the priest walked through the door held open for him. Stepping out onto the small brick platform, the Professional quickly looked about. The courtyard was deserted as he had hoped it would be. He walked directly across the small square to a barred doorway. There was a brass striker in the center of the heavy wooden door and he used it to create three sharp raps. The sound echoed in the space behind the door.

In a few seconds a face-high square opened. The priest held up his identity card for examination. The wooden square slammed shut. From behind the door came sounds of movement; the latch was released and in another moment the door swung open, allowing him to pass through. It was one of the many privileges of being a member of the staff—the use of any and all doorways opening onto the library.

In ten minutes Father Kottmeyer was busily unwrapping the package. Inside a rigid styrofoam shell was everything he needed; silicone base ink, specially prepared packets of cards, a microtransmitter, and an ultra-high-frequency oscillator. He would hide the equipment in his workman's chest. Soon, at the right moment, he would climb the steps to the altar of the Sistine Chapel and implement the final stage of the scheme—the rigging of the cardinals' Conclave ballots. Everything was proceeding as planned. Now he could rest.

A lone nun waited outside the Vatican bookstore until asked to vacate her spot by an apologetic uniformed guard. "Sister, we have to close now. You'll have to leave."

The nun smiled and turned. At the closing gate she glanced back into the courtyard. It was vacant. She hurried off across the piazza, entering the first curio shop that displayed the TELEPHONE AVAILABLE sign. In moments she had dialed the number of the Russian Embassy in Rome.

"Hello. Embassy of the Soviet Socialist Republics. Can I be of service?"

In flawless Russian the nun began, "Security. Priority Four. I want to speak to Comrade Jvari!" The only reply was the telltale electronic sound of the interoffice switching of telephone equipment.

A full minute passed. The sister's eyes were intent on the movements of people near the booth, ensuring that no one paid undue attention to her. Her heart beat rapidly. The walk from her position outside the bookstore had been swift. Beads of sweat ran down her chest and onto her breasts beneath the layers of black cloth. The agent would be happy when this assignment was completed.

Suddenly the line cleared and a familiar voice spoke. "Sister, is that you? Acknowledge."

"Yes, this is Sister Six. The dawn holds a thousand faces, yet I was unable to pick out the one of our Lord."

"Any other leads?"

"None. The delivery of the Bibles was as planned. No incident, no discovery. I can only guess that receipt has been accomplished. There is no reason to believe otherwise. Any further instructions?"

There was a momentary silence. Then, "No, Sister Six. You have done as instructed. Pray everything goes as planned. We will be in touch."

The phone went dead in her hand, the voice replaced by a steady hum. As she departed she spied a vendor selling a particularly beautiful photograph of Pope John and picked it up. It was 2,500 lire, half the Vatican bookstore's price. To her the savings would more than compensate for its lack of official blessing. Taking it to the counter, she placed three 1,000-lire notes on the glass surface. The cashier placed the item in a paper bag, then handed the nun one of the 1,000-lire bills. "Two thousand for you, Sister." Here, there was even a discount for religion.

"Bless you," she replied. The Pope's picture would be a small memento to take with her upon her impending reassignment to Moscow.

Major Jvari of the KGB switched off the small tape recorder on the desk top. In five minutes he had coded the conversation and was running it off onto a high-speed tape.

In the office next to his was housed a ultra-high-frequency, single sideband microwave radio whose antenna was aimed directly at Moscow. With the prepared tape and a signal unit he went into the room. The machine's operator looked up without a word. The major handed him the tape and the young man placed it in the transmitter. Next Jvari handed the operator a small recognition box, which was placed in the proper place on the transmitter board.

The major watched the digital clock on the face of the machine as it counted up toward 6:29, then reached for the transmit button. The operator turned away as he had been taught to; no one but the sender knew the precise second when his compressed message could be sent. That knowledge provided a clear control. 6:28:50 . . . 6:28:51 . . . 6:28:52 . . . 6:28:53. His finger depressed the sending key. In a microsecond the message flashed to KGB headquarters in Moscow.

The operator turned back and removed the two items, handing them to his commander. Ten seconds later a beep confirmed the message had been received and recorded. Jvari turned and dropped the tape into a shallow, acid-filled container, assuring its complete destruction. He walked from the room without a word having been uttered.

The adjusted time on the digital clock at KGB headquarters, Moscow, read 6:28:53. The operator quickly traced the listing of times on the tables before him. 6:28:53 was to be sent directly to the chief of the Secret Police, Gvozdetskii. His fingers reached carefully and hurriedly for the tiny cassette. He packaged it and quickly wrote the code-name for Dmitri Gvozdetskii on the envelope and receipt, then caught the attention of a courier who hurried over.

"Straight to the director. No stops."

The young man saluted and ran off, relieving the operator (much to his appreciation) of any further responsibility.

In five minutes Dmitri Gvozdetskii understood that the Conclave plan was in motion, and that he was, thus far, powerless to control its progress. He chose not to inform Chairman Shaposhnikov that his Professional was still on the job. "No, let the man sweat," he thought. "He'll know soon enough."

He placed the tape of the conversation between the nun and Major Jvari in the top drawer of his austere desk, locking it. The chief then pushed himself away from the desk and stood up. There were other pressing matters that needed his immediate attention.

Chief Inspector Maggiore had left word that Detective Barzini was to stop by his office before he left for the day. It was a meeting neither man would keep. By 1:00 P.M., the chief inspector was involved in security at the Vatican. Lorenzo had a reprieve, at least for the moment. He realized that he would be free to pursue his killer for at least a week or so because of the recent religious tragedy. However, just as soon as the new Pope was chosen, Maggiore would be upon him once again, and he would be looking for results. As of now, there was nothing but theories.

Barzini felt he had reached a dead end. The jaw fragment had lead nowhere. The only other piece of possible evidence was a small plastic ring that a priest had forgotten in a room in Ostia. But what was it? Its significance still eluded him.

He began to walk out of the building. As he reached the first level he stopped in his tracks. "If anyone would know," he reasoned, "it would be Carlo the fence." Carlo Bonano, small-time "purchasing agent," had disposed of anything and everything in his assorted career. Barzini hurried to his car, his fingers toying with the ring sealed in a small plastic pocket. There was something more to this tiny bit of plastic than met the eye; he could feel it.

He reached the battered vehicle and jumped inside. The engine burst into life. He threw the car into gear and it lurched off in a cloud of oily smoke. At the first intersection he made a quick right from the center lane, oblivious to the gestures and curses of the drivers he had cut off.

Fifteen minutes later the Fiat pulled to a halt in front of an out-of-the-way tailor shop. The detective hopped out and looked about the seemingly deserted street. He tugged on his collar, which seemed too tight around his overripe neck.

Walking directly to the closed shop door, he opened it without knocking. A tiny bell rang somewhere in the rear of the small establishment. He walked to the counter and leaned warily against its dusty surface. From behind the dingy curtain that separated the shop from whatever lay in the back, footsteps moved toward the opening.

His eyes traveled to the source of the steps. A meaty hand grasped the curtain and drew it aside. There framed in the dim light of the rear room was Carlo, all 250 pounds of him. The man was awesome; his hands were the size of meat cleavers, his chest as broad as a barrel, and, as he was fond of proclaiming, there wasn't an ounce of fat on him. A broad smile of recognition broke over his suspicious countenance and his eyes began to twinkle as soon as he recognized the detective. Barzini had used Carlo from time to time to cull information about the local toughs. Nothing really important, just enough to keep the contact viable in the eyes of his superiors. Bonano was repaying Barzini for a favor from a few years back—the detective had helped arrest a young *capo* who had dishonored his daughter.

"Hello, Barzini," shouted the muscular Bonano, his features alive in a scarred and creviced face which was highlighted by a bushy, upturned mustache.

"Carlo, how are things treating you?" Bonano clasped his hand a little too firmly and smacked him on the shoulder.

"No complaints." The man walked around the counter. Lorenzo never ceased to be amazed at the fence's physique. He had the playfulness of an overgrown puppy, yet with arms like a blacksmith's, he could easily break a man in two. "Eh. Tailoring's slow these days." The mustached smile broadened.

"Tailoring? Are you kidding? You couldn't sew a button on your underwear if your dick was hanging out." Barzini always kidded Carlo—they both knew the truth about his occupation. But each served a purpose to the other; Barzini got what he needed from Carlo, and in turn the fence was protected by the detective. In Italy, everything has its place.

"By the way, Lorenzo. I never, ah, got to thank you for giving that nice kid a break, eh? You know, he didn't know the watches weren't kosher."

"Yeah, yeah," said Barzini. "When the hell are you going to stop using those kids as runners? I mean, they're getting younger and younger. Next time you'll have to get a cop to help them cross the street." Even Barzini was enjoying himself. For a moment he'd almost forgotten the reason for this visit.

"Look, Carlo, you get a lot of stuff passing through this . . . tailor shop." He reached into his pocket and removed the small plastic ring. "Ever come across something like this?"

Barzini dropped the plastic bag with its black object into the oversized palm. Carlo took a few steps into the front doorway and held it up to the sunlight. After a long minute he turned back to the detective and held out the ring. Barzini took it from him gingerly. "Well?"

"Perhaps, ah . . . probably I could find something like it."

"I don't need the object itself, I just need to know what it is," said Barzini.

"What it is, ah!" He shrugged his massive shoulders. "Some sort of ring. Come off, ah, like a telescope, camera, binoculars. A retainer ring. Yeah, maybe even a Japanese clock. Eh. Probably a camera.

"Why Japanese?" Barzini questioned.

"Why? Size. 45mm. Pretty common on some cheap Jap stuff. Yeah, a camera."

"Or it could be a telescope or binoculars."

"Could be."

A camera seemed plausible. The apartment was directly opposite the burned-out flat. Maybe the priest was really a private investigator hired by some husband or wife to gain evidence against the other spouse for a divorce or the like? Photographs would make good evidence in court. Or maybe it was blackmail.

But there were too many flaws in that reasoning. This case was no mere marital squabble; the details clearly pointed toward a more complex scheme. And, why would an investigator hypothetically in disguise, utilize a cheap dime-store camera? Wouldn't he have better equipment than that?

Well, then; binoculars, cheap ones: possible. A cheap pair of glasses would be sufficient for spying across the thirty meters between the two buildings. Cheap binoculars? Available, disposable, attract no unusual notice. It wouldn't be too difficult to pick up a pair at any outdoor market; even Ostia must have one.

Leaving the fence after thanking him, Barzini cruised to the nearest empty phone booth and dialed the Ostia police to find out where one might purchase a cheap pair of binoculars or a camera. After a dozen or so double rings, an officer answered. He was able to name a few likely retail shops, but made Barzini's task simple with his final suggestion.

"Actually," he said, "you'd be better off at the beach market. It's mostly industrial stuff, tools, paints, nails. You know, anything they can steal from work finds its way there."

"And when is it open?" questioned Barzini.

"Almost any time after working hours."

"Thanks. You've been a big help."

"Sure, any time for our friends in Rome."

Barzini reasoned the killer had not brought the equipment, whatever it was, with him. If he had, then the quality of the item would have been superior. Since the ring came from an inexpensive piece of hardware, it had probably been purchased on the spot and then been disposed of immediately after its need had been fulfilled.

He drove toward Ostia lost in speculative thought, the speedometer reading over 90 kilometers an hour, well above the posted limit for that stretch of roadway.

He was not far into his mental cogitations when the sound of a siren rose from somewhere behind him. His eyes glanced to the rearview mirror and spied a white police motorcycle quickly overtaking him, its revolving blue light barely visible in the afternoon glare.

His foot eased off the accelerator; the laboring engine slowed. The motorcycle officer drew alongside and motioned him to the dirt shoulder, the two vehicles pulling off onto the dry red dust. Barzini reached into his pocket for his identity card as the officer stepped off his cycle. He held it up to the open side window just as the policeman approached, summons in hand.

"Okay," began the sweating policeman, "do you know the . . . " It was then that he caught sight of the detective's card. He came to attention and gave a half salute. "Sorry."

Barzini cut him off. "Don't worry. It was my fault. I was thinking about something else and . . . " His hand opened in a familiar gesture.

"Where are you headed?" asked the officer.

"To Ostia. Say, do you know anything about the open air markets there?"

"Sure. Me and the kids go there for our sports equipment. Good prices, and you can always bargain!"

"Every day?"

"Only the beach is open every night. The other one is . . . "

Barzini interrupted. "I'm only interested in where you might buy a cheap camera."

"Okay, the beachfront, like I said. It should be beginning at about five-thirty or six. You got a few hours? Need something for a big case or something?"

The detective looked up, surprised. "Yes, in fact. How did you know?"

At that moment a car full of youngsters sped around the bend, cutting into the oncoming lane. When the officer spotted it he swiftly saluted, ran back to his motorcycle and jumped on. He kicked over the engine and sped off. A pattern of dislodged pebbles showered Lorenzo's already battered car.

Barzini's hand grasped the ignition key and started the engine. The car had just begun to roll forward when the front end suddenly dropped. He gunned the engine and the rear wheels spun, but the car didn't move. Finally he threw it into second gear and the light Fiat lurched forward. A familiar thumping sound greeted the engine's efforts. Lorenzo recognized it immediately: His car had a flat.

The detective got out and walked to the hood, passing the crumpled tire. It was as dead as a tire could be, useless.

His hands found the hood release and pulled the lid. Trapped heat was all that greeted him. In the place where a spare tire should be, there was none. He was stranded.

Barzini turned in disgust and walked to the side of the road, putting his thumb out in the internationally understood request for a ride. After ten minutes of increasing agitation, he was still standing there; no one had bothered to stop. It was another fifteen minutes before a farmer gave him a ride into Ostia. By chance, the farmer was headed to the markets with a load of melons, intending to arrive there just as the workday was coming to a close.

The beach spread out in a bed of black powder that ran along the roadway past a semi-circular plaza of gray concrete. The intersection of Via di Mar and the ocean was the westernmost portion of Mussolini's ambitious, if unsuccessful, effort to modernize Italian roads and rail lines. While Mussolini garnered, among his many epitaphs, the myth that he "got the trains to run on time," his highways invariably ended at the sea. Via di Mar was no exception. The fascist was killed in 1945 on the fifth anniversary of the completion of this very plaza.

Barzini's tie had long before been deposited in his jacket pocket, his collar opened wide at the neck. He looked anything but an Italian detective. A grimy shirt evidenced its second day's wearing. In a way, his informal appearance acted to his advantage, putting people more at ease. He had none of the harshness usually associated with the Italian police.

The detective waded into the growing throng of hawkers and sightseers. In late summer both natives and tourists flocked to Ostia as a retreat from the hot Roman weather. On this Friday the crowd was unusually large, as the temperature in the city was pushing record-breaking highs for the season; in its wake the city dwellers had left the streets to the American tourists.

At the periphery of the plaza was a stand of open-backed trucks loaded with fresh fruits and vegetables. Housewives busily stuffed produce into their shopping bags and hurried back toward home, intent upon starting the preparation of their evening meal. Tourists likewise were busy with their purchases—lesser quantities of fruits to be deposited in hotel rooms and consumed the following day at the beach.

Lorenzo passed them by. His eyes played along the rows of fabric peddlers, then to the stone wall that was the outermost limit of the impromptu market. Along the parapet were hundreds of vendors, each with his own tiny "shop"—a towel or bit of cloth spread across the width of the waist-high wall. As he walked along his eyes kept a lookout for signs of a camera or lens salesman. So far there was none.

From time to time vendors took a step toward him with a piece of rumpled merchandise. "Looking for a toaster?" He declined.

His eyes fastened momentarily on a precision set of calipers, obviously of high quality: "5,000 lire." Barzini waved his hand in disinterest. "4,900 lire." The chubby vendor followed him down the aisle.

Barzini turned. "Hey, no thanks, okay?" he said with some irritation.

"Yeah?" the vendor responded indignantly. "Who the hell do you think you are?"

"A cop!" Barzini hissed.

"A cop your ass!" the man guffawed, belly quivering under

his sleeveless T-shirt. "My mother is more of a cop than you are."

"She probably is," Barzini replied, to the amusement of those witnessing the conversation, and continued down the long row. As he left, the vendor placed his thumb on the roof of his mouth and pulled it out in the detective's direction.

A few minutes later, Barzini came upon a vendor who had five cameras lined up for sale along with other sundry items. The detective's eyes played over the wares—American Instamatics. Their fixed lenses were too small to match the ring he now withdrew from his jacket. He held out the plastic object to the teenage merchant. "Do you know where I could find someone who might be selling a camera with a lens this size?"

The slick-haired young man took the ring and inspected it gingerly. "45mm or so. Maybe one of the other guys. Could be an old Minolta." He returned the retainer ring to Lorenzo. "But it's a cheap one. Why not replace it with one of these?" The man picked up the nearest camera and waved it at Barzini, who politely declined.

In an hour he had covered only half the wall, with no luck. He had attempted to fit the ring onto a dozen different lenses and holders, finding nothing even remotely similar. He was beginning to feel that he was searching for a shy Cinderella with this odd glass slipper.

Just before he reached the very center of the plaza, he came upon a display of three Japanese 35mm cameras. The vendor appeared as unkempt as the tired detective.

Once again Barzini displayed the plastic ring. "Would this fit onto any of the cameras you have here?"

The unshaven man took the object in his hand, turned it over once and frowned. "Not a chance." Barzini reached for the ring. "It isn't from a camera," the man said.

Barzini winced. "Not from a camera?"

"Of course not." The middle-aged man reached into the cardboard box at his feet and took out a pair of binoculars. "It comes from one of these." He offered it to Barzini.

The detective grabbed for the glasses, almost dropping them in his haste.

"Careful!" shouted the vendor. "If you break them it'll cost you. They're not cheap."

Barzini held out his hand for the ring. The merchant dropped it into his palm. The detective then fit the ring snugly onto the outer lens; a perfect match. "You got a lot of these?" he inquired.

"No, that's my last pair." The vendor's eyes gleamed as he broke into a broad, crooked-toothed smile. "It's a beauty, isn't it? Since it's my last one, I'll make you a special deal. Fifty thousand lire."

Barzini hadn't paid him any heed. "How many pair of them did you have?"

"Hey," the man complained, "you want to buy, or talk?"

"Talk," Barzini said as his eyes came up from the binoculars and struck the vendor's. "How long have you been selling them?"

"You from the sales tax commission or something?"

"Something."

"You a cop?"

Barzini held out his identity card. The vendor grudgingly matched the picture with the man. "A cop. Wouldn't you figure. Look, how would I know if they're stolen—some guy gives me a bargain on a dozen a few weeks back, I take it; I don't ask questions. Hey, I gotta make a living too, right?"

"You have more of them?" Barzini prodded.

"Yeah, I got plenty of them. Between you and me, they're dogs; don't sell much. I don't think anyone else on the strip even bothers with them. Say, am I in trouble, or anything?"

Barzini reassured him, "Listen, I don't care where the hell they came from, I just need to know who bought them."

"You got a killer or something?"

Barzini didn't care to field that question. "Just answer my questions. That way you'll be rid of me."

"Okay," said the vendor, shrugging. Already eyes were turning in his direction and he was beginning to feel uncomfortable. It wasn't healthy for a dealer in questionable goods to be seen talking to a policeman. "What do you want to know?" he mumbled.

Barzini placed his hand on the man's shoulders and drew him aside confidentially, both of them facing the sea. "I'm looking for someone—a man or a woman—who might have bought these same glasses in the past week or so. Can you remember any of the people who bought binoculars? Anything at all."

The vendor thought for a while, then nodded. "Well, nothing special. Let's see . . . I only sold four pair. One was to a couple of Americans, kids on holiday—bargained me down to 30,000 lire. Then there was Anthony who wanted a pair for his kid. And a week ago I sold a pair to a priest. There was one more . . . "

Barzini's hand closed on the man's shoulder. "A priest?" he questioned.

"Yeah, a priest. I think the last pair was sold to . . . "

"Just tell me about the priest," Barzini broke in. "Do you know him?"

"No. He isn't from Ostia. In fact, I think he was from somewhere in northern Europe, like Germany maybe. His Italian was pretty good, but you knew it was school-learned."

"What did he look like?"

The puzzled vendor asked, "What's so important about a priest?"

"Just tell me what he looked like," the detective ordered.

The man gazed at the water, trying to recall the image. "I really can't tell you too much about him, except that he wasn't very old; like his mid-thirties. And he was built good. Could've been an athlete: big, tall." The man gestured broadly with his arms.

After a moment he continued. "I don't remember his face much, he might've worn glasses."

"What color was his hair?"

"Light. Not *quite* blond or gray, just light."

"Anything else?"

"Nope, I don't think so. He was all business. Knew exactly what he wanted and what price."

"Did he say where he was staying?"

"No, nothing."

Barzini had nearly struck out. "Could you give a police artist a couple of hours to come up with a likeness of the man?"

"I don't think I could."

"Listen, we're working on something and I need your help. I can get it one of two ways."

The vendor looked distressed. "Hey, look, I don't want any trouble." He glanced around. By this time everyone knew he was speaking to a cop. "You're going to ruin me. I told you whatever

I know, now give me a break, eh? So I sold a pair of binoculars to some priest . . . I didn't break no laws."

"Hey, Bud," the detective interrupted in a stern voice. "If I wanted to discuss breaking laws, I'd have plenty to say, *capisce?* But right now I'm talking 'information,' so be a good boy and rack your memory, *okay?* Before I start talking 'summons' or 'confiscate suspicious goods,' got me?"

"*Okay, okay.* What else can I tell you? This guy was no fool; like, he wouldn't take damaged merchandise and he had plenty of money, but he still had to bargain."

"Money?"

"Sure. He kept on chiseling me down and down. And all the while you could see he had money. All you had to do was look at the ring he was wearing. And he was no fool either; he paid me what the glasses were really worth."

"I see." Barzini was trying to digest this new information, to compose an image of who, or what, he was up against. "A ring? Anything special about it?"

"Yeah, I noticed it; big, heavy." He made a gesture with his fingers to signify a bulbous shape. "You know, like a pimp's ring—real deep gold, big diamond stuck in the middle. Expensive, I thought, for a priest."

"A large gold ring with a diamond in it?" repeated the detective.

"Big diamond, stuck all the way in; with, like engravings around it."

"Okay, good. Anything else?"

The vendor rubbed his fingers against the heavy stubble on his chin and shook his head. Lorenzo figured that he'd pumped this guy for all he was worth. There was a point to stop pressing, he knew, before people started inventing answers just to get rid of you. "Okay, Bud. I'll consider this a favor if I happen to run into you again under different circumstances."

The man nodded and turned away from the policeman, quickly gathering his wares. The evening had ended earlier than he had intended it to. "Look, if it's okay with you, I'm going to get out of here. By now, you've ruined any chance of making a sale anyway."

Barzini didn't answer. Turning his back, he slowly walked away, oblivious to openly hostile glares of surrounding tradesmen.

He adjusted his collar. The evening had begun to close in on him, a growing chill penetrating through the dampness his clothing had absorbed during the day.

The detective walked the five streets to the train station. He had decided not to return to his car. It was more important to get back to Rome than to recover the battered vehicle. He'd report its breakdown to the Vehicle Control Section, who would send out a tow truck . . . if vandals hadn't stripped or burned it in the interim.

Barzini was only a street away from the station when the train whistle blew. His pace immediately picked up, first into a trot and finally into a flat-out run. He reached the platform just in time to watch the train's lights recede down the tracks into the darkness. It was only then that he felt the first pangs of hunger jab at his stomach. It had been nearly twenty-four hours since he'd eaten. Lorenzo slumped onto a damp concrete bench, its chill sending a shiver through him. He took the next few minutes to catch his breath and to compose himself and his thoughts.

A priest had rented the flat opposite the site of a murder; a murder performed with professional expertise, with the same grisly earmark of the Roman jaw-fragment dismemberment. He had purchased binoculars to spy on the couple. Clearly, this priest was deeply involved. He had reported nothing to the police, and he had vanished the moment the crime was committed. "Could a priest really be mixed up in a case like this?" wondered Lorenzo, deeply disturbed at the sacrilegious implications. "How can it be?"

As if in response to his questions, the hollow sound of footsteps approached. An old padre was tottering toward him, wearing an old hassock and using a cane. When he reached the far end of the bench, the priest sat down, clasping the cane with both hands in front of him. Barzini studied the man, who appeared to be at least eighty-five. His face was weathered and wrinkled. Barzini's eyes drifted to the man's hands. They were as brown, worn, and gnarled as the cane that supported them.

And then it occurred to him: Priests don't wear rings! This was the key—the suspect wasn't a priest after all, he realized. Some bastard is using the garb of a priest to do his bloody work. Lorenzo was suddenly burning with righteous anger and indignation.

The killer had gone to a great deal of trouble to disguise his work; something crucial had to be at stake. This puzzle was too damn complicated to be simply a killer's attempt to throw off the police. Each item, each bit of evidence convinced the detective that there was some master planner at work. The total dismemberment of the body in Rome had alerted him to the experienced hand. The jaw fragment with its "Eastern bloc" fillings created international associations, as did this bogus priest's supposed accent. Now the discovery of the unidentifiable bodies in Ostia linked the two cases inextricably.

It was a puzzle that had as yet no answer. There were forces involved that the Roman cop had not begun to fathom. He was adrift in a pool of enigma.

A driving rain began to pelt the concrete platform, biting coldly through his already damp clothing. Lorenzo's eyes searched for shelter from the tiny yet stinging blows. The platform provided none.

He glanced toward the priest at his left, who sat unaffected as if free from mortal needs and endowed with everlasting serenity.

Lorenzo drew his collar up against his neck, for what it was worth. The next train wouldn't arrive for another ten minutes.

13

Of the 264 Prelates since Linus I succeeded St. Peter in A.D. 67, forty-five did not survive the first year of their tenancy. Pope John XXV had been the forty-sixth to succumb shortly after donning the triple-crowned tiara that symbolized the power of the Papacy. Of the previous forty-five, six were murdered, one died of wounds suffered during his participation in the Guelph-Ghibelline civil wars, and one, John XXI, expired in 1277 when a Vatican ceiling chose an inopportune moment to collapse.

As usually occurs upon the death of a Pope, all official business ceased during the interregnum. As soon as the official announcement had been made, three cardinals oversaw the ceremonial breaking of the Pope's ring. This emblem of papal authority had to be destroyed to prevent possible forgeries of state documents. It had been minted and presented to Pope John just thirteen days before his death.

An old Roman saying, *Morto un papa, se ne fa un altro*, was immediately followed. Just as soon as the Pope had been laid to his eternal rest, the College of Cardinals would convene to elect the 265th successor to the ring of St. Peter.

As the word of John's death spread around the globe, the scarlet-robed members of the College of Cardinals began preparations to assemble in Rome. Some had been interrupted while still in transit, having not yet returned to their homes after the previous election. Daily "congregations"—the earliest meetings of all cardinals present in Rome—were already planned. Ten days after the funeral, on October 1, the Conclave would commence. One hundred twelve eligible cardinals were expected to attend. Already names were popping up as favorites to become the new Pope.

From a window high above the plaza that fronted St. Peter's, the Professional looked down on the gathering multitude. The weather was again hot and muggy. Italian Red Cross wagons were being set up, their operators preparing for the casualties exacted by the sun when it reached its zenith. In the line already that stretched for one and a half miles, talk turned to the major candidates: Corrado Pappalardo, Salvatore Ursi, Giuseppe Bennelli, and the clear favorite, fifty-five-year-old Aloisio Pignedoli. Even at his young age, Pignedoli might emerge with the largest single bloc of votes. However, it was doubtful whether he'd garner the required seventy-five votes on the first few ballots. If his initial showing wasn't strong enough, his chances could easily wane and another candidate might emerge. Observers were betting on a lengthy Conclave.

As for now, the throngs were gathering to pay homage to John. By noon of the second day, the Pontiff's body was lying in state in the frescoed splendor of the Clementine Hall in the Apostolic Palace. His bier, draped in folds of violet silk, was inclined at the foot. He seemed almost to be resting. On his feet were a pair of glove-leather slippers; the brightness of his red robe completed the pastoral composition. In a few minutes members of the Vatican staff, Father Kottmeyer among them, would be allowed to enter in advance of the general public.

The frail Bishop Bartoleme seemed weighed down with the robes of his rank of office. The director of the Vatican's archives and library was certain to be named a cardinal by the next Pope. With the heavily tinted glasses he wore to protect his eyes from the light and the impressive costume that outshone the man, the doddering albino presented an almost sinister appearance as he led the staff to pay their respects. Father Kottmeyer trailed much to the rear amid other members of the staff of the Holy City.

The seven-hundred-year-old doors of the Clementine Hall opened slowly and the line of officials began to inch forward. Fifteen minutes later Father Kottmeyer took his first in a series of steps that led to the body of the Pontiff. The frescoes shined serenely down on Pope John, reminders of his native Florence, home of a thousand frescoes of equal splendor.

Father Kottmeyer watched as Bishop Bartoleme went to his knee to offer a silent prayer for his friend. When he rose there were tears on his cheeks. It was the first overt emotional expression the Professional had seen the aged bishop exhibit.

When his turn came, the assassin outwardly displayed the attributes of his priestly person to perfection. Kneeling, he made the sign of the cross, as his superior had done before him, and seemed to offer a silent prayer.

His eyes played across the Pope's folded hands, the fingers folded around a small black cross and interwoven with rosary beads. The Professional fingered his own personal symbol, the crested golden ring bearing the insignia of his heritage. He had become accustomed to folding his hands in front of him when necessary to shield the ring from detection. But he would not remove it; it was his symbol of self-respect, of honor, of rank, of family pride.

The kneeling father crossed himself again, then stood. He folded his hands in front of his chest and mumbled the holy words he had rehearsed. It would be another fifteen minutes before he was able to return to his cell and begin the important work ahead. All would have to be ready before the Conclave began—the chalice, the electronics, the ballots, the cardinal. He would require access to the most closely guarded areas within the Apostolic Palace and the Sistine Chapel. His cloak of black would have to serve him well.

Cold winds came roaring into the eternal city, bending the dark green cypresses, seeking out and awakening the sleeping detective. The thin damp sheet pulled against his chest offered scant protection against the sudden chill.

A shuttered window slammed against the stone facade of the outside wall; he bolted upright. The turmoil of sleep spilled over into the reality of the day, his mind still groping for the wisp of a dream that had clouded his mind under cover of night. A black figure had taunted him, mocked at his efforts to capture it. Was the figure a man, or an emissary of the devil himself? The image of the proprietor of Hell entering his mind and ensnaring him gave Lorenzo pause. Unconsciously he crossed himself, causing the rumpled sheet to fall away and exposing his sweating frame to the chilled air.

The relentless materialism of the world he lived in had relatively little appeal to Lorenzo. He was born to be a policeman, to enforce the law, such as it was, relentlessly, like Sisyphus repeatedly pushing the boulder to the top of his ancient peak. While others had risen within the profession, Barzini would never advance beyond the top of his personal hill—and, like Sisyphus, he found that even his highest achievements brought only fleeting recognition.

He had never succumbed to the ambient sloth, the bureaucracy of the police department, never bent to its nepotism or its hierarchy. He had risen as far as one could without being tainted by cynicism, without becoming part of the corruption of the higher echelons. But even if he could never reach the pinnacles that others aspired to, he would break this case. It had gotten into his blood, into his very soul, and the thought of being ordered off it was intolerable.

The wind rose, hurling the window against the building's facade once again. Lorenzo stood up and hurried to where it slammed against the outer wall. He reached out, attempting to grasp the wooden frame, just as a final gust caught the swinging shutter and threw it full open, shattering the glass and sprinkling the street below with shards. He caught the swinging frame and finally secured it. The sky was dark.

A chill wind blew into the flat through the broken pane. Barzini hurried into the bathroom, closing the door securely to seal the cold out. But the wind found the small space beneath the door, sending a draft into the shower where Lorenzo had sought shelter under a cascade of steaming water. The coldness prompted him to wash and shave with maximum haste.

In fifteen minutes he had gulped down a small breakfast, rummaged through his flat for clean clothes, and was ready to dash off to check out his latest hunch. The unknown priest or poseur, he figured, had to be placed at the scene where the two children had first discovered the jaw fragment. If he could prove a connection between the Rome scene and the Ostia murder site, then he had more than a simple murder or murderer on his hands. Then the chief wouldn't dare take me off it, he thought. But it was always possible that the chief really saw him as merely a bumbling fool, just as the detective's immediate superior, Paluzzo Antionelli, did. If so, Maggiore would reassign him to some inconsequential investigation and assign one of Antionelli's shining college graduates to what would have been proven a major case. Lorenzo swore to himself he would not allow that to happen, even if it meant withholding information.

At that moment he heard the front door close upstairs. His alluring new neighbor, Theresa Manzillo, was leaving for work. Barzini grabbed his suit jacket and hurried outside without waiting to lock his door, rushing to the stairway in order to catch up with her.

As he turned the corner of the stairwell, he froze; she was walking down toward him, arm in arm with a distinguished-looking man. Theresa was laughing and chatting with him attentively, not noticing Lorenzo until they nearly faced each other. "Oh," she said, nearly jostling the policeman, "Detective . . . Detective Bar . . ."

"Barzini!" he shouted.

She was startled by his tone. "Yes, Barzini." Her companion stepped forward, a square-jawed, crew-cut man of military bearing.

Lorenzo turned his attention to the young man as Theresa introduced them: "Detective Barzini, this is Iori Jvari. He's my fiancé."

"Fiancé?" Lorenzo questioned.

The man held out his hand to the detective. It was seconds before Barzini accepted it. "Er, I see. I'm so pleased to learn of your engagement," Lorenzo responded, a little too gamely.

"Yes, Iori and I have just recently become engaged," she smiled toward him. "He's a military attaché."

"Attaché? . . . At a foreign embassy?"

"Yes, the Russian Embassy. I am so pleased to make your acquaintance," he replied in thickly accented Italian.

"Yes, so am I," Lorenzo lied. The younger man's engagement to Theresa was another blow to his already battered ego. He hesitated a moment, then took a step toward the couple, exhibiting an enormous smile. "Congratulations . . . congratulations to both of you!" He grasped first the man's hand, then Theresa's. "Sorry I can't stay and chat, but I have to get going. I'm in the midst of a very important case."

"Ah, vat kind of detective verk do you do?" questioned the Russian in an accent thicker than borscht.

"Homicide," glowered Barzini as he disappeared down the stairwell with a wave.

In twenty minutes Barzini had checked into his squad room for the day's assignment. Antionelli had assigned both him and Giorgio to undercover crowd control at St. Peter's Square. It was the same assignment they'd pulled the previous month—boring and uneventful, except for keeping an eye out for pickpockets. Last month he'd been relegated to guarding a rarely used side entrance to the Vatican archives. Very few outsiders even knew the entrance existed, and with the generally beefed-up security around the Vatican, only a totally lost tourist or mourner ever stumbled across it. All those allowed to use the entrance had official Vatican identity cards.

Lorenzo and Giorgio walked through the massive, hushed crowd that filled the piazza, thousands upon thousands of persons waiting patiently to form the single line of humanity that would inch past the body as it lay in state.

As a boy Lorenzo had waited overnight in this same square after the death of John XXIII. His father had held him when he fell asleep, and in the morning they had walked together into the great church to view the man whom God, in His infinite wisdom, had taken from the mortal world. The feeling was the same now, as it had been then. There was something about this place that transcended time. There was purpose in his being here.

The two detectives stood to the right of the cathedral where the police had erected a series of barriers. Access to the small courtyard was blocked just beyond the massive wooden gate that would later open to admit but one mourner at a time. Uniformed officers huddled in small groups, talking and smoking. As the two detectives approached, the closest policeman barely looked up. Barzini and D'Annunzio flashed their identity cards and the uniformed officers raised their hands in a disgruntled half salute. The men had been on duty throughout the night and were impatient to be relieved.

Lorenzo looked around for the ranking officer. There didn't seem to be one in the vicinity. He took a couple of timid steps to the closest group of policemen, clearing his throat twice before they turned away from their conversation.

"Any of you know who's in charge here?"

A smile curled across their collective lips. Then a corporal volunteered a bit of sarcasm: "If you can find him, please let us know. He was here . . . ten hours ago."

"You mean he hasn't been back since you guys first went on duty?"

"Nope. He usually gets lost on a 'tough' assignment like this one. You know, he doesn't want to get involved when the bad guys get to robbing and killing." The smile turned into a laugh.

Lorenzo backed off, saying, "Well, my partner and I will be checking inside if he shows up. Just let him know where we are. Okay?"

"Sure. There's nothing in the court. But if you want to check for yourselves. . . . " He shrugged.

A second policeman spoke up. "And if you find our sergeant in there with a nun, send him out." His partners erupted into sustained laughter.

Barzini had already turned to leave when the round of laughter flooded the area. He looked back. The officers returned to their huddle, laughter continuing unabated. It must have been a long night.

He motioned with his head to Giorgio and his fellow detective fell into step beside him. They walked through the police barricade and squeezed through the narrow opening leading to the small courtyard beyond.

The cobblestoned yard was surrounded by gray stone structures, the sunlight barely peeking through an opening between the buildings. It was silent . . . almost as if God were holding His breath, waiting to inspire an event that would bring the ancient yard into the present. The absence of life of any sort made for an emptiness that the two detectives' bodies were unable to fill. They walked through its antiquated austerity like invaders from an unspeakably tumultuous future. Their steps on the smooth stone sounded against the walls, echoing like a dying heartbeat.

Lorenzo and his partner had been here little more than a month before. Nothing was different. The silent, stately courtyard had challenged time for more than four hundred years. Its stones had outlived a score of Popes, wars, hopes, and follies of man. Their humble elegance rang with a simple proclamation: The faith that had inspired all this would surely continue.

The two men studied the various doorways that faced the ancient piazza. Giorgio walked toward the trio of arches, checking the one that led to the Vatican bookstore, then the pair marked MEN . . . WOMEN. All were secure.

Lorenzo took Giorgio's cue and shuffled to the single barred door directly across the yard from the bookstore, set into a heavy archway, secured by three brass hinges. It bore no exterior handle and could only be opened from the inside. He reached out to test if it was locked. As his hand came to rest on the door's edge, the sound of a lock turning startled him. The heavy door swung inward, leaving the detective openmouthed.

His eyes peered into the semi-darkness, trying to interpret the twin shapes framed in the narrow entranceway. Suddenly the first ray of sunlight flooded over the uppermost rim of the building to his right, blinding him for the moment. His hand rose to shield his straining eyes as a voice inside the passage inquired, "Can I help you?"

"Yes . . . I mean, no. I'm a policeman." He held out his identity card. "I . . . my partner and I have been assigned to check this area. Who are you two?"

The two men stepped outside onto the small stone platform. The shorter and elder spoke with slight annoyance.

"We're members of the Vatican staff, officer."

"Ah, might I examine your identification, please?" Lorenzo requested in his usual apologetic tone.

The taller priest handed over his Vatican identity card quickly; the older one fumbled in his tunic for a moment, finally producing his with a mutter. "Is that all, officer?" the younger one inquired.

"Yes . . . yes. Sorry, but I'm sure you'll both understand the need for . . . "

"Of course, officer," said the older priest, interrupting the officer's apologies. "We understand that security is necessary."

"Thank you," replied the detective as he returned the cards to their respective owners, "Father Krebs and Father . . . Kottmeyer." He read the names as he handed back the passes. The two continued on their way as Lorenzo rejoined his partner.

"Any problem?" questioned Giorgio.

"Of course not. Come with me, Giorgio. Everything's fine. Let's get back to the piazza. Maybe we'll be able to find that damn . . . " he caught himself. Red-faced, he turned to the smiling priests. "Sorry about that, Fathers. But . . . "

"It's all right, officer. We understand," said the younger man.

Leaving the courtyard, the pair of policemen looked about. The same officers seemed to be on duty as when they had first arrived, indicating that their commander had still not returned. Giorgio decided to begin making the rounds of the great piazza, as they had after the death of Pope John XXIV—probably what the ranking officer would tell them to do if he were there. What else would they be assigned to? "Might as well get to work," he commented and hurried ahead.

Lorenzo nodded, but his attention was lost in the spectacle of sunlight breaking across the great piazza.

"Lorenzo!" called Giorgio. "What the hell is holding you up?"

"I'm coming. Just keep you shirt on, Giorgio," shouted the elder detective. He ran to his partner, his voice dropping as he drew alongside. "What the hell are you shouting for? We don't want everyone to know we're cops."

Giorgio laughed. "Are you kidding? What the fuck do you suppose they think we are, a couple of fairies?"

Lorenzo looked around, hoping no one was listening. "Giorgio," he pleaded, "we're in the Vatican. Please, clean up your language." His partner only smiled and clapped him on the back.

"Sure, sure. But who the hell . . . heck is going to hear? We can't even find the goddamn C.O." Giorgio kept walking. His eyes were on the line of people waiting to enter the cathedral. He wasn't looking for a mad gunman, a thief, or a pickpocket. Soon his roving eye came to rest: There, half-hidden in the midst of a mass of dark-clothed mourners, was a woman's face of extraordinary beauty.

Framed in black, the woman's eyes peeked out at him. Delicate as a fawn's, to Giorgio they seemed to whisper intimacy. He would not have been more awestruck by her beauty had the Holy Madonna herself been waiting among her mortal flock. He stopped to face her, and she must have realized he was staring; she turned and lowered her head. Giorgio took two timid steps in her direction, hoping to catch another glimpse of her captivating eyes.

"Giorgio. What are you up to?" called Lorenzo from just behind the police buses parked alongside the central first aid center. "Come on, Giorgio. I've got some important business in here," he said as he disappeared into a fenced-off area that contained temporary toilets.

"All right. I'll be right there," replied Giorgio, his eyes turning for the briefest of moments toward his partner. In that moment, the queue began to move. Just as suddenly as she had appeared, she disappeared. Frantically he searched along the snaking line. The black garments of the women blended into a single mournful mass. Hands were held in front of faces in prayer as the people moved along. Giorgio began to run along the line, his eyes darting from one face to another, but he could not find her.

The column wound slowly forward. Like a swimmer frantically diving after a dropped jewel, Giorgio dove into the crowd again and again, only to come to the surface dazed and empty-handed when Lorenzo's voice called out to him.

"Giorgio, the sergeant's in here. Come on!"

The detective began to walk toward his partner, stopping every few feet to look back at the line. The trail of indistinguishable mourners continued their slow procession. "Like a madonna," he sighed with a shake of the head.

At the reception area he and his partner were joined by a burly uniformed sergeant clutching a cup of coffee in one hand, and filling his round face with some oily pasta with the other.

The heat of the sun burned into their shoulders. The day was going to be a hot one, Lorenzo thought, hoping for an indoor assignment, yet knowing better.

Giorgio turned the corner of the makeshift fabric fence, and with Lorenzo followed the sergeant to the canteen truck. The sergeant was railing unabashedly against the assignment, the department, the city, the food. Barzini grabbed a short pause to interject. "I know just how you feel. Too many days on the street, right, Sarge? So how about working inside today?" he coaxed.

The sergeant laughed. "I didn't know you'd been promoted, Barzini."

Giorgio turned his attention back to his partner muttering, "Just like a madonna . . . a goddamn madonna."

14

Bloodshot eyes peered out through the glass panels to the great plaza below. The scarlet-cloaked figure hadn't changed position for the past hour. Gradually the dawn had cast its first scorching rays of light upon his face, replacing the shadows of night, causing the silver in his hair to glimmer about his tormented face. His hands were clenched as one before him, the barest hint of an object held between his delicate fingers. The object burned deeply into his palms, searing with a symbolic heat, not a physical one, but one that could scar like a burning brand.

Bohuslav Tabor had been brutally resurrected in the earthly form of Brandano Cardinal Michalovce. They were one and the same—a secret buried for more than thirty-five years, now disinterred and returned to haunt him, torment him, entice him. Bohuslav had been a fighter, a pillar of strength, but a transgressor. Michalovce was something less, merely a man.

A vision floated in the space between the small cell's windows and the plaza below; it was her picture once again. His mind attempted to grasp the timeless beauty of the woman's face, to caress her delicate features, to kiss open her lips, to whisper closed her eyelids. But each time she came into focus, each time he almost grasped her, the woman fled. He had been haunted by memories of her since the small packet had been brought to him by his aide.

Eight weeks earlier he had been summoned to a fateful meeting. There he learned that Bohuslav Tabor and his long-buried past had risen again. Unbelievably, they had somehow discovered the secret so carefully concealed for all those years, and using it had offered Michalovce only two paths: complete destruction, or tainted glory. All he could manage to do, since choosing the latter, was pray for the Lord's forgiveness.

In the passage of time, he hoped they had somehow forgotten him, or perhaps dropped their insane plot. But the too-early death of John XXIV had not altered their plans. Behind the Kremlin wall the plot to use him had merely skipped a beat, then gone on as John XXV followed his brother Pope to another life. Sometimes Michalovce wished he had the strength to join them, when death seemed the only alternative to doing their bidding.

A week ago, an inner voice had beckoned him from a sleepless bed to the windowsill. Pushing aside the smooth panes of glass, he had climbed onto the ledge and looked down to the piazza, its concrete surface unyielding. Yet he had been unable to take the final step. He'd stood there for two hours, neither stepping forward to doom, nor backward to safety. At the approach of dawn he had responded to a soft knock on the door, retiring into the cold room to admit his aide. And so he had failed at death even as he had failed at life; choosing to live a lie, he was haunted by it.

His eyes fell again on the long procession of mourners that seemed to stretch on for eternity, like black rope drawing him ever deeper into the miasma. He was faced with two opposing avenues; first, to come forward to a council of cardinals and admit he had lied—had sinned and hidden the sin for forty years. Or second, the gleaming ring of St. Peter beckoned, and in his despair he was comforted by the thought that perhaps this was God's method of testing him. In moments of secret pride he even wondered if this was His way of choosing His earthly representative.

He could feel the early morning heat coming off the concrete three stories below. Heat waves already distorted the Roman skyline as he looked out toward the city, as if God's anger were punishing the ancient capital.

Movement below caught his eye. A lone figure hurried haphazardly along the inchworm-like gyrations of the black line, as if in confusion or near-panic. Perhaps he was a security officer who had seen something out of order. From here, man's petty concerns seemed insect-like.

A hollow knock reverberated from the hard bare door of the cardinal's cell. It was followed by a second, and a voice from the hallway just beyond the wooden barrier: "Cardinal . . . Cardinal Michalovce, are you up?"

The Cardinal didn't move. He was rooted to this place in time and space. If he could, he would turn into a pillar of salt.

"Cardinal Michalovce . . . please!" This time the voice conveyed a sense of urgency, which finally registered. "Cardinal . . . Cardinal!"

"Yes, I'm coming."

A deep sigh could barely be heard from the other side of the door, followed by a voice that sounded somewhat calmer. "Cardinal. . . . "—the tone was almost apologetic—"Your Eminence, you have to attend the cardinal's mass in fifteen minutes."

"I'll be ready," he whispered, nearly swallowing his words.

The cardinals paid their simple respects to Pope John, and made their various statements to the world's press expressing how much their colleague had become indispensable both to the Church and to the cardinals themselves.

"Too soon," said a tearful Jamie Cardinal Win of Manila.

"God has willed it, as painful as His will is," consoled Cologne's Hans Cardinal Hoffner.

New York's Francis Cardinal Burke joined his brothers and said, "God cannot be questioned. Yet it makes it no less a loss."

"The ways of Our Lord are disconcerting to the human perspective," was the calming thought of Milan's Renato Cardinal Buzzonetti.

To a man they wept as they laid John to rest. But at the furthest reach of each mind was a question they could not still so completely: "Who will be chosen Pope?" The question would remain unanswered through the coming week.

As it had been for his predecessor, the funeral Mass would be held outdoors; the setting of broad stone steps at the venerable basilica would be simple, and the service brief. This had been the Pope's expressed wish, and the Princes of the Church would make certain that the request was fulfilled to the letter.

Once the funeral was over, the 112 Princes of the Church eligible to vote on the selection of his successor would convene the ancient rite of Conclave.

The simple cypress casket lay on the marble pavement, the summer's sun giving its surface a faint glow. A single candle stood as a beacon on the edge of the tapestry laid out to cushion the warm wood. Cardinals clothed in blazing scarlet, bishops in somber purple, priests and nuns along with dignitaries from a hundred nations, and 75,000 of the faithful filled the square framed by the grandeur of St. Peter's.

Sorrowful Latin chants fell from a thousand lips to embrace Bernini's magestic colonnade. John XXV, the Pilgrim Pope, had begun his final journey. Steaming bodies pressed forward to catch a glimpse of the casket as ten stout pairs of hands bore it across the square. His body was lovingly carried inside the basilica and placed in a crypt adjacent to his most recent predecessors. The following private interrment was reserved for the closest friends, relatives, and a handful of Vatican dignitaries.

Within hours of the clearing of the square, the process of succession had begun in a ritual that could be traced back nearly nine centuries. The cardinals who were present were already engaged in the search for a new Holy Father. Soon other Princes of the Church would join them for the inevitable political maneuvering. The prayerful debates would then be followed by the formality of the election Conclave.

The cardinals would remain sealed in the Sistine Chapel until one man was chosen "Il Papa." When that would happen no one could predict. Surely no one expected the choice to be a simple one, without a clear-cut favorite.

Of course, less than two months before, John had been chosen on the fourth ballot. But the problem now was more complex than it had been then. He had been the single figure who might have lead the Church away from an uncertain future, while healing the widening divisions among the faithful. Could God provide yet another? Only one of the cardinals could even imagine that a different unseen power would make the agony of decision irrelevant.

Hours after Pope John had been laid to rest, maintenance men began the process of preparing the Sistine Chapel for the Conclave. The 112 cardinals, supported by their staffs of confessors, doctors, cooks, pharmacists, barbers, dishwashers, and various workmen, would all be subject to the most rigorous security. Of course, complete secrecy of all details was sworn under pain of excommunication. This threat of eternal damnation aside, officials were subject to intense additional scrutiny. Each nook and cranny of that ancient Renaissance chapel would be twice electronically swept. As an added precaution, all phones had already been disconnected, save the one under heavy guard reserved for the most dire of emergencies. Food, prepared by the most trusted cooks, was passed to the cardinals through a series of revolving hatches designed to circumvent any contact. All notes recorded during the Conclave were required to be burned before the announcement of the new Pope was made.

Thus, all that actually occurred during the days, weeks, or perhaps months of the Conclave would remain in total secrecy for years to come—theoretically, forever.

The College of Cardinals would follow the protocol that had been established centuries ago. Each cardinal would submit his candidate's name by formal ballot. He would approach the altar to pray and to repeat his vow of secrecy, then lay the ballot on the plate that lay across the golden chalice. With both hands he would be required to tip the plate so that the ballot would drop into the cup in full view of all his brother cardinals.

After each of the 112 Princes of the Church had "cast his ballot," the results would be counted aloud by three "scrutinizers." If none of the cardinals emerged with the required majority vote of two-thirds plus one, a second ballot would be taken forthwith. If still no cardinal had been chosen by the requisite margin, the Conclave would retire for the morning, to resume the procedure on the same afternoon. No conversation would be heard in the interim; all concerned would observe a vow of strict silence outside of prayer. The day's ballots would be bound together, doused with oil, and burned until completely consumed. The fire gives off the traditional dark black smoke that signals to all eyes intent upon the chimney of the chapel that the Conclave has not yet prevailed in its task.

If the first three days of ritual balloting produced no winner, the fourth day would be set aside for prayer and meditation. Rested, the cardinals would then embark on a second series of three days' balloting.

But this time the selection of the Pope would not require any protracted delay. The little-known and unlikely choice of the Czech religious leader, Brandano Cardinal Michalovce, would

slowly emerge to achieve the necessary majority on a predetermined ballot. Without the fathomless precision of God's design—with, rather, only the machinations of power-mad mortals—
this result, it appeared, had already been ordained.

The sky was too perfectly blue. Clouds lofted high, as if afraid
to clutter God's Baroque tapestry. For Bishop Galen it was a day
of decision. Ever since Father Hacha had passed him those notes
of damnation, the bishop had understood that the moment of action would someday arrive. It was his duty, as churchman, and as
man.

Pope John XXV had barely been laid to rest when the West
German clergyman reached the decision to relieve his soul of this
terrible burden. As if in response to the cries of his heart, the
great bells outside pealed forth a mournful wail.

The thin envelope burned as a brand in his jacket pocket. It
was crucial he didn't lose the "documents;" he felt that they had
been entrusted to him by the guidance of an unseen hand.

The sounds of workmen dismantling the remains of the open-
air funeral accompanied him as he walked through the center of
the great piazza. Its simple altar and hundreds of seats provided
for the world's dignitaries were almost gone. And vanished were
the mourners, as well as the cardinals.

The cathedral stood sturdy against the contrasting sky, loom-
ing ever larger as he approached. The bishop's knees nearly lost
their strength as he took the first tremulous steps up the marble
entranceway. Just inside, past the ever-present workmen silently
polishing the marble colonnades and surfaces, were the official offices of the Vatican. He approached the entrance and displayed
his official pass to the guards, who saluted as he approached.

"Bishop Galen?" One of them read the name and compared
the photo of the white-haired clergyman with the lined and dignified face before him. "Can I be of service, Sir?"

The bishop took a moment to respond. "Yes . . . I'd like to
have directions to the Office of Vatican Security, please."

"Security, Bishop?" said the officer, apparently finding the
request rather unusual.

"Correct. I have official business with the director of security."

The officer permitted the clergyman to pass, then stepped
alongside to accompany him. "If you'd come with me, sir, I'd be

happy to show you the way." The tall, square-boned bishop nodded his thanks.

"Here you go, Bishop Galen," said the officer, who then saluted, turned on his heels and left the German bishop before an imposing door marked "THE DIRECTOR OF SECURITY."

His hand felt clammy as it grasped the metal handle and swung the door in. As he looked inside, he thought at first that the office was deserted. This was all too impossible; he doubted he would ever pay such a visit again.

Then from down the hallway flapped the sound of approaching sandled feet. In another moment in tottered a priest, shriveled and bowed nearly in half by the ravages of time. The bespectacled relic peered up over the rim of his bifocals, surprised at the presence of a bishop in his office. "Yes . . . can I help you?"

The West German clergyman thought of departing, but the old priest did not move from his path. Finally Galen stammered: "I've come to see the director. But, since he isn't here, I'll come back."

"To be certain. Yes. If you've come for Bishop Pironio, you'll find him busy for the duration of the Conclave. Certainly, until then," chattered the ancient priest as he hobbled into the office, "I'm in charge certainly, until his return, you see?" His shriveled lips smiled up toward the standing bishop, as he gestured with a slow open hand, indicating the complete vacancy of the office. Clearly this bent and feeble priest had been assigned the none-too-taxing duties of message-taking, filing, mail collecting, and the like during the Conclave. "Of course, I might be of service perhaps, yes? If you'd care to tell me why you wish to see the good bishop." The pinched old man filled the momentary pause obligingly. "Oh, yes. Have I mentioned? No, I don't think so. I am Father Datuk, Bishop Pironio's assistant."

After introducing himself, Bishop Galen followed the slowly moving priest through a closed door and into a smaller office. Father Datuk crumpled into a wooden swivel chair behind a massive desk more ancient, if possible, than he. The elder priest pushed aside one of the many stacks of files and looked out through the channel he had created. "Now, how can I be of help?"

"Are you certain that Bishop Pironio couldn't find time to deal with . . . with a problem I have?"

"I'm afraid that would be totally impossible." The priest's head nodded incessantly as he spoke. "Of course, you see, if you'd care to make an appointment, for . . . let's say the fourth week after the Papal nomination?"

The old priest's simple offer bit like lion's teeth. "No, it cannot wait." After a long pause, Bishop Galen withdrew the envelope from his pocket and leaned forward to drop it on the center of the priest's desk. "Here. It is now entrusted to you, and thus to Bishop Pironio. Please comprehend, if you can, the seriousness of this matter. Transfer it to him at once." The bishop now placed his hands on his knees and, after pausing as if to add some further remark, stood up. "I cannot stress the importance of bringing this envelope immediately to his attention," he added finally with a patriarchal sigh that was half relief, half resignation.

The priest picked up the damp sealed wrapping and turned it over once. There was nothing written on either side. "Of course, yes. I see. And what is in this . . . this packet?"

"Four documents that the bishop will be most anxious to examine." Bishop Galen walked to the doorway, then paused to caution, "and intended only for his eyes."

The priest turned the packet over yet another time, his head bobbing with either comprehension or senility. "Aha. Yes, I see. Yes. But Bishop . . ." He rattled the envelope with his stringy, ancient hand. "Inside. What is inside?" he repeated. This time there was no response. The bishop had already passed through the doorway, his strides clacking briskly down the corridor.

Father Datuk returned his attention to the envelope. Curious, yet careful, he would not open it. He intended to present it to the director at the first opportunity. But for now his energies were channeled to the numbering and filing of the mountain of perfunctory reports left to his care. He pushed the packet to the corner of the desk. Lifting the nearest yellow folder from the top of the pile, he was soon engrossed in his snail-paced collating. Hours later the mountain of manila folders had been sorted into a dozen stacks scattered over the desk, with no thought to what might lie buried underneath.

A solitary sanitation worker in the dull green Vatican maintenance uniform was diligently polishing the marble floors outside the Vatican's security office. Although he scarcely lifted his eyes from his labor, no visitor to the office could escape his careful scrutiny. At 10:47 Bishop Galen had approached with the guard, who—by obligingly addressing the prelate by name—had merely confirmed his identity. Moments later the familiar Father Datuk had entered the hallway from the opposite direction, and met the bishop at the office door.

The sanitation worker had moved as close to the door as seemed prudent in an attempt to overhear their conversation, but had found it impossible. He'd noted, however, that their business was concluded in less than five minutes.

As the bishop exited, the workman removed his cap in a gesture of respect, acknowledged only by a preoccupied smile.

Less than ten minutes later the stocky workman gathered his pail and mop, deposited them in a storeroom, and left the Vatican's grounds. Once outside St. Peter's he headed for the nearest phone booth, and dialed the Soviet Embassy in Rome.

"Security. Priority Four. Comrade Jvari." As usual, there was no reply from the operator. The sounds of electronic switching equipment flooded the receiver, and in a moment:

"Password, please?" The voice was firm and authoritative.

The workman replied, "Brother Six. Your bishop has appeared."

"Observations?"

"Some agitation upon entering that was not evident at departure. Short visitation, met with number eight only, for less than quarter hour. That's all." Only a short silence followed.

"We expect your return to the fold." The line went dead.

The solidly built workman withdrew from the phone booth, lighted a cigarette while casually glancing around, then disappeared into the crowd.

Captain Iori Jvari had been waiting for this call for the past two days, never questioning its meaning. Now he picked up the secure line to KGB headquarters—Moscow, and in moments was speaking to Dmitri Gvozdetskii. He repeated the message precisely as given—"Your bishop has appeared"—and offered the supplementary observations.

After a moment Gvozdetskii spoke, "Please shut down the operation, Captain."

"Yes, sir." There was no question. "I'll see to it at once."

"Good job, Captain," his chief uttered before breaking the connection.

Jvari smiled, pleased with the turn of events.

A thousand miles away, Dmitri Gvozdetskii sat back in his chair. "He's passed it on. No doubt about it, Michalovce's days are numbered." He made a mental note to meet with Colonel Torchnoi in the next twenty-four hours to begin setting up his "special services"; he would proceed with his counter-insurgency. Having monitored the movements of the documents closely, he was now in a position to permit their disclosure, should Shaposhnikov's plan threaten to succeed. He still expected the chairman's coup to fail on its own. But if it didn't, there were methods to tilt the balance of power subtly in Gvozdetskii's favor; there was always Colonel Torchnoi.

The approach of night found Father Datuk still preoccupied with the folders. Suddenly finding himself late for Mass, he scurried shakily from the office and locked the door behind him.

The night air had quite a nip to it as the aging priest hurried along the side of St. Peter's. The summer had rapidly drawn to an end. Colder days would follow.

A single row of high-backed chairs and linen-covered tables lined each of the two long walls of the Sistine Chapel. In twelve hours a garrison of cardinals would file into the ornate room to convene the ancient rite of Conclave. The room had already been swept clean by Italian security forces searching for any electronic devices. Now a second team of experts was performing the same operation even more painstakingly. Once they were finished, a squadron of armed guards would be stationed outside the single entrance to prevent entry to any and all.

Such security had always been more than sufficient protection against tampering with the sanctity of the Conclave. Mainly, such a threat had come from an overly nosy Roman press; more recently the Church had armed itself against actual physical danger from extreme right- and pseudo–left-wing terrorist cells, which had proliferated alarmingly in inflation-ravaged Italy. This convention might have been a prime target for such publicity-hungry fanatics, and perhaps even for radical political factions vying for influence within the Church itself. But these had been the only forces Vatican security had faced—until now. Now, a more devious and manipulating menace lurked unseen.

Only minutes before the team completed their assignment, a tall priest-workman had entered the chapel unobtrusively, carrying a workman's wooden tool kit. Unnoticed, he slipped a silver object into a corner trash bin, then walked across the room to the altar unheeded, his identity card conspicuously attached to his lapel. It seemed perfectly natural for an authorized workman-priest to be putting final touches on some item at this last minute, so the members of the security team continued their jobs, allowing the priest free movement. Everything was now timed with scrupulous accuracy; there were five minutes to complete this task.

The Professional used the opportunity to rehang the tiny Michelangelo the art-forgers had been hired to restore. It might be decades before anyone noticed it was an impeccable forgery. As he rummaged through his tool kit, the imposter's eyes were not on its contents, but rather on the last of the policemen as they finished checking their designated areas. When assured that they were paying no attention to him, he picked up a two-liter plastic container of black fluid, carrying it with a cloth as one would some cleaning agent. Three minutes remained.

At the side of the altar a small enclosed table had been set up, on top of which was an identical container, likewise filled with black liquid. With exceedingly deft sleight of hand the exchange was effected without a break in stride. Returning to his tool kit, he filled the empty spot with the ink-container he had just taken. Specially formulated silicone ink had now been placed in its stead. Two minutes remained.

As he moved across the room to check the lighting on the masterpiece, the Professional produced from his box a stack of tightly bound cards. There were precisely 112 bits of cardboard in each packet. Four double packets were bound with a single ribbon, each set of four corresponding to a day's balloting. One minute thirty seconds.

The priest covered the packets with the cloth he still carried and passed once more by the table at the altar's side. There, without a moment's hesitation in his movements, he exchanged the existing bound cards for his pre-treated duplicates.

There remained one last task, for which he required a minimum of thirty seconds.

He waited, counting down the last ten seconds. At zero a piercing buzz sounded through the open space. The security men froze, their hands searching for their weapons.

"There—in the case, a bomb!" the nearest officer yelled. He leaped to the Professional's box, frantically rummaging through its contents. Everyone else jumped for cover a safe distance away. "Shit!" he proclaimed resoundingly. "It's only a workman's wristwatch." His hand raised the buzzing alarm aloft for all to see.

During this planned diversion, the Professional had instantly gone to work. Atop the altar, beneath Michelangelo's timeless tableau, *The Last Judgment*, was the gold chalice. As the clamor from the diversion held all eyes elsewhere, he deftly turned the relic on its side and carefully stripped away its felt base. From deep within his clothing he swiftly withdrew a small oblong sphere no more than five centimeters in diameter. Quickly removing the smooth cellophane covering on its contoured surface, he pressed it tightly into the base of the chalice. During the precious seconds while all attention was focused on the opposite corner, the Professional's deft hands covered the rim of the base with a sticky substance and replaced the felt backing. Surreptitiously eyeing his work, he could find no sign the chalice had been tampered with. Everything had gone as planned, in perfect sequence.

He now returned to the tiny framed masterpiece whose rehanging had provided the excuse for his entry. He adjusted it finally with a leveling gauge, smiling at his good work, and collected his tools to depart.

Within half an hour the chapel was sealed. Any check for a "bug" would prove fruitless, as only transmitters could be detected, not passive receivers.

The previous morning, 112 cardinals had gathered in St. Peter's Basilica to pray for divine inspiration. Guided by a homily delivered by the French Minister Jean Cardinal Vilot, the Princes of the Church prepared to use their intellects and inspirations in the days ahead. John, the candidate of compromise, was gone, choosing his successor would be no easy task.

"Our Lord Jesus Christ has shown us how to follow His way," Vilot said. "He leaves us freedom for the working of our intellect and will to interpret His holy scripture." The statement was intended as more than merely a guide; already the subtle politicking had begun in earnest.

When the Sistine Chapel had been sealed shut by the security forces, the cardinals met for a second time. This time the site was the smaller Pauline Chapel.

When the meeting and prayers were complete, the Princes of the Church, followed by a staff of eighty-eight, would march two-by-two into the Sistine Chapel. They would file along the parallel walls and take their assigned places at the long beige, felt-covered tables beneath the magnificence of Michelangelo's ceiling fresco, *The Creation.* The physical pain the master had endured in completing this masterpiece could be compared with the intellectual agony many of the cardinals expected to be subjected to.

Less than an hour had passed since the master of ceremonies, Virgilio Noe, had stood at the door of the Sistine Chapel and quietly commanded: *"Extra Omnes."* It was the order for all unauthorized personnel to depart. Minutes later the doors were closed, locked, and sealed. The cardinals, along with their staffs, would not emerge from their walled citadel until led by one robed in white, the 265th successor to the throne of St. Peter.

The favorites: Corrado Cardinal Pappalardo, a strict traditionalist; Salvatore Cardinal Ursi, older and more conservative still; Giuseppe Cardinal Bennelli, nearing eighty; and young, energetic, fifty-five-year-old Aloisio Cardinal Pignedoli, a dark horse because of his forward-looking revisionist policies, but a charismatic favorite among the general populace and among the Church's minorities. Pappalardo and Pignedoli were seated side by side, almost as if to demonstrate that they were running neck-and-neck. As the speakers intoned their nominations there were tremendous admonitions. Tension rippled through the room. Deals were made; there were exchanges, threats, promises in order to further the cause of one candidate or another. While there was no debate within the Sistine Chapel itself, as ordered by Pope Paul in 1975, this did not exclude the cardinals from praising at length the various candidates' merits. During meals, taken in the Borgia Dining Room where luxurious Pope Alexander VI had entertained world figures in Renaissance splendor, the prelates would have still another opportunity to quietly exert influence and form necessary alliances.

All discussion was muted under the thick blanket of utter secrecy. Pope Paul's decree had specifically excluded any and all assistants and had silenced the many tipoffs and leaks. There would be no reports—of progress or otherwise—until the time-honored signal of white smoke marked a fruitful conclusion.

Late that morning the first ballot was taken. One of the three presiding cardinals walked to the small table beside the altar and untied the first of four pre-counted sets of ballots; walking down the wall of tables he dropped before each cardinal a single card with the words *Eligo in Summan Pontificem . . .* ("I elect as Supreme Pontiff. . . .")

Upon signal, each of the 112 prelates raised a feather pen to record his choice, using ink that had been poured into ink wells from the container thoughtfully supplied by the Professional. Each cardinal then folded his card in half.

Now, each cardinal in turn stood and walked to the altar, hands grasping the ballot before him. Beneath the magnificent *Last Judgment* each man declared, "I call to witness Christ the Lord who will be my judge, that my vote is given to the one who before God I consider should be elected." And each deposited his card on the plate perched upon the golden chalice, then, facing Michelangelo's fresco, tipped the plate for the ballot to drop into the sacred cup.

The balloting completed, the cardinals bowed their heads in prayer. As his companions prayed, Cardinal Michalovce slipped his hand into his tunic. His fingers found a small plastic box and turned it so that his thumb was in a position to depress the small button at its center. He remained poised for what seemed like an eternity, until the prayer's conclusion. Then his thumb fell full on the button, pressing it with all the strength his body could muster. Half of him still wanted to crush the instrument and bring his spiritual torment to an end.

A tiny microwave signal of negligible power reached out for a distance of twenty meters, designed to be undetectable outside of the chapel. Inside the chalice, the small receiver picked up the signal and triggered the attached micro-oscillator, planted securely in the vessel's base. Perhaps only heavenly beings could detect its sound, for it operated beyond the range of human hearing. The silicone ink reacted instantly to the oscillatory motion.

The ink, which had appeared dry to the naked eye, was not. In fact, it had never been wet. Silicone, a slippery synthetic substance, moves freely upon extreme agitation.

The oscillator jarred the ink from each card's surface and set it in motion in tiny rivulets of black. Flowing across the ballot, it sought out an imperceptible magnetic thread that had been carefully woven into the card. Each card had been previously threaded with a candidate's name, each in a different hand, to a specified, predetermined count.

In a matter of seconds, the ink had completed its course. When the oscillator ceased, the liquid and magnetic thread had fused as one. The age-old sacred ritual had been circumvented.

When the cardinals ended their prayer the plate was lifted from atop the chalice. The first scrutinizer lifted out a ballot, unfolded it, and noted the choice on his tally sheet. The second overseer likewise noted the selection, then passed the card on to the third member of the committee, who read it aloud:

"Aloisio Cardinal Pignedoli," he called.

Eyes darted about during the hushed murmur that followed. For some there was exultation, for others only tense anticipation. Cardinal Michalovce's face showed relief. At least the first vote had not been cast for him.

A half hour later the count was complete. Pignedoli had garnered an impressive fifty-four votes and his liberal rival Pappalardo but twenty-eight. The arch-conservative Ursi received ten, and Cardinal Kee from South Korea six votes. The choice of Kee appeared to be a budding protest by members of the Third World at their seemingly small representation in the College of Cardinals. Aging Bennelli's scant four votes appeared to be a clear signal that the Princes desired a longer, more stable reign. And notably, French Cardinal Vilot received four; this was considered a surprise for a non-Italian. Half a dozen others received only a single vote apiece. Cardinal Michalovce was not among them. Cardinal Pignedoli allowed himself the luxury of a tiny inner smile. He could not have known that these results had been predetermined—by men.

Only a scant quarter hour after the completion of the first unsuccessful ballot, the second was called for. An hour later its results revealed what appeared to be a trend.

The falsified balloting made it appear as if the conservative factions had failed to rally behind Pignedoli. Their vote remained split: Pignedoli fifty-six, Ursi eight, and Bennelli four.

But Pignedoli's liberal counterpart had not gained either, slipping to twenty-two votes. Only the Third World nations had picked up a few, with Kee finishing at eleven. Cardinal Vilot scored eight votes, giving rise to the feeling that this was a reaction to Italy's domination of the Papacy. Three other votes varied, including a single ballot cast for an unlikely Czech candidate. Only the new nominee paid any heed to the lone ballot.

Thus the first morning's balloting had drawn to a close. After prayer the cardinals would retire for refreshment. They would reassemble in the Sistine Chapel at 2:00 P.M. to pray and vote once again. If there was no winner after the two afternoon ballots, the cardinals would retire for the remainder of the day. In the hallways, the anterooms, the courtyard, the true politicking that usually decided the next Pope would take place.

Three hours and two ballots later, no Pope had been chosen. The last ballot showed still greater turmoil among the traditionalists, with only the Third World and small factionalists rallying together.

It seemed that Pignedoli was still the favorite, but now with only forty-seven votes. The elder Bennelli appeared to have dropped from consideration entirely, for he received but a single vote; the conservative Ursi remained active with eleven votes.

But Pappalardo, the likely liberal contender, barely equalled his previous score. Korean Cardinal Kee and French Vilot each reached a surprising fourteen votes, seeming to represent sentiment for the anti-traditionalists. Michalovce's three votes still appeared inconsequential.

By this vote the trends had been established. The cardinals appeared to be deserting the failing conservative and liberal ranks in favor of the Third World's Kee, and the anti-traditional Vilot. But Michalovce, now with nine votes, began to emerge as an alternative. Heads shook with murmurs and prayers, as the day's exhausting ordeal drew to a close. Following tradition, the ballots were gathered, along with all notes written during the afternoon session. One of the cardinals passed a thread through the 112 pieces of thin cardboard and deposited them in the tiny stove at the corner of the chapel. Outside there would be no mistaking the inconclusive outcome.

Black smoke wafted out of the tiny smokestack at the corner of the great basilica as the afternoon's 224 cardboard ballots were consumed. It was the signal that the day's balloting had ended fruitlessly. In minutes the assembled masses in the great square began their treks home. They would return in the morning, anxious for the new day's selections to begin.

At a corner of St. Peter's stood a tall young priest, his eyes fixed upon the thin column of smoke that snaked forth, to be dispersed by the powerful wind. To the others the dark puff bespoke failure, but to him it signaled clear confirmation of success.

Deep inside the Kremlin's walls anxious eyes watched a television screen tuned to the inter-European network, showing the smoke that rose from the small stack. Dmitri Gvozdetskii smiled. He was joined by Chairman Shaposhnikov and Marshal Tukhachevski. The three rulers had glasses of cold vodka placed before them, and drank deeply. Each was already foreseeing victory; each planned to claim it for his own.

Detective Barzini was just leaving the station when he met the chief's secretary, Angela Cardone, in the hallway. He half-waved a salute to the young lieutenant as she passed by him and continued down the hallway. Three steps beyond she suddenly stopped and turned around, calling back to the detective as he passed, "Hey . . . you, wait a minute!"

Lorenzo spun about at the sound. "Me?" he questioned, bringing his hand to his chest.

Lieutenant Cardone stood waiting, hands on her shapely hips. His eyes were elsewhere, running along her upper torso, following the rise and fall of her full blouse, as he approached her. She gave him a few brief moments to eye her, then, when she felt like it, she cut his gaze. "The only thing you should be looking at are these bars." She pointed with her chin to the symbol of rank on her shoulder.

"Yes, uh, sir." Barzini shrugged.

"As I was saying, Barzini, the chief has been leaving messages for you all around the division. Don't you ever pick them up?"

Barzini had purposely been avoiding Maggiore whenever possible. "Well, I've been working on something really big. I'll get in to see him just as soon as I can."

"Not as soon as you can, Barzini. Tomorrow, is that understood? When you get back from the Vatican tomorrow, you report directly to me. Clear?"

"The Vatican again?" he questioned. "You mean the new Pope hasn't been chosen yet?"

"What do you expect, Barzini? It's only the first day. You're probably going to be there for quite a while," she said.

"But I have a case to work on."

"Why is it that you always seem to work on one that leads nowhere?"

The detective cut her off. "Leads nowhere? Are you kidding? I'm on the edge of breaking this one. . . . "

The lieutenant raised her hand, stopping him from further comment. Taking a step backward, she said, "Now, Barzini, you'll have more success watching my rear than you did my front." With that she walked away, leaving the embarrassed Lorenzo frozen in place. Which didn't preclude his watching her backside anyway. Between undulations he realized he had little time to waste.

In fifteen minutes he was standing on the street where the school children had found the neatly packaged evidence that a crime had been committed. It was important that he come up with some lead, some clue to prove indisputably a concrete tie to the Ostia murders, so he could remain on the case in Rome.

The street was nearly deserted; it was dinnertime in Rome. The city's inhabitants had retreated to their apartments, leaving the streets to the garbage, the flies, and a detective named Barzini.

Lorenzo looked about. Mounds of garbage seemed to grow in place endlessly. The sounds of evening life tumbled out the hundreds of windows that opened onto the street. As he had done before, the detective reexamined the entire area. For some unknown reason he was drawn back to the building line. There were a number of basement doors, service entrances and curtained cellar windows. The curved cobblestone street was perfect as a drop-off point; everything seemed planned for someone who might want to remain undetected.

Lorenzo suddenly remembered the burly janitor who had attacked him for going through his garbage the day the crime was discovered. He walked along the building's face until he reached the cellar apartment door, cut three steps down below street level. Alongside the doorway was a series of five half windows, the closest fully open.

Barzini leaned over and looked inside. There, seated at a kitchen table, was the fat janitor gulping down a bottle of vino. The red liquid dribbled down his chin, staining his already filthy undershirt.

A heavy-set woman came into view. She was dressed in a sheer nylon slip, her sagging breasts overfilling its top. She took the bottle from the man and drank deeply. Neither one spoke. She went behind her man and cradled his head in her more than ample bosom. The tips of her breasts suddenly sprang to life, protruding visibly through the slip. He responded by turning in her direction, his tongue reaching out playfully to lick at the nipple through the thin fabric. She pressed his head toward her forcefully as he began to suck on her nipple and mouth her breast. His hands groped for her thick waist and tugged the slip upward.

Barzini continued watching for the moment, forgetting about the purpose of his visit. The spectacle both attracted him, and filled him with revulsion. Like Rome, their vigorous lust outstripped their dilapidation. Suddenly a cat screamed a few feet to his right. It was quickly joined in an animal chorus by a second. Barzini bolted upright.

After he composed himself, straightening his tie and jacket, he banged on the unpainted door. The sounds of groping hands and mouths issued from the room. Barzini knocked harder, not stopping until it produced the desired response:

"Okay. . . . Who the fuck is there? . . . Go away!"

Barzini began pounding once more, this time without stopping. The janitor screamed out, "I said cut it out or I'll break your cock off!" But the sound didn't cease. Barzini heard a chair thrown across the room, then the door latch being undone. When the door opened, the pounding stopped. There in the doorway was the janitor's chunky frame, nose to nose with the detective, his jaw thrust forward belligerently. Barzini calmly leaned against the door-frame, identity card displayed with his left hand, his right hand in his jacket on the butt of his automatic. In all his years on the force the detective had never had to use his gun; he intended to keep it that way.

The janitor stopped, read the identity card, then looked hard into Lorenzo's face. He grumbled finally, "What the fuck do you want?"

Barzini replaced the card in his pocket and stepped back onto the street. The janitor followed. "Look, if it's about the fight with Tony, I didn't start nothing, see?"

Barzini shook his head and motioned the beefy janitor toward the spot where the youngsters had discovered the wrapped jaw fragment. "I'd like to ask you some questions about the piece of a body that some kids found a few weeks back."

"Questions? Are you kidding? Hey, I told them cops when it happened that I didn't see nothing. What the fuck do you want me to remember?" He threw his tattooed arms up in exasperation. "Do you know I was just about to eat when you started knocking down my door? And I don't mean pasta, neither." His overfilled belly began to quiver at what he thought was his private jest. He spat.

"Yeah, yeah . . . but I still have a couple of questions, unless you'd rather discuss that fight with Tony?"

"Awright. Like what kinda questions?"

"Simple. Did you see anyone that morning—or before—who didn't belong in the neighborhood?"

"You gotta be kidding," answered the janitor. "There's thousands of people in this neighborhood I don't know. What you really want to know is if I saw the guy who chopped up whoever's bones were in that bag."

"Well?" asked the detective.

"Well your ass. How the hell could I see anyone do anything? I live in that goddamn cellar. Crap. Can anyone see anything from there?"

"But you saw me."

"Sure, cause you were where you didn't belong."

"And?"

"And what?"

"Was there anything, anyone else where he, or she, didn't belong?"

The janitor began to turn away. He caught himself in an instant.

Barzini screamed at him, "And?"

"And I also saw this priest rummaging for old clothing in the same cans."

"What priest?"

"A priest. That's all. Like I said, this tall guy . . . this priest, he was going through the garbage, I think."

"When?"

"It was a lot earlier . . . like really early in the morning. But why the hell are you interested in the priest. They're always scavenging for the vagrants."

Barzini pressed the point. "Tell me about the priest. What was he wearing? What did he look like?"

The janitor began walking back to the cellar apartment. "Hey, look. What's so important about the priest? Don't tell me he chopped up the guy in the bag? C'mon."

Barzini grabbed the janitor's arm. "Just tell me, dammit! If I have to, I'll write up enough violations on this garbage heap to keep you and the landlord busy for a year."

The janitor turned just inside the apartment, his hands grasping the door jambs. "The priest, right? Who the hell knows? He was just a priest. A big blond priest. Okay?"

"You have any idea who the priest is? Is he from the neighborhood?"

"Nope." The burly workman folded his arms across his chest.

"Is there anyone you can think of who might know of him?"

"Nope."

Barzini asked a few similar questions and received identical responses. He realized he had pushed this character as far as he would go. There was no point pressing his luck; he had gotten what he was after. Offering a nonchalant thanks, the detective hurried off.

"Yeah, thanks. . . . " The janitor slammed the basement door closed. "Thanks for nothing."

In the first hint of light, the faithful had already begun to assemble in St. Peter's Plaza, hoping to be present when the white smoke proclaimed a joyous omen to the world.

Priests and nuns joined the growing multitude, among them a lone, tall, handsome priest whose darting eyes saw everyone, but met no one's.

As the sun climbed into the heavens, anxious eyes strained to catch a glimpse of the roof of the Sistine Chapel. The small tin smokestack was, as expected, without a sign. No ballots would be taken for at least three hours. Still they watched.

Suddenly a window opened; its reflection sent a murmur through the crowd. People stopped in their tracks. The only ones who were moving were the plainclothes policemen on the lookout for pickpockets. Crowds such as this one invariably drew them as honey would bees.

The priest knew exactly how much time would pass before Cardinal Michalovce would be proclaimed Pope; it would be yet another day. And he had other more pressing things to attend to than to waste his time searching for a wisp of smoke that wouldn't come. He walked casually away from the crowd, careful not to draw attention to himself. This time he left the great cathedral behind. He would return to his apartment just across the Tiber River. From there he would prepare for his planned flight. Soon the bogus Father Kottmeyer would vanish even more completely than the original priest had, several weeks ago.

He left the Vatican's grounds at the instant the sun broke through the rapidly vanishing clouds. The powerful rays absorbed by the black hassock he wore, warmed him.

The priest's steps speeded up. He was one of the few persons walking away from the Holy state. Everyone else was moving in the opposite direction. He smiled, for he knew their vigil would be fruitless this day.

15

Swirls of heavy fog blanketed the great piazza, distorting the dawn's glare. The incandescence created an ocean of haze that glowed over the gates to St. Peter's. Behind the sealed doors of the Sistine Chapel, the players awaited their cue.

The Czech cardinal had lain awake the entire night. His bloodshot eyes roved absently over the white plaster of his cell. When the first shards of brightness pierced his window like glinting rapiers, his hand rose to his face to shield himself from their accusation. The entire night he had lain, prostrated before God, grappling with his conscience. He could find no comfort. The last vote of the previous day had given him a total of nine, eight more than his single vote in the second balloting. He alone bore the heavy weight of knowledge. Like the prophets of old, he could foretell the final outcome—but his prescience was a curse from men, not a gift from God. Surely he held the future of the Papacy in his own slender hands. He could only pray that the ultimate power would intervene.

An hour later, the 112 Princes of the Church had completed their solemn morning prayers and silently breakfasted. Now they filed two by two into the Sistine Chapel to search their souls for inspiration once more. Each took his position before his high-backed seat, his hands clasped before him in prayer. "Oh Lord, we beseech you through our fervent prayers for your divine guidance in selecting your earthly representative." Perhaps, thought the withered Michalovce, such guidance would arrive.

Cardinal Michalovce's eyes relentlessly roved over the Michelangelo frescoes and the hanging masterworks of Botticelli, Pinturicchio, Perugino, as if beseeching these aged sentinels to relinquish their private wisdom. He didn't notice that his Christian brothers had completed their prayer and were already seated until his neighbor quickly tugged on his tunic.

Now, once again the scrutineers passed among the cardinals, placing a card before each. The signal was given, the choices penned, the ballots cast.

After all had performed the ritual, the call for prayer was made. Once more the Czech cardinal's hand slipped from his lap and sought out the tiny control unit within his tunic. With weakening will, his finger was drawn to its indented surface. But even his hesitant touch was sufficient to activate the unseen oscillator.

When the prayer was completed, one of the three scrutineers began the count. This time when the first name was read, a slight whisper buzzed about the chapel:

"Cardinal Michalovce."

His name was now uttered more frequently through the course of the ballot-counting. Pignedoli still led the field, but with ever-eroding figures. Other conservative votes were fragmented between Ursi and Bennelli. The energetic Italian liberal, Pappalardo, had not gained. Rather, it appeared, the liberal votes were allying with those of the non-Italians, the Third World, the anti-traditional. Clearly neither Kee nor Vilot could realistically expect to win despite what appeared, in the rigged balloting, to be early strength. These had been merely "protest" votes. Now it would appear that those voters sought a more likely candidate. A cardinal outside of the mainstream tradition. Someone who was not so liberal as to alienate the conservative votes. A candidate from outside Italy to satisfy the Third World and progressive factions. A lean, silver-haired cardinal from Eastern-Bloc Czechoslovakia: Michalovce!

To the observing eye the momentum of the election seemed logical, rational, purposeful. In reality, it was ineluctable; by now Michalovce had garnered twenty-six votes, a shoulder above any candidate but Pignedoli. The tide had begun to turn.

Even as the cardinals conferred on the results, the tampered ballots were strung together and placed in the potbellied stove, where they would repose until the conclusion of the morning's last ballot.

Cardinal Vilot cautioned his brothers about the rule of silence, but more than a hundred pairs of eyes were silently speaking, searching, arranging. Michalovce's gaze had fallen to the tabletop where it remained until the next card was placed before him.

The pounding at his temples was such that he barely heard the call for the cardinals to make their next choice. He summoned all his strength and wrote another's name in a wavering scrawl. The feather pen slid from his hand in futility.

Once again there was the call to proceed to the altar and place the ballots into the chalice before peers and the Lord.

This time Cardinal Michalovce seemed frozen in place. His heart pounded within his chest until it seemed it would fight its way out of his flesh. He tried to discipline his racing thoughts, composing them through the only method he had ever known, fervent concentration on the image of the Lord. He fought not to grasp at the tiny electronic mechanism still hidden in his tunic. He tore his hand away from his breast, not caring if anyone happened to notice. Taut fingers, returning to the mechanism, trembled before the nub at the center of the box.

When the rumbling incantation abruptly ceased he found himself dizzy from the tension. His dazed face glimmered with trembling pearls of water. He was not even sure if he'd pressed the button:

"Cardinal Pignedoli" was the first name called. Again, "Cardinal Pignedoli." But the third ballot rang out: "Cardinal Michalovce." And the fourth and fifth alike. The pattern was clear. As the counting progressed, Michalovce emerged as the compromise candidate, challenged only by the faltering Pignedoli; the others had fallen by the wayside.

The scrutineers droned out ballot after ballot " . . . Michalovce . . . Cardinal Pignedoli . . . Cardinal Michalo . . ." When an anguished voice broke the silence.

"Stop!" The Czech cardinal thought that the words had escaped his own gaping lips.

It was Cardinal Pignedoli. "Cease! I demand to be heard!"

All eyes focused upon the heretofore clear favorite. He walked out from behind the table and strode directly for the Czech cardinal. There were tears in his eyes, tears of pure joy. His hands opened wide in a gesture of divine inspiration.

"*Annuntio vobis gaudium magnum. Habemus Papam!*—I announce to you a great joy. We have a Pope!" An electric hush bristled through the Chapel. Cardinal Pignedoli fell to his knees. No one moved.

Cardinal Vilot took the first tentative steps to join his colleague. There were tears in his eyes as well. The French prelate, who had only yesterday become the opposition's favorite, was today joining in an occasion of inspired revelation: selection of the Pope by spontaneous acclamation. Soon Pappalardo, Ursi and Kee rose to join them.

Cardinal after cardinal followed the pair until the trickle grew to a crimson wave. The papal electors had clearly made their choice.

The seniormost member of the electoral College of Cardinals, Benjerio Cardinal Assicion, raised his hands in a vain attempt to quell the mounting intensity. He stood before a crying Cardinal Michalovce and shouted, "Do you accept the throne of St. Peter?"

The long space of a heartbeat that followed seemed like a ripple of eternity until the cardinal dropped his trembling hands from his face. He looked into the sea of familiar faces before him. His mind, torn between exaltation and doubt, tense from fear and dizzy from sleeplessness, brought him to the breaking point. Had he even touched the device? His reeling brain could not be certain. The question spun dizzily through his thoughts. But had they elected him in spite of the balloting, by acclamation, by an inspiration, a vision? Then God's will was truly served. The thought pealed through his mind like a faroff cathedral bell, a response to his fervent prayers. The word rolled from his lips; he looked into Cardinal Assicion's eager countenance and answered: "*Accepto.*"

The Princes of the Church burst into a sustained display of ecstasy. Their joyous applause rebounded from wall to sculptured wall.

In the midst of their exclamations, Senior Cardinal Assicion's deep voice called out the second question:

"By what name do you wish to be called?"

Michalovce hesitated only briefly; this would be the third name he would have in his lifetime. Then, with a solemn gesture, he replied, "Alexander . . . Alexander."

The lean and silver-haired Michalovce—the new Pope—walked from behind the long table. One by one all 111 cardinals came forward to pay homage to *Il Papa.*

Before he dressed in the waiting white cassock, one task remained; to proclaim to the waiting world that a new Pope had been chosen.

The ballots had been threaded together. Though the count had never been completed, all pieces of scrap paper were collected, and under the watchful eyes of the scrutineers and revisers, the documents were placed in the corner stove. Doused with the ritual oil, a flare was lit and inserted. Through the chimney, to the world outside, curled the first soft billow of pure, pure white, unfolding like the petals of a rose.

A banderole of smoke grew atop the Sistine Chapel. Excited voices and pointing fingers proclaimed its sighting. As the wind slowed and the wisps became clear, the entire square grew silent. Then a whisper, growing to a roar, rumbled forth—a new Pope had been chosen! *"Il Papa . . . Il Papa,"* the shout echoed from ten thousand throats. In moments fifty thousand others joined in until the cry became a thunderclap. The cornerstone of the giant basilica, laid in 1506, shook with the rolling sound. It flowed out of the plaza and down the Piazza San Pietro like a flood, engulfing additional faithful who raced forward and took up the cry.

The spaces around the great Bernini colonnades were soon filled to capacity. For those who could not press toward the church the Maderna fountains became a vantage point. Everyone shouted for the appearance of the new Vicar of Christ.

Then at last the Senior Cardinal Deacon stepped out onto the central balcony of St. Peter's. His words were those used by Cardinal Pignedoli in his moment of inspiration, *"Annuntio vobis gaudium magnum.* We have a Pope!" The crowd responded with a great shout of joy.

The cardinal continued, " . . . the Most Eminent and Most Reverend Brandano Lord Cardinal Michalovce, who has taken the name Alexander."

That was the moment the entire world learned a Czech had been named Pope. Even in the shock and muttering was the beginning of a cry of joy. It rose in intensity until they shouted as one:

"*Il Papa . . . Il Papa . . . Il Papa.*"

The chant went on without stop until the white Mozzetta came into view. It was almost beyond imagination that a non-Italian had been chosen. That it had happened would be attributed, at least in part, to the goal of his immediate predecessor: the movement of the Church into the twenty-first century. A non-Italian offered hope of worldwide unity for the future.

Cardinal Michalovce strode out onto the balcony, beaming. The crowd greeted him with his name . . . "Alexander . . . Alexander . . . Alexander."

It was mid-afternoon when news of the selection of the new Pope was relayed, via satellite, to the Soviet capital. Chairman Maksim Shaposhnikov had left strict orders to be immediately informed of its results. At the moment the announcement flashed on German television, the chairman was engrossed in a planning session with his economic advisors. (Projected grain production was down 20 percent from the prior year—something to be reckoned with.)

"Chairman?" called a voice on the intercom. "If you turn on the television, German transmission is reporting the papal selection."

Maksim walked to the wall screen, switching on the pre-tuned receiver. A German-speaking commentator was droning on, before a background of the Vatican, about the history of the Papacy. The camera flashed the wisps of white smoke.

Neither Chairman Shaposhnikov nor the commentator had a long wait before the doors on the central balcony parted and the Senior Cardinal Deacon stepped out. The chanting crowd nearly drowned out the newsman until the cardinal raised his hands, calling for silence. When the multitude obeyed, the silence was frightening. The thousands in the great square, along with untold millions around the world, held their breath.

" . . . the most Eminent and Most Reverend Brandano Lord Cardinal Michalovce, who has taken the name Alexander."

A smile came over the lips of the Soviet leader. His eyes

closed almost in prayer. It was over, the plan was successful; his position as chairman was secure.

The other men present in the room began to question one another, "The Czech? How is it possible?"

Shaposhnikov spun about, his back facing the screen, and said, "Gentlemen, please take note. The Czech Cardinal Michalovce has been chosen as Pope. I believe that we have all just witnessed the beginning of a new era for us." He caught himself, not wishing to overflow in his enthusiasm. "And I think, for today, this meeting shall be suspended." He turned and walked out, rubbing his thick palms together, unable to conceal his grin.

Marshal A. A. Tukhachevski had just watched a Helicopter Assault Group destroy a series of discarded trucks and plywood huts. He was approaching the lead ship, which had landed not thirty meters from him, when a young aide grabbed at his elbow. The Marshal leaned over as the officer shouted into his ear over the roar of the ship's twin jet engines, "Marshal, an important call for you."

The slender lieutenant held his cap down on his shock of light blond hair as they turned away from the ship's downwash and sprinted back to the marshal's staff car. The marshal jumped in, pressing the receiver to his ear. "Tukhachevski here."

"Marshal," the faint voice answered, "Michalovce has been chosen."

"Please repeat the name," the marshal requested.

"Michalovce, Marshal . . . it is Michalovce! He has taken the name Alexander. Congratulations, sir!"

There was no reply. Tukhachevski replaced the receiver and began to laugh. His aide looked in without understanding what his general found humorous. But to the marshal it didn't matter if the entire army thought him daft; he had chosen the winning side—Shaposhnikov had come through, the old fox!

As the marshal got out of the car, beaming, his boyish-looking lieutenant straightened to attention. Tukhachevski brought his hand down on the surprised officer's back, sending him reeling forward before snapping back to attention.

"Come on, Lieutenant. This is a day for joy." The muscular former cosmonaut slapped him again. "I know how I can bring a smile to your face. As of this moment, Tbilisi, you're a captain!"

Thunderstruck, the only response the young officer could muster was a half-swallowed, "Thank you, sir." But his words were eclipsed by the sudden roar of the twin motors picking up power, as the marshal ran toward the ship. The aide sprinted after his commander; by now, he too was sporting a smile.

Ten minutes after receiving confirmation that Cardinal Michalovce had indeed been chosen, Gvozdetskii and Colonel V. Torchnoi, known as "Kichkine" to his subordinates, were deep in conference. Kichkine was anything but the "little one" the name implied. Rather he was lean, muscular, and brutal—one of the most feared of the KGB's special operatives.

"Colonel," began Gvozdetskii, "our contingency plan is no longer merely an intellectual exercise. Have you been able to make the selection?"

The colonel needed few words. Both he and his chief had been over this ground before. The colonel had earlier narrowed the list of subjects to two individuals, their psychological profiles making them both prime candidates. Only this morning he had eliminated one. "Yes. I have selected."

"Good," said Gvozdetskii. "Will he be ready?"

"Yes!"

"Then, proceed. Cardinal Michalovce must never gain the triple tiara."

"He will not, Comrade Director."

The conference was at an end.

The office of the Vatican director of security seemed vacant. Detective Barzini called out, "Is anyone there?" There was no one. He walked inside, looking about. It was crucial that he gain access to the personnel files, and pictures of all priests assigned either to the Rome Archdiocese or to the Vatican itself. He would be able to eliminate all but those between the ages of twenty-five and forty. This would still leave hundreds, if not thousands, of records to sift through, but since his priest had been seen in Rome, not far from the Vatican, there was a good chance his face would be among the file photos.

The sound of rustling papers drew him to the inner office. In front of two tall windows a yellow folder was suddenly thrown atop a mountainous pile of similar documents.

Lorenzo called out, "Excuse me, I'm from the police."

There was no response.

Barzini walked around the desk. On the other side he found an old priest working furiously on a pile of papers. "Excuse me I'm Detective . . . "

The old man looked up. "Who are you?" he questioned. "What do you want? Can't you see the office is closed? We have a new Pope. Everything must wait. Come after . . . next week."

Barzini took out his identification and held it out so that the priest could squint at it.

"He? So you're a policeman. I see. But it doesn't matter. Come back next week!" The priest began to return to his work.

"Sir. I have urgent need of assistance! I'm working on an important case that cannot wait. It's essential that I speak with the director at once."

"Clearly, young man, that's impossible," prattled the shriveled priest. Bishop Pironio is too busy with security preparations."

The old man stood; bent nearly in half, he reached the detective's mid-section. "I'm Father Datuk, Bishop Pironio's assistant. I'm afraid I'll be the only one you'll be able to speak to this week. So, if it's urgent, you'll have to deal with me."

Barzini had hoped for a security officer, but he was desperate; Father Datuk would have to do. "Father, I'm working on a murder investigation and . . . "

"Murder? Why come here? Do you think the director knows of murders?"

Barzini was taken aback. "No, Father. I'm afraid you don't understand. I'm working on a murder investigation and I think one of your priests could help."

"One of our priests? How possibly could a priest be of help to the police department?"

"Er, it's possible that he might have seen the killer," Lorenzo lied.

Father Datuk sat down, facing the detective. "Now then, how might we be of help to you? Why don't you simply ask this priest your questions?"

"Because I don't know who he is. Our witnesses can only give us a skimpy description of the priest. I can only guess that he's a member of the Roman Archdiocese. He was in the area and didn't seem to be sightseeing. So," Barzini continued, "I wonder if I could go through whatever pictures or physical descriptions you have of the priests assigned here? This priest must be located."

Father Datuk turned back to his mound of work. "Priests? Are you aware just how many priests there are in Rome? Clearly, it's an impossible task. And a general description? Why"—he flapped his hands in front of him—"see these folders? There are twenty thousand assigned to teaching duties in Italy alone."

"Twenty thousand?" answered Barzini. Indeed, it seemed impossible.

"What else do you have to go on?" questioned Father Datuk.

"Not too much, Father," said the dejected policeman. "I only know that he is tall, and aged from the middle twenties to under forty."

"Fifteen years, my, my. As I said, impossible," answered the elderly priest. "What else might you know about him?"

"Not much, Father. A young priest was seen walking in the area of a killing a few weeks ago. It's taken me until now to find that out. As for a description, there isn't anything too clear. I was hoping that something might come to me by looking over some of your identification shots."

"Surely. All you have to do is go through all the red folders. That way you'll only get priests, not bishops, monsignors, cardinals, or Popes. Of course, some of these pictures might be twenty years old."

"Twenty years old?" Barzini was bewildered.

"Oh, yes. Or more. A priest doesn't need a new picture unless he transfers, or gains a higher station."

At that moment the phone began ringing. Father Datuk reached for the instrument. "Hello. Yes, Bishop. I'll be right there." The father instantly forgot about his visitor and gathered up a series of documents, stuffing them into a worn leather briefcase that rested beside the desk. As he stood he returned his attention to the officer. "Remember, the red folders only, yes?"

Five hours later, an exhausted Lorenzo Barzini had all but given up. The task was truly impossible. He picked up the pile of folders he'd just gone through and was carrying them back to the shelf when the sound of papers scattering on the floor stopped him. Sighing, he put the red stack down on the nearest seat and bent to retrieve the fallen documents. Lifting the envelope from the wrong end, its contents, several photocopied documents, slid out and fluttered to the floor. The seal that had held it closed had apparently come undone when it fell.

With an exasperated mutter he knelt to collect the scattered pages. Only then did he notice the curious Russian lettering stamped in red across the top and bottom of each page. Some of the words looked vaguely familiar—the same thing was written in several languages. Slowly the meaning began to dawn on him: *Top Secret.*

He spent the next several hours carefully studying the Czechoslovakian documents, gradually piecing together their meaning. He learned that the documents dated back to the war, 1943, 1944, 1945. And there was a name . . . Brandano Michalovce . . . the new Pope.

The name was thrice accompanied by another, Bohuslav Tabor. He determined that they were linked together—both names were circled in red as if Michalovce and Tabor were one and the same.

The last page was unmistakable. It was a ledger of unions in marriage. No matter what language it might be written in, it could not have been clearer, Bohuslav Tabor had taken Anya Anelovicz as his wife.

The slow dawning of comprehension left Barzini dumbfounded. If he had read the documents correctly, the new Pope might well be an imposter . . . at least known by another name. And what made it even more incredible, if he understood correctly, Bohuslav Tabor—who was also Brandano Michalovce—had married!

Lorenzo finally replaced the folder on the desk, carefully placing some yellow folders on top of it. He turned to leave, then stopped, wanting to look at the sheets once again. No, he thought, it was all too impossible; they were probably forgeries . . . they had to be. It was possible the Vatican was investigating these bogus documents.

He made the sign of the cross on his chest, then left the musty room and closed the door behind him.

Canticles echoed faintly through the hallowed halls surrounding the Sistine Chapel: a choir practicing for the coming investiture.

A chilling wind had swept down from the north during the night. It whipped about the buildings, foretelling the approaching winter. The halls lost their last remnant of summer's warmth, replaced by a chilled dampness which would remain for the next six months. More fortunate Romans spent their winters at Napoli.

A dark figure stalked triumphantly in the passages between the Vatican library and the Sistine Chapel. He was dressed as a priest, this cerebus in human guise. The workman-priest had devised everything perfectly. So far no problems had arisen, no deviations from the expected. Never prey to laxity, especially with complete success so close at hand, he was now taking inordinate care to be on guard.

By 5:30 P.M., the choir had finished their work, their harmonic echoes evaporating in the chilled night. The Swiss Guards completed their final sweep of the passages; by 7:00 P.M. only authorized personnel remained inside. With the new Pope awaiting investiture, all in the Vatican would sleep deeply through the long night.

Now, down the deserted passages, the workman-priest walked calmly toward the chapel. There should be no one to question him or to interrupt his task. The hallway was silent and he trod lightly. The Sistine Chapel's doors were padlocked with a huge iron ornament. After examining it, the Professional withdrew a small leather case of master steel picks from his overalls. Looking at the keyhole once again, he selected a spindly tool and inserted it into the small space. After a few moments of delicate exertions the ancient padlock gave way. The heavy ceremonial ornament had not been intended to bar an expert's passage.

Once inside the chapel he moved directly to the altar, requiring only a couple of minutes to retrieve the small electronic receiver hidden in the chalice base.

The heavy golden goblet was still in place, not scheduled to be removed until morning. After turning the goblet on its side, the Professional carefully removed the felt backing and began to loosen the oscillating apparatus so as to remove it undetectably. He did not see the lone figure at the chapel doorway.

Ninety-year-old Father Mostrianni had spent the past five years in a world of his own. He had long ceased to be of productive service to the Church, yet the institution still had room for him here, protected, behind the walls of St. Peter's. The priest would spend hours on end seated complacently at the back of the great cathedral, relishing the beauty of a thousand young voices as they practiced their hymns, soaking in the wash of harmonies as one might bask in the rays of the sun. Then, when the choirs left, he would wander through the hallways. Tolerated because of his age and senility, he could be found walking at almost any hour, lost in silent fantasies.

This night he began his random wanderings in the set of passages that led to the Sistine Chapel. His step was without weight, and almost soundless. As usual, the priest walked barefoot, whether from forgetfulness or symbolic devotion, no one ever knew.

In fiction lies only the specter of reality. In Father Mostrianni's confused mind, perhaps he was following the footsteps of some long-departed Holy Father; his pilgrimage through these deserted halls was a journey through another time. The devices of his imagination were infinitely more powerful than those of his senses. In the inner recesses of his clouded brain, he was seeking a pathway to heaven. Indeed, the Angel of Death needed to search no further than this emaciated ancient for its next victim.

Now, as he turned a corner and stopped, he found the doors to the chapel were open. Inside, at the far side of the room, beneath the panoramic the *Last Judgment*, a priest knelt, it seemed to him in prayer, holding a golden chalice. The senile father decided to join this young priest in silent contemplation under the altar, or perhaps to offer to sing him a hymn. His steps barely touching the cold floor, hands clasped in front of him, he approached the back of the working figure.

The man had evidently completed his prayer. He carefully repositioned the golden goblet and placed something in his overall's pocket. Father Mostrianni innocently moved closer, his shallow breathing lost in the vastness of the room. He raised his hand and placed it on the man's shoulder while at the same time allowing the first note of a hymn to escape his throat and find his lips. It was the last sound he'd ever make.

Instantly the man spun like a startled jaguar. With lightning reflex, his hands lashed out their icy axe of death.

The Professional had replaced the felt liner and had glued it in place. He was turning the chalice right side up when he felt the presence of someone else in the room. He purposely hesitated, prolonging his turn until he could feel the faint rhythmic pattern of breath. Like a cat knows, he knew the other's position. He tensed.

A soft hand found his shoulder; he reacted without thought. He spun, right hand slashing down on the fragile priest he found staring up at him. The man's mouth was open but the sound that barely escaped his lips died there. Perhaps it was a protest; it mattered little.

The heel of his hand struck the priest across the bridge of his nose with a dull, sickening sound of crushing bone.

As the priest fell, the Professional's arm caught the man's neck in a vice-like grip and, without hesitation, snapped the spinal column.

The priest's head lolled limply backward on the broken neck. The Professional swiftly wrapped his kerchief around the face to prevent any seepage of blood.

He let the priest slip from his grasp and fall silently to the floor. The room was empty; the man had been alone. Old and spent, he had posed no danger. But now his withered form created a problem: Where to hide a dead man?

It was important that the body would not be found inside the Sistine Chapel, for with such a discovery questions would follow, questions he couldn't afford to have asked.

To the right of the chapel's doorway, perhaps ten meters away, a stairway led down. A velvet rope stretched across it prevented its use. There was no time to waste.

The Professional seized his victim and carried him outside the chapel. He positioned the old man face down on the sixth step, his feet dangling off the first. The rope was broken from one pillar and placed under the body. Next, the Professional grasped the rosary beads in his hand and tore them from the priest's neck. The beads exploded from the thin wire and fell bouncing off the steps to the landing below.

He stood back, grasped the wire tightly at both ends, and pulled it, along with the remaining beads, sharply across the upright banister post. The glass beads shattered, showering tiny slivers of glass. The effort left a vivid mark on the dark wooden post; any investigation would show that the priest had somehow lost his footing and had slipped down on the closed-off stairway, his rosary beads catching on the upright banister post. Result: a snapped neck. The man's smashed nose would be attributed to having struck a wooden tread. Now, unwrapping the kerchief, he allowed the blood to begin trickling along the sixth step. Everything seemed right.

The Professional returned to the doors of the Sistine Chapel. He carefully closed them and was about to replace the lock in its original place, when he stopped. His mind had discovered a flaw.

He hurried back to where the dead priest lay and surveyed the scene. There was a crucial element he had not attended to. He bent over and raised his fist, then brought it down sharply on the edge of the upper step, splintering it. He reached for the priest's left foot and moved it in line with the cracked tread.

There now could be no other conclusion but that the priest had failed to see the flaw in the upper step. He thus tumbled to his death; may God protect his humble soul.

16

Lorenzo Barzini had arrived at Vatican security before the sun was fully up, determined to discover a picture of this man, or to eliminate the possibility that the killer was truly a priest.

At ten minutes after ten that morning, Father Datuk burst in on the seated detective, his face distorted with fright. "Officer," he wheezed, gasping for breath. "Oh ... oh ... I am so glad you're still here."

Lorenzo jumped up, offering his seat to the hysterical man. "Sit down, Father. Please ... what's the mat—"

"He's dead, Father Mostrianni is dead," gasped the priest.

"Dead? ... Where? How?"

Tears streamed down the priest's pinched face. "By the Sistine Chapel. When we went to the chapel, to take the golden chalice, oh ... oh ... one of the guards found him." The bent priest offered a trembling sign of the cross on his chest, over and over again. "Oh ... Oh my Lord. ..."

Barzini inched forward. "How did this happen?"

"Oh, I don't know," sobbed Father Datuk. "He must have fallen." The policeman nodded.

"He was such a gentle soul, always listening to music. Father Mostrianni had been a priest, for, my God, nearly seventy years. He only knew one purpose, to serve our Lord, Jesus Christ."

"Take me to him," said the detective quietly.

The old father rose slowly, still sobbing for breath, and tottered with the detective out of the office. "The police were called," he said, head bobbing.

"Just in case," was Barzini's answer.

When they reached the Sistine Chapel, a small crowd of curious priests and guards had already gathered. Barzini didn't have to shout; the presence of Father Datuk was enough to clear the way for the pair.

Two familiar faces greeted Lorenzo as he approached the stairway. "Hey, Barzini. How come you're here? I thought we caught this one?"

"I'm just an observer," answered the detective. "I've been following a few leads down here when I got the word that a death had occurred. Just thought I'd protect the scene until you guys arrived. Got anything, Cambio?" he inquired of his round-faced associate.

The squatting detective rose and pointed down at the dead man. "Broken step. Poor old guy was probably walking down the hallway"—his hand indicated the probable path of Father Mostrianni—"and he didn't see this rut."

"Fell; rope gave way; bang. The damn thing wasn't too strong." Cambio caught himself. "Sorry, Father . . . I mean about the damn."

Father Datuk could not bear to survey the scene. He waved his hand, assuring the detective forgiveness.

"Well," Cambio began anew, "the old guy fell, broke his neck." He puffed his jowls. "The blood? Looks like he kind of slid on down and busted his nose to boot. On the . . . " he counted, "sixth step."

Barzini nodded, turning his attention to the scene. "What's all this?" he queried, pointing to the scattered beads.

"Humph," pouted Cambio, "glass—I don't know."

Barzini knelt to examine one. "Rosary beads." On the steps, half hidden by the body, he found the remainder of them. "A necklace; looks like it was torn in the fall." Cambio stood flatfooted, hands folded across his paunch, eyeing Barzini with some suspicion. It didn't take long for the latter to complete his theorizing.

"Here, look on the banister-post." Barzini found the mark left there intentionally. "Looks to me like his beads caught here as he fell; they left a groove where they snapped."

"Yeah, and his neck snapped with 'em," deduced Cambio finally.

"Seems pretty likely," nodded Lorenzo, concluding his thesis solemnly.

There was a commotion at the rear of the milling crowd; a stretcher was being passed through. Cambio's partner climbed the stairs and began to direct the stretcher's movement. Barzini didn't pay much more attention to what was happening; the blood dripping over the lower steps was making his stomach turn. He sat down on a stone bench nearby to clear his head.

Who needed this interruption now? He had precious little time as it was. Someone sinister was hiding behind the robes of piety, and he was determined to find him.

"And now this happens," he muttered. "They'll probably want me to fill out a report. And they'll want to know what in heaven's name I was doing here. *Mamma mia!*" He struck his forehead with his palm in disgust.

Then it occurred to him: Perhaps there was some connection here. Could the old priest really have twisted his ankle, fallen through the rope and caught his necklace on the railpost? If his neck had snapped back, how had he bloodied his face as well? Lorenzo leaped up to examine the scene once more. The attendants were already positioning their stretcher. Cambio had drawn the chalk outline, and was about to instruct them to move the body.

"Hold it a second!" he shouted and clambered forward.

Barzini bent over to scrutinize the corpse once again. The padre was face down, a puddle of blood around his face, the rope caught beneath the body. "Exactly where it should be," he mused.

His eyes traveled to the priest's feet, then looked up suddenly. "Father Datuk," he called. "Please come here."

The priest walked to where the detective was kneeling. "Yes?" he asked, averting his swollen eyes from the spectacle.

"Father, this man isn't wearing shoes. Hasn't anyone asked where they are?"

The priest smiled sadly. "He wouldn't be, Detective Barzini. You see, Father Mostrianni's mind wasn't always, ah, con-

centrating on such worldly matters. For a number of years now
he has been leaving his shoes and socks in places he couldn't remember."

"Thank you, Father," said the detective. The priest turned
away.

Barzini's attention returned to the man's feet, and then to the
splintered step. Here was the problem. How could this slight,
barefoot man possibly have done this much damage to the
wooden tread? There seemed to be no marks on his feet!

He looked closer ... his eye caught a hint of a gouge per-
pendicular to the flow of the shattered wood; it was out of place.
He bent over even further, kneeling with his face practically
against the floor. Something caught his eye: a faint glint. It was
unmistakable: Something golden had clearly scratched hard
against a black-iron nail, made visible in the cleft of the cracked
step. No featherweight, barefoot priest had broken this wood. It
had been cloven by a heavy blow from an object tooled in gold.

Barzini stood up stiffly, his head reeling with the implication
he alone could fathom. This was no accident, he thought. No, it
was *him*; the priest ... the one with the golden ring. The man is
here within these hallowed walls.

The detective's eyes searched the thinning crowd suspiciously.
He studied each face. Something inside him was certain he'd
know, if they met, who it was.

White-suited attendants began covering the body before lifting it onto the stretcher.

Barzini started walking. In a few steps he passed the open
doors of the Sistine Chapel and looked inside. Directly across the
room, resting on the far altar, was a golden chalice. He paused,
then walked on. His mind was clouded with darker visions. As he
made his way back to the Vatican's security office he grappled
with the intuitive truth: The killer was a priest. This man had
violated his contract with God; Thou shalt not kill. He knew it
was a thesis no one would believe ... not until he brought the
man in.

His footsteps echoed against the stone walls. His legs ached
with his tense fear. Such a man might kill again, before Barzini
could stop him.

There was still no face to supplement the description. The detective plunged into the mountainous pile of Vatican records with renewed, obsessive vigor.

Her face burned with intensity: pale skin, almost translucent; slash of dark lips; the vivid, searing black of open eyes. Their meeting was anteprandial. He willed it so.

She had waited for nearly an hour in a sparsely furnished room, with no window, no light, just visible darkness.

A sliver of fluorescence cut through the black like a razor. The hallway timer lit a single 20-watt bulb outside her doorway to show her visitor the way. The pupils of her dark eyes remained open wide despite the glare. Moments later, without sound, the saber's edge of light under the door was suddenly broken by a dark form. The sound of a metal key slithering in the tumblers of its lock meant that it was he.

She walked to the left wall and switched on the overhead fixture to bathe the room in incandescence. She returned to her seat on the end of the high padded bench, and waited.

As always, the handle turned slowly, the door swinging open in minute degrees. The man slipped inside, peered slowly about, then walked directly for her "My dear. Ritsa. How lovely you look today."

She remained mute, her eyes looking through him. Her lips quivered.

"Ritsa . . . Ritsa, are you there?" he intoned gently, in a droning voice that never wavered.

Her eyes were empty.

Patiently he grasped her chin, as if he were grasping a familiar utensil.

"Ritsa," he beckoned once again. "Ritsa, listen to my voice. You can hear nothing but my voice . . . nothing at all." Her eyes closed, her body tensed. "Concentrate on my voice . . . concentrate. You will do exactly as I tell you. Do you hear me?"

Her head bowed, a wisp of raven hair falling across her face; she made no attempt to brush it away. She possessed only one thought, one direction, one dedication—to follow.

"Ritsa." She raised her head, eyes remaining closed. "You will take the evening plane to Rome to attend the investiture.

You will stand, from first dawn on the morning of the ceremony, in the first row in the great square of St. Peter's.

"When the ceremony is complete, and the Holy Father wears the high-pointed white tiara, he will walk through the great square. You must prostrate yourself before him, kiss his feet, and press your hands against your breasts. That is all that is necessary. Can you do this for me?"

"Yes," she answered. There was nothing sinister in her response. Her words fell innocently from her lips, with a sad, gentle softness to her voice. "I will do as you ask."

"Good, my child," he said. "Remember, you must press fully on your breasts as you fall before him."

"Yes," she said without prompting.

Slowly he lifted her shirt, his fingers running lightly across her smooth belly. She made no motion of response; her posture remained stiff. Raising the thin fabric entirely, he revealed two soft mounds jutting high from her young chest, their tips taut and protruding.

His firm fingers lightly circled them, then pressed deeply into the soft flesh. He could feel the devices implanted there; it would soon be time to activate them.

He leaned forward, his face entering the harsh circle of light cast by the single shaded overhead bulb. It was a face of iron eyes and cold disdain that did not match the soothing monotone of his voice. "Ritsa, when I leave, at the closing of the door, you will begin to awaken. At that time you will not recall our meeting, nor what has been said between us. Yet you will act as I have instructed. Repeat that to me."

Her eyes opened for the first time since he began speaking. They showed no flicker of the woman burning behind them. "I will act as you have instructed."

He was satisfied. She would perform.

His hands continued to toy with her small, firmly pointed breasts. Applying pressure, he steadily forced her down against the padded benchtop. She lay back stiffly. The chief would be very pleased with his progress, thought Colonel Torchnoi. Gvozdetskii would probably promote him. His hands moved lower, pushing up her skirt, gripping her knees tightly and spreading them wide apart. . . .

Detective Barzini walked along the cold passageways between the Sistine Chapel and the offices of Vatican security. He was faced with a dilemma. Undoubtedly a man in priestly robes had been responsible for the killings of at least four persons. That "priest" might well lurk somewhere within the walls of the Vatican. But how could the detective uncover his identity? There was one thing he felt sure of: Whoever this devil was, his picture could be found in the files he was looking through. What he lacked was one clue that would single out the right man.

The tired detective sat before the mammoth pile of personnel folders; his energy was waning. His hand sought the top document, placed the folder on the desk and opened it. He read it aloud:

"Father Dominic Panzzio, age forty-nine; No. His eyes scanned the vital statistics. Too small, too old, too well known.

He reached for the next one. Then a curious thought crossed his mind. Whoever he was, he would probably be a newcomer to the Vatican. Of course—an unknown; a foreigner, perhaps, who wouldn't be familiar. He'd spoken perfect Italian, one had said—book-learned Italian.

"The steel fillings," he shouted. His words rang out in the empty room as the fillings' Central European origin sprang to mind. That bastard within these walls. Soberly he sat down; with all other leads exhausted, now it was time to play a hunch. His hands raced through the piles of records once more. This time he was looking for a specific profile. His suspect had to be relatively young, tall, with access to the innermost corridors of the Vatican, and with one additional essential element: he should be European.

Five hours later, the detective had run through all the possibilities. Before him were photographs of three suspects. Each one fit his profile.

It has to be one of these, he thought. One worked in registry, the second was a translator, the third a member of the Vatican library. Each suspect had been at the Vatican less than a year. The oldest was thirty-six, the youngest twenty-nine. Each had been born in Eastern Europe; all had access to the area about the Sistine Chapel. There was only one way to eliminate any of them, or to confirm just who was the killer. The old-fashioned way.

Barzini scooped up the photographs and slipped them into his jacket pocket, then rushed through the outer doorway, nearly knocking over Father Datuk, who was hobbling into the office. "Sorry, Father," he called as he spun past.

"Certainly, my son . . . " answered the bewildered priest. He turned and watched the detective run down the hallway and disappear into a stairwell.

Fifteen minutes later, the detective was bashing energetically on the basement apartment door, just meters from where the schoolchildren had found the packaged jawbone fragment.

"Who the fuck is it?" a gravelly voice rumbled from behind the cracked and peeling barrier.

"Detective Barzini! Open up, I have to speak to you for a few minutes."

"Get your ass out of here," bellowed the janitor. "Come back tomorrow. I'm too busy to talk to you now."

Barzini pounded on the door jamb. "Open it now or I'll kick this goddamn thing down." Lorenzo was surprised at his own words, but they got the desired reaction. Within the apartment a chair scratched against the concrete floor. The door was thrown open.

"Okay, cop. What do you want this time?" Behind the janitor a thin girl, hardly in her teens, stood half hidden by his bulk. Barzini's eyes searched her face. She pulled the ragged robe about her neck, trying to hide her nakedness. "I asked you what the hell you want from me? Didn't I tell you everything I know?"

Barzini glowered back at the janitor. "I want you to look at some pictures."

The man laughed. "So you want to give me art lessons, do you?"

"Hey, look, you clown. I don't want to give you anything but a week in the can. Either you help me, or I'm going to run your ass in for . . . for fucking a minor—a felony, *capisce?*" The girl's face disappeared behind the janitor, whose thick fingers were massaging the stubble on his cheeks.

"Okay, cop. Let's look at your pictures."

The detective stepped into the cellar apartment and walked to a ceiling light. He glanced back as the girl scurried from the room clutching her clothes. Barzini spread the three photographs on the food-encrusted table. "Come over here, creep," he said. The janitor walked to the detective. "Now look at these three guys. Recognize any of them?"

The janitor studied the three photos. "These guys are priests," he said.

"Very good. Now, do you recognize any of them?"

"Maybe," he answered.

"I said," Barzini's voice was steady and strong, "do you recognize any of them? You asshole, you better come up with a straight answer. No bullcrap or I'll have your hide. Was any one of these guys the priest you saw at the garbage pails that night?"

"Like I said, maybe. I told the other cops, it was dark that night. I hardly even saw the guy."

"And?" Barzini fumed.

"I can't tell for sure. But I do know it wasn't this one. His hair is the wrong color. And his face is too thin." The janitor picked up the other two photos and handed them to Lorenzo. "It could be either one of these guys. That's the best I can do for you. Okay?" He belched.

Two hours later, Barzini's car skidded to a halt in front of the outdoor flea market that backed on the sea. Jumping out, he waded into the crowd, heading directly to the back of the square to find the unkempt vendor that had sold the binoculars to the bogus priest. It didn't take long. When the man spied the detective pushing through the milling mass of humanity, he quickly turned away.

But the detective had already spied his workman's cap and was walking toward him. "Glad you're here," said Barzini. "It saves me the trouble of looking you up at your house."

The vendor tried to gather up his possessions. The detective's hand came down on the small bundle stopping him.

"Listen, detective, why are you back here to bug me again? You want to ruin me or something?"

"No," answered the detective. "In fact, I only have one question for you this time. If you cooperate, I get out of your hair, fast."

"All right," grumbled the anxious vendor. "Ask, ask!"

Lorenzo dropped the three photographs on the concrete wall. "Look at these three men." The man glanced at the pictures, then turned back to the detective.

"So?" he questioned.

"So, was any of them the priest you sold the binoculars to?"

The vendor turned his attention back to the photos. A crowd had already gathered and the vendor played to his new-found audience. "So I'm gonna break a big case, huh?" He grinned, spreading the photos apart and scrutinizing them dramatically. Finally, after scratching his chin, tilting his cap over one eye and doing his best Mastroianni imitation, he picked up one and flipped it to Lorenzo. "This is the guy."

Barzini looked at the snapshot. "Are you sure? Or did he just look like this one?"

"Nope. If I tell you that's the one, then that's the one. Nobody gonna say Nino Palmero makes mistakes, eh?" He pointed to his chest with both thumbs for the benefit of the onlookers, who playfully grunted their approval.

"So I broke a big case, huh?" he shouted after Barzini, who nodded his thanks with a wry smile and left the clump of vendors to their camaraderie.

Lorenzo sat in his car gazing at the picture the vendor had selected. Square-jawed, light-haired, tight-lipped, but the subject's eyes glanced to the side. It was the priest who worked in the Vatican library as an art restorer: one Father Kottmeyer. Could it be him? wondered the detective. It fits; he has access to almost anywhere. But why the Sistine Chapel? He still couldn't figure it out.

He started the car and pulled out into the traffic. The vehicle leapt noisily ahead, picking up speed. The Madonna on the dash rattled with the old Fiat's vibrations. Lorenzo turned onto Via di Terni, then suddenly slammed on the brakes. Behind him there came a squeal of tires as another car avoided his rear bumper by scant centimeters.

"Hey, you asshole," shouted the other driver. "Get that junk heap off the roadway."

Lorenzo paid no attention to the driver's obscene shouts. He was captivated by his thoughts. Pulling over, he turned off the engine, as the irate driver behind him careened ahead.

Barzini's ruminations concerned the fire that had been set to mask the twin killings, and the solvents. It has to be him, it all fits. The priest is an art restorer. He works with solvents and the like. Whoever those people were, he thought, they had to be disposed of. Art forgers? Whoever they were, one thing was certain: They had served their function.

And the jawbone. Who would have that belonged to? A mystery. Another victim, yet another piece to the puzzle. Fillings from Eastern Europe. This priest comes from Germany. Another match? Or was Father Kottmeyer an imposter? Could be. If this killer had disposed of the real priest, and had taken his place, it was in order to have access to the Sistine Chapel. But why?

In that moment, Lorenzo's mind had once again glanced across the tip of that iceberg; and once again veered away. The Sistine Chapel . . . the election of the Pope . . . the documents revealing Cardinal Michalovce's dual identity. These were connections that boggled his mind. Michalovce: a cardinal from Czechoslovakia, an Iron Curtain state. There were too many disturbing implications to this train of thought. Barzini crossed himself twice and promptly resolved not to pursue this kind of reasoning any further.

The morning sun pierced the fast-moving clouds in flashes of bright intensity, struggling to dispel the lingering coldness of the night. Even as the sun rose higher, the stone steps of the majestic Cathedral of St. Peter's retained their chill. An exhausted Lorenzo glanced at his watch; it was 7:30 A.M. It would be another half hour before the Vatican's official offices were open and he could be admitted. The detective spent the time scrutinizing each face that passed him.

When the bells tolled eight, the heavy bronze doors opened slowly. He hurried through, flashing his police identification, and ran up the far stairway toward the office of Vatican security. The door was locked.

"Detective Barzini." An aged voice rattled from down the corridor.

"Hello, Father Datuk," he said. "I was waiting for you."

The tiny padre approached, inserting a key in the lock with some difficulty. "After you, Detective Barzini," said the priest.

They entered. "Some coffee, my son?"

"No, Father. Please. I'll only need a minute of your time."

"Certainly, what is it?" questioned Father Datuk, finally noticing the detective's agitation.

"Father, I want to find one of your priests."

"To be sure. Which?"

"This one." The detective held out the photograph of the bogus priest.

Father Datuk took the single photo from Lorenzo and held it inches from his face.

"I know him, certainly; he's Father Kottmeyer, a fine new addition to our staff. Yes, in fact, Bishop Bartoleme, the library's chief administrator, just commented that Kottmeyer was the brightest star in his stable. Such beautiful work he did on the little Michelangelo in the Sistine Chapel, Bishop Bartoleme is . . . "

"Where can this Kottmeyer be found?" Barzini interrupted gravely.

"Right at this minute? My goodness. Most probably in his cell on the second level, I should think. But then again, he could be completing his morning prayer and breakfast. Certainly, by eight-thirty he would be in his workroom. No later than nine, do you think?"

"Where's that?"

"Yes, oh, attached to the library."

Barzini jumped up. "It's nearly eight-thirty now. How do I find his room?"

"Oh my," stuttered Datuk. "You can get there by turning right outside the office. Take the second stairway. I should think it would lead you directly to the library."

"And the priest's cells?" demanded Barzini.

"They're right at the end of that corridor. Goodness, I don't see . . . What all the fuss is? . . . "

He never had time to finish his query. Lorenzo had already dashed out.

The Professional had awakened to a ravenous hunger that accompanied the stirrings of victory. He packed all his priestly garb, along with the micro-oscillator, and silicone ink, into a neat, tight package. It would be disposed of in a nearby apartment-house incinerator he'd selected. A tiny explosive-incendiary device would be included to ensure complete consumption.

He patted his breast pocket; his travel documents—a passport and a one-way, first-class ticket overseas. The plane was scheduled to leave at 10:30 A.M., the same hour that the triple tiara was to be placed on the head of Pope Alexander. Everything would be completed before his departure.

All that remained was a last check of the workshop, to ensure that there was nothing to investigate when Father Kottmeyer was reported missing. He would vanish with all traces, like a wisp of smoke in the wind.

By now the piazza would be filled to overflowing with those lucky enough to have gained entrance during the long night. Members of the clergy would be arriving in astounding numbers to witness the ceremony. A single priest would go unnoticed. As for the identity of Father Kottmeyer, this day would be his final priestly pilgrimage.

The detective worked his way swiftly down the hallway, reading each printed nameplate along the walls. Halfway down he came to the one that said "FATHER KOTTMEYER, LIBRARY STAFF." His hand found the automatic he kept in his trousers pocket, finger wrapping tightly around the handle. Lorenzo knew he was after a professional who killed with hesitation.

He hesitated, aware suddenly of the echo of his feet in the narrow corridor, of the sound of his own breathing. Carefully he pressed his ear against the heavy door, but all he could hear was the pounding of his own heart. Through the thickness of the wood he could not detect a sound within.

Lorenzo swallowed, his stomach churned; he realized that there was no one else to make this capture but him, no other time but now, no other way but hand to hand.

Gritting his teeth with the resolve of that thought, he slowly raised his gun to his shoulder, his arm cocked, the barrel close to his cheek, pointing upward. His other hand reached quietly for the door handle. Sure fingers pressed ever so slightly on its latch. He crouched down low.

With one swift fluid move, his sturdy hand released the latch, his shoulder threw the door open, and he burst somersaulting into the room. He came out of his shoulder-roll in perfect position— feet solidly on the floor, both hands outstretched with firearm in combat position. Poised for action, he whirled in one direction, then back in the other.

There was no one in the room.

He lowered his gun and massaged his painful shoulder. This had been an entrance he hadn't utilized since police academy days.

Looking about, he found only a small bare room. He examined all four walls and the wooden dresser. Everything was neat, spotless. Barzini was hard-pressed to say whether anyone had occupied it recently. It reminded him of the room in Ostia: too clean to be normal. Turning to leave, Lorenzo's last glance noticed the shadow of a small object under the bed. He bent down and peered below. Hidden in a corner was a small package. He grabbed it, placed it on the bed, and tore the paper open.

Inside were some priest's clothing, a bottle filled with some black liquid, and a small disc-shaped electronic device. Lorenzo closely examined the ridged, metallic object under the cell's single light. It revealed an elaborate mechanism, obviously sophisticated, its purpose unknown to him. Around one edge was a rectangular adhesive patch, partially torn away, indicating that it may have been attached to another object, then removed. His finger ran thoughtfully along its edge. He held it up to the light; there seemed to be writing along the curved surface.

The letters were foreign, but not entirely unfamiliar. He searched his memory: they weren't Greek or Cyrillic. "Czech?" he wondered, remembering the lettering of the documents he had seen. Then the answer came to him: Like the words stamped *Secret* at the top of those pages—they were Russian! Whatever this complex device was, it was of Russian manufacture.

The implications made him dizzy. This exotic device aroused the gut suspicion that there was mischief afoot more devious than impersonation, of greater gravity than forgery, more sinister even than murder. The implication of this Russian clue tolled in his mind like a cathedral bell in the distance: espionage!

Now the revelations of the documents regarding the Czech about to be ensconced as Pope burned ever clearer. What was this killer doing, disguised as a priest, stalking the inner corridors of the Vatican? What was the purpose of the complex Russian mechanism? What was the meaning of secret Soviet documents indicating something terribly amiss in the background of the Pope? As the questions mounted they pointed steadily, ineluctably in only one direction. It was a train of thought he would have little time to follow through.

The sound of firm footsteps down the hallway drifted into the small room. Suddenly aware of their approach, he stepped back and drew his gun. The steps grew louder. His hand grasped his automatic tightly. A single bead of cold sweat ran down his nose and fell onto his lips. As the steps came nearer he moved the barrel down to bear on whoever would walk through the doorway. He held his breath.

The steps stopped short.

It was perhaps only a heartbeat that elapsed between the halting steps and their equally swift sudden retreat in the other direction. In that moment Lorenzo realized his assailant had responded to the anomaly of the open door. Lorenzo jumped out of the room, gun in hand. He could see a priest's back receding rapidly down the hallway.

"You . . . priest!" he shouted.

The tall man spun for a fraction of a second and returned Lorenzo's gaze with an eye of ice. Even then the detective knew it was a face he'd not easily forget. Before he could even consider pulling his trigger, this demon in holy garb had vanished into the stairwell with the reflexes of a cat.

Only the word "Halt" choked from Lorenzo's lips like a plea to a world gone berserk—uttered far too late.

Lorenzo's steps clattered along the corridor after the priest. He pounded heavily toward the staircase and down. Below him he barely caught sight of a swift figure in black, retreating through a lower archway.

Two landings further down, Barzini was still in close pursuit. He was surprised at his speed; only righteous anger and pounding adrenaline could drive his middle-aged frame through the widening corridor like this. The priest had turned the corner toward the great hall just seconds ahead of him.

A moment later Lorenzo broke into the lighted hall, sweating heavily. He holstered his gun under his arm. There were too many people hurrying to their destinations, preparing for the aftermath of the investiture; too many priests milling in clusters, or moving through doors and corridors.

Lorenzo spun in all directions, fearing that he'd lost his quarry. To the forefront of the main hall were rows of massive wooden doorways. Barzini grasped instinctively that there was where the priest would head—out into the crowd. Lorenzo started in that direction but cut his steps short. It was too far, he realized, eyeing the fifty meters to the door. If the priest had run, he would have attracted attention. And if not, the detective should have caught sight of him leaving—a clever ruse! Barzini whirled and headed in the opposite direction, half running toward the rear of the hall. He had gone only a few steps before a tall priest, shielded behind a cluster of colleagues in the shadow of a rear column, broke away, rushing down the nearest stairwell with an alert Barzini in hot pursuit.

The Professional's feet took several steps at a time, jumping to the first landing—whoever was giving chase was already in the stairwell. By the time the Professional had reached the second landing, the other man was not far behind. Labored steps indicated he wasn't a young man. If the Professional could put enough distance between him and his pursuer, he could lose himself in the growing crowd gathering in St. Peter's.

He had taken his pursuer down several levels, below the main floor. Now he would lose him in the catacomb-like lower passageways, and head for daylight. Or better still, he could use these dark turns to reverse this chase—revert from hunted to his usual role of hunter.

He had led his pursuer to territory of his own advantage. The Professional was already familiar with these passageways; the hunter, he reasoned, was not.

Clattering steps behind him signaled his adversary's proximity. He ducked under an archway before a narrow wooden staircase and flattened himself behind the abutment of the turn. A small sharp instrument flashed in his hand; his assailant had only to turn this way.

Lorenzo had somehow made the last landing. His chest burned from the lack of oxygen. It had been many years since he had attempted such physical activity. Youth was on his suspect's side.

He emerged into the darkened passageway. To his left was the longer route; he chose to go to the right, his shoes ringing steadily toward the opening where the Professional waited.

The detective's steps slowed. He glanced back over his shoulder to be sure no one lurked behind, his gun clenched in a sweaty hand. He moved forward.

The deep passageway was quiet and dim; the first of many archways drew nearer. Lorenzo realized that if the killer was still in these passageways he was motionless—hiding, or lying in wait. The last thought caused him to halt just steps before the darkened archway. He waited. Only his hearbeat sounded in the silence.

Suddenly a sharp ping echoed from the darkness a dozen meters ahead of him. Instantly he ducked, then threw himself flat against the curved wall. As he did so he heard the sound of footsteps bounding up the wooden stairs beneath the archway just to his right.

The Professional, having heard the heavy tread suddenly halt, realized that it was time for action. He held a button tensed between his thumb and forefinger. He had just torn it from the sleeve of his habit. Now, in the moment of stillness, he flicked it sharply with his fingers and wrist as far down the passageway as possible. In the second of distraction caused by the noise, he turned and bounded up the nearby wooden stairs, only a heartbeat before his armed pursuer emerged.

There was one landing between flights. The old staircase led only to a heavy door entering onto a series of larger hallways and public chambers. The Professional moved swiftly through them.

There to his right were four confessionals, their black curtains concealing those who had chosen to make their peace with their Lord. He angled for the last one; the shroud swung from its restraint.

The detective jumped up the lengthy wooden staircase and out onto the ground floor corridor. He could see his man dashing ahead of him. Lorenzo began to half run, half stumble. He fought for breath; it was slow in coming, but still he closed the distance to the killer.

The man turned another corner. Barzini knew his strength was nearly gone as he burst forward. If he didn't catch him in the next hundred meters, he never would. He reached the corner and swung around it. The killer was gone.

His heart pounded and his stomach knotted. He stopped. Off to the right he spied a series of confessional booths; the curtain of the last one was moving. Lorenzo's hand raised the gun chest high.

Cautiously he approached the booth. Sweat soaked through his clothing, his face was blood-red from exertion.

He stood in the doorway, struggling to prevent his panting from betraying his presence. With agonizing slowness, his hand parted the curtains, then suddenly dove into the unlit booth, going for the occupant's throat. A stifled protest barely escaped surprised lips as Lorenzo forced the man out, the gun's muzzle brought to bear at eye level.

A terrified old Italian gentleman was torn from the dim interior of the confessional. His feet barely touched the floor as Barzini, veins and muscles bulging, held him off balance. The man's face was aghast with fear; enormous eyes agape at the muzzle of the gun jammed squarely in his face.

"*Mamma mia,*" the man whispered, his eyes never leaving the weapon.

Barzini exhaled heavily and dropped the man back into the booth. The old Italian burst into a litany of *Hail Mary's* instantly. He had just paid a peculiar penance.

The detective ran from booth to booth, tearing open each curtain. His killer had vanished.

17

The Lord had chosen to provide Michalovce with a cool but sunlit day for his coronation. The chill of October lingered crisply in the air; the sun shone fully. One hundred thousand people had packed the great piazza before the grandeur of St. Peter's. Some had waited throughout the night to be assured a better vantage point.

Lost amidst this sea of faces was one of a hauntingly alluring girl, a foreigner to Rome who had arrived in the Eternal City only a couple of days earlier. The woman seemed calm, detached. She had waited hours on end, eyes fixed on the cathedral, seated on the pavement with thousands of others.

Italian soldiers approached and took their stations, forming a gray line that defined the route of the future Pope. One young man in uniform looked at her, in awe of her beauty. He nudged a companion and pointed her out. "So?" his friend taunted. "Do something."

He took up his comrade's suggestion and approached the girl.

"Quite a crowd," he smiled, but received no response. "A bit nippy to have waited so long, eh? You must have waited all night to be up this close." He shuffled nervously, awaiting a response.

She turned her head toward him finally, but uttered nothing. Her eyes met his; they showed no expression. Dismayed, the guard returned to his post moments later.

"Nothing doing, Paulo." He shook his head. "I think maybe she don't speak Italian or something. Maybe she's deaf."

"Or maybe you're dumb," his friend kidded, still gazing at

the dark-haired pale-skinned beauty. It would be a long morning.

On this day Ritsa Esja, student, had one purpose. Her thoughts narrowed until they pounded in her brain like the waves upon the seashore. The Pope's return from the coronation ceremony, wearing the high pointed hat of stark white that indicated his ascension to the Papacy, would be her cue to act. The sight of the pointed rank of office would inspire a need in her far beyond human emotion. Only that image, passing before her, could trigger her reaction.

The multitude had swollen to enormous proportions. Every corner of the Piazza San Pietro teemed with onlookers. Soon white-robed members of the enormous choir began filing to their places. The crowd pressed forward as the ceremony neared commencement.

Twenty minutes later, world notables began taking their places. Alongside them sat members of the Italian cabinet, the President, and dignitaries of the Church. But movement from the central portal of the cathedral stole the attention of all present. A scarlet-cloaked cardinal emerged and walked forward with measured paces. Soldiers came to attention at this signal that the ritual had begun.

It took a full ten minutes for all the members of the College of Cardinals, Vatican bishops, monsignors, priests, and staff members to pass through the doorway. The procession filled and engulfed the area before the cathedral, unfurling like a flag out into the square. A reverent hush settled over the faithful.

Finally, entering suddenly, an exalted player was on a great stage, Cardinal Michalovce stepped out into the sunlight. As he appeared a shout rang forth, sustained for moments until it broke into a joyous chanting of his name. The walls of the piazza reverberated with sound. The Pope-to-be held out his hands in a gesture of humble acknowledgment. The crowd responded.

Ritsa Esja watched from the first row near the very center of the piazza. The Holy Father wore but a skull cap atop his silvered head.

The mortal who would soon be coronated as Christ's Vicar descended the stone steps from the cathedral. The choir conductor's hands came down. The echoes of angels poured forth in response. Michalovce stepped into the square.

A sweating and tired Lorenzo Barzini walked to the side exit of the basilica. Police nodded in acknowledgment as he passed through security without a word. His face was etched with stern and worried lines.

He had returned from the Professional's chamber with his first few physical clues under his arm: the package of clothes, ink, and the small disc-shaped electronic device.

Only a hundred meters away, on the far edge of the cathedral, the investiture was about to begin. Once again the crowd grew quiet.

Lorenzo's eyes squinted from the strong sunlight as he turned to view the scene. He paused a moment, then began walking away from the building. Suddenly the bells of the city's thousand churches began to ring on cue.

Lorenzo stared in awe from the cathedral's side, obtaining an unobstructed view from this restricted, distant vantage point. But his reverence did not swell the way he expected it to. Rather, as he watched the tiny figures cloaked in dignity, he saw them suddenly as tainted, bloodied, besmirched with the corruption of intrigue and falsehood.

The panorama before him was of pastoral splendor and magnificence. But it was the rising tide of Lorenzo's anger and frustration that caused tears to well in his eyes. Something was wrong here that might never be set right. The ringing of the bells did not inspire devotion in him; they seemed to toll the end of his last refuge of purity. Lorenzo's thoughts turned in that moment to the killer he had stalked. Looking out at the spectacle, at the panorama of steeples echoing with the joy of mingled bells, he swore before God to track him down.

Chairman Shaposhnikov had requested their presence at 2:00 P.M. It was to be his hour of triumph, one he had labored over for the past four months. Everything had turned in his favor, and now he intended to impress that fact upon the defense minister and the chief of the Secret Police—to reaffirm his position as apex of power within the party, and thus the nation.

Marshal Tukhachevski was beaming. His large hand dwarfed

a brimming glass of vodka, which he brought to his lips with increasing regularity.

Gvozdetskii was more subdued. He found an over-upholstered armchair and sank into its recesses. His eyes darted from under a sunken brow, avoiding the direct stares of the other two men, waiting for an opportune moment. Hopefully his vigil would not be too long, for his future—and perhaps his very life—depended on events he could no longer directly control.

Shaposhnikov walked to the armchair and held out a glass of clear liquid. "Drink, my dear Dmitri. We have much to celebrate." There was only the barest trace of mockery in the old fox's voice. The Secret Police chief took the glass, nodded, and forced a thin-lipped smile at his superior. "In a while, Comrade, we will have gained all we bargained for, and more. Mother Russia will finally hold sway in the very walls of our staunchest opponent. What more could we wish for?" He held up his glass, and motioned the others to follow his example. The three men raised and drained their goblets, each toasting his own success in their silent rivalry.

Gvozdetskii's face reddened as he swallowed the burning liquid. He hated vodka, but how could any true Russian admit to that shortcoming? When I become Premier, he thought, I'll outlaw this vile brew.

"Come, Dmitri," shouted Marshal Tukhachevskii as he grabbed the bottle's neck, "have another drink. Your glass is empty."

Dmitri's hand covered the top of the glass as the Marshal walked toward him. He had no intention of becoming the drunken fool; that was a part Comrade Tukhachevski seemed to relish playing "No, Marshal. Someone has to keep his wits about him."

Tukhachevski stopped, laughed, and drained the remainder of his glass. He immediately poured another portion. "See?" he said holding the glass aloft. "A soldier knows how to hold his vodka." He tilted his head back and threw the contents down his throat in a single gulp, then headed toward the table intent upon breaking open the seal on another bottle.

The chairman diverted him from the liquor table saying with

a pat on the back, "Tukhachevski, sit, the celebration has not yet begun." The marshal responded to the firm undertone of the chairman's otherwise cheerful tone.

Shaposhnikov took his place behind his massive desk. The others turned to face him.

Dmitri Gvozdetskii's eyes roved across the inebriated marshal, then turned slowly toward the chairman. Like electric beams their gazes fused. Time was suspended for the pair; only their willpower wrestled. Shaposhnikov stared with the forceful gaze of experience, the knowledge of certain victory. Gvozdetskii's eyes answered with the burning brand of unbridled ambition, the flickering fire of treachery. Only the monotonous clicking of the chronometer above the television screen wall broke the crypt-still air.

Tukhachevski sat, awed by the battle of nerves. The vodka hadn't dulled his senses so much as to allow him to miss the contest.

A shrill buzz pierced the electric circuit that sparked from the two men's eyes. Neither moved. Finally Tukhachevski stood and answered the intercom for them, handing the receiver to the chairman.

Shaposhnikov did not take the phone immediately. His stern gaze remained riveted to his adversary's for just long enough, before he turned away.

"Yes!" he shouted angrily into the unit.

"Chairman?" the voice answered. "You wished to be informed when the network began the Pope's coronation."

"Then it's begun?" he asked.

"In less than a minute, Comrade Chairman."

Shaposhnikov hit the television controls. The room's lights dimmed, the huge hanging screen rapidly illuminating. The etched faces of the three were soon bathed in electronic light, as the ritual they awaited unfolded before them.

Dmitri tightened his jaw and hid all traces of anticipation. Torchnoi had promised the Czech would never reign as Pope. He allowed himself the luxury of a cigarette to quell his agitation.

The cardinal began to walk across the piazza. Gvozdetskii waited. There was still time, he hoped, impatiently.

Moments linked into minutes and still the cardinal continued. Gvozdetskii's teeth bit into the filter, severing it. The cigarette fell into his lap.

His eyes returned to the screen. Thus far there had been no incident. He could feel a vein throb at his temple as the tension rose. The Czech cardinal seemed to beam with energy as he obviously relished the cheers of the crowd. The waiting was intolerable.

He took a series of deep breaths. Torchnoi had never been wrong before.

The bells of the ancient city sang out the joy of the moment. A new Holy Father had been crowned. Thousands of booming voices reverberated with a sound that would only be equalled, perhaps, by the election of Alexander's successor.

The Czech Pope held his hands aloft to the heavens in thanks. It was his moment, and he meant to share it with the multitude, the entire world. He turned and faced the great undulating sea of faithful, and they roared their response. Michalovce was now and forever Alexander. "Long may he reign," they shouted.

The Pope offered his prayer, his benediction. The throng accepted. He faced in each direction offering the sign of the cross. A hundred thousand pairs of hands and tear-brimming eyes followed his lead. He gestured dramatically, just as his predecessor Pope John XXIV had. The homage was not lost either on the crowd or on the reporters who recorded each step, each motion, each small gesture. Alexander would be a Pope of the masses, it appeared. His flock would be universal.

Ritsa Esja waited. She watched the procession from the steps of St. Peter's, but remained calm. Her heart beat fiercely when she saw the new Pope, but he did not yet draw, from the inner recesses of her mind, the trigger impulse to prostrate herself before him. Except for the white skullcap atop his thinning hair, his head was bare. Her movements followed the surging crowd about her, crossing herself whenever they did, waving with them, applauding as they. Nothing could suggest she harbored anything but adulation for the Vicar of Christ the Lord deep within her bosom.

Stirred by the sound of the bells that signaled the coronation, the crowd became electrified. They responded to some unseen stimulus from the direction of the new Holy Father's approach. A crushing wave of humanity surged forward, sweeping her with it. He was nearing. Her angel-like face raised with determination. Tiny droplets of salty sweat appeared where none had been before.

The roar of the crowd made the very ground tremble. She struggled in vain to see him.

The Holy Father rejoiced in his hour of supreme exultation. His steps were sure, firm against the hallowed pavement of the piazza. About him swarmed his followers. An elderly man burst forward, threw himself on his knees before his new Pope.

Alexander halted in front of the tearful worshipper. The man bent over, planting a tender kiss on the Holy Father's feet. The guards struggled to restrain the surging, beseeching crowd.

Drawing his follower upright, the Pope kissed the old man on the forehead. His high pointed hat fell to the ground, but the Holy Father made no effort to retrieve it, so taken was he by the man's gesture.

The great crowd responded as an orchestra of emotion, with a symphony of adulation. Alexander was forging a bond that would secure him their hearts. He came to them, the shepherd leading his joyful, obedient flock.

An aide rushed to the fallen hat and picked it up, brushing it off reverently as the Pope walked on. Hurrying to Alexander, he held out the symbol of the Papacy to the new incumbent. The Pope waved him off, having no need for such adornment.

Each moment his march was interrupted by others who burst through to caress the Pope and prostrate themselves before him. Each time he knelt down and brought the faithful upright to kiss his or her head. Any lingering doubts as to whether the Italians would accept one who was not their own were surely laid to rest at this moment.

The procession wound slowly about the Maderna Fountains; hands pressed forth to touch His Grace at every step. The march continued toward the great obelisk in the center of the piazza. It was there Ritsa Esja was waiting.

Maksim Shaposhnikov's face beamed with relief. Michalovce had been pronounced and crowned. It was a *fait accompli*. Though the stakes were enormous, the Old Fox had cast the die; the roll had won his point. At his age this was his last chance to stave off the forceful challenge of the younger man. If he'd failed, there would have been little to live for. With the consolidation of power he had earned on the heels of this victory, Gvozdetskii could be dealt with from a position of strength. In the days of Stalin, the remedy would have been swift. But now the Central Committee would be more generous. Dmitri was not only ambitious, but was also brilliant and ruthless. These qualities would save him; the party had need of such people. Yes, he would be taught a lesson, and forced into the background for years perhaps, but would eventually return. Maksim was certain of that.

Gvozdetskii watched the screen with keen but hidden interest. As the Czech walked from St. Peter's, he edged forward on his seat.

By the time the rite was complete, Dmitri had succumbed to tensions he could not suppress. Michalovce was Pope; Torchnoi's man had not come through.

"A toast!" called Tukhachevski suddenly. The effect of the vodka had partially worn off. "A toast to . . . Comrade Shaposhnikov!" He turned to the seated chairman, raising his glass. Shaposhnikov accepted the marshal's acclaim, and Gvozdetskii mechanically followed the marshal's lead. The three raised glasses, then drained them. Gvozdetskii, increasingly frantic, kept a furtive eye on the screen.

Maksim walked up to the set and lowered the raucous sound. He stood, in his moment of supremacy, framed by the huge screen's panorama of St. Peter's. Even without sound the picture pulsed with the joy of the multitude. For a moment, he shared it.

At that instant the Pope bent to kiss an old man, his peaked hat falling to the ground. Dmitri watched in horror as the Holy Father waved off the aide who tried to replace it on his head.

She'll never do it! he nearly shouted, terrorstruck. Without the trigger . . . everything is lost.

Shaposhnikov's eyes were on the large screen just a meter before him. From time to time, various members of the faithful broke through the police lines and ran up to the Holy Father, falling on their faces, kissing his feet. The Pope's response, the raising of each, obviously made the thousands gathered to pay him homage delirious with joy.

Alexander stopped for an instant. Seizing the chance, his aide walked behind His Holiness, replacing and adjusting his fallen hat. Gvozdetskii's breath hissed out sharply with relief as he watched. The Secret Police chief's eyes went from the marshal to the chairman to check that neither had noticed his agitation. He turned away from the screen, relief making him unable to watch for a moment.

The procession moved on; yet another broke from the crowd. This time it was a woman with flowing black hair who ran directly, almost frantically through the line toward the Holy Father. He raised his hands as a gesture for her to come to him and not to fall on the pavement. She paid him no heed.

The woman threw herself on the ground before him. The crowd roared. Shaposhnikov could not hear their joy for there was no sound, merely a picture.

The chairman smiled as he raised his glass to his mouth.

The woman's lips touched His Holiness. Her hands were pinned under her; she caressed him tenderly.

The chairman's throat burned with the thin fire of success and liquor.

The screen burst angrily with a flash of vivid light. A column of heavy smoke filled the view.

The glass slipped slowly from the chairman's hand, and shattered.

Barzini's hand found the door handle of his police car. He took a last look back at the Vatican. Its walls failed to muffle the sounds of joy from the piazza beyond. In his moment of despair and failure, the detective hoped that a bolt of lightning would strike him that very instant. It was about to strike elsewhere.

The killer had slipped out of his grasp. He'd search for him, as long and as hard as necessary, but for now he tasted only the bile of defeat.

Lorenzo swung the Fiat's door closed behind him and started

the engine, the tired muffler coughing and spewing fumes. Lorenzo peered over the dented hood. He'd thought he'd heard a greater noise than the grinding of his auto's clutch. Beyond the buildings that encompassed the Holy City a thick column of black smoke rose into the cloudless sky.

He got into his car. A minute later the high-pitched sound of police horns filled the air. The detective watched as a bomb squad truck passed. The apparatus raced in the direction of the Vatican, disappearing as it turned the far corner on two wheels. Other emergency vehicles followed in an unending stream.

Barzini jumped out of the car and began running in the same direction as the vehicles. He waved to one, holding out his identity card, praying it would stop. It did not. He cursed the driver as he continued running. Whatever this was, he thought, it was a police matter.

He raced back uphill to his higher vantage point from the far side of the cathedral. After chugging heavily for several hundred meters he turned the last corner to see the unfolding scene of carnage. In the distance the smoke was lifting as the curtain of La Scala does before an opera's opening. Bodies were scattered across the blood-soaked concrete. The crowd cowered back, leaving a circle of complete desolation. The screams of hysteria and confusion caused those nearest the explosion to flee helter-skelter in panic. Then, from every direction, columns of gray-suited soldiers began forcing their way through.

The horrified onlookers were an unwieldy mass. Those in the rear were not yet certain what had happened, and pressed forward. Those in the middle attempted to escape in terror. Unable to make headway, the military began frantically throwing people aside.

Deep in the pit of his stomach, his very bowels . . . deeper still—in his soul—Lorenzo realized that he alone might begin to grasp what had really occurred. The loneliness of that realization terrified him.

The image of the undulating, panic-stricken mob coursing forward and scattering back like the whirlpool of God's vengeful flood was one that would forever be etched indelibly upon the memory of one Lorenzo Barzini, officer of the law.

Heart pounding, Dmitri Gvozdetskii trailed a bewildered Marshal Tukhachevski out of the chairman's office. Neither man spoke. Each was buried in divergent personal thoughts. The old man had stood frozen, ghost-white, wavering dizzily. They had thought he was having a seizure. But no, he had finally seated himself and waved them out.

Now the corridor was void of all sound, save that of their footsteps striking the hard floor. Armed guards came to attention, returning to parade-rest only after the pair had passed. The two men walked slowly down the hallway bathed in sterile blue-white light, neither speaking to nor glancing at the other.

As they reached the first intersection, they faced each other for an instant. Only their eyes spoke; each read what was in the other's mind. The messages were clear, concise and complete. They turned away and began walking in opposite directions.

Five seconds later a single gunshot pierced the stillness. The guards unslung their machine-guns, threw open the chairman's door, and rushed inside.

Both Gvozdetskii and a sobering Tukhachevski spun about. They froze in place, neither man attempting to return to Shaposnikov's office. Twenty paces apart their eyes fused.

There were shouts from the chairman's office: "Call an ambulance! He's shot himself! Quickly. . . . "

A loud alarm began to clang. In a moment other security men raced down the hallway to Shaposhnikov's rapidly filling office. Again the shouts: "He's dying! He's dying, I tell you!"

Gvozdetskii's sharp eyes pierced like a rapier through Tukhachevski's soul. The tall marshal felt his blood turn to ice. He attempted a weak nervous smile, barely succeeding.

When Gvozdetskii broke his gaze, starting to turn back in his original direction, Tukhachevski's huge body snapped suddenly to attention, his right hand crisply saluting. He waited. . . . Dmitri Gvozdetskii nodded, then walked away. The sound of his footsteps was soon lost in the distance.

Epilogue

Face lined with tension and fatigue, eyes scorching with determination, Lorenzo Barzini raced up the steps to police headquarters. His face was bathed in sweat and his clothes blood-spattered after more than thirty-five hours of intense, almost frantic questioning of witnesses and victims. He had not paused in that time to catch his breath.

The piazza had writhed like the pit of the *Inferno*. Bodies everywhere; some trembling with agony, some motionless. All through the night the cries echoed, a wailing cacophony of grief, pleas, harsh commands and moaning prayers.

Conflicting reports had already circulated world-wide. All that could be ascertained was that the newly invested Pope had been assassinated by some crazed individual. Though rumors would abound and theories would be propagated, as in other assassinations, this was all the world would ever determine with certainty. Only Lorenzo Barzini's suspicions were grounded in truth. He alone sensed the carefully cloaked hand reaching out from the East to tamper with Roman piety. Slowly the detective began to trace the pattern of the strands interwoven in this tapestry of death, deception, and intrigue.

He negotiated the last flight of stairs and made for his chief's office, energy all but consumed. As he reached for the door it swung open, as if by its own power. He stumbled forward, barely catching himself in time. Lieutenant Cardone's hand withdrew from the doorknob as she stepped back startled.

"Oh! Barzini. . . . "

Lorenzo didn't allow her to finish. "Is the chief in?" he demanded, rushing past her.

Her face went red. "Yes. What do you . . . "

Before she could compose herself he had crossed the anteroom and thrown open Chief Maggiore's door. Inside, Ugo and his deputy were huddling over a set of street maps. Paluzzo Antionelli bolted upright at the stormy entrance.

"Barzini, what goes on here?" Chief Maggiore was taken aback by the detective's wild-eyed appearance.

But Lorenzo simply strode inside and laid both hands flat on the chief's massive desk. "Ugo, I know why the Pope was killed." He spoke calmly.

Deputy Chief Antionelli stepped between the detective and Maggiore. "All of us know why. It was the act of some crazed woman; a replay of the tapes shows that."

Barzini's hand grasped Antionelli's shoulder and stared hard into his face. The smaller man withdrew. "Chief," Barzini began, turning back to the elder Paluzzo, "it wasn't that simple. Nobody is explaining why; nobody is making any connections. Did she act alone? Whom was she working for? The explosion was powerful enough to kill fifteen and maim three dozen others; that young kid didn't make that bomb herself. So who is involved in this conspiracy?" His questions were met with silence. "Chief, I think I know some of the answers."

Ugo Maggiore's face revealed only a guarded interest. His deputy's countenance was more skeptical: "Yes? What is your theory?" he challenged.

"Not theory, Antionelli, fact," Barzini snapped back. "She is only the tip of the iceberg. The culmination of a line of murders. You see, an agent, probably a Russian agent, was loose in the Vatican. I'm not sure of his exact purpose but it undoubtedly involved the Pope, *this* Pope, and I think it included blackmail."

"Blackmail? To what purpose? Barzini, you sound like you're on another planet." Antionelli's mouth curled upward as he spoke.

The chief raised his hand to make Antionelli stop taunting the detective. Then he turned his attention to Barzini. "Lorenzo, come." He offered him a seat. "Please, sit down."

"No, I don't need a seat. I'm telling you that the jawbone fragment here, the killings in Ostia, and the death of that priest a couple of days ago at the Sistine Chapel are all related."

Paluzzo motioned to Angela to close the door. He had no desire to be heard outside the chief's office. "Barzini, what are you talking about?"

Lorenzo heaved an enormous sign of frustration and tried to begin at the beginning. He explained the ties between the cases in Ostia and the bone fragment here, pointing out the indication of a priest in both. After voicing his suspicions concerning the death of the old priest on the staircase, he explained his discovery and indentification of the bogus priest, described his hair-raising chase. Chief Paluzzo listened patiently, but when Barzini told of the documents, and discussed his suspicions of tampering or blackmail, the chief's impressions began to coincide with Antionelli's skepticism.

"So this priest got away?"

"Not a priest—an agent, a provocateur."

"All right, an agent then, but he's gone." The chief's question was answered with a nod. "So you haven't any evidence, anything concrete to substantiate this claim."

"No, I . . . "

"Of course he hasn't," interrupted the slight deputy. "How could there be? It's a fantasy, a concoction to account for his wasted time."

"Here, both of you, look." Barzini withdrew the disc-shaped mechanism he had discovered in the Professional's cell. "It's a low-frequency generator, or so the lab tells me. Of Russian manufacture and certainly not available here. I found it in the priest's cell. . . . "

"What purpose does it serve, Lorenzo?" the chief inquired.

"I don't know. But it sure as hell wasn't used to count rosaries. Something big is going on here and the pieces are sitting right in front of us. I tell you there's a murderer loose and I have no doubt that he and his people are behind this bombing."

"All right, all right, Lorenzo, suppose it's true—where does that leave us?" The chief was losing patience. "What do I do, start arresting every priest in Rome?"

"Look, Ugo; I have his picture and his profile. . . . "

"And I have a headache, Barzini," Antionelli broke in, "from listening to this hare-brained tale about blackmailing the Pope. As for this . . . thing, it looks like a device one would use to massage his back . . . "

"Massage his back?! This is a complex piece of equipment! No cords, no power pack, no transmitter! But it emits . . . "

"Lorenzo. The past few days have been rather draining on all of us." Ugo put his hand on the detective's shoulder. "I think we all need a rest. Why don't you take some time off?"

Beside himself, the detective walked to the windows and looked out. The street bustled with midday traffic. His eyes traveled across the Tiber to the dome of St. Peter's. It was all there, if only they would listen.

"I'm telling you. It was him . . . a priest . . . an agent. He was responsible for everything. He planned it all, the killings, probably the killing of the Pope and more."

"More?" Antionelli questioned with a patronizing tone. "You mean there's even more to this?"

Lorenzo whirled to answer but could find no words. His eyes spoke for him. "Please, Ugo. You've got to believe me. I tell you a killer, disguised as a priest, was responsible."

"You mean it was a priest and not a woman who killed the Pope?" Antionelli chided.

"If he didn't, he was part of a far-reaching conspiracy that did. That girl who got her guts blown all over the piazza was probably a poor dupe. Duped by someone powerful enough to dupe you too, and get away with it!" His eyes never left those of Antionelli.

"What do you mean, Lorenzo?" Maggiore asked.

"I mean a hired killer, a professional agent, was given this assignment . . . maybe by the Soviets—if those documents and this device point where they seem to. Whatever that job was, it resulted in five deaths . . . and the Pope's assassination."

Antionelli scoffed. "And why would the Russians kill Alexander? What ungodly purpose would it achieve?" He turned away from Barzini and spoke to his chief. "After they finally got one of their own in office. Why the hell would they kill him?"

"I don't know!" the detective screamed. "But they did!" His eyes pleaded for them to believe. He was exhausted. "Consider, Ugo. I know it all sounds like the ravings of a madman. But you've known me for twenty years. I may not have been the best officer you ever had, but I am an honest one. I'm telling you that for some damn reason the Russians killed him." Barzini finally sank into the empty seat. He had to admit to himself that in the end he was stumped for the reason behind this complex conspiracy. If the Russians were manipulating Michalovce, why would they have him killed? He could not have known that greed for power within the Kremlin had caused one faction to foil the successful scheme of another.

Chief Maggiore and his deputy moved to a corner of the room where they conferred for a moment. The chief nodded solemnly and then returned to the detective.

"Lorenzo," he began, placing his hand on the detective's shoulder, "we both think you could use some rest. Maybe a week or two off would . . . "

Barzini bolted upright. A vacation was the furthest thing from his mind. A dangerous killer had to be found, with or without their help.

"*No!* There is no time. As we're speaking he's making his escape. I have his picture. If you call Interpol . . . the border police; everyone has to be on the lookout for him. I tell you, we are wasting time!" Barzini stood facing his two superiors. "Damn! Can't you see your nose in front of your face?"

The chief drew closer to the frazzled Barzini. "Even if it were true, Lorenzo—and for all I know it is—what do you expect me to do? Call out the National Guard? Break a story like that to the newspapers? Who would believe it? It would start an international incident—don't forget, I can be fired too! Listen, Lorenzo. People don't want to deal with that kind of hysteria. They want to believe that a crazy woman acted alone. Can't you just let it lie?"

Lorenzo threw the chief's hand off his shoulder. "Let it lie? Not for a minute! If I can't get your help, then I'll go after him alone."

Paluzzo Antionelli decided the fiasco had gone far enough.

"Barzini, you'll take that vacation as the chief ordered. If you don't . . . "

Lorenzo didn't have to hear another word. His hand reached into his breast pocket and extracted his leather identity case. He let it drop from his hand. It landed flush on the desk, the sound akin to the closing of a heavy book.

There was no need to speak further. The tired officer left his automatic on the table and walked calmly toward the door. Behind him, Ugo Maggiore called his name.

Lorenzo stopped and turned. "Chief, what else can I do?"

No reply was necessary.

A tall, dark-haired gentleman waited on line at the Canadian Immigration Center's receiving area. The government officer called to him, "Next."

He walked to the booth, presenting his Canadian passport and Immigration form.

The officer opened the booklet and compared the photograph with the man standing before him. "Dr. Abraham?"

"Yes, I'm Dr. Abraham." The man smiled pleasantly, blue eyes twinkling behind his horn-rimmed spectacles.

"Did you have a nice holiday in . . . " the officer looked down and studied the single exit visa, "Italy?"

"Beautiful" was the answer, in precise tones tinged with a European accent. "Italy in the early fall is everything they write about, and more."

The customs officer turned the leather suitcase on its side to examine it. "Do you have anything to declare?"

"No . . . ah, yes, a few paintings—reproductions. Rather good work they do in Italy."

The customs officer examined the few framed prints without noting the luster of a small, finely crafted Michelangelo. "What about that ring?" he asked finally.

"The ring? It's been in the family for nearly two centuries. It was my father's. A family crest—all that remains of such things. His finger ran lovingly over its surface. There was a jagged edge, a flaw that hadn't been there before. He held it up to the light. A bit of the raised surface had been damaged. He made a mental note to have it repaired at the first opportunity.

"Can I please see it?" the customs officer requested.

The doctor slipped it off and handed it to the waiting officer. In a moment it was given back, the uniformed man commenting, "A beautiful piece. The panther is so strikingly sculpted. Take care of it; that diamond must be valuable." The officer stamped the passport and handed it back to the doctor.

The doctor picked up his bag. Adjusting his glasses, he glanced at a newspaper carried by one of his fellow passengers. The headline read:

NEW POPE KILLED BY CRAZED WOMAN
ATTACKER & NINE OTHERS DIE IN BLAST

With only a flicker of hesitancy, he strode toward the pneumatic doors that led to the terminal's exit. They closed behind him with a hiss.

And behold an angel of the Lord from heaven called to him, saying: Abraham, Abraham. And he answered: Here I am.

GENESIS 22:11